TREASURE
Love,
TREASURE
DISAPPOINTMENT

TREASURE *Love,* TREASURE DISAPPOINTMENT

Different Ways and Experiences "Why" You should
Look Up to God for Guidance and within
Your Soul for a Soul Mate to be Found

CHAUNDA GAINES

Copyright © Chaunda Gaines.

All rights reserved. No part of this book may be reproduced in any form or by any electronic or mechanical means, including information storage and retrieval systems, without permission in writing from the publisher, except by reviewers, who may quote brief passages in a review.

ISBN: 978-1-63649-252-0   (Paperback Edition)
ISBN: 978-1-63649-253-7   (Hardcover Edition)
ISBN: 978-1-63649-251-3   (E-book Edition)

Some characters and events in this book are fictitious. Any similarity to real persons, living or dead, is coincidental and not intended by the author.

Scripture taken from the Holy Bible, King James Version (Authorized Version). First published in 1611. Quoted from the KJV Classic Reference Bible, Copyright © 1983 by The Zondervan Corporation.

Book Ordering Information

Phone Number: 315 288-7939 ext. 1000 or 347-901-4920
Email: info@globalsummithouse.com
Global Summit House
www.globalsummithouse.com

Printed in the United States of America

TABLE OF CONTENTS

Introduction xiii

Relationships 1
The Men 7
The Other Men 100
    David 101
    Damon 104
    Dennis 106
    Dale 107
    Daniel 108
    Dominique 109
    Derek 111
    Darrell 112
    Darnell 114
    Detroit 116
    Dempsey 117
    Donnie 120
    Donald 122
    Devon 124
    Demetrius 125
    Darwin 126
    Dashaun 129
    Duane 134
    Deacon 137
    Duncan 141
Women's Experience 144
Pamela's Conclusion 161
Steps To Treasure Love 168

A Virtuous Woman 177
Twelve Commandments.. 180
Poetry of Love 181
Relationships.. 182
Thank You's 183

This is Chaunda Gaines, the author of the spiritual inspirational self-help book, "Say What Loneliness?"

The author came from the school of hard knocks, the streets. She has the Zeal, Zest, and Zealous attitude of making it as a writer. She grew up in Third Ward, Texas, and a native Houstonian. She experienced things she believed before her time. She can relate to the pain and hurt you may be going through in your life, wanting to be loved by someone. Now she's writing about relationships adding a little lemony twist to it. You can call her by her short name "cg" or "red" whose coming right back at you with "Treasure Love Treasure Disappointment."

The author keeps it real, simple, and does not sugar coat her words but writes with a sincere heart to help you know how to value a relationship, when to get out of one, how to save the relationship you're into if that's what you desire, and how to walk away or work with the relationship you're in. This book is going to give you the direction to get to where you want to be in a relationship. This book is about how some men treat some women and the author offers suggestions on how to help you salvage your relationships and appreciate who you are with. She also knows how it is to be happy, but never really experience happiness one on one with a man yet. This book can show you how to get there, find happiness, accept what you've been through, learn from your mistakes, move forward, put the past in the past, and move onto your greatness without giving your bad relationships any thought because it did not work out.

As she was growing up, she always heard from others that relationship is what you make of it. Each relationship Pamela was in has helped her grow spiritually, physically, and emotionally which affect her soul and whether that relationship benefits her or not.

Your soul consists of what are in your mind— your emotions, intellect, and your imagination. Sometimes a relationship can be so painful and can hurt you really bad inside and outside, which destroy who you are and what you've become right now. Then some relationships can make you happy, contented, and fulfilled. You can be in love forever with your mate and spending a lifetime with them. Sometimes you can determine how your relationship is going to turn out with how your mother and father raised you. If you didn't like your parents' relationship, you can change the relationship you're in and make it better by making adjustments that suit your specification so it can grow and last forever. All it takes is an effect and willingness on your part to work at your relationship at every moment of the day. It's like you have to yield to the Holy Spirit and be obedient to God's word in order to have a blessed life, a blessed relationship, and a blessed marriage. The author wants to save your marriage or relationship by teaching you how to avoid many mistakes and stay married until death do you part. Sometimes it may take seconds, minutes, hours, days, weeks, and months to work out the problem or issue that you have with each other. Just don't give up and throw in the towel. Just keep in mind that the Devil comes to conquer, destroy, and kill marriages. This could mean your relationships or marriages.

This book will be dealing with different relationships that Pamela went through her entire life with different men, how they treated her, and the choices she made trying to keep them or leave them when she has already given all that she could give of herself. Yes, it is about making the right choices when it comes to welcome a man in your life. There are plenty of life lessons to be found in this book to encourage each and every one of you to stay with the man, give the man another chance, or leave the man that you are with altogether. You might want to compare your relationship with one of hers and turn the relationship into how you want your relationship to be that could last forever like your forefathers set before us back then, staying with their wives until they passed away. This is how our relationships should be today. Pamela wants you to realize that when you are in a relationship, you should be with a man that the Lord wants you to be with, that's in His Divine Will, not who you want or choose to be with, so you can receive all the blessings in your life that the Lord has set up in your pathway, for you to travel down. The choice will be yours. Lots of us go to clubs to meet someone to be in our lives. Men know this. Most men think we, women, are desperate and lonely. Some men think we're filling those seats at the bar for us to be picked up by them to have a one night stand. Ladies, one night stand with a man will not keep him coming back because you had sex with him or allow you to be his new woman in his life. When you go to clubs, you need to have the right mindset. You are going to have fun, and just get his telephone number and call him back the next day, next week, or in two weeks. Then you can see where the relationship will lead. This way, you can find out more about him as an individual. Just remember, men love sex and brain. You can't be with a man and don't have sex with him. He's going to get sex from somewhere else. So don't be naive. If a man is not sleeping with you, he's sleeping with somebody else. In some relationships, some situations are different. For instance, there are open relationships wherein couples sleep with other partners. They know about it but allow it, thinking that this will spark their own sexual intimacy with one another. Just hope that the other partner doesn't fall in love with one of those partners outside their marriage that they are swinging with because then it becomes an issue. Pamela solely talks about sex because sex is what turns a man on. When sex is not involved, then your marriage will be in that high percentage divorce rate. Sex is what a man likes and what keeps him with you. You have to be creative with sex when you are in bed with your man. Just don't have up and down sex. You have to make it interesting to the point of giving him some brain. If you don't include brain in your sex, he's definitely going to get another woman to give him some brain and pay her very well to do it. This will be money taking out of your household. There's another situation where women take care of their men. It could be because of low self-esteem in them, or they just don't want to be alone. This will allow your man to take advantage of you and take you for granted. When you come home from work, he might be gone somewhere. You may have to come home, cook, clean the house, do the laundry, vacuum, wash the dishes, iron the clothes, and check the mailbox, but your man still won't work. When you get home, he won't even be there. If he's there when you get home, he doesn't even show you any appreciation from working on a nine-to-five job. When it comes time for sex, he might say, "not tonight, baby," or "I'm too tired, honey. Maybe tomorrow," but keep in mind that he doesn't work. If this is the case, your marriage might be in trouble.

Pamela experienced some of these above. Men Pamela had a relationship with left a disaster in her life when they broke up with her, and she had to live from place to place after trying to pick up the pieces of her life when these men were done with her. Pamela was just a sweet girl and too trustworthy. A man tells her anything, and she would always believe him. She would always put her heart in it and would always be the one to get hurt. Pamela had been through so much in her life, but the light of God always shined in her face. She knew she had favor with the Lord. God would make things better for her one day. Pamela kept believing and having faith in what God had revealed to her in visions through her dreams. Pamela knew her day would come where everything would flow right in her life for a change because God would walk side by side with her making sure that it does.

As you read this book in every step of the way, you will find out how men treated Pamela and what these men were looking for from her. So you will know what a man is looking for from you when you become involved with one. You will be able to relate to her hurting and pain when men left her. The author wrote this book also to help you learn that if your relationship doesn't work, don't blame yourself, don't beat yourself up, don't bottle up all your whys and why not inside you, as to why it didn't work, but just remember that you gave it all you had. You exhausted all your avenues, revenues, efforts, and came out empty but you still have the lessons learned from those relationships you were into and not to make those same mistakes again and again, or over and over, but look up to God for guidance and within your soul, for a soul mate to be found.

This is a story about a young lady named Pamela. This book is about the many men she became involved with and found out about the ups and downs of many marriages and relationships she had endured. In all of her relationships, she never knew what to expect, what the outcome would be, and how they would end, but she went into each of these relationships fresh, thinking that they would last forever. The many men she became involved with, the men she thought would treat her right, only to become miserable, dismayed, lied to, and most of all, they brought her disappointment in life, but she stayed regardless if the men were in love with her or not. She wanted the relationship to work. She didn't want to be alone. She had to come to grips with herself when the relationship became sour, and there was nothing else she could contribute to make the relationship better. She came to a roadblock forcing her to walk away from them or men walked away from her to go to other women thinking that the grass was greener on the other side. Pamela had to face some hard facts about the men she was involved with. Some men were just no good. Some men would lie. Some men would cheat because they saw their dad cheat on their mom, and their mom stayed with their dad no matter what. Pamela felt that you have to make the best out of what you have, and wondered where the good men are. She could not find one good man on her road. This is how bad Pamela's luck was. The men that left Pamela always wanted to come back to her when they realized she was a good woman after being with other women they thought were better. Pamela did not take them back because she did not do sequels. She learned that a leopard never changes its spots. The author wrote this book with the hope to help you work at your relationship, stay in your relationship, weathering the fires and pitfalls that arise or just walk away altogether in your relationship or marriage, knowing that you did everything you could possibly do to make it work. The author outlined every man she became involved with that turned out to be a treasure or a disappointment. She also outlined the twelve commandments that you can follow to improve your relationships and marriages. The author hopes that you can learn something from her mistakes to make your relationship better in "Treasure Love Treasure Disappointment." This is why she provided the different ways and experiences on "why" to look up to God for guidance and within your soul, for a soul mate to be found. He is out there somewhere, and you just got to be patient and wait on the Lord.

INTRODUCTION

PAMELA'S WORLD WAS ALWAYS TURNED UPSIDE DOWN WHENEVER love was involved. Here's why. Pamela was always less fortunate than most ladies. She experienced sleeping in her car because she was so heavy in debt due to helping other people and not herself, which left her homeless. She experienced being hungry for three weeks without food. She was in and out of relationships with men, not able to hold onto steady relationships.

Pamela felt someone cursed her. She also experienced not having clothes to wear to work but only two pairs of pants and two blouses because everything she had was in storage due to her living from one place to another. Her clothes were in the back of the storage against the wall, and her furniture was in front. It was hard for her to get to her clothes in the back. Pamela never experienced love because every man in her life either cheated on her or left her for another woman. They told her that while they were walking away from her. She was a good woman, but they had to do this and be back if it does not work out.

Pamela experienced riding a bus for a year because she did not have enough money to get her car fixed. If she missed her bus, then she had to walk miles to get home. She was always talked about, humiliated, and put down all the time by people whom she thought had loved her. Pamela was abused physically, mentally, and emotionally by some of the men she became involved with. She also experienced being a servant to a man she once dated. She had to bring his food to him on a tray when he yelled, "Yo." When it came to washing his clothes, he would throw them at her. She would go pick them up and wash them.

Pamela was really messed up mentally, but she survived. She knew that if she stuck it out and stay strong, everything would be okay for her. Pamela had been through a lot. Some things just got the best of her. You would not know it if you just look at her if she was going through anything because nothing would show on her facial expression, but inside she's hurting so badly, and only her and her God knew that. No one else did by just looking at her. Pamela kept a smile on her face in spite of it.

When she was forty-eight years old, Pamela's mom told her that she had a different dad. Her mom withheld the information out of spite. She despises Pamela as a daughter because she was a career-oriented, and she knew where she was going in life. She set goals for herself to reach. Her mother wanted her to be nothing because she was disappointed with her own life. Her mom wanted Pamela to become a prostitute or a drug addict so she could degrade her in front of other people and her friends and make her feel like she's nothing.

Pamela was a loving and caring person and showed deep compassion for others. She had the patience and a listening ear for any person that came up to her. Pamela had that outgoing personality about her that stood out. Pamela learned to love herself. She realized that she looked for love in all the wrong places. She looked for love in the sanctuary because this was God's house. She felt a man in God's house would be living his life right and doing "what thus says," the Lord. She was obedient because she respected God's Word but just to be disappointed later because some men in God's House of Worship were just looking for sex and a good time.

These men in God's House of Worship used God's Word for their own benefit or purpose. She realized that some men who weren't even associated with God were better men than those in the church house. In other words, these men didn't go to church and profess to love God and be a Godly Christian man. They were only concerned about how much money they have, and want people to notice their outward appearances and the position they hold on their jobs and in the community. They weren't putting on any heirs. They were just being themselves, and Pamela appreciated those men that were real. She felt that if you are a Christian man, you need to act like one and treat a woman right like you would want Christ to treat you. In Pamela's heart, she knew she was a better woman than the way men treated her.

Pamela had a dream of becoming a famous author one day no matter what she'd been through, no matter how hard she fell to the ground. She kept getting back up, knowing she was going to make it one day. As she recalled when she was a little girl, she was kidnapped and raped. Somebody came through the window and took her while she was sleeping. The police found her by the railroad tracks. This man, made her suck and sat on his penis. She remembered crying and wanting her mommie because this man had hurt her so badly. Then one year later, she was hit by a car coming from school. Pamela was in a cast from her waist down for two years. It was like tragedies follow her somehow. As she was growing up, she didn't know that what can happen to you in your younger years may follow you in your older years. When she was a teenager, she was molested by her mother's boyfriend. It was one mishap after another. When she came of age, she got married, not truly knowing what marriage was all about. What it meant to be married and how it is to be a wife.

How in the event that you have disagreements with one another, you shouldn't leave but stay until the problem is resolved because once you leave the trust leaves. Sometimes in marriage, you can never get the lost trust back. Just stay there and rough it out because the argument you have will dissolve in itself eventually. One thing about Pamela is, she didn't have anyone to tell her about a girl growing up and the things that come into play in a person's life. She had to find out the hard way on her own, making plenty of mistakes along the way, which truly cost her in her life.

Pamela was a very beautiful woman. She had beautiful eyes that could hypnotize you. She had those million-dollar legs that could keep your eyes watching her walk. Her walk could make a man say, "damn, I wish she was mine." The walk that could show the movement of her body over yours when she's in bed with you. She had a pillow talk voice that could make a man want to take her to bed. She had long beautiful weaved hair and long eyelashes. She couldn't help how God blessed her body. Sometimes she thought her body was her curse. Pamela wanted a relationship with a man. She wanted to be loved by a man. She wanted to be married.

She wanted a man to know what he wanted when he saw her marrying her right off the top, not hesitating one bit.

She didn't want a man to date her for months or years. When you marry someone immediately, your love grows and strengthens you as one as you learn each other's ways. This kind of bond connects quickly between both of you, resulting in a lasting relationship. Pamela loved a well-dressed man from head to toe. A man dressed well but doesn't live like he dressed.

This is what Pamela got in trouble with. He didn't have the house or the furniture to go with his clothes. He didn't have the job he said he had. The man drove a nice fancy car, but the house didn't line up with his car. She found these things out when she dated them. These men were very deceiving to Pamela, which caused her focus to shift on the wrong characteristic that a person possessed. Pamela focused on a person's outward appearances instead of the inside appearances of a man. The type of man Pamela met on her road was sheep in wolf's clothing.

Pamela was just looking for a man to be a man. Pamela lived in an environment of alcoholics, drug addicts, and some are sexual molesters. Pamela was truly scared mentally when it comes to men and relationships. Please let's not forget marriages. Keep in mind every man who dated Pamela wanted to marry her or shack with her. It was like she had an "M" written in the middle of her forehead, saying, "marry me." Every marriage, Pamela had ended up in divorce. She felt that it was not her fault that in her many relationships, marriages didn't work out.

She gave all that she could give into each relationship. Love hurts when you're the only one giving love back, but in the end, she knows that God is going to bless her with the perfect mate. She just got to hold on and believe in the Lord and have the patience for the Lord to put the right man into her pathway. Pamela had many relationships with different men. One day, she said time out because she kept making the same mistakes with men she became involved with. In Pamela's experience, men just wanted to bone her and keep her between their legs and on her knees but didn't want her to be part of their world.

Pamela knew she was much more than that. See, men thought Pamela couldn't handle living in a big fancy house, driving a fancy car, putting her on his life insurance policies, and handle his money without him being scared she might steal it all or give it away to help her family or leave him altogether with nothing. Pamela was a good woman with Godly values. Now with God's help and by keeping Christ first in her life, Pamela's healing inside because the love she had from men brought scars inside of her heart. She never was happy. No man truly took care of her like how she felt a man should.

So now, Pamela is trying to heal her soul within her spirit. Hoping that one day the man she always dreamed of and hoped for will come her way. Pamela had always been a fighter when it comes to love. The men may have knocked her down, but she just gets right back up. She seeks love in her life as well as security. Pamela believes and has faith in the life that she always dreamed of having. She knows God is going to see her through because there's nothing God can't make happen for her. The Lord has been there for her from day one through the pathway he outlined for her to travel through during her course of life.

The next man Pamela becomes involve with will see that she'll always treasure love and treasure no disappointment with him. As you continue to read this book, you will find out whether Pamela treasure love or treasure disappointment. What she learned by being in those relationships she was in and how those men will make you think twice by being involved with them. She gives examples, pointers, solutions, and encouragement to try to make a relationship work or just walk away and wipe the dirt off your feet for endurance.

"Where the heart is at, where the heart is treasured."

RELATIONSHIPS

RELATIONSHIPS ARE SOMETHING WE ALL WANT IN LIFE. We strive to get it and almost do anything to keep it. Relationships are started when we yearn as individuals to want, miss, or long for someone in our lives. There are many relationship books in the market, but no one truly can tell you if your relationship will last, end, get better, worse, or you will be bitter, happy, or sad. One thing Pamela can tell you is God knows what you are enduring in your relationship.

If your relationship is evenly yoked in Christ, the relationship will probably last forever until God calls you home. It does not mean that you won't have problems in your marriage or relationship, but you have to work at anything just like you go to work every day and try to do your best at your job to keep it. You have to work at your relationship like this if you want it to succeed. So both partners can be the way each partner wants them to be. Relationships should be a lifetime commitment between you and your mate.

So whatever struggles and pains you may experience behind being in a relationship, just endure it because if the relationship is bad, the relationship can't stay that way all the time. The relationship will eventually get better. Sometimes in relationships, we can be our own worst enemies, and sometimes we can be our very best enemy. It's all in the mind. A relationship can be with a person we are involved whether it's common law marriage or just being a longtime girlfriend or boyfriend.

It could be for love, money, sex, or numerous reasons, for companionship or not wanting to be alone or to venture out to find somebody in our lives. Keep in mind that love is tricky, and the disappointment in love can hurt you so bad. We do crazy things and make stupid choices in trying to make our relationships work when there's nothing to hang onto. We, as individuals, sometimes long for having a relationship that can bring happiness, joy, longevity, regardless of the ups, downs, and pitfalls that come in a relationship that can last forever like our grandmothers and grandfathers had back in the day.

A relationship like this is not hard to reach, and if you can withstand the struggles, pain, and crying without giving up or leaving each other, you can make it and survive. Then the relationship becomes worth it. It's really all about how you start out in a relationship because that's how it will end. Every relationship a person is into is a give and take situation. It's compromising and not compromising, it's forgiving and not forgiving, it's being trustworthy and not trustworthy, it's being honest and not honest, and not a liar or a cheater, it's coming together of the minds and working together, not separately.

Nobody truly has the perfect relationship or marriage even if they say they do, because it's going to be something that the person is not bringing to the table in the relationship and is lacking in something he or she is not aware of yet. It takes a whole lot that goes in a relationship, and sometimes we can miss out on what's important.

In a relationship with each person, we get to know his likes, dislikes, mood swings, personality, attitude, and goals, and we might even test him in areas that he's weak, especially with his temper. When you're in a relationship with someone you love, you wonder if your relationship can survive anything if love exists and if so, then nothing else really matters. In relationships, you have to share responsibilities equally or somewhat meet the person halfway.

You need to tell a person the first time you meet him with what you are expecting in a relationship, so you'll know where it's headed and whether you want to take the relationship any further or you just want to end the relationship. Once you ask the right person you want in your life with all the questions you need to have answers to make a relationship, you could treasure love, and just maybe this could result in a relationship or marriage. Pamela realized some relationships and marriages she was in were treasured with love, and some were treasured with disappointment, but they did not last forever.

It was either a breakup or it'll end up in divorce. She had to go back to square one, re-group, and scrutinize herself as to why her relationships and marriages did not last. Was it her fault? So she can get it right the next time around. We need to ask the man we want in our lives questions. How do you know whether or not you can have a successful relationship with me? What do you think it takes to make a relationship work out? Why do you want to be with me? How can you and him stay together in a relationship when there are bad times and hard days?

What would be the right ingredient you think goes into a relationship? How can we, as a couple or marriage mate, cut out the bitterness between one another and the arguments we get into? Do you think I should have just given it into you to avoid disagreements or just talk it out? After the sex is over, what else do you think we will have in common? If I take you home with me, what makes you extraordinary compared to the next man? What are you bringing to the table as to why you should be my man? Will voicing my opinion and speaking what's on my mind hurt the relationship? If you are a jealous individual who follows the person you love everywhere she goes and always wants control of her, do you think this will hurt the relationship?

Will spending time and being busy together with me help the relationship be successful and lasting? Having other affairs and being a swinger while you're in a relationship with me, how do you benefit from those outside the relationship?

Being very submissive to you in a relationship, will this cause you to stay with me and treat me right? What can you do as an individual to prevent the person you have a relationship with to go on the outside for a younger mate when you are with this person for years? What makes your man smile and happy with you? What's his outlook and persona in life? Ask his family members or someone he's close to if he treated his wife, common law, or girlfriend like a queen and pampered her and why they broke up.

Always stay in God's good character and do not let a man take you out of your character with God if you see yourself cursing on a Sunday because your man is accusing you of being with another man. He's calling you degrading names constantly, putting you down where he tries to lower your self-esteem. You need to ask yourself, do you need to be with him? Evidently, for him to treat you like that, he must be insecure with himself, or has he been with another woman? If your man hits you or has a violent temper, which consists of throwing things at you or trying to whip you like you are his child like your mom or dad did when you were a child.

Do you think you should stay or leave him? We have to remember God is a God of love at 2 Corinthians 13:11. If we love God, we love ourselves. If God does not verbally, mentally, or physically abuse you, should you let someone else abuse you? Because all of the above would be out of God's character. We need to stay in God's character as Christian, believer, or persons where Christ lives in our minds and hearts. Sometimes being a good woman could be a curse. Some men love to be with women who complain all the time and women who are garden tool. Some men may not appreciate a good woman being in their lives. When a man knows you love him, he'll take you for granted like he doesn't care about your emotions and feelings or gives you some consideration for the way you feel about him because you love him.

If you're a single woman, your sexual desire takes over your body. Don't give in and have sex because you crave for it. Make sure the person means something to you. Don't have sex with someone you just met. Just wait until you get to know the person. Don't have sex with a man because he goes to your church, a minister, a deacon, or a pastor. Sometimes these men can be deceiving for one's own fleshly desires. Please make sure everything is done in God's goodness and grace. Get to know the person and let God bless your relationship or companionship.

Relationships take endurance, which consists of enduring the hardships, tests, arguments, cheating, lying, falling in and out of love with one another, paying bills, blaming game, hitting your loved one, and definitely money problems. In relationships, you've got to bring everything to the table for it to succeed. Couples need to make sure that the responsibility of maintaining and keeping a relationship does not fall on one person only. The majority of the women today want a man to be like them and have their backs for a change instead of them always having his back when dilemmas come into play in their lives.

In relationships, you can date a man forever and think you know him, but you never know a man until you live with him or get married to him because that's when you are going to find out about the real him. If a man is around you twenty-four-seven, he can't keep hiding his feelings, attitudes, and ways inside for too long. They got to come out, the real him. When you're in a relationship, everyone wants honesty from the person you're involved with. Some men you claim to be with or married to may have a girlfriend on the side. What the wife can't perform in bed like you want her to, the girlfriend can do whatever to satisfy you in bed. The girlfriend can do whatever to please your man the way he wants it.

When you think about it, no man can be faithful to one woman unless Christ dwells within his soul. It is what it is. Sometimes you want to believe that your man is faithful to you only, but if you pay close attention to him for one day with what he does, you might be disappointed. We live in an imperfect world, so what makes you think your man is perfect and flawless from fleshly desires? Relationships are complicated if you don't meet the right man. In relationships, what a woman misses is a man's love. Don't run behind them. Don't call them all day long. Don't run to their houses unannounced. Only come to his house if both of you are in agreement with your schedules. If he doesn't show you that he loves you and cares about you, you won't be hurt by his action. This man truly needs to measure up with your specifications in order for the relationship to work.

One true thing you can't deny is you want to be happy with the one you are involved with. The key to a relationship really is happiness. Then there's love, but sometimes love may not be enough in a relationship. We want both love and happiness and not either-or. If we're lucky, we can get both love and happiness, whether the case may all depend on how you make a relationship work and what you are going to put into it for the relationship to stay strong, last forever, maintain happiness, and endurance.

In relationships, there are choices to be made. They may be easy or hard, but the choice is yours. But when you love someone, that's what makes the choice tough to make. Stick to your guns, and the choice will be okay. In love, if you are in a bad relationship and it's not working out, let it go. Sometimes love brings pain. If there's no pain, then there's no mending of your heart and mind. Then you know what you are not going to put up with the next person.

You have to realize also that a relationship can work, and it depends solely on you. Let's set the record straight. The grass is not greener on the other side. Your significant one sometimes leaves because he thinks the grass is greener on the other side. The other person that loved them is usually the one that gets hurt. It seems like the other party just doesn't care about their feelings. When the significant one gets with the person, they left their mate for. Things are not what it seems to be on the other side. The significant one was deceived on the other side, but the significant one gave up a person that loved them. The significant one did not realize this until the other party was no longer in his life. When they get with the person they left you for, and the significant one finds out that this person just flat out lied to get them over there to the other side. This person may not have had a job. The person may still have been married. The person may have told him she's pregnant but keeping a secret that he may not be the father. The person may still be in love with someone else besides you. The person could have AIDS/HIV and forgot to tell you until you left your mate, who probably was disease-free, and you stop having sex with.

The person could have been living a double life, had an alias name, and not the person you thought to be. The person's home might be in foreclosure, or he could be just leasing a home instead of owning it. The person may be behind in his car notes, or his vehicle is about to be reprocessed. These are some things the significant one could have left you for the grass being greener on the other side. Whatever the reason the person drew you to them, be careful not to give up the other person unless the relationship is over and the candle has been burnt out completely and cannot be re-lit. If you leave a person, make sure the other person on the other side is not playing with you like you played the person you were with.

By all means, don't leave the other person because you're not having sex anymore, or the communication with one another has ceased. You can always make these two things come back into your relationship if you both put forth an effort. Try to re-establish the relationship you've lost. This sometimes is hard to do because pride gets in the way. Pride can hurt you. Pride always gets the best of a person and a relationship. A person's pride is their ego. Let's be mature about our decision to leave someone for another person because we think the grass is greener on the other side but only to reap what you sow for leaving a good person.

A vase that you drop and becomes broken can be fixed and repaired and put back together. Those little pieces can be put back in place, but it just takes time. Time heals every wound that been hurt so deeply. So, if your significant one makes it back to you and you are still in love with him, forgive him for leaving you. Forget how he left you and move forward together in your relationship that was meant to be. By all means, do not get back together with him for vengeance because vengeance is the Lord in due time at Deuteronomy 32:35.

By all means, leave the past in the past because you can't move forward, bringing up how he left you for another woman thinking the grass is greener on the other side because it's always lies and deceit that lives on the other side. It takes the Lord abiding in your relationship, time, effort, patience, endurance, along with respectfulness, and love in your relationship for it to be how you want it to be.

THE MEN

Jamal was an amazing love in Pamela's life. Pamela met Jamal at a skating ring and was her first love. Pamela always dreamed of having this type of love in her life when she was a little girl. Despite all the mishaps that came her way that Pamela endured in her life. Jamal was a heavy-set guy, medium-toned brown skin, and very smart. Jamal had his head on his shoulders right and loved going to church. Jamal's faith was a Baptist. Jamal had a love for his mother and his brothers. Jamal's family was a close-knit family where mom had control of her sons, but that was okay with Pamela. She just loved that man.

His mom was a very sweet and loving mom. Everything in the house, like utility bills and credit cards, wasin Jamal's name. When the holidays came, his mother had everything cooked. She knew everybody loved to eat at the dining room table. They all looked up to him as head of the household since his father had passed away. His family accepted Pamela as part of their family. This was very important for Pamela to be accepted by his family. In Pamela's world, Jamal gave Pamela her first real kiss. Pamela enjoyed the kiss to the fullest. The kiss was like eating cotton candy-like lips sticking together.

There was no sex involved in their relationship. It was simply innocent and cute. Jamal and Pamela started seeing each other on a regular basis. Jamal was Pamela's age, not someone older than her. Jamal and Pamela kissed, shopped, went to church together, went to church activities for the youth, hung out with his family, friends, and went to the movies all the time just about every weekend, both of them were doing stuff together. They would also take long walks around the neighborhood. Jamal took Pamela to the carnival when the carnival came to town. He took her to Astroworld on the weekends. Jamal took her always to her favorite eating place McDonald's, where she always ordered a big mac, a large fries, and a chocolate shake. They ate together like two lovebirds. You would never see Jamal without Pamela on his side. They would have family dinners at Jamal's house along with his brothers, their girlfriends, and they all seated at the table talking about everything that went on with them during the week.

Pamela's father loved Jamal. In reality, Jamal was the perfect son-in-law a father would want for his daughter to be with. He never rushed Pamela into having sex with him. The love Jamal and Pamela had, was like a Cinderella's love.

Only in a fairy tale, a love you could treasure and never treasure disappointment. Of course, Jamal asked Pamela to marry him in his bedroom. He put this two-carat wedding ring on Pamela's finger. Pamela said yes, yes, and yes. She jumped up for joy in his bedroom. She hugged him and kissed him again and again. Then after that, Pamela asked Jamal, did he get her father's permission? He told her, yes. Pamela just smiled, hugged, and kissed him again. Jamal started making wedding plans. His other brothers finished high school with honors. They all had girlfriends that they had been with for years. Each of them was making wedding plans with the love of their lives as well.

That night, when Jamal took Pamela home, her sister met her at the screen door. She told her congratulations on your marriage to be. When Pamela looked at her sister, she looked upset instead of being happy for her. She said "I'm very happy for you. You know me and Jamal are lovers. I love him, too. He should be marrying me, not you." Pamela told her sister, "You're lying, you're just jealous no one asked to marry you." "I'm telling you the truth I just want you to know. So there won't be any secrets between you and him. The cat is out of the bag now," replied Pamela's sister.

So Pamela called Jamal and told him what her sister had revealed to her. Jamal did not deny it on the other end of the telephone. Pamela just started crying and crying until she couldn't cry anymore. Pamela fell asleep that night, still sniffing and crying in her sleep. Pamela cried for a whole week. One day when Pamela woke up from her sleep, her father and her sister wanted to talk to her together at the table. Her dad was telling her to go on with her wedding plans because Jamal told him what happened between Pamela's sister and him. Her dad told Pamela that Jamal truly loves her, and he wants to marry her in spite of everything that happened. Pamela's dad told her that everybody in the church knew it's supposed to be a wedding and what is he now going to say as to why a wedding is not going to happen.

They're talking and gossiping inside the church. Pamela wasn't thinking about her father's reputation at the moment. Her dad was only thinking about his reputation inside the church because he was a pastor and holding his head up high without any crooks in it. Pamela asked her sister while she was seeing Jamal how did she hook up with him when they were together all the time. He would call her when they were not together. "I met him, and he would pick me up at the corner." Pamela said, "Why?" Her sister didn't reply. Pamela said, "You must really hate me as your sister. What did I ever do to you for you to do this to me?"

If you love me, you would have never seen him or came on to him knowing your sister was seeing him. Pamela told her dad, she loves Jamal. She doesn't want to marry him with all her heart because she has her boundaries, and he crossed the line. When a man she loves sleeps with her sister, trust is thrown out the door and that she could never trust Jamal. She needs to be able to trust a man she's going to marry. She asked them to respect her decision, if nothing else. Pamela felt in her heart that she couldn't trust Jamal.

Now Pamela had a broken heart. She was destroyed by both of them emotionally and mentally. Her sister told Pamela, she's sorry. Her sister told Pamela, she won't ever sleep with him again. She has her word. Pamela said it's too late, and the damage has been done. Pamela felt her sister should have kept that dirty little secret to herself, maybe taking that secret to her grave. Pamela realized she would never have that fairy tale marriage she always dreamed of having. Her sister and her fiancé took that away from her. Now Pamela was bitter and angry. She wanted revenge. Believe me she got it by never telling anyone why she didn't marry Jamal when she is questioned. After this point, Jamal kept calling and calling Pamela. Pamela never answered any of his phone calls.

One day, he came by to see her. She would not answer the door. Then another day, Jamal came by to see Pamela. She only spoke to him through the door screen, not letting Jamal in the house. Because she knew if he would touch her and hold her in his arms, and give her a kiss, Pamela would have probably ended up forgiving him. Her pride wouldn't let her let that happen. She asked Jamal, how could you have done this to her. It was downright nasty sleeping with her sister. "What were you thinking? One thing I know, my sister is beautiful, and no man could resist her." Jamal said, "Please forgive me, Pamela, I love you."

Pamela just slammed the door in his face. Her sister was gloating in the background. Pamela treasured disappointment. You know, usually, if someone is your first love, this love is a treasure for a lifetime, and if you're disappointed, this can have a lasting effect on the road that you travel in your life. Pamela was very profoundly hurt inside of her heart. It was like her love began to dry up. When you're young, and in love, you give love all you got. Every ounce of your breath whatever it takes, especially when this is your first love. A person can be a scar for life when they're hurt in a relationship when you put every ounce of your soul into it.

Pamela wanted to kill them both for whipping her heart out, but bitterness took over her soul. Being hurt by love can make you do foolish things without thinking. Pamela felt betrayed by both of them. Pamela could never trust a word from her sister's mouth ever again or believe and trust Jamal. Jamal, on the other hand, treasured love with Pamela regardless of the wrongdoing he had done to her. See, he couldn't have sex with Pamela because he respected her and wanted to have sex only when they got married already. On the contrary, he really couldn't wait. He had sex with her sister instead. All he had to do was to talk to Pamela and she would have had sex with him before the marriage because she loved him.

Just maybe he was twisted in his line of thinking to have sex with the other sibling until he marries the other sibling.

Pamela never forgave her sister and Jamal for that dirty deed the both of them had done together, but she knew she couldn't ever trust her sister with any of her men in her life, for fear of her trying to sleep with them. Eventually, she forgave her sister, but she never forgot the dirty deed.

It's easy to forgive because Christ forgives us of our sins on a daily basis, but you don't forget what wrongdoing a person did to you. Jamal must don't have a conscious as to his actions. Jamal did not value Pamela as a person because he would have never hurt her like that. He still wanted to marry Pamela in spite of what he did.

Jamal was a low-down dirty dog trying to have his cake and eat it too. It seemed like for Pamela, Jamal wanted to marry one sister and the other sister for his sexual pleasures. Where was his moral code of conduct since he went to church on a regular basis? Jamal seemed so sweet and loving on the outside, but he had a corrupt heart in the inside even if he didn't mean to hurt Pamela like he did.

Was Pamela supposed to overlook this and marry him anyway? See, love comes with respecting the other person's feelings before you make a mistake that could be devastating to that person. You could have avoided hurting the other person's feelings only if you had respected her. In other words, think about the acts you're going to commit before you do it, it might devastate your partner. Will you consider how she may feel? Do you think your loved one had feelings for you at all? See, Pamela could not forgive Jamal at all. Since this was the love that Pamela treasured the most, this marked the turning point in her life. It is where Pamela's heart became heartless to love, and love was destroyed and taken away from her soul.

In Pamela's mind, Jamal was her knight and shining armor, one that swept her off her feet with the nice picket fence home and children. She dreamed about having from him a marriage that could have lasted forever if it had happened. So what Pamela did was just marry another man on the rebound, not knowing anything about him. See, love hurts, and we all deal with hurt and pain differently. Later on, in Pamela's life, she ran into Jamal at the club. He told Pamela, he married a woman he did not even love and had grown children with her after Pamela refused to marry him. Pamela and Jamal left out of the club together, but before she left, he gave Pamela his number to call him. Pamela called him the next day. He came over to Pamela's apartment, and both of them had sex. The sex was rough. Pamela didn't get off with him. Pamela had to end up going to the emergency room because she was hurting badly below. The doctor asked her had she been raped because her insides were torn up, and she had a venereal disease. She told the doctor she had consented sex. The police came into the hospital room where Pamela was wanted to get the name of the person she slept with. She would not give his name to the police because they were going to charge him with rape. The next day, she called Jamal to let him know he gave her a venereal disease, and he needed to let anybody he had sex with know so they can go get them some penicillin pills to be clean again. Pamela never saw or spoke to him again after that.

Pamela met Jerome through her girlfriend. She would always spend the night at her girlfriend's house every weekend. Her girlfriend was her best girlfriend forever. Jerome was medium height, medium built, medium complexion, and had the cutest little dimples in his cheeks. He was a smooth talker, and when Pamela would go to Jerome's house to visit his sister, she would always see Jerome with a different woman. Jerome was a pimp. Pamela found this out through her best girlfriend forever, his sister.

Jerome's sister told Pamela he never did finish school. When Jerome saw Pamela, he fell in love with her at first sight. Jerome was definitely a victim caught up in a circumstance of betrayal by what Jamal did to Pamela, whom she truly loved. Jerome started seeing Pamela every weekend. He was spending a lot of time with Pamela, so she won't hurt so badly. Then in a conversation they were having, he asked Pamela to marry him. Pamela said, yes. Pamela just married him on the rebound from being hurt by

Jamal. Pamela did not know anything at all about Jerome. What Pamela loved about Jerome was his smooth rap that could just sway you away once he started talking, which could have you falling deeply in love with Jerome.

One night, Jerome and Pamela went out in town. He asked Pamela if she would stand on the corner for him. Pamela replied, "I'm an educated woman. I can get a job" and said no. "I will not stand on the corner for you or any man for that matter. Jerome, you do not need to be doing this for a living because you can end up dead on these streets. Don't you know another pimp out there could hurt you behind the girls you put on these corners? You're going to have to be out there day and night to make sure your girls are all right. Since you don't have a job, you're going to have to be out there at night with your girls to make your money." Low and behold, one night, when Jerome came home, he was sweating and talking fast. Pamela said, "Jerome slow down because I can't understand a word you're saying."

Jerome told Pamela, this other pimp had been eying his girls and put a gun to his head and wanted his prostitutes. If he didn't do it, he was going to die on the spot. Pamela told him, "It's time for you to let it go and move on to something else." Jerome told Pamela, "I don't have any experience in a job. What do I do?" Pamela said, "First, you need to get your G.E.D." So Jerome went to school at night. Pamela helped him study for his G.E.D. He did complete the class and passed the test. This took about six weeks. Once he did this, Pamela went out and bought a newspaper for him to look for a job. The first job he went on an interview hired him. He was a welder, making good money. Jerome was excited because he never worked anywhere before but only with those girls on the streets. He told Pamela, "You gave me good luck and changed my life for the better. No more street life. Let's celebrate." So Pamela played his favorite song, "Sarah Smile."

Jerome loved working for a living. He also loved to listen to old school music and smoking his weed. Jerome always told Pamela that she was a beautiful woman, and he loves her. Jerome told Pamela, "You know you are a woman with your head on your shoulders right, very intelligent, and a very smart woman." Jerome was eight years older than Pamela. Pamela and Jerome lived in an efficiency apartment where the living room turned into a bedroom. There were a small kitchen and bathroom.

Pamela enjoyed her relationship and marriage to Jerome. They had a lot of fun together. Jerome bought her clothes on top of clothes. He would take Pamela to plays, clubs, parties, movies, and out to eat at restaurants. Jerome studied with Pamela to pass her driver's test and taught her how to parallel parking so she could pass her driving test. Jerome taught Pamela to drive and bought her first car. He would take her to the grocery store and taught her how to make groceries. Jerome had lots of patience when it came to teaching Pamela anything. She passed her driving test the first go-round. Jerome was very excited for Pamela.

Jerome also taught Pamela how to cook and how to clean up a house. Pamela did not love Jerome as much as she loved Jamal, but she married him, so she was very much determined to make it work. Pamela became religious and brought Jerome with her to church. Jerome was a yes man when it came to Pamela. Actually, he was the perfect man for Pamela. Jerome and Pamela would make all their church meetings all the time during the week. They were at church every Sunday. They would study the bible at home as a family. Jerome and Pamela truly loved the Lord. Then for recreation Jerome would take Pamela fishing.

And of course, Pamela did not know how to fish. You guessed it. Jerome taught Pamela how to put bait on the hook to catch a fish. She loved catching her some catfish. Jerome also taught Pamela how to catch crabs in the water. They both would put the crabs in a bucket of water. With the crabs, Pamela would fry them in the deep fryer or make a gumbo. After a couple of years went by, Pamela got pregnant. She was so excited and Jerome too. After she had the baby, things started to change between them. Jerome took the attitude of ownership where a man states I got her, hook line, and sinker. She's mine now I own her. After the baby became three months old, Jerome started slapping Pamela around and beating her.

When Jerome would come home from work, he would tell Pamela, "shut that baby up because I'm stressed out, and if you don't get some quietness in this house, I'm going to beat the hell out of you. So, make the baby stop crying." The beatings continue even after the second baby was born. The physical abuse kept continuing. Pamela never fought back and let him continue to beat her because she loved him. To Pamela, it may not make sense, but Pamela felt the word love is a strong four-letter-word, and it will cause you to get your butt whipped day and night without thinking of putting him in jail and fighting back.

Pamela continued to stay married to Jerome despite his violent behavior hoping that one day he would stop. Pamela would always remember the vows she made to him. When you say vows, you need to keep them. This means you fear God. You will always stay in a marriage no matter what comes or prevails. Pamela knew she shouldn't have been married to him on the rebound. Because of that action, she felt she was reaping what she sow because of her bad choice. Just maybe if Pamela would have dated him for a while, she would have seen his dark side. After years passed in their marriage, Jerome started sleeping with another woman in the church.

Pamela was only aware of one whom she caught him with. Jerome slept with one of Pamela's best girlfriends named Rachel. Jerome was the type of man Pamela never wanted for anything, such as clothes, costume jewelry, or anything she desires. Pamela stayed in the malls, this particular day, she was all bought out. Jerome gave Pamela five hundred dollars to go shopping for her and the kids. Jerome told Pamela to make sure she and the kids stop and get something to eat before they come back home. Pamela said, "Okay."

As Pamela got into the car driving down the street, she and the kids reached their destination to the mall. Pamela told the kids, "We really don't need anything in the mall, so let's go to McDonald's and eat. Pamela ordered two happy meals for the kids and watched them play on the playground. After they finished eating and were all played out, Pamela put the kids into the car and headed home. Pamela walked into the house and heard some noise coming from her bedroom. Pamela put the kids to sleep in their bedroom. Then Pamela opened the door to her bedroom. Low and behold, her husband and Rachel, whom she told her everything that went on between her and Jerome, was on top of her husband, buck naked. They were very surprised to see Pamela open the door.

They did not hear Pamela come into the house. So, Pamela just shut the door and went into the kitchen, allowing them time to get dressed. Pamela didn't get mad. She was just surprised by her best girlfriend's actions. Pamela went into the bedroom and asked Rachel, "How could you do this to me at my house? Did you forget we have kids?" Pamela came up to her, slapping the hell out of her. Then Jerome jumped in to stop Pamela from whipping her butt. Then Jerome started beating up Pamela in front of Rachel. Pamela never looked at Rachel the same again. Pamela left him. Jerome was downright disrespectful to have brought that woman in their house and slept with her in their bed.

Pamela thought to herself, out of respect, they should have gone and gotten a hotel room. Pamela left for two months but came right back home to him after. Pamela forgave Jerome for cheating on her. You know, we as women always forgive the man once or twice for cheating. When Pamela came home, Rachel came over. Pamela noticed that Rachel was high as a kite. Pamela looked up to Rachel. Pamela loved Rachel very much as her BFF. So she forgave Rachel for that adulterous act she committed. Pamela asked Rachel, "Why would you hurt me like this?" She told Pamela that her husband's back hurts and can't perform sex sometimes. Rachel told Pamela, "I never meant to hurt you."

Pamela told Rachel, "I'm going to be honest with you, Rachel." Pamela told Rachel, "You don't have to do the things you're doing to yourself." Rachel told Pamela, "You don't know the half of it, but I'm not only a liar, a cheater, but I'm also a drug addict. Sometimes I can't help myself, Pamela." Pamela told Rachel, "You have a husband who's a good man who looks beyond your faults because of the love he has for you. Don't you know you have the perfect marriage? Your husband is the best husband any woman can have."

"He keeps you well dressed. He takes you to the finest restaurants. He keeps you spiritually knowledgeable, plus he's a pastor at the church." Pamela said, "You know what girlfriend, don't you ever come to my house without your husband. If you do, I'll never speak to you again." Rachel said, "Thank you, Pamela, for forgiving me and giving me a second chance with our relationship." Pamela said, "One more thing, don't you ever betray me again because the next time I'm going to make sure your husband finds out as to what you've done."

Four weeks later, Pamela received a phone call that she was coming over and needed to talk to Pamela. Once Rachel arrived, she told Pamela some shocking news. She just left from having sex with a man, and they were doing drugs. "Pamela, I'm a drug addict addicted to drugs." Pamela looked at Rachel, just stunned with her mouth wide open. Pamela always had this image of Rachel. She was just a person you would look up to the way she carried herself. Pamela asked her, "Does your husband know about your sex habit and your drug addiction?" Rachel said, "No, he doesn't." "Rachel, he needs to know, so your husband can get you the help you need. So you can stop having sex with these different men and get off with those drugs." Then Rachel said, "Thanks for listening to me and not judging me." That's what she'd always loved about her —she had a listening ear and a forgiving heart.

Then Rachel left. Pamela would always see her at church and say hello to her. Eventually, she left her husband and died a tragic death in the end. She was walking along the sidewalk, high as a kite. Rachel stepped off the side of the road when car hit her, spattering her body parts all over the streets. God doesn't like ugliness. In the end, she died a horrible death because you can't serve two Gods who are the Lord, and Satan the Devil. You have to make a choice.

In the end, it can cost you pain, regrets, and even your life. Now, let's get back to Jerome. Jerome's behavior pattern didn't change. He continued to beat Pamela and cheated on her. Pamela, over and over again, would forgive Jerome and just kept moving. Pamela was not the type of person who would throw things he had done back in his face, but she was the opposite.

She left the past in the past. She let it go and moved onto the next phase in her life. She loved Jerome tremendously. At first, when she married him, she didn't love him. She knew love comes in time. The thing about Jerome cheating on Pamela is that she always caught him cheating and knew whom he was cheating with. Pamela and Jerome's sister were always best friends. Pamela went to a house party one night and met her sister-in law's friend. Her sister-in law's friend, named Theresa, was there. She did not know who Pamela was married to.

Nor did Jerome and his sister know that Pamela knew Theresa. Theresa was telling all the women and her friends at the house party about this man she met at her friend's house. She was going to marry him out of the blue.

Pamela asked her what this man's name whom she's going to marry. Pamela said to Theresa, "So this has been up with you? Catch me up, girl. I haven't seen you in love for a long time. You still look good, girl." "Pamela, I met a wonderful man. We have been just kicking it for a while now. We have so much in common. We are so compatible." Theresa said, "I haven't been this happy for a long time." Theresa ran up to Pamela and gave her a hug. "I'm going to be married just like you."

"What's your man's name? It seems like we started talking about something else." Pamela asked her again, "What was his name?" She told Pamela, "His name is Jerome." Then Pamela asked her, "What's his last name?" Pamela's eyes got big and wide because she said his last name was Jackson. Pamela said to Theresa, "That's my husband you're in love with." Theresa said, "That can't be. There are a lot of men with the name of your husband." Pamela asked Theresa to show her a picture of him. Pamela looked in her purse to see his picture. "Is this the man you're in love with and hoped to be your husband?"

Theresa said, "Yes, he's the man." Pamela said, "You know you are seeing my husband." "Pamela, he told me he was single." Pamela told Theresa, "Well, he's not, girl." Theresa was so apologetic. Pamela took Theresa to the side and asked her, "Did you have sex with him?" She said, "Yes, many times. Pamela, I even met his mom, and she did not say anything." "Now, Theresa, I do expect you to stop seeing my husband."

Pamela told Theresa, "When you date a married man, you miss out on your blessing from the Lord. Because if he's cheating on me with you. When he gets with you, he's going to cheat on you with somebody else. Now Theresa, surely, you don't want to go through this repeating vicious cheating cycle."

Theresa told Pamela, "You've always been a good friend to me. You always gave me good advice in my life. My life was truly blessed because I listened to you." Pamela told Theresa, "Thank you for being truthful with me because you surely didn't have to be." Then Theresa told Pamela, "I will not come over to your sister-in-law's house anymore. I will not answer any of your husband's calls. I will definitely stop seeing him as of today." Believe me, Theresa was not just talking, but she did everything she told Pamela she would do. Theresa asked Pamela, "Why do you think he cheats on you all the time?" Pamela replied, "We used to do everything together, had plenty of fun, but after I had his children, he no longer desired me sexually. Now he beats me instead of having sex with me."

See, Theresa had a conscience unlike so many women out there, and she valued her relationship with Pamela, and she wanted the Lord to continue to bless her. Theresa was also deceived by Jerome lying about his marital status. Pamela was assured had Theresa known about his marital status, she would have walked away from him. Theresa's first husband had cheated on her, and Pamela was there to console her in her time of need. Now Jerome's behavior pattern did not change. Jerome continued to beat Pamela and Pamela continued to allow him to. Pamela asked Jerome about his relationship with Theresa, and he did not deny it.

The next day, Pamela left Jerome. Jerome chased Pamela and the kids until they came back home. Pamela and the kids were gone for three weeks this time. Jerome truly loved Pamela, but he couldn't keep his penis in his pants. These church women were chasing him like he was single.

They wanted him as their man. The next day, Pamela went to the mall, where she met this gay man. He just came up to Pamela and told her his whole life story. But before he continued, Pamela asked him his name, and he said it was David. David told Pamela he was working with the FBI trying to bring down this drug pin.

David never told her any names of anybody. He just wanted Pamela to escort him on any dinners at the finest restaurants, dates, and parties. David told Pamela, "You are a very beautiful woman, and you would be perfect for this." Pamela said, "Sure. I think this will be fun for me." David told Pamela that he'd be leaving out of town today. He asked Pamela for her phone number. Pamela wrote her phone number down on a piece of paper and gave it to him. Pamela told David about how her husband cheats on her with some women in their church. David and Pamela kept in touch by the telephone. David was a classy man, very well dressed, and well-mannered, just a proper type of man.

David made Pamela strong and to take her life by her hand. David told her to stand up for herself and stop him from beating her. When David would come back to Houston, he would call Pamela, and they would go to dinner. He taught Pamela how to eat, he taught her which fork to eat with, how to cut her meat, how to wipe each side of her lips once she put food in her mouth and how to get out of a car with her legs closed. He wanted her to be classy like him so he could put on an impression with the drug pin. This way, he could get closed to the drug pin and bring down his operation.

Then once his mission was completed, Pamela never heard from him again. Jerome continued to beat Pamela and made her feel real low like everything was her fault because he wanted to be with other women. Until one day, Pamela told Jerome she was not taking any more of his beatings ever again. Jerome just laughed at her and walked into the other room. Then one day later, Jerome, just out of the blue, hit Pamela on her face. Pamela didn't even do anything to him to cause him to hit her. Pamela picked up the iron and struck Jerome on his knee. Jerome fell to the floor because he couldn't walk. Pamela took him to the emergency room. He lied to the nurse about his accident. Jerome told the doctor he fell off a ladder and landed on his knee.

The doctor had the nurse bandaged his knee and gave him some crutches to walk in. Pamela told him when they got back home that she was going to leave him for good, but Pamela was just talking to hear herself talk.

The next time, Jerome gave Pamela a black eye. That night Pamela boiled hot water on the stove. While Jerome was lying down in the bed asleep, Pamela poured hot water on his back. She was very scared. Pamela made up in her mind, and the madness had to stop. The madness did stop because once Pamela poured boiling water on him, Jerome never hit Pamela again. Sometimes you have to fight fire with fire. Pamela didn't want her children to think that it's okay for a man to hit a woman.

Finally, everything was good between the two until Pamela heard him talking to a woman again. She asked Jerome, "Who was that?" He lied and said that he was talking to his sister. Then the phone rang again, and Jerome answered it. Pamela picked up the other end of the telephone. Pamela heard the other woman tell him she loved him. Pamela asked Jerome, "Who is she?" Jerome told Pamela, "She goes to the church where we attend. Her husband just passed away, and he left her everything." "So, you're consoling her? Have you slept with her, Jerome?" Jerome wouldn't answer her. Pamela said, "I'm talking to you." Jerome still did not answer.

Pamela told Jerome, "Why can't you stop cheating?" Pamela said, "I'm going to leave you for good. There's no coming back this time around. I'm sick of this mess. I deserve respect in this marriage. I have feelings, Jerome. Who in the world do you think you are?" So, Pamela went into the bedroom and started packing her clothes. Jerome went into the living room. Then he came up from behind Pamela and tied her hands behind her back and sat her in this chair. Then he tied Pamela's hands to the back of the chair for a whole two weeks.

Jerome told Pamela, she was not leaving him. For some reason, he knew Pamela was serious this time. Pamela said, "Well, you act like you don't want to be married. What do you want me to do?" Pamela said, "I've done all I can do in this marriage to make it work. I don't know what else to do." Pamela could not call anyone to rescue her. Her children were scared to untie her of fear of catching a whipping until Pamela's father realized he hadn't heard from his daughter. Her father called Pamela at work and did not get a response. Her father sensed something was wrong. He called everybody he thought Pamela could have called. Everyone told Pamela's father they have not heard from her. Her father and cousin stopped by the apartment where Pamela lived.

Pamela's father rang the doorbell but didn't get an answer. He looked into the window and saw Pamela tied up to a chair. Pamela's dad took the screen off the window and told Pamela's kids to unlock the lock on the window. Once the kids unlocked the window lock like Pamela's father instructed them to, he told them, "I'm so proud of my grandbabies." Pamela's cousin climbed through the window. Pamela's cousin went to the door and let her father in. They untied Pamela, and her father told her, "You have to leave this place, or he will kill you." Pamela left and went to get a U-Haul. Pamela's father and cousin moved her things out of her apartment and placed everything in storage.

Pamela and the children stayed with her father, and never went back to Jerome. Not Ever!! When Jerome's lease was up on his apartment, he moved in with this lady from the church. The next day, Pamela filed for a divorce. Jerome became very devious to Pamela and took all the money out of the bank account. Then he took her car, so she and the kids had to catch the bus and walk miles to get to the babysitter. One day, when Pamela got off of work and went to the babysitter to pick up her kids, they were gone. Jerome took her kids from her. Jerome's mom went along with Jerome when they had taken Pamela's children from the babysitter, never letting Pamela talk to them on the telephone or seeing them for a whole year.

Jerome was a skimmer. When the divorce was finalized, the judge ordered him to return the children, the car, and some furniture to her within twenty-four hours, or he would be put in jail. Jerome was a cold-blooded man because while they were going through a divorce, he was living with another woman, and Pamela was made out to be the bad person. In the end, Pamela prevailed because her babies were returned to her. She was rewarded sole custody.

She couldn't believe her eyes how big they had grown. From then on, Pamela moved on with her life without Jerome. Pamela did not treasure disappointment because she truly loved Jerome.

The only thing also that was treasured as a disappointment is the marriage did not last forever like the TV pictures Pamela watched, like Coming to America, Cinderella, and Snow White as a little girl. The pictures made Pamela think you would be with your prince forever and live happily ever after. Pamela thought all marriages would turn out to be and end up like a fairy tale marriage lasting forever. With Jerome, trust went out the window with his cheating. Jerome kept getting caught time after time until Pamela got enough of it. She just couldn't forgive Jerome anymore.

At least, Pamela was able to walk away with no regrets in her marriage, no second-guessing herself in the marriage whether she should have stayed in the marriage for the kid's sake. Pamela was done, finished, and there was nothing left within her to give the marriage any more chances or tries. Pamela was all tried out,, which helped her to move on, never looking back at what could have been. Twenty years later, Pamela saw Jerome at her daughter's house. It was coming on him and his wife's twenty-two year anniversary. They were renewing their vows. Pamela told Jerome, "You and your wife were meant to be together. It seems like you both have the kind of love that lasts forever, which holds two people together. Jerome never said that he loved his wife. He just said that she held him up financially.

Pamela replied to him, "It's got to be more than that because of the years you two have been together. You know, love had to keep the two of you together even if you don't want to admit it to yourself." Jerome said,

"You haven't changed a bit. You are still as beautiful as ever." Pamela said, "Thank you. You haven't changed a bit but bald at the top of your head." Everybody in Pamela's daughter's house laughed. Pamela left her daughter's house and went home.

Pamela stopped at a gas station one morning to get gas. She saw a Dolly Madison truck parked on the other side. This tall, dark-skinned man had the cutest dimples in his cheeks, his teeth were pearly white, and he had a pop belly. As Pamela walked by him, he spoke to Pamela, saying to her, "Good Morning." Pamela went into the store to pay for her gas.

As Pamela was going over to pump gas in her car, he walked up to Pamela and gave her his business card with his telephone number on the card.

He told Pamela that his name is Jerry. Pamela said, "Hi, Jerry, it's my pleasure to meet you." He asked Pamela if she likes donuts. Pamela said, "Yes, my favorite donuts are the coconut kind." Jerry gave Pamela six-packs of Hostess coconut donuts. Pamela told him, "Thank you." Pamela became fascinated by him. She couldn't wait until the next day so she could call him. Both of them talked for hours and hours on the phone. He was telling her about himself, how many times he had been married, why he broke up with many different women he became involved with, how many children he has. and how he wanted a better paying job. He told Pamela that he was married and separated from his wife at the moment.

Jerry told Pamela that he met his wife at a strip club dancing on a pole. He went on to brag how he dressed her from wearing whooshed clothes to conservative clothes, how he got her shopping at the top department stores, how he moved her out of the ghetto into a house in the suburbs. He told Pamela how he jeweled her up with diamonds, fancy rings, diamond bracelets, necklaces, with totaling one carat of diamonds on up. He also told Pamela how pretty his wife is, and how she's refined and has class now, and how he made her into the woman that she is now.

So, Pamela asked him, "If you did all these making her into the type of woman you wanted her to be Jerry, why did she cheat on you? Why would you still not talk to her?" He told Pamela that he caught her in bed with his best friend. She hurt him real bad inside. He said that instead of killing her, he beat the crap out of her instead. The next day, he moved out of the house, moving his clothes and some furniture into an apartment. Jerry said that she wiped out his bank account. He told Pamela that he had a hundred and fifty-five thousand dollars in the bank. Before Pamela knew, it was already three o'clock in the morning.

Pamela told Jerry that she was sleepy, and she was going to bed because she had to get up and go to work the next day. Jerry went on to tell Pamela that now she is divorcing him and trying to get his 401k from his job. Pamela told him, "Some women just want a man's money without loving him. It seems like you might have loved her dearly, but she didn't love you back. All she probably was interested in was your pocketbook." Jerry told Pamela, "You might be right, but I made her who she has become now."

"I guess she's your masterpiece." Pamela laughed because she never heard a man speak that way about a woman. Pamela felt his wife was his trophy. Pamela knew most men who put their wives on a pedestal, and nine out of ten, they cheat on them, and then they leave them for another man and clean out their bank account. Then their soon to be ex is heartbroken like they never saw it coming. Pamela and Jerry talked on the phone for hours before both of them met. One day Jerry got off of work early and asked Pamela to come over to his house.

So, Pamela went to his house. Jerry gave Pamela directions to get to his apartment. Pamela got lost because she has no sense of direction. Even if Jerry draws her a map, she would still get lost. After Pamela being lost for forty-five minutes, Pamela finally arrived at his apartment. Pamela knocked at his door. Jerry told her to come in, and Pamela did. Once she was inside his apartment. He introduced Pamela to his wife, and Pamela said hello, and then Jerry told Pamela that she could sit down on the couch.

Once Pamela sat down on the couch, his soon to be ex said that she guessed she'd be going and left. Pamela being a direct person, asked Jerry, "What was that all about?" "If your wife was here, I could have come over some other time." He said, "I want my wife to see the beautiful woman that I'm dating because I wanted my wife to let him come back home." "Once she took a glance at you, she could become intimidated by you." Pamela told him, "You are wrong for that because this could have been a catfight, especially if she was still was in love with you."

"Jerry, you put me in the middle of this mess without knowing about what's going on." Jerry fixed Pamela a drink and started feeling all over on her. Pamela got hot as a firecracker and ended up in bed with him. He wanted Pamela to go down on him and suck on his brain. Pamela told Jerry that she didn't know how to suck his brain. Jerry said that he thinks it's time for her to learn a new sex trick. Jerry told her how to do it, where to put her mouth, how to go up and down, lick all around his brain and how to lick his head in the middle like a lollipop.

Jerry said, "This is what most men like." He said that he would give her a grade of a "B" plus. As both of them continue to see one another, he told Pamela that she'd get better in time. Jerry also said, a man likes a little foreplay before he put it in your vagina. Jerry went on to say you can hook a man by doing this because his wife or mistress might not go down on him at home. Some men get with other women for the sole purpose of getting something different than what he's getting at home. Pamela told Jerry that she is only looking for fun and sex. Jerry said, "You come to the right place."

Pamela let Jerry be her school teacher, and every time she saw him, he wanted her to suck his brain with whip cream, jelly, and syrup. Every time she saw him, he always had her sucking his brain differently until she became a pro and started making him scout sperm everywhere. Jerry would go back to work and tell his co-workers about Pamela going down on him and how beautiful she was. Pamela was so attracted to him that what he said to his co-workers didn't bother her at all.

Jerry was the type of man that Pamela always wanted in her life, so she decided she was going to hang with him no matter what. As several months went by, Pamela met his first wife and daughter. She was light-skinned, very bright, with long beautiful curly hair, which was all hers. Both of them had a beautiful daughter. She told Pamela to be careful of him because she went to prison for him having drugs in his car, which was his. She took the rap for him. She told Pamela that she told the cops the drugs were hers, but the drugs were really for him.

She told Pamela that she was crazy for taking the rap for him because he never sent her any money or came to see her in prison. He just moved on with his life and with other women like she didn't exist. She went on to say that she gave up ten years of her life, and she couldn't get it back. She couldn't get a job because she has a felony on her record. She could only prostitute herself now to make money and take care of her kids or sell drugs, which she hoped won't land her back in prison. He won't even give her some money to take care of his child, so just be careful of him.

Pamela told Jerry what she said, and he did not deny it. Jerry said that it was true, but he couldn't go to jail because he had so much at stake. He was trying to get a job back then. See, Pamela will do anything for him, and She would do it because she loved him no matter what. After that, he took Pamela home. Then the next weekend, he took Pamela to see his mom, sister, and brother. His mom was tall and skinny. Jerry looked just like his mom except that he was on the heavy side but tall. His brother was light-skinned.

Jerry said that his brother got all the breaks in life because of his skin color. Jerry's mother told Pamela that she was very pretty, but Jerry doesn't come around as much because he is ashamed of his family. He always wanted a better life than his mom could give him. His mom said that Jerry was raised in the ghetto in a small shack of a house. He barely had enough food to eat. A lot of times, all her children ate were bread with ketchup or mayonnaise.

Jerry had to wear second-hand clothes that the neighbors gave him or at the goodwill stores. So, when he comes home, this house reminds him of his childhood life. He doesn't want to be reminded, so he doesn't come home to visit much. "Would you like something to eat or drink, Pamela?" Pamela replied, "No, thank you." Pamela and Jerry stayed at his mom's house for about three hours. His sister was helping him fill out an application at a well-known beer company that had several positions open.

Then two weeks later, he got a job there. Pamela and Jerry went out clubbing, dancing, and out to eat just celebrating every weekend with him having a new job and making more money. Jerry loved to go to clubs and to dance with Pamela. Whenever they dance, somebody from the dance crowd would always go on the other side of Pamela and be dancing with them. Pamela could dance, and men would always stare at her and wanted to dance with her. Jerry never had a problem with that.

He loved to party with Pamela. He loved the attention Pamela received from men, like he got off on that. Even though Jerry got the job at the brewery company, he and his trophy wife still got a divorce. His ex-wife left him because she felt that the grass was greener on the other side. Jerry started at the bottom of the brewery job and worked his way to the top until he became a manager over everybody. His whole outlook on life started changing. He bought himself a BMW, dressed in designer suits, and wore expensive shoes, diamond rings on his finger, and a diamond watch on his wrist. Pamela liked seeing Jerry's makeover as a sophisticated businessman.

Pamela and Jerry dated for a long time, but he never asked Pamela to marry him. But instead of Jerry coming to Pamela's house, he always wanted Pamela to meet him at some sleazy motel somewhere out of the city limits, like on the other side of town from where he lived. As both of them were making love one night, his phone began ringing. He answered the phone and said hello. Once he finished his call, he told Pamela that it was his wife on the telephone. She was having a baby boy.

Pamela said, "When did you get married? Why didn't you tell me until now? You're having a son at this point." Pamela was livid because he lied to her. She thought he would marry her for all the time they had spent together. He was on charade around town with Pamela, and he was married. She told Jerry that she was good enough to screw but not good enough to be his wife. Pamela asked, "What does your wife looks like?. "What does she do for a living?" He replied, "You know she's high yellow. She's a marketing representative for a major company." He heard her speak at some of her presentations with other companies.

"She's remarkable, witty, and smart. She has a good head on her shoulder." Jerry told Pamela that he knew what she was thinking. Pamela said, "You have no possible idea what I'm thinking." She told Jerry that he was a low-down dirty dog to lead her on like she does not mean anything to him. Pamela told him that he never even considered marrying her after all the times they spent together and all the things they've been through. He told Pamela that she was too dark for him, plus she does not have a degree and hold a professional title. Besides, he was buying a two-story house in a prestigious neighborhood.

"Pamela, you are not used to that type of lifestyle." He said, "Pamela, you're my garden tool. Maybe one day, you will get lucky but not today with me." Jerry hurt Pamela's feelings so bad she started crying. Jerry told Pamela that he was sorry for those hurtful words. He didn't mean to hurt her feelings, but they know that all they have or will ever have in common is sex. Jerry said to Pamela that she could never be part of his world. So, he hoped that she could deal with that, but they have good chemistry. He also told her that he was still going to see her. Pamela was so mad. She didn't even answer him. After that, he took Pamela out to eat.

Pamela was silent the whole time during dinner. When she looked at him, she rolled those big, pretty eyelashes at him. When he took her home, she told Jerry no more. She stopped answering his calls. She stopped sleeping with him. Pamela thought to herself she could have made him happy, but she figured that his love was elsewhere and not with her. After a year and a half went by, Jerry showed up at Pamela's job and asked for her at the switchboard. Her co-workers were asking her, who's that man. He's good looking, and they wanted to talk to him. Pamela went to the front desk to see who was there to see her. She was amazed to see Jerry. She asked him, "what brings you here?"

She told Jerry that she was surprised to see him. He said, "Will you have lunch with me?" Pamela said, "What the hell? Yes." She went back to her desk to get her purse. One of her co-workers asked her, "Is that your friend?" Pamela said, "Yes." Her co-worker said for some unknown comment that she knew he was coming to see her. Pamela smiled and left with Jerry for lunch. He took Pamela to eat seafood because he knew this was Pamela's favorite food. Pamela asked him at the table with what was going on in his world. He said that he and his wife haven't been getting along, and both of them have separated.

He asked Pamela if he could start seeing her again. Jerry asked, "Pamela, what was going on with you? Pamela said that she's just raising her two daughters, going to church, work, and back home. Pamela said, "That's it, my daily routine every day." Jerry said, "Do you have a man in your life?" Pamela said, "No man yet." Jerry told Pamela that he has been grieving over her. Pamela said, "Right." Jerry said that he has not been able to move on without her. Out of nowhere, Pamela said that, of course, he could see her. Pamela and Jerry started seeing one another and spending time together again.

When Jerry wanted to spend time with Pamela, he would call Pamela to meet him at his job. Once Pamela arrived at his job, he would get into Pamela's car, and both of them would go to a motel and have sex. Then he would give her money to buy her a gift and gas up her car. This became a regular routine of Jerry with Pamela. Then one evening, he had Pamela take him to these projects in the hood. Pamela said, "Who lives in the projects?" He said, "You will see." They arrived at the apartments in the projects. Jerry got out of the car, turned to Pamela, and said, "Are you coming?"

Pamela said, "Okay." She got out of her car and went in with him. He knocked on this door, and an elderly lady opened the door and asked them to come in. It seemed like she was expecting him. Once both of them are inside the house, she asked Jerry if he did serve those child support papers since he has moved up in the world. She told Jerry, "It's time for you to take care of your daughter now, she's in the eleventh grade, and you haven't done anything for her. She looks exactly like you. She's graduating next year, and you won't even own up to it that she's your daughter. This is the reason why we're going to court, Jerry."

She went on to say, "It's a shame we as women have to take a man to court just to get him to take care of his own flesh and blood." Then his daughter came out. She said, "Hello." Pamela was surprised to see her because she looked just like her daddy from head to toe. Pamela asked Jerry in front of everybody, "Are you trying to deny her? She looks just like you." Jerry laughed. His daughter replied, "He has always denied me." His daughter said, "Do you know why?" Pamela asked her, "Why do you think that he has denied you all these years?" His daughter said that because her skin is dark.

His daughter said to Pamela, "You too are too dark for my dad, also." Pamela laughed and said, "You are absolutely correct because he has always married yellow skin toned-women." Pamela told his daughter, "Your dad has never mentioned you to me." She has known him for a long time. His daughter said that she really wanted to get to know her dad, but her dad never wanted her around because of her skin color. She said that when she graduates from school, she's going to cosmetology school. She said she loves to do hair. Pamela told his daughter that she could make a lot of money, especially if she builds up her clientele.

Jerry and her grandmother were talking about what his plans were going to be for his daughter. Once their conversation was finished, Jerry told Pamela that he was ready to go. Pamela got up and gave everybody in the house a hug, and said, "Goodbye, it was nice meeting everyone." Pamela and Jerry left. Pamela told Jerry, "You are a piece of work." She went on to say that nothing ever shocks her where he is concerned. Pamela told Jerry, "You are full of surprises."

Jerry told her to drive the car over there to the motel, and so they can spend some time together before she takes him to his car at his job. They checked into a motel, and while they were making love, Jerry told Pamela, "my wife is having another baby. She is nine months pregnant, and she's going to have a baby boy. Pamela, I lied. We are not separated. We are still together, but she can't have sex right now until the baby comes." Jerry told Pamela that he loves his wife. He has always enjoyed the sex Pamela had with him and this is why he came to her job to find her.

Pamela told him for once that she gets it. She understands him now. Pamela told him, "Thank you for letting me know who you really are." Pamela told Jerry that now she also knows she was just someone he could sleep with when he couldn't get it from his wife. Pamela told Jerry that he always got what he wanted when it came to the kind of woman he wanted to be, with but that's okay. Life is a learning experience. Jerry told Pamela that one day she's going to find the right man in her life to share her world with.

Jerry also told Pamela that within ten years from now, he felt within that she will be climbing to the top of the ladder in her career. Pamela told Jerry that she'd always loved him from the first time she saw him. Pamela said to him, "I wished it was me whom you were married to and having your babies." Pamela said that she couldn't take any more from him. She was going to walk away from him completely this time and never look back. This might be hard for her, but she's going to do it. Pamela also said that she knew he really did not care about her because he has his other life over there at his home. Pamela got out of bed, then she took a shower with Jerry, and put her clothes back on.

Both of them left the motel, and Pamela took Jerry back to his car. She kissed him goodbye. From then on, Pamela never answered his telephone calls or saw Jerry again. Pamela treasured disappointment with Jerry. Pamela was crazy about this man and was hoping to have a future together with him. Pamela fell in love with him, not him in love with her, and that hurt inside her heart. His love was an experience for her. She realized that you don't always get what you want or desire, but at one point in life, you have to wake up to the situation at hand.

Pamela woke up realizing that he was never interested in her even though he had known her for a long time because he kept passing her up in marriage. So, marrying other women like Pamela wasn't good enough to be in his world, only good enough to give him brain and sex. Pamela had to see the situation as it was and move on with her life.

Pamela met Jack at her work office. Jack was a mail courier and delivered mail to different companies. The ladies loved him when he came into the office. The ladies kept up with his schedules at the precise time of the day. He would be coming to the office to drop and pick up the mail. Jack was a tall, dark skin-tone man. He had plenty of gray hair on his head, and he was medium built. Then one day, Jack just stopped by her desk and told her good morning. Then Pamela looked up at him and told him good morning also.

Every time he would stop by, Jack would always tell Pamela, good morning. Then one day, Jack took the plunge and asked Pamela for her telephone number, which Pamela wrote down on a piece of paper for him. Pamela didn't answer any of his phone calls until Jack gave her his telephone number. Jack asked Pamela, "Why did you not answer my phone calls?" Pamela said, "Because I felt like you were married. Since you have given me your number now, I'll talk to you already." Jack and Pamela talked for weeks and months.

Pamela told Jack where she lived and told him she has two girls. Then one day, Jack just turned up at Pamela's doorsteps with his clothes. Pamela told him, "I like you but not like this. I have children, girls, I just can't let you move in like that. So, what's going on with you, Jack?" Jack told Pamela, "I left my wife." Pamela replied, "So, Jack, you are married? Wow!" Jack replied, "Yes." "Jack, what made you leave your wife?" Jack told Pamela, "We'd grown apart. This is what happens when you spend a lot of time and years with one woman."

Pamela said, "But what makes a man grow apart from his wife?" Jack told Pamela, "I was with my wife for ten years but never married her. I have a ten-year-old son. The woman I'm with has eight kids." Pamela replied, "You've been living or shacking with a woman that has eight kids? Were you crazy? So, she hooked you by getting pregnant to keep you?" Then Pamela asked him, "Do you love her?" Jack replied, "I loved her at one time, but love has faded away." Jack told Pamela, "The woman I'm living with is a nagger, controlling, always bossing me around, and spending all my money."

Jack told Pamela that the first time he laid eyes on her, he fell in love with her. Pamela's response was, "Oh, really now. That's smooth. Jack, you can stay the night. We will take this one day at a time." The days turn into months, and Pamela's children loved him. He became like a second father to Pamela's children, taking them to carnivals, parks, to the zoo, movies, go-kart rides, help them with their homework, and read children's books to them. He would listen to her kids talk about Pamela. What Pamela liked about him, he would correct the kids and would tell them to never talk about their mom to anyone. If you can't say anything good about your mother, don't say anything at all. Jack was very good with the kids, and Pamela was very moved by this.

Pamela said in her mind if the children like him, then he must be a good man. Then one day, Jack took Pamela and her children to meet his family on a Saturday. Pamela and her children met his father, mother, his sister, his three brothers, their wives, and their children. Pamela and her children also met his cousins. It was like a family reunion. Jack had a close-knit family. They truly welcomed Pamela and her children. It was like they knew her already.

Jack's parents kissed her and welcomed her into the family. Jack's brothers' wives also welcomed Pamela. His sister was wonderful, and his brothers gave her a hug. Jack was smiling, showing those white teeth of his. Then after Pamela met his family, Jack took Pamela and her children to meet his best friend for his approval of their relationship. They liked Pamela also. Pamela learned that Jack met his best friend in jail. He protected Jack so that no other inmates would take advantage of him while he was serving his time in jail. As a couple of weeks went by, a lady started calling Pamela's house.

Pamela just ignored the calls because she thought it was probably a wrong number, but it turned out instead to be Jack's baby momma. So, the next time his baby mama called, Pamela picked up the phone and said hello. Jack's baby mama's name was Anita. She was crying on the other end and cursing Pamela out at the same time for taking her man. She even told Pamela that Jack was a child molester, but Pamela did not believe her.

Pamela told her to calm down, and they should talk like adults. Anita told Pamela, "You know, Jack and I have lived with one another for ten years, and one day he just walked out on me. This must have been when he moved in with you." Anita said, "I don't know why he left me, Pamela. All I remember him saying to me was, we have problems which he couldn't deal with anymore." Pamela asked Anita why she stayed with a man for ten years, and they never got married.

She said to Pamela that she got pregnant in order to keep him there with her. Pamela told Anita that she really didn't know he was married or was common law married because he didn't have a ring on his finger. Pamela told Anita that if she knew he was married, she would not have ever let him move in with her and the kids. Anita told Pamela that she loved him and has devoted her whole life to him. Now he's gone. Pamela said, "Whose fault is that?" Pamela knew that if the conversation continued, there could be drama between them. So Pamela ended the conversation by saying goodnight. Then Jack walked in. Pamela told him that she just got off the telephone with Anita. "She sounded so messed up behind you." Pamela told him, "I lied to her about knowing that you were together for ten years."

Pamela asked Jack why he lived with Anita for so long and didn't marry her. Jack replied that she had too many kids with different men. He was not going to marry a woman like that. Pamela left the conversation alone. Jack and Pamela grew closer. Then one day, on her birthday, Jack proposed to Pamela less than six months of them living together. Jack put a two-carat diamond ring on Pamela's finger. His sister orchestrated the whole wedding. Pamela found a lady to make the cake. The cake was going to be pink, and this was Pamela's favorite color.

Pamela found a photographer to take pictures of her wedding. She asked her cousins to sing at her wedding. Pamela also found a place where she could rent her wedding gown because Pamela could not afford to buy one. At the wedding shop, Pamela rented her wedding gown, the veil, the shoes, and the girdle. The color of the wedding dress was off-white layered with ruffles. The shoes were beautiful, and they shoes were off-white with pearls beaded all over each shoe. This was Pamela's first wedding ever. Pamela had a bridal shower and a rehearsal dinner, and did her own invitations and sent them to everybody she knew.

Pamela and Jack had a big church wedding. Pamela's father married them since Pamela's father was a pastor. Everybody who Pamela knew was on her big day. Everyone her husband knew was there also. It was a beautiful wedding. One Pamela will never forget in her life. The only dip in the wedding is they could not afford a honeymoon somewhere or a hotel room. They went back to their apartment, drank champagne, and made passionate love like it was their first time ever. Now two days before the wedding, Jack's baby mama was trying very hard to stop the wedding.

When Anita found out the day that they were getting married, she wanted to whip Pamela's butt for taking her man. Pamela laughed at her on the telephone and told Anita that she knows where she lives. She told Anita that she's not scared of her. The next day, Anita sent a certified letter to Pamela, stating in the letter that Jack had slept with one of her daughters. She needed to watch her girls around him. Pamela immediately dismissed this entirely from her mind. Pamela felt that Anita was trying to pull out one last straw to stop their wedding or make Pamela have second thoughts about marrying Jack. After their wedding day, everything was good with Pamela and Jack. It seemed like Pamela's life was fulfilled. Jack was the perfect stepdaddy to her children. Jack even bought Pamela a house to raise her children. They lived close to his family. Jack and Pamela were so very happy. Now Jack began to change when his son started coming over to the house. His son was very angry that his father married Pamela instead of his mom. His son began to lie on Pamela all the time, and his father would believe him over Pamela for some strange reasons. His son told his dad that Pamela would not let him eat, and Pamela called him a bad name.

Pamela did not defend herself in front of his son because she believed this was between her and his father, not him. She did not want his son to think that he caused friction between them. So, Pamela spoke to Jack once he went home. See, some step-children like to start confusion to see two parents get into it, to show the other parent that father believes me and not you. Jack's son knew just how to manipulate his father. See, Pamela believes a child should stay in a child's place. Pamela told Jack that she fed his child, and he ate everything on his plate, and he even got seconds and thirds.

"Your son can eat. He has a big appetite." Pamela told Jack that she surely did not curse at his son or called him a bad name, and he can ask her children. Pamela told Jack that this is the first time she ever met his son, and now she knows he is a big fat liar. Jack slapped Pamela in her face, and Pamela slapped him back. Jack said that he knows she didn't say those things his son said she did. Jack said that he loves his son. His son just wants all his time and attention when he's with him. His son feels that he left his mother for her. Pamela told Jack, "You did."

Jack told Pamela that his son sees us as a family with your girls. He's probably jealous somewhat. Jack told Pamela that he'd speak to his son about telling the truth. Pamela replied, "Thank you." From then on, Pamela would watch herself when his son would come around. Pamela always had her guard up when his son would come over to the house. His son would always start some kind of friction between the two before he leaves and go back home. Jack would always slap Pamela behind when his son would tell his father something, which was a lie. All his son would do is laugh at Pamela and lick his tongue out at her.

Jack would really believe anything his son would tell him, and would always fight with Pamela behind his son's lies. Pamela knew she had her hands full with his son. Now Jack started staying out all night on Friday nights, gambling, drinking, and smoking weed. This started after they had been married for two years. Jack would go into a rage sometimes and started breaking up everything in the house. Then if Pamela cooked, all the food would end up in the kitchen sink or on the wall. The next day, Pamela would have to clean up everything he broke and threw on the wall. Jack would just sit on the couch, drink his beer, and watch Pamela clean up his mess.

Then he would want to have makeup sex. Despite all he put Pamela through, she loved Jack. They would fight all the time because his father would always beat his mom. He thought it was okay to do that to Pamela the same way. Jack was a good stepfather to Pamela's children, and this was the reason why Pamela tried so hard to hold on to him. Pamela and Jack would fuss fight and make love on a normal basis every weekend. Jack became very comfortable in their marriage with this type of arrangement. Jack started coming home in the wee hours of the morning. Then Jack started coming up short with the house note money.

Pamela made sure the house notes got paid even when Jack couldn't pay it. Pamela never questioned anything until he started bringing women to her house. When he was off work during the week, Pamela noticed that when she got home, her bed was all messed up. Before Pamela would leave for work, she would always make up the bed every morning. Pamela would wake up early in the morning, get up, and clean up the whole house. Pamela would notice if anything were out of place. There would be times when Pamela would walk in her bathroom and always noticed a towel on the floor. She knew that she didn't put it there.

Then Pamela would always notice the top was off of her perfume. Pamela waited two weeks before she mentioned it to Jack. Jack just blew her off like she didn't say anything at all. Then one evening, when Pamela and the children were home, the telephone rung and on the other end was a woman. She was telling Pamela that her husband should be pulling in the driveway in about two minutes. She also told Pamela what he was wearing. Pamela would never see Jack get dressed on his off days. Pamela didn't know what type of clothing Jack was wearing.

She described what Jack had on to a tee. Jack had some blue jeans with a white T-shirt. She described everything, just right. Pamela told her, "You might be sleeping with my husband, up in my bed and in my house. You will never have him until I decide to let him go. He's still sleeping with me. Everything he's doing with you in bed, he's doing it twice and better with me." Pamela lets her know that she calls the shots here with him, and until she decides to leave him, then she can have him. Then Pamela said, "Let me tell you this and think about this hard and long just like he's cheating on me with you, he's going to cheat on you with somebody else. That's just how the cheating cycle is, but you probably already know this."

Then Jack pulled up in the driveway in two minutes just like she said. It did not take a rocket science to figure out that she lived nearby, maybe around the corner. When Jack came into the house, Pamela said, "Your woman called and let me know that you would be pulling up in the driveway in two minutes and told me what you would be wearing. Do you have anything you want to say, Jack?" Jack said, "No." Jack wouldn't even discuss anything with Pamela. He just asked her, "Was dinner ready?" Pamela fed him, and nothing was discussed about the matter. Pamela was very upset with Jack, but she didn't show it. Pamela thought that he loved her. Pamela thought their love would last until time indefinitely.

She never thought in a million years that Jack would cheat on her. For what? Pamela always tried to keep him happy and satisfied, even in bed. She was very shocked that he was cheating on her and the woman was calling her house. He must have given her their house number for her to call him. How disrespectful had Jack become to Pamela? Pamela let four days go by before she brought it up again. She told Jack that her marriage means a lot to her. She put a lot into this marriage. "How do you feel about our marriage? Are you going to keep seeing this woman? Are you going to work on our marriage?"

Pamela told Jack, "See, everything is going well with us. See, Satan the Devil knows this. Now you are letting the devil win. The devil loves to break up the couple's marriages. The devil is using her to do it. After she breaks us up Jack, she's not going to want you either. See, Jack, some women want a man because they're in a relationship. Once she breaks that up, she's not going to want you because it's a game she's playing. All she wants to do is break up our happy home. After she accomplishes breaking us up, she's going to move on to someone else." Pamela pleaded with Jack to think hard about them and don't let her destroy what they tried so hard to achieve and accomplish in their marriage. Jack just ignored Pamela and started sleeping in the other room of the house. Jack stopped having sex with Pamela and stopped contributing to the house note. Jack started staying out later and later, even coming home the next day. Then he started hanging out with friends who didn't mean him any good. His best friend called the house one night and told Pamela that Jack was doing drugs, and she needed to leave him. Each day, Jack's behavior pattern was changing. Pamela was so hurt deep inside her heart because she loved him so much, and she wanted her marriage to work.

Then one day, her daughter came home from a basketball game at school. She told her mom that when she came home with her classmate, Jack was also home. Her classmate asked her if Jack was her dad, and her daughter told Jack in front of her classmate that Jack was her stepfather. But Jack told her classmate that he was her boyfriend. Pamela asked her daughter if Jack was drunk. Her daughter said, "No." Pamela replied to her daughter, "Honey, I'm sorry if he embarrassed you in front of your classmate. I'll have a talk with Jack when he comes in. I'll find out where his head was at." Pamela asked her daughter if Jack ever touched her.

Her daughter said, "No." Pamela said, "Are you telling me the truth? I don't want you blaming me later if somebody touched your private spot." So Pamela's daughter said, no again. Pamela told her daughter, "Thank you." Pamela told her daughter that she's going to have a long talk with Jack tonight. Pamela's daughter told her mom, "Please don't get beat up tonight." Pamela immediately thought back to the letter his ex-wife had sent her the day before her wedding. Pamela thought that maybe he did sleep with one of her daughters. Anita was okay with that, but Pamela was not about to let that happen with any of her girls.

Because in Pamela's mind, no man was going to take her girls' innocence away from them until they are ready to give it up to the person they fall in love with. When Jack came home that night, it was around eleven o'clock. Pamela stayed up waiting for him. When Jack walked in, he was high and drunk. Pamela just asked him, "Why did you tell my daughter's classmate that you were her boyfriend when you're her stepfather?" Pamela said, "Wouldn't this have been more appropriate for you to say?" Jack replied that he was just playing with them.

Pamela said, "You don't play with my daughters like that because you're a grown man." Pamela said, "Grown men do not make statements like that to young children." Pamela asked Jack, "Do you want this marriage? Because I'm sick of you bringing your woman to my house and screwing her in our bed." Jack told Pamela, "Leave then, there's the door." Pamela went into her bedroom, went to sleep, and left Jack on the couch. Pamela told Jack that if he wouldn't straighten up his act, she would leave him. Pamela had to get herself a second job to make sure all the bills get paid. See Pamela was the type of woman who tries and makes a marriage work regardless of the situation.

But one particular night she had a feeling something terrible was going to happen. Pamela got out of bed, and it was around twelve o'clock p.m. Something just woke Pamela up out of her sleep. Pamela felt for Jack in the bed, and he wasn't there. Pamela got out of the bed and checked on the girls, and they were asleep. As Pamela was walking out of the girls' room, she noticed Jack in the dark of the living room with a gun in his hand playing Russian Roulette. Pamela said that she knows he's crazy now. "Jack, please put the gun down." Pamela also was noticing that Jack was putting the gun in his hand to his head and was actually pulling the trigger. Jack was trying to blow his brain out.

Pamela turned on the light and noticed that Jack was high as a kite. Pamela told Jack, "Please put the gun down because if you kill yourself, it will be very devastating for my girls to witness your brain all over the place. Jack told Pamela that he's going to kill himself and everybody in the house tonight. Pamela turned the lights off and quietly picked up her car keys. Pamela went into her children's room and woke them up and told them to grab some clothes. The children and Pamela climbed out of the window and ran down to Pamela's girlfriend's house down the street. The next day, Pamela went back to the house for the girls to get ready for school and to pack them some more clothes until Pamela can get the rest of their things out of the house.

A week went by, and Pamela went back to the house to get some more clothes, but the locks were changed. All of Pamela's clothes, jewelry, children's toys, and furniture were inside the house. Jack told Pamela that if she wants anything in the house, she has to let him know so he can be there to watch her take what he wanted her to have. Jack told Pamela that he was keeping all of her jewelry and furniture. The only thing she could take would be her kids' bedroom, their clothes, and her clothes. Pamela said to herself that he's crazy. Pamela came up with a plan to get her stuff out of the house. Jack would call Pamela's job every day at around twelve o'clock in the afternoon to see if Pamela was at work.

When Pamela got paid, she told her boss lady that she would not be there tomorrow because she was going to break in her own house and get her furniture, clothes, toys, jewelry, and appliances out of the house. She had scheduled a moving company to be at the house around ten o'clock in the morning. Pamela asked her boss lady that she could answer her phone if it rings and say that she's in a meeting until she gets all of her things out of the house. Pamela also told her that she would call her as soon as the movers move everything out of the house.

The night before the move, Pamela went to her parents' house and told her dad that she was going to pick him up at seven o'clock in the morning, he was going to help her pack up her furniture out of the house and to bring his gun with him in case there's any trouble. Pamela's dad asked her, "How are we going to get any furniture out of the house if you don't have any keys?" Pamela told him, "Don't worry, we will be able to get in. Just trust me." The next day, Pamela had the children, her dad, and the gun inside the car. They arrived at the house at eight o'clock in the morning, just right about Jack had left the house for work.

Pamela called her boss lady to make sure that she answers the phone on her desk and to let her know she had made it to the house. She would call her back when everything was out. Pamela had her girlfriend looking out for her in case Jack comes home while they were moving. Her best friend was going to call Pamela on her cell phone if he drove up in the driveway, and Pamela's dad had the gun in his pocket in case there is any trouble. Pamela went on the side of the house, broke the glass window with her shoe, unlocked the window, and raised the window up. Pamela had one of her daughters crawl into the window to unlock the front door. Her neighbor next door told Pamela that she was going to call the police.

Pamela told her next-door neighbor to call them because her name is on the lease.

Pamela told her next-door neighbor she and her kids just want to get their stuff out, and they'll be gone. The next-door neighbor said, "I'm sorry. Go ahead and do what you need to do." Her girls packed up their room. Pamela packed up the kitchen, bedroom, and the living room found her jewelry and packed up the bathrooms. The movers came around ten o'clock in the morning. The movers were on time, and Pamela explained her situation to the movers. She then told the movers that they need to have everything moved within one hour. Believe her. Everything was out in an hour. Pamela, her dad, and the girls helped the movers move everything they packed on the moving van. When everything was on the moving truck, Pamela's girlfriend down the street went inside her house. Pamela locked the house back up.

Pamela called her boss lady, told her that she was done moving, and no need to answer her phone anymore. Pamela moved everything in storage until she saved enough money for a deposit on an apartment. Later that evening, Pamela's girlfriend walked outside, got her a chair, and waited for Jack to pull up in the driveway of his house. Pamela's girlfriend had Pamela on the phone to tell her his reaction. Jack came home, pulled in the driveway of the house, and came back outside, scratching his head and mumbling words. You know he was outdone, rrobably wondering how she was able to outsmart him. Never underestimate a woman because they can always outthink a man when she feels like she is being pushed against a corner.

The only things the girls forgot were their stuffed animals and the baby patch dolls in the attic. They were crying two days later for the stuff animals they left behind. Pamela never went back to Jack or gave him a second chance with her. She divorced him quickly fast and hurry. Pamela treasured disappointment because she wanted her marriage to work, but the disappointment turned out to be a treasure in disguise because Pamela learned how to be a good wife and how to love with her heart. She never cheated on him. She was faithful and true. She learned to be a good mom to her children instead of being someone in a nightclub on the weekends. Pamela also felt that some men think with their brains below instead of their hearts.

See, your heart stores the love inside. The kind of love would have kept the two together because that love would have prevented him from hurting the other person. Love for the other person can be your conscience. Six months went by after the divorce, Pamela ran into Jack in the grocery store. He told Pamela that he was so sorry for taking his marriage for granted. Jack told Pamela that she was right. "The other woman never loved me or wanted me. She just loved the hype of breaking us up." Pamela asked Jack, "Was it worth it?" Jack said, "No." It was the biggest mistake that he ever made because he had everything right at home. Jack kissed Pamela on her cheek and told her that he will always love her forever.

Pamela met Jason at a washateria. Pamela was washing clothes when Jason came in with two of his cousins. He was a heavyset man with an earring in his ear, he had pearly white teeth, and he was a medium skin toned man. Pamela was sitting down, waiting for her clothes to dry. Pamela asked him what his name was. He told Pamela that his name was Jason. Then he gave Pamela his cell phone number and asked her to call him whenever she got a chance. Jason went over to the washing machine and put his clothes in the washing machine along with the washing powder to wash them. Pamela's clothes finally finished drying. She waved at Jason and told him goodbye.

Pamela went home and cooked dinner for her children. Pamela waited two weeks before she called him. So it would not seem like she was desperate or easy. When Pamela called Jason, he remembered who she was before she could tell him. Pamela was truly shocked that he remembered her. She thought she was going to have to go down memory lane, but she didn't have to. Jason asked Pamela what she was doing. She said, "Nothing." Jason said, "Why don't you come over?" Pamela said okay, but her children will have to come because she did not have a babysitter. Jason said, "Bring them with you."

Jason told Pamela that she has the cutest kids. He gave Pamela the direction to his house. As Pamela proceeded to go to his house, she got lost, and she called him and told him she doesn't know where she is. He asked her, "Do you see a street named Caldwell?" Pamela said, "Yes." Jason started telling Pamela what street to turn on to get to his house. As Pamela arrived there, Jason met Pamela outside in the driveway. He spoke to her children, and Jason told them, "Hello." They told him, "Hi." Pamela and the children walked up to his driveway and into his house.

Jason told Pamela that his wife left him for another man, and she just walked out on him and left him the house. He didn't want the house without her. Jason said that he's so hurt and he just doesn't know what he's going to do without her. Jason told Pamela that he couldn't even work or think right on his job. Jason also told Pamela that he gave her everything.

She never had to want for nothing. "Pamela, I mean nothing." He loved her more than life itself. He said, "I gave her the whole world, yet she had the balls to walk out on me." Pamela asked Jason, "Do you and your wife have small kids? Or do you have grown children?" Jason said that the last child just graduated from high school. Now, he'll be going to college. "Who knows Pamela, maybe she stayed until the last child finished school."

"Pamela, it seems like she had this planned." Pamela asked Jason, "Did you work all the time around the clock? Did you spend any time with your wife? Did you tell her that you love her while you were together?" Jason told Pamela that he worked all the time around the clock to give her and his kids everything. "You know Pamela, she cleaned me out." Pamela said, "What do you mean?" Jason told Pamela, "She went to the bank and took every dime that was in the checking and the savings account." Jason told Pamela, "That's okay because I expected my wife to do this." Jason turned to Pamela, "How do I live without her?" Pamela's children were sitting on the couch, watching TV. Jason and Pamela were sitting at the table. Pamela told Jason that she knows it's hard. Pamela told Jason, "You have to take one day at a time."

"Jason, it's not going to be easy. You could have sex with another woman to get over your wife. This is what most people do, but this will probably not work for you but only cause you more problems. This is what some people do to fill the void and pain that they feel when someone they loved has left them. Jason told Pamela that women run behind him all the time because he's a manager and makes good money, but he loves his wife. Jason told Pamela that when he walked in the washateria and saw her, the Lord told him that he could talk to her about anything. "You would help him sort everything out." Pamela told Jason, "Thank you. You're a good guy, Jason." Pamela said that she hates how he's going through something like this. Pamela told Jason that she's not looking for a relationship with him. He can just talk to her about all his problems. She'll help him resolve them, and she'll be the shoulder that he can cry on. Jason said, "Okay."

He said how his wife could leave him when he gave her everything in the world. She had access to the money at the bank. She drives a Lexus, she has diamonds, and he means big diamonds on every ring of her finger. She buys top of the line everything. She wears brand name clothes, purses, and shoes. When he's home, he tries to give her all of him. He guessed that wasn't good enough. Pamela told Jason that sometimes a relationship could run its course. People get married for all sorts of reasons. "Maybe in your case, maybe you weren't home enough. Maybe your wife got tired of being home by herself." "You know, Pamela, I'm going to retire from my job soon. I'm going to see if she will come back home."

Pamela told Jason that it sounds like a winner to her. "Go get your wife. You know Jason, marriage has sunshine, rain, and storms, and we all have to go through them some time or another." Pamela said, "You really truly love your wife, I can tell." Pamela got her children, left, and went home. After that, she didn't hear from Jason again until a month later. Pamela was the type of person who is trying to give Jason some time to sort his matters out in his life. She knew that all they will ever have in common is friendship because he was married and still in love with his wife. Jason called Pamela one night, crying around 1:00 in the morning. Jason said, "Pamela, help me. I need help." Pamela said, "Where are you? Jason."

Jason gave Pamela his address and gave her directions to his place. Pamela arrived at his apartment. When Pamela came into his apartment, there were three men and two ladies sitting on the couch. Pamela said hello to everybody, including Jason. Pamela said to Jason, "What the hell is going on with you? Who are these people? What type of help do you need?" Jason said, "These three dudes are my homeboys. These two women are the people I'm kicking it with." Pamela said, "Really now." Pamela said to Jason, "What happened to you? You lost weight. You're skinny. How did you lose so much weight? I can guess what these three dudes are doing for you—Keeping you doped up and getting you to spend up to your money. Just admit it, Jason. Just because something has saddened you, you turned to drugs for a solution." "Pamela, I love my wife. I retired from my job. I called her and told her that, but she still would not come home." "Then, she told me we're divorced." Pamela said, "What? How could that be possible? She got a divorce without your signature, and without you both going to court?" "I surely did not know I was divorced until she informed me. As I remember Pamela, I signed a bunch of papers without reading them. We have been together for twenty-two years." Jason told Pamela that he called his ex-wife and told her that she could have the house, and he'll move all his things out. She said okay to that. "Pamela, I truly love my wife, and it really hurts so bad inside. I do not know how to cope with this."

"Pamela, I know you are not going to like what I'm going to say. By doing drugs right now, drinking alcohol until I'm drunk and sleeping with those two women at the same time, helps me to keep my mind off my wife. This is how I'm coping for now." All Pamela could say to Jason, she's sorry he is going through this. She doesn't know what else to say to him. Pamela said to Jason that she sorry for his sorrows. Jason told Pamela that he couldn't sleep because he misses his wife a hell of a lot. Pamela tried to console Jason by saying, "in time, Jason you will get over her and be able to move on in with your life. The pain you are feeling inside right now will go away in time. After the incident at his house, Pamela would only talk to Jason on the telephone.

Each time she spoke to Jason, he was out partying at some club or at some friend's house doing crack. One night, Jason invited Pamela to one of his friend's party. They treated Pamela like they knew her already like she was part of their circle. This probably was because she was Jason's friend. It was a nice party until they started doing crack. So, Pamela left and told Jason goodnight. That was not Pamela's kind of party. Jason called Pamela the next day and told Pamela he apologizes for inviting her to that kind of party. Pamela replied, apology accepted, but don't you do that again. Pamela told Jason that she was going to say this again, and that she's sorry for his pain. "Don't let your wife make you turn to crack. There's more to life ahead, Jason.

She knows that you may not see this right now, but in time you will. Your wife has moved on with her life, and you should do the same. She knows it's hard right now, Jason, but you gonna have to do this sooner or later. Please, please, Jason, stop doing crack before you're hooked.

After this, Pamela didn't hear from Jason for months. Pamela felt Jason was probably mad at her, but Pamela never did pick up the phone and call Jason because their relationship was only friendship. Jason only wanted to be friends with Pamela. A person he could talk to about his problems and how he was feeling because his wife had left him. This is how Pamela accepted their friendship.

Pamela did not put anything else into it, but what he told her up front. Pamela was the type of person who listens to him attentively. After five months went by, she finally heard from Jason. Jason asked her to come over to his new place, and gave her directions to get there. As she arrived, he met her outside and brought her up to his townhouse. He opened the door and asked Pamela to come in. Pamela sat on his new leather sofa. Jason thanked her again and again for being there for him. Jason said, "Because of all I've been through, I finally stopped doing crack. I just woke up one morning and said no more. I did it, Pamela, I stopped doing crack. Just like that."

"Not only that, Pamela, but I also stopped having sex with so many women that I don't even know. Just because I was hurt by my wife." Having said all of this, Pamela met his lover. Jason introduced him to Pamela. Pamela said, nice to meet you. Pamela was not shocked. He turned to another man because this happens when a woman hurts a man so badly without talking to him in their marriage or relationship before she walks out the door. Just leaves without any warnings. Pamela told Jason, "I'm so happy for both of you. Jason replied, "I knew you would be happy for me."

"Pamela, you were truly a real friend to me in my time of need." Pamela told Jason, "now, I don't have to worry about you anymore. It seems like you found your way." Jason said, he surely did. Pamela left and went home. Years later, she met Jason at her office building, driving a metro lift for the handicap. He still looked the same but had more gray hair, and he was thin, but he looked happy.

Jason told Pamela, "I would never forget you as long as I live. You were truly a friend indeed." In this relationship, Pamela just treasure true friendship. There was no love treasured or disappointment.

Pamela would have loved him and have went further, but it didn't. Jason stated upfront what he was looking for between the two. Sometimes you meet somebody, and they may not want a relationship with you. They may just want to be friends. Pamela was just glad he picked her to talk out his problems and not somebody else. Pamela listens to Jason closely. She felt like she was his psychologist. She advised him to the best of her ability. She did not lie to him to get him to be with her. Instead, Pamela let Jason know he could trust her with anything he needed to get off his chest. On some roads, you travel, and you meet people, and you will find out that friends is hard to come by. If you have a friend, cherish the moment you have together. In this relationship, Pamela was only there for a moment for Jason to share his deepest feelings and to advised him correctly to the best of her ability.

So Jason would not commit suicide. Even though he and his wife did not get back together. This showed Pamela that there are men out here in the world that truly love their wives and know how to take care of their wives materially also. You just have to be patient and wait on the Lord to send you a good mate like this man was. Pamela hopes one day, she could experience treasuring love in a relationship with no disappointment. Jason truly, truly, loved his wife more than life himself. There's a lesson to be learned here, but there was no communication.

Communication could have salvaged their marriage if she let him know how she felt. Where was Christ, no one thought about going to their pastor for counseling to save their marriage. The trust went out the door, never coming back in the marriage. She had moved on with someone else. Jason was never the same again. He turned to another man for the love that he lost with his wife of twenty-two years. At least he found happiness with someone which Pamela was happy about, which were her main concern for him.

Pamela met Jeremy through her girlfriend friend. They were supposed to meet at a club, but Jeremy didn't show up. Pamela had herself together from head to toe. She found out he worked for the railroad, made good money, and been on his job for over twenty-five years. She really wanted this man. Jeremy called Pamela and apologize to her for not showing up because his daughter had gotten married. Pamela excused him this time. Jeremy set up another date for her and her girlfriend to come over. Her girlfriend and Jeremy were friends. They went on a double date at Jeremy's apartment. Her girlfriend and her date made out in one of his bedrooms.

Pamela and Jeremy just talked to get acquainted first. They became friends first, then lovers, then husband and wife. When Jeremy made love to Pamela for the first time at his apartment, it was magic. The chemistry was amazing. Jeremy was a perfect fit for Pamela. Jeremy and Pamela fell in love with one another at the same time. He was the perfect match. They were on the same common ground. Keep in mind, Pamela was sort of a yes woman.

She would do whatever a man wanted her to do. Within six months, Jeremy asked Pamela to marry him, she said yes. When they went to the Jewelry store and picked out rings, he bought her a three and a half-carat ring.

It was huge on her finger, and she couldn't believe it. She kept looking at her finger. She was in a dazed. When she and Jeremy got married, she didn't know much about Jeremy. Her father married them at her Dad's house since Pamela's father was a pastor. Pamela learned Jeremy as each day went by. Jeremy would come home at weird hours working for the railroad. Once Jeremy comes home from working, Pamela would have to get up out of bed, fix his plate of food, then warm it up in the microwave and then sit at the table until he was finished eating. Then he would go take a shower, come to bed, and they would make sweet love. This was the kind of sweet love that made Pamela scream all the time when she climaxes.

Jeremy knew how to love her. One thing Pamela loved about him was he paid all the bills in the house. He was a real man, not fifty-fifty like most men out there. When he would tell Pamela to do something, she would do it, no questions asked. Jeremy would take Pamela to see his mom all the time. She loved Pamela and she would always say to Pamela that she was like an angel. For some reason, Jeremy didn't like this. He stopped taking Pamela to see his mom. Maybe because Jeremy's mom got close to Pamela because she knew her son married a good woman that loved him. Jeremy had three children, and Pamela only met them once because Jeremy was very particular when it came to his children. His children got so close to Pamela and her children to the extent that his daughter was telling Pamela all her deep dark secrets that her parents didn't know about what was going on with her.

His two sons fell in love with Pamela's daughters because they were just as beautiful as Pamela. Once, his children went home and told their mother what a fantastic day they had with Pamela and Jeremy's new wife. This was the last time Pamela saw them. The thing with his ex-wife was, Pamela had to deal with her calling her house every morning like she wanted him back. She would call her house like five o'clock in the morning like she didn't have a man. When she and Jeremy were married, she put him out of the house for another man.

She moved the man in Jeremy's house, and they weren't even divorce. Now by his ex-wife doing this, this caused tension between Pamela and Jeremy because he still had feelings for her. Whatever his ex-wife would tell him about the telephone calls, Jeremy believed every word she would say. They started having problems in their marriage, but Pamela loved the ground Jeremy walked on more than life itself. He knew this. Jeremy started staying out late at night saying, he was working late, but he wasn't. Then he would come home and fuss at Pamela for no reason at all. Then on top of that, he stopped calling Pamela at night when he was working. Pamela knew he was cheating on her, but she loved him.

Women would call her house all the time and hang up in her face. Then he told Pamela when he's at home, do not answer the phone. Pamela said, okay. He told her only to pick up the telephone only if she sees his cell phone number on the telephone or his children's calls. Pamela did whatever he told her to do like a puppet on a string. Not only this, but she also had to put up with women calling the house who went to his church, and they were married. These married women from the church had a relationship with Pamela's husband. These women were at church every day of the week if the church doors were open. Then Pamela had to contend with him going on vacations with other women though he would never take her on vacations with him. She would find out from the other woman. One day she came home, she came in and answered the telephone.

This woman out of the blue told Pamela she just came back from Jamaica with her husband and told her "Just ask him." She knew it was true because when she confronted him, he couldn't look her in the face. Then he would start fussing at her about picking up the telephone. They lived in an apartment. Then Pamela had to contend with him sleeping with a woman living in the apartment complex. One time she was taking the kids somewhere, the kids saw another woman get into his truck and parked her car on the side of the road. Pamela hit his truck and was ready to whup that woman's butt. Pamela picked up a brick on the ground and threw it at Jeremy before Jeremy could beat Pamela home.

Pamela broke up everything that meant something to him in the apartment because she was sick of him accusing her of cheating on him when he knew he was the one cheating on her. Pamela cut up all his clothes, broke a lamp his grandmother had given him, she turned the TV over and broke it. She cut up all his pictures on the wall. Then later on, during the week, Jeremy went to the store and replaced everything Pamela had ripped to pieces and broke up. Jeremy threw Pamela and her kids out of his apartment for another woman and divorced Pamela.

But stupid Pamela still loved him. Pamela tried to commit suicide behind Jeremy. She loved the ground he walked on and could not see her life without him. She swallowed a whole bottle of sleeping pills. It must not be destined for her to die that day because a friend of hers stopped by and the door was open. He walked in and went into Pamela's room and found her lying across the bed, moveless, and the pill bottle on the floor. He immediately shook her, stood her up on her feet to walk, but he still couldn't get a response from Pamela. Then he pressed his hands on her chest until she threw those pills up out of her stomach. Then she finally started coughing and coming to herself.

He told her, "Never in life try to take your own life behind another man because he's going to move on with his life, losing no sleep behind you and not even thinking about you. What would you have accomplished by taking your life? Pamela, always remember that if you are dead and gone, he'll still be living, going on with his life, never even thinking twice about you. What about your children? They need you not that man you're trying to take your life for." But stupid Pamela stilled loved him no matter what. Two years later, Jeremy and Pamela started seeing one another again. Jeremy told her how sorry he was and how much he loved her.

Pamela felled for the yokey-dokey but could never remarry him because once a cheat is always a cheat. Pamela felt they did not make it because she loved the ground he walked on. She put him before the Lord. That's why bad things in her life started to happen to her. Everything in her life went topsy-turvey or to mess. This man brought her all the way down emotionally and mentally. She ended up having nowhere to go because he put her out of his apartment once again. This time, she had to start living with people because she couldn't get her own apartment because of co-signing for someone else whom broke the lease on an apartment failing to tell Pamela. The amount owed was four thousand dollars, and she had to pay this back first before she could get an apartment. It took her months to do this.

Then the Lord made a way for her. She accepted a job promotion in another city and was given a huge package deal, which got her caught up financially, which allow Pamela to get on her feet once again. Then when she started the job a month later, Pamela's father passed away. This was a very sad point in her life because Pamela's dad was her best friend, always there to pull her out of situations. Pamela had to head back home to prepare for her father's funeral. She dropped a call to Jeremy and told him what happened, and Jeremy definitely ran to be by her side. Little did she knew Jeremy was trying to wren his way back into her life by taking advantage of Pamela's vulnerability.

He even succeeded because Pamela ended up marrying him a second time only to head for heartbreak again with Jeremy. Jeremy lived in Houston, and Pamela lived in Austin. On the weekends, she would have to travel to see Jeremy. He would tell her he would be in Austin watching her apartment and leave without letting Pamela know he was there. When she would always come to see him, he was never there. When he would come home, she would see him on a Sunday, but it would be time for Pamela to head back home to Austin to get ready for work. One weekend when she came to visit Jeremy, a woman called the house and revealed to Pamela that she and her husband went on a cruise to the Bahamas.

Pamela asked her, "Do you know who am I? She replied, "No." Pamela told her, "Well, I am Jeremy's wife." "You're lying because he's not married. We went on a cruise together," the woman on the other end retorted. Pamela told her, "Just because you went on a cruise with a man doesn't mean he may not be married." Pamela said, "I understand how excited you may seem to be with him and the idea of going on a vacation together. But remember, if he did this while he was with me, once he gets with you, he would do the same thing with you like he did to me. Then after the phone call, a woman stopped by to spend the night. Pamela invited her in, and Jeremy was there. She asked, "Who are you? You must be the maid."

Pamela said, "Ssorry to disappoint you but I'm the Mrs., Right Jeremy? Jeremy said, "Yes she is." You should have seen Jeremy's face when this woman walked into the house.

You could have bought him for a penny. This woman kept apologizing to Pamela for disrespecting her. Pamela told her to stop apologizing to her. She mentioned to her that she lives in Austin, right in front of Jeremy. Pamela told her, "I only come home on the weekend. So, I understood you thought he was single. You can have this good-for-nothing brother because he's nothing but a liar and a cheater." Pamela walked out of his life for good this time, never looking back or having any regrets. Jeremy claimed he loved her, but he didn't. He just didn't want any other man to have her. He put his feet on her head, crushing her so she could not grow or be anything in life. Jeremy felt like Pamela did him wrong.

He always blamed Pamela for what he had done wrong. His definition of love is two fools feeling sorry for one another. Later on, as years passed, Pamela heard from him admitting to her once again, he was sorry for how he treated her. He was sick with old age, high blood pressure, going blind in his eyes, and he wasn't seeing anybody because he couldn't get his penis up anymore. He told Pamela, all these women wanted was his money and not him. Pamela really could not converse with him too long because he hurt her real bad. She always remembered the old saying, a leopard never changes its spots. Pamela treasured disappointment in this relationship because she loved this man and tried to put up with whatever he did.

But this man was a dog, couldn't remain faithful, and be true to her like she was with him. In this world we live in, Pamela realized that some men couldn't be true to one woman. Pamela tried to accept this about him, but in the end, she couldn't deal with it anymore. Pamela knows Jeremy will not ever in life find a good woman like herself who accepted the good, the bad, his ugly ways, and his faults. This were love, no doubt. The way Pamela loved Jeremy was truly loving a man for who he is and not who you want him to be by trying to change him.

As of today, Jeremy has never remarried. No woman has ever wanted to be with him nor marry him. Jeremy still calls Pamela every three months to see how she's doing. He took trips by himself all the time, alone. He told Pamela that she'll always be his wife. He said that in their marriage, there were no fingers to be pointed at. Both of them needed maturity in their relationship. He felt like Pamela was never shown love in her life, and she did not know how to accept love from someone else. He said, he made life about her, and she could not accept this.

He said most men took advantage of her in sex instead of loving her as a person. He had his hang-ups, the fact he had to raise and buy clothes for his brothers and sisters. Then he sent them to college to get their degrees, which he was never able to get. He said he missed out on his childhood life, which he could never get it back. This is why life to him was a big party. He just didn't know how to stay with one woman.

Pamela was having lunch at her favorite seafood restaurant on Saturday, around two o'clock p. m. when Johnathan walked into the restaurant. Johnathan asked Pamela if he could sit with her. Pamela said, yes. Both of them had lunch, talked for hours, and exchange telephone numbers. When Pamela had arrived at her apartment, Johnathan left her a message for her to meet him at a club on the sixth street. Pamela did just that and met him. When she walked into the club, he had a hat on, jeans, a shirt, and his alligator boots. He was dressed to kill. Pamela loved his gray ponytail, and he looked like a black Frenchman. Pamela fell in love with Johnathan at first sight. He was a suave kind of fellow that swept Pamela right off her feet.

Both of them danced the night away. It was about two o'clock in the morning, and the club was about to close when Pamela proceeded to leave then Johnathan asked Pamela if he could spend the night because he had a long drive home. Pamela said, "Yes, of course, follow me." She gave him directions to her house just in case he got lost. Johnathan walked into Pamela's apartment and noticed how nice it was. He said, "Thanks for inviting me to your home, Pamela." Pamela said, "You're welcome. You can sleep on the couch."

Pamela began to get him a blanket, a sheet, and a pillow to make a bed for him on the couch. She went and got into her bed. Then later, Pamela told him, she hasn't been with a man in a while. She told Johnathan that if he was not comfortable on the couch, he could come and get in bed with her. Johnathan did just that. Both of them made mad passionate love. He even went down on Pamela the first night. From then on, he was driving to Austin every weekend to see Pamela. Pamela would drive to Sabine to see him every chance she could get.

Both of them started talking on the phone every night until the wee hours of the morning. Sometimes they would meet up at the club on the sixth street every Saturday, drinking, and dancing. Johnathan always drunk Hennessy and a glass of water. Pamela would always drink gin and orange juice. Both of them were clicking in all areas and just had everything in common. Johnathan loved sex in every way. Johnathan was very fascinated with Pamela's body and how she made him feel. Pamela was glad she had someone to party in the club like she does.

Then one day, he asked Pamela to drive out to his place on the weekend. Johnathan was taking Pamela all around his friends. All his friends were clubbers and love to party. All of Johnathan's friends were close-knit. Johnathan and his friends do everything together. All his friends, including him, had their own business, degrees, and some of them had retired from the army. Johnathan's friends were true real people. All his friends shown Pamela lots of love and welcomed her in their circle. Pamela met his mother and father on a Sunday afternoon. His mother always cooked dinner on a Sunday, and all of her children would come over and eat. Pamela met his brother and his wife. She met his sister and her husband. Johnathan's mom didn't really take to Pamela, but she guessed that if her son liked Pamela, she'll like her too. Johnathan's family gave Pamela lots of hugs and kisses on her cheeks. They really welcome her into their family. The next Sunday, his mom invited Johnathan and Pamela to her church. Everybody at his mom's church, she knew, embraced Pamela with love. Pamela dated Johnathan one year before she moved in with him. While she lived with Johnathan, both of them club together, danced together, shared everything with one another for as what went on with them from morning until both of them went to bed.

If Pamela went to the restroom, Johnathan would be right there until she finished with her business. Pamela liked this about Johnathan because she felt like he really truly cared about her. The relationship was perfect, just the way Pamela always wanted a relationship to be. Johnathan and Pamela communicated together, ate at his mom's house every Sunday after church, partied at his friend's house, got drunk together, listen to music together at home, and made mad compassionate love. Both of them had the same opinion about everything. Both of them didn't make a decision about anything unless they had discussed it with one another. Both of them were just compatible in every aspect you could imagine, and they were a perfect match.

Pamela started visiting different Methodist churches until she found the one church where she felt at home. She became an usher in the church, and then she became the President of the Women Ministry. Pamela became very active in the church. She loved the Lord and loved being close to the Lord in his house of worship. Johnathan came to church sometimes. He was not that active in going to church, but you could find him on the golf field. Johnathan loved to play golf. Johnathan would go and play golf with his famous friends during the week and on the weekends. Johnathan would receive phone calls every morning from his men friends to go and play golf.

As time passed by, it was getting close to Christmas. Pamela had to leave and go home to Houston on Christmas Eve to visit her family for the Holidays and be Mrs. Claus, bringing gifts. It was hard for Pamela to leave Johnathan behind because he wasn't going with her. Pamela drove back home to Sabine on Christmas day to be with Johnathan. When she arrived, Johnathan had cooked. He made a gumbo creole style, and Pamela ate her heart out because she was hungry. After Pamela finished eating, Johnathan fixed Pamela a glass of wine. Then he surprised her with yellow roses, Pamela's favorite color. Then he got on one knee and put a four-carat wedding band on her finger. Then Johnathan asked Pamela to marry him. She said, "Yes! Yes!" with excitement. Pamela gave Johnathan the biggest kiss ever, and both of them made mad passionate love.

The next day, he told his parents that he and Pamela were engaged. His mom wasn't really thrilled about it. You could see it on her facial expression. But then she got a grip on herself and pretended to welcome Pamela into her family because his mom knew her son was in love with her. She did not want to lose her son to Pamela. Then Johnathan's friends found out about their engagement. His friends gave them an engagement party at the club. Then Johnathan's best friend told Pamela out of the blue, "You know, Johnathan is gay." Pamela laughed at him and said, "Yeah, right." "He eats a ton of her pernana. So, how can he be gay?" Pamela laughed it off, went back on the dance floor, and danced with Johnathan.

She totally dismissed what his best friend said to her and never thought about it again. Johnathan was very wealthy, and Pamela did not know this until he told her on the dance floor. As Pamela was living with Johnathan, she found out he was a computer geek also. He kept up with his stock and knew how to maneuver his stock around, keeping his money climbing. He would play computer games, poker, dominoes, twenty-one in the chat room. He was always having conversations with other people in the chat rooms. Johnathan was a music lover and would burn CD's and put oldie music on the CD's.

Pamela and Johnathan lived with one another for one and a half years before both of them got married. Johnathan asked Pamela if she wanted a big church wedding. Pamela said, she just wanted a small house wedding. Johnathan said, whatever you want. Pamela started planning her wedding, but she had to go on a business trip to Florida first. Once Pamela arrived in Florida, she was training some ladies on the company computer system. One lady told her she was going to be married for only one year. The man that God was going to send her, she was going to meet him traveling. Pamela became very upset with this lady. So, Pamela just walked away from her desk. She let someone else finish her training. Pamela never forgot what she said to her. Pamela flew back home once Friday came and started planning her wedding.

First, Pamela ordered the cake from the bakery. The cake was white with pineapple filling. Second, she went looking for a dress which she found in a department store. The dress was a purple chiffon dress. Then she found some black satin shoes to go with her dress. She ordered a purple bouquet of roses, and a red rose for the groom at the florist shop. Then Pamela went to Sams to get some hor d'oeuvres. Then she went to the grocery store to get some fruit to do a fruit tray. Next, she went to the liquor store to buy a bottle of Don Perrion Champagne to toast at their wedding.

The next day, Pamela called her pastor at her church to marry them, but her pastor was sick, so he asked his wife to marry them. Then Friday came, Pamela got up that morning, this is the day Johnathan and Pamela were getting married at 12:00 in the afternoon. She jumped up and down on the bed because she was very happy because she was getting married today. Johnathan cooked breakfast for Pamela, and both of them ate. After this, Johnathan helped Pamela set the table for their wedding. Both of them put the cake, bottle of champagne, a fruit tray, hor d'oeuvres, and spiked punch on the table. Then the guest started arriving. The first person to arrive was Johnathan's mother. His mother brought a veggie tray, and Pamela set the veggie tray on the table. Johnathan's mom started taking pictures of how beautiful the table was set up. Then his mom kissed Pamela on her cheekbone and told her "Welcome to the family." Then Pamela's brother arrived with his wife and two children plus Pamela's nephew. Then Pamela's daughter arrived. Then Johnathan's best friend and his wife arrived. Then finally, the pastor arrived to marry Pamela and Johnathan. She was running late. It was a small wedding, and Pamela loved small weddings. She did not want anything big and fancy. She loved simple things and was very happy and in love. After the marriage ceremony, everyone who was there hugged and kissed them. Then they ate and drank punch —All of them taking pictures of the bride and groom for keepsakes. Then Johnathan and Pamela cut the cake and fed the cake to each other. Then the both of them open the bottle of champagne and everyone at the house toast to them. After the wedding was over, everyone left and headed for home before it became night time. Pamela put on her sexy negligee.

Both of them finish the bottle of champagne and made passionate love to one another. Pamela knew she found the man of her dreams whom she could grow old and die with. The next two days, both of them went on their honeymoon to the Bahamas. Pamela had a blast on her honeymoon with Johnathan. While both of them were on their honeymoon on the cruise ship, a woman was trying to flirt with Pamela's husband. The woman had too much to drink and was drunk. Pamela tried to hold her temper, so she went to her husband and asked him nicely to get a handle on his wife. Pamela told her husband that this was their honeymoon. The husband was very apologetic.

Pamela and Johnathan went to the club and dance until two o'clock in the morning. This was a honeymoon Pamela never forgotten. She was very happy. When they returned home, Pamela noticed Johnathon started moving his clothes into the other bedroom where the Fulton sofa, computer, and the stereo is located. Pamela asked Johnathan, "Why are you moving out of our bedroom?" His reply was, "I gave you my last name, and I was getting too old to have sex on a regular basis." Pamela just accepted his answered and moved on. Then one morning, she heard Johnathan in the shower in his bedroom. She hopped in the shower for Johnathan to tell her rudely to get out. Both of them used to take showers together all the time. Slowly but surely, Johnathan started to change.

But one thing for sure, he never stopped cooking for her. Both of them always went out every Friday to dinner. Both of them still had sex only when he wanted too or when he was in the mood. Pamela and Johnathan still did everything together. Pamela loved her connection with Johnathan. Both of them talked about everything openly, walked to the park together, club together, visit family together, went to the grocery store together, and the shopping mall together. The only thing both of them did not do together was going to church together. He was not a church-going person like he said he was. Pamela was okay with that. After the word had spread around that the both of them were married, his ex-wife called the house and wanted Johnathan to pay child support and to start spending time with his seven-year-old daughter on a regular basis.

Johnathan went to pick up his daughter from Austin, one Saturday morning and brought her to the house where they lived, and Pamela gave her a hug. Pamela and his daughter went across the street from the house and went to the stop-n-go to get ice cream. Then both of them went to blockbuster and picked out some movies to watch. Later in the evening, both of them took baths. His daughter put on her pajamas. Pamela put on her negligee with shorts underneath. Pamela and his daughter watch movies until she fell asleep. The next morning, Pamela got up and cooked breakfast for everybody before his daughter left to go back home to Austin. Pamela's husband drove his daughter back home to Austin. Later that night, her mother called Johnathan and told him that this would be the last time he'll see his daughter because Pamela had on a skimpy negligee and the fact she did not put on a robe over her nightclothes. When Johnathan told Pamela about the conversation, Pamela just laughed and said she act like a jealous ex-wife. His ex-wife was just mad because he married a younger woman. His daughter connected and had fun with Pamela. As time went by, his daughter came over every other weekend. His daughter loved Pamela. After two months of marriage, Pamela started putting her money in with Johnathan. Johnathan paid all the bills in the house. Pamela began to notice each time she got paid, she never had any money in the bank.

When she would get home, Johnathan would tell Pamela that she had no money in the bank. Johnathan would also tell Pamela not to spend any money because there was not any money to spend. Pamela asked him, "How would I be able to get my nails and feet done?" She also asked him, "Will I have enough gas to get to work?" Johnathan's reply was, yes. But what Johnathan didn't know, Pamela would call the bank each time she got paid. The bank would tell her her husband made a withdrawal from the bank. Pamela accepted this and moved on. Johnathan and Pamela kept their lines of communication open. Johnathan would tell Pamela how his whole week went on Fridays and Saturdays. His conversation with Pamela was more like a friend instead of his wife. Johnathan even told Pamela, how he came onto his supervisor describing how big his private part was against a broomstick.

Pamela asked him, "Are you gay? "I'm your wife, not your best bud. There so much you can tell me, and so much you can't, and there's a limit." Pamela got heavily involved in church to keep her mind off of things at home. Pamela noticed at home that Johnathan was getting a lot of calls from men early in the morning around seven o'clock in the morning on the weekend, interrupting her sleep for him to go and play golf. Johnathan always played golf. They would go to the bar, drink, play darts, listen to music, or play the pinball machines. Johnathan would spend time with Pamela also. Every Wednesday, both of them would go bowling with a bunch of husbands and wives. Pamela could not bowl. The bowling ball would run on the outside instead of the middle of the pins. Pamela always had fun bowling.

This is what Pamela loved about Johnathan because both of them just had pure fun together. Johnathan was working in Austin also at dell computers. Johnathan was a computer geek, where he could put together a computer with no problems. One day, Johnathan went to work and passed out. Johnathan had an anxiety attack, and Pamela had to leave work and go pick him up from his job. When she arrived, he had a busted lip and a bruise over his right eye. After that, he could not go back to work. Pamela was worried that if he took the long drive to work in Austin, he could pass out behind the wheel on the freeway and kill himself. Johnathan began to find work in the city where he didn't have to drive far.

Johnathan started looking for work in the small city of Sabine. There were not too many jobs hiring in Sabine. He would put in one application after another. Until one day, he put in this application at this plant that packaged food for restaurants and grocery stores. He got hired because he knew the manager. So, Johnathan started to work on a Monday. Pamela was very excited for Johnathan. Both of them went to their favorite Chinese restaurant and went to Johnathan's favorite bar for drinks afterward. Monday came, and Johnathan was excited, and he enjoyed working at his job. Johnathan always looked forward to going to work. He would tell Pamela everything went on his job if a woman would flirt with him, if there was a catfight between two women on the job. If somebody was a newly hire. If somebody could not meet their quota for the day and what the consequences would be. If they let somebody go or fired anyone.

Then one particular day, Johnathan got off of work, he called Pamela and told her he was going to the bar to have a drink with one of his co-workers, and he would be in late. You know, Pamela was agreeable to that. When Johnathan came home from the bar, he told Pamela everything they would talk about from A thru Z. Friday night came, Pamela and Johnathan went out on the town to a nightclub. When both of them came into this club, Pamela noticed some men in the club knew Johnathan and was talking to them as both of them were walking in the club. He found them a table, and Pamela sat down. Johnathan went to get Pamela a drink from the bar. He brought Pamela a drink back to the table and left. Johnathan went to the bar to buy him a drink. His friend paid for his drink, and Johnathan stayed at the bar talking to his friend.

Then other men came up to the bar talking to Johnathan and buying him drinks. He just forgot about Pamela at the table. Right before the club closed, he came back to the table and danced with Pamela. Then both of them left the club. Pamela and Johnathan loved the club scene. Both of them loved to drink and dance in the clubs, and they would arrive home drunk, then both of them got into bed. Johnathan reached over to the nightstand, got some KY gel. He said to Pamela that he wanted to try anal sex with his wife. This is what he got this night. Even though Pamela was drunk, anal sex was very uncomfortable for her. Pamela's line of thinking was if her husband wants anal sex, then he needs to be satisfied.

Pamela thought that she might as well do it and act like she like it. Pamela had the attitude that she'll do anything to please her man. For her, it is whether her husband gets it from her than someone else. When both of them would make love, anal sex became a part of their sex life. Anal sex was always an uncomfortable thing for Pamela. If Pamela liked something, then Johnathan liked it too. If Pamela liked something, and Johnathan many not like it, then he would pretend that he liked it too. Pamela and Johnathan had so much in common in so many ways. It was sickening sometimes that two people had so much in common like it is too good to be true.

Wherever Pamela would go, he would always turn up there even if it was just visiting a friend, grocery store, even out to eat or if she were at a club. He would appear out of nowhere. This was okay with Pamela because she admired him wanting to be with her wherever she goes. One Friday night, Johnathan called Pamela from a friend's house and told her to drop by. Usually on a Friday night, when they're not clubbing, Pamela would go to bed and watch TV, but this particular night, it seems like the Holy Spirit wouldn't let her do her regular routine. She got up, got dressed, and left to go to Jonathan's best friend's house. Once she arrived there, she spoke to Johnathan, his best friend, and his co-worker. Apparently, he really wasn't expecting Pamela to show up. He was very nervous, and Pamela has never seen Johnathan like this way. His friends were playing pool, but Pamela noticed something strange between Johnathan and his co-worker. Johnathan and his co-worker couldn't keep their eyes off of one another, like the both of them were in love. Johnathan's co-worker said that he was going to leave and go home. As his co-worker was about to leave, both of them shook hands and almost kissed. This was when Pamela jumped in between them to stop this from happening in front of her. Pamela knew who he was because Johnathan would talk about him all the time. His co-worker was Johnathan's whole conversation at home, she would know every little detail about him, and she had never even met him before, until that night.

This was the same night the pastor called from the church and asked her if she could do the deserts for three hundred people for a funeral. Pamela said, okay. Pamela served the bereaved family at the repass. They, in exchange, personally thanked her. She told them they were welcome. She left there, went home, and went to bed afterward. Lately, Johnathan began spending his time at the bar until ten o'clock in the evening every night and every day of the week. He started taking his showers in the other bathroom. He also started sleeping in the other bedroom with the sleeper sofa if he came home from the bar late. Pamela was busy with the church that it didn't disturb her that much. She figured it probably was a phase he was going through in the marriage. Something too, she felt, will pass. Johnathan even though he was acting funny.

He would still tell Pamela everything was going on at the bar. To Pamela, it was like listening to a soap opera but could not see the faces. Once Sunday, Pamela went to church. The person who handled the finances let Pamela know she had a check bounce. Pamela was shocked because she made good money. She should have had money in her bank to cover the check. When the church was over, her girlfriend called her over to introduce her to her fiancé. She told Pamela, "Johnathan has been bragging in the bar how he handles and spend your money, how he's in charge of all the money that comes in the household. He spends your money buying everybody drinks at the bar at your expense and talks about how stupid you are." She told Pamela, "Johnathan should not be over your money."

She suggested to Pamela to put half her paycheck into their joint account and the other half into her account. This is what Pamela ended up doing because when she confronted Johnathan, his reply was, he took the money out of the bank and put into his account to pay the bills and forgot to leave money in the bank to cover the check. Pamela asked Johnathan, "Why did you take money out of the bank account?" He replied, "I always take it out because someone has to save for a rainy day. I put it in my bank account for both of us." Pamela, the little submissive wife, said, "Okay." Pamela did not go into anything with him about putting half and half into the bank accounts. Pamela just did it and not consult him because he made a check bounced when there was enough money in the bank to pay for the check.

Plus, he made Pamela look bad in the church with a bounced check given back to her to make good of it once the money was changed over. Johnathan suspected Pamela's attitude was changing toward him. Johnathan started following Pamela wherever she went, too, more so than ever. The only exception was he did not follow Pamela to church. Once the church was over, this older lady called Pamela to her car. The old lady told Pamela, "You're a bright young lady and a city girl, right. Pamela, you need to go to this bar where your husband hangs out. Take a look around and notice what you see. If you walk into a place, you do know how to discern your surroundings, right. Please make sure your eyes are open and not close. You helped my family a whole lot during the funeral." She did not know where she would have come up with the money to feed all those people. She felt obligated to her some kind of way for what she did for her family. The old lady said, "I want you to go to this bar, look around, and put on your city smarts." Pamela told her, "Okay, I'll do just that. When Pamela got off of work, she went to the bar where Johnathan hangs out at. Pamela followed the direction the old lady had given her. She got lost but came back to the starting point and followed the direction again. Pamela came right to the bar, and as she got out of her car, she saw Johnathan's vehicle. Johnathan's vehicle was a green four-door Sonata. Pamela walked into the bar, but she did not see Johnathan.

So, Pamela looked around the bar. She first noticed the game machines, then the pool table, and the dartboard on the wall. Then secondly, she noticed some men in the bar. Then thirdly, she noticed just one woman at the bar. She still did not see Johnathan. Then she sat at the table, just noticing the people that would come into the bar. Then she realized that this was a gay bar. Then her play mother showed up because she saw Pamela's car from the freeway. Pamela drove a four-door marooned Volkswagen Passat. Pamela's play-mother asked Pamela, "have you figure it out yet?" Pamela said, "Yes. So, my husband Johnathan is bi-sexual or gay. How long have you known?" Pamela's play mother said, "ever since I met him ten years ago. This is why my husband and your husband would argue all the time. Because Pamela, you are a very good and sweet woman. You deserve to know your husband's lifestyle, whether or not Johnathan wanted you to know.

My husband and I wanted you to know also. Then all of a sudden, Johnathan appeared. Johnathan came out of the men's restroom with another Caucasian man. When Pamela turned her head around there, Johnathan was talking with this Caucasian man. Once Johnathan noticed

Pamela, he came over to the table. He was very nervous and started sweating like he was about to have an anxiety attack. Johnathan asked Pamela, "what are you doing here? And How long had she been here? Pamela responded, "I have been here since six-thirty this evening. I saw your car but no sign of you. Pamela also responded by saying, "I came by to surprise you, have a drink with you, and to also see how you're spending your time away from home.

Johnathan sat at the table with Pamela, her play mother, and her play mother's husband. All of them had a couple of rounds of drinks. Then they all left and went home. Once Pamela and Johnathan arrived at home, Pamela did not let him know how she was thinking until the next day. She asked Johnathan if he like men. Johnathan charged at Pamela and said, "Don't you ever ask me something like that. Even if I am, you have to deal with it. You can shop until you drop." Johnathan said, "I'll buy you a townhouse. Please don't leave me." From then on, he would follow Pamela everywhere she would go. Pamela started scheming. She called her mom from work and told her the situation.

Pamela's mom put nine hundred dollars in her bank account so she could move back home to Houston. Pamela decided she was not going to be married to a man that loved men, too, because Pamela did not want to die from getting AIDS. She did not want to take the chance. Pamela decided to leave Johnathan. This is how she did this. The moving company was going to be at Pamela's apartment at nine-thirty in the morning. For some particular reason that day, Johnathan wanted to call in sick on his job, but Pamela talked him into going in. So, Johnathan asked Pamela, "Why haven't you left for work yet?" Pamela told him, "I had some bad cramps. I'm going to go to the doctor up the street." Pamela said to Johnathan, "I need to get some pills for my cramps to go away."

So, Johnathan followed Pamela to the doctor's office. Pamela was so intense because she did not know how she was going to get rid of Johnathan. Pamela played it off, went into the doctor's building, and went to the doctor's office. Then Johnathan left and went to work. Then after, Pamela left the doctor's building, went back to the apartment, and started packing up the apartment. So, when the movers came, everything would be ready to go. Pamela's best friend from her job came over and helped Pamela pack up her apartment. It was storming this day. Pamela got nervous because they got everything packed up, and the movers may have to reschedule due to the rain. Just as Pamela was thinking this, then the mover's called to reschedule. Pamela talked them into coming in the rain.

The mover's got everything out by twelve o'clock that afternoon. Her best friend left when the mover's arrived. Pamela kissed her on the cheek and told her goodbye. Pamela and the movers left and headed home to Houston. Pamela left Johnathan, the other bedroom, table with chairs, and a complete bathroom set. Johnathan was also left with Pamela's car, the green Sonata. Johnathan did call Pamela to come back and sign over the titles to the car to him. Pamela drove down to the bar where Johnathan told her to meet him. Pamela asked him to close out the bank account. Johnathan did just that.

Pamela never heard from Johnathan again. But Pamela did go to the doctor to get tested for AIDS and HIV. The test results came back negative. Pamela's doctor did ask her why she wanted the test done. She told the doctor the man she was married to was bi-sexual or gay. So, Pamela had to be tested for a whole year because her doctor reported her to the City Health Department. Each time Pamela took the test, the test came back negative. Pamela treasure disappointment because she thought that finally, she found the man of her dreams because both of them had everything in common with one another. In the end, Pamela felt like this marriage was too good to be true. She believed something had to go wrong in the relationship because two people just can't have everything in common without something going wrong in this society, we as individuals live in. Pamela treasure disappointment because she thought she met her mate, wherer she could grow old and die together once the Lord called them home.

Pamela did all the right things to make a marriage work only to find out the husband she was married too was bi-sexual or gay. She loved him wholeheartedly.

Pamela didn't want another failed marriage under her belt. Pamela just couldn't accept his lifestyle, and once she opened her mind, eyes, and heart to what was actually going on in her marriage. See, Pamela always accepted whatever Johnathan did and moved on. Her love for Johnathan blinded her eyesight. Pamela couldn't stay with a bi-sexual man with fear of contracting AIDS or becoming HIV Pamela knew this was a death sentence. Pamela wished that Johnathan was true to himself, accepted how he was, and stop living a lie. By Pamela being with Johnathan, she realized how to determine if you are married to a bi-sexual man.

If the phone calls you received at home were from men calling early in the morning. If he decides to move out of the bedroom into another room and nothing is your fault. When sex doesn't matter to him but wants to have sex with you once or twice a month, if at all. When he no longer wants to take a shower with you or don't want you in the bathroom when he's taking a shower. If he likes to have anal sex with you when making love, then he has gay tendencies. So, ladies, be careful because the man you could be with is gay. Just keeping it real. When he boldly talks constantly about another man, and this would be his whole conversation,especially entertaining in gay clubs. Pamela was deeply hurt inside her heart and could not move on in her life for years. Pamela knew she would always love this man because he understood her so well. He knew exactly what she was thinking, her likes, and dislikes. When Pamela moved to Houston and five years went by. He would not sign those divorce papers only if Pamela signed a waiver forfeiting everything she was entitled too. After so long, Pamela decided to sign, losing everything. She did not want to stay married to him forever. He lives in one city, and she lives in another. Once Pamela signed the waiver, she never heard from Johnathan again, but to only hear from his friends saying he drives a metro bus and he has never re-married. He still hangs out in gay bars.

Pamela was so down and out in her life. She crossed a bad crossroad in her life. Pamela lost everything she ever had all behind, helping her immediate family. Before Pamela knew it, she didn't have a pot to piss in and a pan to throw it in. When Pamela looked back at her life, she saw how she took a lot of things in her life for granted, especially marriage and money. These were the very things you need, want for, and desire in your life. See, God was not the number one in her life. Everything she lost this made her rely on God above more so because after everything was said and done. He was the only friend she ended up having in the whole world. All her immediate family turned their back on her and started talking about her like a dog.

Pamela's family and friends were saying how stupid she was, and she shouldn't have helped anybody but herself. These were the people she helped financially that landed her broke. None of them would lift a finger to help her. Pamela had to live from place to place, sleeping in her car. She kept moving like there was no tomorrow. She had no food to eat. She was starving from day to day on a daily basis. She had a mother, had money, and lived in a five-bedroom house liked River Oaks, but she wouldn't let Pamela come back home to get on her feet. She was the type of mother who helped other people like her friends but not her kids. It's like she wanted her kids to fail in life and not succeed so she could belittle them, low rate them like they were nothing. If you were down and out, she would talk about you like a dog to your face then kick you out of her house. Her mother wouldn't even give Pamela money to help her get on her feet, knowing she had a job to pay her back. Pamela's mom would feed her if she had a way to her house to eat, and after that, you had to go. Get out of her fancy house and go live on the streets. When you come around her during the holidays, she would talk about you and your personal life to her family and friends. You don't even know some of those people. It's like she was just putting Pamela's name out there badly to her family and friends. Pamela, in spite of and how bad her mother treated her, she stilled loved her mother so much, but she just couldn't understand her and her ways. All those people that Pamela's mom was talking about to about Pamela began talking about her too. After being faced with this during the holiday, Pamela realized she had nobody to turn to but the Lord, realizing what mistakes she made and if she had to do it all over again. She would only look out for herself and not other people. She realized if God bless you with anything, then the blessing was for you and not to give your blessing away to anybody. This made Pamela to become a selfish little witch. When you ended up learning a lesson in life of how you ended up where you are, And what lead you to get into the situation you're in, you kinda take this attitude. Now let's see how Pamela got out of the dilemma she's in. She was driving down Sentra street when Pamela kept passing this church for three times already. The church looked new, but the church was one story, gated, and fenced in and had a quite few cars in the parking lot. There was lots of land, and lots of trailers at the church where they held school for the kids and the young people. The second time Pamela passed the church, she was going to the Family Dollar Store. The third time she passed the church, Pamela saw their sign telling you the name of the church, the days service were held, when the church met, and the time of church sermon would be speaking on Sunday. Pamela had on a hundred -dollar pantsuit, very nice and dressy. As the pastor began talking, he looked at her and said that in his church, you dress up in a dress or suit but not pants or jeans.

    She was very impressed and said wow to herself. This was a pastor very truthful and told you how it should be. Pamela said to herself. This is the type of church she likes to become a member of. Pamela came back Wednesday night for Bible Study. She really enjoyed it. This person was the minister, pastor, teacher, and mentor wrapped up all in one. Everything he preached about, he backed it up with a scripture. Pamela knew right then that this would be her church until the day she dies. Before the church was over, the pastor was closing in prayer. Pamela felt this body behind her. She always was a little psychic. Pamela could always see things in her dreams. She could sense if you were a bad or good person by touching your hand.

She could also look into your eyes and know what type of person she's dealing with. When Pamela opened her eyes from saying "Amen" to the closing of the prayer, this man was standing behind her and ask her what she wanted the church to do for her. She said that she's trying to get on her feet and keep it on solid ground and hoping God will bless her with a book contract. We had an eye to eye contact. He said to her, "You keep coming here, and God will bless you with that contract and everything else." Pamela felt so ecstatic and good about where she was. So, that Friday, Pamela came back to Bible Study. The church had a bible study twice a week on a Wednesday and Friday.

As Pamela walked into this church, this nice man looked up at her, he said, "You're back," and introduced himself to her as Joshua. Pamela introduced herself to him as Pamela. He twisted his head like he was shocked to see her, and then he acted like he knew her. Joshua was a very well-dressed man. His shirt matched his tie. Joshua had on a linen suit and shoes to match. She could not take her eyes off of him. Pamela looked at his finger to see if he had a ring on his finger, but he didn't have one on. She thought maybe he's single. Still, he was a good-looking man to her eyes. The Lord had revealed to her in a dream. He was sending a spiritual man to help her get on her feet. Pamela must have passed her test and made the Lord pleased above with her. She certainly has to admit that the Lord certainly picked her up when she fell all the way down. Pamela's car broke down at church.

Pamela asked Joshua to take a look at her car. She knew she had no money to fix her car at that time. Joshua offered to pay to get her car fix, but she wouldn't let him. Joshua asked her, "What can I do for you to get you on your feet? She told him she needed to wash her clothes. Joshua picked her up that afternoon around three o'clock in the evening and washed her clothes for her. He was looking at her underclothes to see if he needed to buy her some more, and he said, "You're alright." Pamela was kind of embarrassed because she worked at this professional company and didn't have enough money to wash her own clothes. Once the clothes were done washing and drying, Joshua took Pamela home, since Pamela's car was not working. Joshua picked up Pamela and took her to work, church and bible study. When he would pick up Pamela for work in the morning, Joshua would have his son with him. Pamela felt his son couldn't be dumb not to know she and his dad was more than friends. See, Joshua told

Pamela that he needed her to sex him up if he was going to help her get on her feet. Pamela did everything sexually; he wanted to be done to him. Pamela became more than a church member to Joshua. As he kept picking her up to take her to church was when her relationship blossom with him. Joshua told Pamela that he was a devoted husband, and he would never leave his wife for her.

When he wanted this relationship to end, he knew how to walk away from her. She just looked at him with her, sexy eyes, and said okay. What Joshua liked about Pamela is sex. He might have been having sex with his wife. Evidently, she wasn't doing it as he wanted her too. He liked Pamela sucking his brain, making him cum, reaching his highest peak, and licking his butt crack. Then afterward, apologizing for getting his cum all over her. One night, she guessed he was so hard up that he couldn't wait to get his clothes off. Pamela sucked his brain and got his cum all over his fine suit he wore to Bible Study. That night, he went home like that, and his wife told him "You bet not ever come home with cum all over your clothes." Then from that day, Pamela realized she knew about her and accepted their relationship.

Sex was probably something she could no longer do to satisfy her husband like she used too. Pamela needed her storage bill paid before she lost all her clothes and furniture. He picked her up on a Saturday, and it was raining like cats and dogs. She had her storage on the opposite side of town. Joshua paid her six-hundred-dollar storage fee, and he paid this with his credit card. By doing this, Pamela felt he bought her. So whatever he wanted from then on, she was going to do whatever he wanted her to do to make him happy. Pamela didn't want to take him from his wife. She knew if he left his wife, he would leave her for someone else. She didn't want that vicious cycle to fall on her. So as months went by, they became very close. They went to the same church, and when the church was over, he would come by the house just to see what she was doing or if it was time for him to be fulfilled. Joshua was an everythreeday man when he needed his brain sucked. They had sex sometimes, but sex was all about him being satisfied, not her. It was okay with her, and Pamela accepted the way it was. As they continue to see one another, Pamela started growing spiritually strong. She started getting closer to the Lord. She knew she was committing adultery. Pamela started becoming very self-conscious about what they were doing because of the relationship she was developing with the Lord. As the sex continued between them, Pamela fell in love with him. They would fight and have arguments between the two. She was really devoted to him like he was her husband. But she wasn't married to him. Joshua, in time, treated Pamela like she was his wife. He took care of her both financially and spiritually. Joshua didn't pay her rent, but he paid the high light bill, bought her groceries, put gas in her vehicle, and paid for her vehicle upkeep.

Then after a while, Pamela started getting sick. Her stomach started getting big, like she was six months pregnant. She started seeing doctors to see if she was pregnant. It took like two months before she could get any results if she was pregnant. While this was going on, Joshua and Pamela started arguing with one another. Pamela would get mad at him. One time when they argued, Joshua told her his wife was devoted to him, and she didn't need this. So, Pamela asked him, "if she was so devoted to you, why are you committing adultery with me?" He didn't answer her, so she figured they had an issue with sex at home. See, he was sleeping on the couch, not in the bed with his wife.

See, Joshua and his wife had been together for fifteen years or more. Sometimes sex goes out of the relationship, and this is when you have to know how to rekindle the flame back up. If you don't, then sex is dead and sometimes your relationship. At this time, Pamela was trying to find out if she was pregnant. He became very arrogant with her and stopped helping her. He told Pamela, "I had done a bad thing and I'm going to pray to Lord for forgiveness for getting you pregnant." Then he started crying crocodile tears. Her heart went out to him. Pamela told him, "I'm not going to tell this to your wife." Pamela mentioned to him, "I don't even know where you live. I don't know your house number, so you do n't have to worry. I'm not going to tell a soul. I can change churches."

Joshua said, "No, I don't want you to do that. I'm going to tell this to my wife. She's going to know because this is her fault." Pamela looked at him in shock. Pamela knew then she knew about her. Pamela knew if she really wanted to break them up, she knew a baby would do it. The following Monday, Pamela called her doctor, the doctor told her the test was negative. Pamela immediately called Joshua and left a voice message on his cell phone. Joshua would never answer the cell phone when Pamela would call because his wife was there. He was the type of man that would never disrespect his wife at home. She was lucky to have a husband like that. Pamela found out she had Irritable Bowel Syndrome. She had to take pills that would make her bowels move. This would blow her up, making her look like she's pregnant.

Pamela and Joshua saw one another for four years. Perfect relationship besides him being married. Sex was great between the two of them. Joshua, on one Christmas, invited Pamela to the church's Christmas party. Pamela wore a long green sequence gown, where she looked like a movie star. That's how her church members treated her. They gave her hugs and kisses because Pamela did change churches and moved to another side of town after all that happened. Some of the church members wanted Pamela to sit at their tables. Joshua had a seat for Pamela at the table with his wife and sister. Once the program started, Pamela told one of the members, "Thank you for a seat at your table, but I'm going to sit with Joshua and his family." You know, church members were watching their table to see if she was going to actually sit with Joshua and his family,

to see if there was going to be any drama from his wife. It was a very awkward situation for Pamela because his wife and sister just spoke and stared at her funny looking. When Joshua came to the table, they began talking to her and making her feel welcome at their table. His wife got her food, and when it came to desert, they made sure she had some. They made sure she got a to-go plate after the program was over. They wish each other a Happy New Year and gave each other a hug, and they all kissed and said goodnight to one another. Then two weeks later, Joshua suffered a major heart attack, which kept him in the hospital for months. Pamela saw him on the weekends because his wife was there on the weekdays.

After he got out of the hospital, it took Joshua three weeks to recover. Then after that, he had another heart attack, then he had two strokes right behind one another, which left Joshua crippled. He was paralyzed on his left side, he couldn't talk, and he couldn't drive anywhere. After this, Pamela never saw Joshua again. He would call her and say Hello and Goodbye. Those the only two words Joshua could speak. Pamela would always let him know what was going on with her. She would always give him an update on her life. After three weeks went by, she never heard from him again. In Pamela's heart, she wished she could take care of him instead of his wife. This man put Pamela on her feet, got her first book published with his own money.

Pamela truly loved him. Pamela's heart was hurt. She always cried herself to sleep because she truly missed him. Joshua showed Pamela how a man should treat a woman and love her even though he was married. Pamela treasured love with this man. She was never disappointed in their relationship. She realized after him that she would never date or become involved with a married man ever again. She knew this was wrong in God's eyesight. Pamela had always been involved with professional men with good jobs. This particular man helped her to develop a relationship with the Lord, put her feet on solid ground, and have a consciousness. Joshua taught Pamela how to study the Bible and how to understand what the scriptures are saying. Joshua always told Pamela that if he's not around, always be biblical conscious of your spiritual need. If Joshua wasn't there for Pamela, he always wanted Pamela to rely on the Lord above to guide her in life. Pamela kept those words from Joshua in her heart and mind. She did just what he advised her to do by keeping her focus on Christ.

Just when Pamela thought love would never exist in her world, there came Jax. Jax was medium built, and he was a loudmouth that you could hear him across the floor. He was tall and wore designer clothes, and his shirt may have cost one hundred dollars. He looked good when he wore his clothes. He had pretty white teeth, and he always wore alligator shoes in every color or Stacy Adams shoes. Pamela met Jax on a Friday night when she had a hell of a day on her job. Then once she was ready to get off of work, she received a phone call to bail her brother out of jail. Pamela stood in a long line with all types of people traveling different roads in life. Funny how they were telling Pamela all their problems they have been through in life. Where they went wrong in their life, how they ended up in jail, and their loved one. Pamela was the type of person has a listening ear for anybody. You could just walk up toward her and tell her anything was on your mind no matter who you are and what. People treated Pamela in life like she was a psychiatrist. That was the type of spirit Pamela generated to others. Earlier during the week, she felt like she was in purgatory or hell at home with family members talking about the mistakes she made in her life. The mistakes she made, which ended her not having a place to stay but staying with other people who just used her for her money.

After she left Harris County to bond her brother out of jail, Pamela got in her car going home, but her vehicle went into another direction. She ended up at a club. She went to a year ago call Seven Times. Pamela decided why not go out and have a couple of drinks since it was happy hour and listen to some soothing music to rest her mind, and Pamela did just that. She went into the club. She found a seat in the back away from the bar like a cuddle shack. Then this party came in sitting in front of her. Pamela watched this party come in one by one. She watched the supervisor of the group buy the whole table drinks after drinks. Then this one guy came in, sat at the table talking and drinking with his friends but kept drinking and turning his head over, glancing at Pamela.

Pamela was on her second drink. Then finally, when Pamela had finished her drink, Jax walked over to her table and asked her, "What are you drinking?" Pamela told him, "An apple martini." Jax had the waiter to bring her two drinks. As Pamela was drinking her drinks, Jax kept turning his head, looking at Pamela constantly. Pamela thought he was crazy for looking at her because Pamela hadn't had a man to notice her in years. Jax had some big pretty hazel brown eyes. Each time he looked at Pamela, she looked at him back. Then this party started leaving. Jax came back there where Pamela was and told her he was going to go next door and get some cigarettes. She mentioned to him, "I'm going to leave around twelve o'clock in the morning."

He said to her, "Do not leave without dancing with me." He wanted to dance with her. Pamela told Jax, "I don't dance." He left again and went to get his cigarettes. When he returned, he looked at her again with those hazel brown eyes. Within herself, Pamela smiled at him because, actually, it's been years since a man looked at her, let alone spoke to her while she was out. People in his party started leaving one by one. Jax came to the back where Pamela was sitting and brought her to the front. Jax asked Pamela, "What's your name?" She said, "My name is Pamela." Then he asked her, "Where do you live?" She told him, "Well, I lived with my cousin, her son, and her husband. "

Jax told Pamela, "I don't know you at all, but you are a very beautiful woman. You must have fallen on hard times for you not to have your own place. He asked her, "What happened?" She replied, "my family was my downfall." She told him, "I'm always a sucker for a sad tale from my family." Her family knew how to get money from her. When she went down to the ground, nobody was there for her. Pamela told him, "I'm staying with my cousin to get on my feet." He said, "I could relate with that, and you're right, its usually your family that can cause your downfall." Some family member doesn't have your best interest at heart because he was staying with his father. Pamela said, "You asked what happened to me. So, what's your story?" Jax said, "I got my cousin a job at the country club. One of my clients I waited on, bought my house." Jax told Pamela, "I'm a waiter and always worked in a country club because I made good money in tips. My tips were big money enough to pay my bills and then some. My cousin started going behind my back, trying to get me fired by telling my manager that one of my customers I waited on, bought my house. My boss fired me for that. Then my wife left me and divorced him because she was used to a certain lifestyle." Jax said, "I lost everything behind a relative. That's my story, and it is what it is." Then Jax started filling on her panty line through her clothes. Jax told Pamela, "You're was going to dance with me before we leave the club and go home." Then he bought Pamela another drink. Pamela was actually in a pity mood, feeling sorry for herself. But she finally danced with Jax. She danced with him on the dance floor in one spot, not really moving to the beat of the music because she really wasn't feeling Jax.

After that song was finished, they went back to the table and talked. Jax told Pamela his favorite singer was Mariah Carey. He loved her music. Pamela was just smiling because every word coming from his mouth made her giggle. Pamela hadn't done this in years. Jax knew Pamela was tipsy. So Jax asked Pamela if she would go home with him tonight. Pamela said, she's not a garden tool, and definitely not an easy hussy. She just met him. In Pamela's mind, she told Jax, "Do you feel like since you bought her some drinks, I'll give up the pernana easy? If you're thinking this, then you're a dead wrong buster." She doesn't know him to jump in bed with him. She hasn't been with a man in five years. She's truly scared because if she goes home with him, he's going to want to have sex with her. Then Pamela asked him, "Do you have protection? He replied, "Yes." So, Pamela agreed because deep down inside, Pamela knew she needed to move on with her life and stop letting herself be trouble about men cheating on her so much. Pamela knew she needed to let everything go in her life that was keeping her from moving forward in her life. She knew deep down inside she needed to feel like a woman again. So, Pamela agreed to go home with him and have sex with him. While they were leaving the club, Pamela told Jax she was hungry. This truck was selling food across the street from the club. Pamela told him she wanted a sausage sandwich. The person got their order gave him his order first.

He gave Pamela some of his sausage sandwich, which impressed Pamela tremendously. The first thing that came to Pamela's mind is he's a sharing kind of fellow. Pamela liked this trait about him. Then they left and went to Jax's house. He asked, "Pamela can you spend the night with me?" She replied, "Yes, but I don't want to disrespect your father's house." Jaz replied, "My dad is asleep. It's okay, Pamela. Okay, if you say so." Pamela went into his bedroom with him. He had a soft bed with fluffy pillows. Pamela told him, "I hadn't been with a man sexually in five years. Jax laughed at her and said, "I do not believe you." Pamela said, "You should because I do not lie. Jax, do you have a latex rubber and some Vaseline because I do not want you to hurt me." Jax said, "I'll get the Vaseline just to please you."

As Jax was putting on the rubber, laughing, and saying to her that she's too old not to have sex. Pamela said, "I work all the time, so I never think about sex because my problems outweigh me, having sex with someone. Jax, do that make sense to you?" He started kissing Pamela, sucking her nipples, and started penetrating his penis inside of her. Jax couldn't get it through, so he had to get up and get some Vaseline to put on the rubber. Jax said, "I believed you now that you hadn't been with anybody sexually. I'm glad you chose me." After they made passionate love, they both fell asleep. Pamela woke up around five o'clock in the morning. She got up and left to go home to get ready for work. Jax walked her to her car and gave her a good morning smack on her lips. They started seeing one another everyday day in and day out.

One Saturday afternoon, Pamela was at Jax's house, and his father came in from work. Jax introduced Pamela to his father and Pamela said, hello. Jax's father told her hello. He showed her every room in the house. He mentioned to Pamela, "My wife had passed away last year. Nobody has been in the living room since then. Come in here, Pamela." Jax's father began to open the blinds and let the sun in, which he had never done before. Jax told Pamela that his dad likes her. Pamela sat in his mom's chair, where his mom would sit in all the time. The sun beamed in the chair, where Pamela was sitting in. Jax dad said, "You have a good spirit. I don't allow anybody in this room." When he looked at her.

He said, "You like a breath of fresh air. It's a pleasure to meet you." So, after Pamela met his dad, Jax took her to his Aunt's house. She loved Pamela. Then he took her to his sister's house. She talked to Pamela all night until Jax said, "Let's go". They went from house to house, visiting all his relatives. Jax fell in love with Pamela. He even wanted Pamela to move in with him at his father's house. But Pamela told Jax, she couldn't because she was living with her cousin. Jax went to where Pamela was staying at her cousin. Pamela invited Jax in her cousin's house, low and behold Pamela's cousin and Jax went to school together. Pamela introduced him to her cousin, husband, and son. Jax went home.

The next week, he came to visit Pamela at her cousin's house. Pamela invited him in again. So, Pamela told him to have a seat, and she was going to the bathroom. When she came out, all hell had broken out. Her cousin told her husband that Jax was flirting with her. Pamela told her cousin, "You're lying." Then her husband said, "Jax, you're not welcome in my house." Pamela said, "Okay." When Jax left, Pamela asked her cousin, "Why would you say that? She replied, "My husband doesn't notice me anymore or want to have sex with me. I wanted him to notice me so I can feel that I still have that whip appeal. My husband rejected me in bed last night, so I tried to break you, Pamela, and your man up with my lies." When the weekend came, Pamela moved out and never went back to her cousin's house ever again.

She moved in with her sister. Jax wanted Pamela to move in with him, but Pamela didn't do it because it was too soon in the relationship. Jax told Pamela two months later that he was going to buy a house. He needed Pamela to come up with twenty-seven hundred dollars. Pamela said, okay. Jax took her to the house he wanted to buy. He showed her the carpet and the color he picked out. He showed her the three bedrooms in the house. Here's the catch, Pamela found out Jax was running a game. He wanted Pamela to give him the money to put down on the house, but he was going to do something different with the money. But how Jax got busted was when Pamela told his dad about the house. His dad told Pamela, "He was a con artist."

Pamela said, "You're kidding me, right." His dad said, "Please do not get caught up in his schemes. Keep your eyes open." He kissed Pamela on the cheekbone. About three months later, Pamela went back to the house. Another family was living there. Pamela talked to the owners and found out they had the house built from scratch. She picked out all the colors, carpet, and design the house how she wanted. Pamela thanked her. Pamela confronted Jax and asked him, "Why would you lie about the house?" He said, "I just wanted a house because I don't want to live with my dad anymore. Pamela said to Jax, "Don't lie. I hope you weren't trying to scam me out of some money because I have been noticing that you have been taking a hundred dollar bills out of my purse every time I get paid. You're not slick buster." Jax was a waiter at a country club. Pamela would always take him to work every evening and pick him up. Jax's father was terminally ill and end up leaving his house to his children.

Jax changed his mind about being with Pamela. All of a sudden, he told Pamela, "I loved you but, all I wanted to have is fun. You're the type of woman who will make a man settle down, do right, and get married. I'm not ready for this right now." This is the shocker part about Jax. While they were dating, Pamela gave Jax her car note money for him to get a money order and send her car note to her financing company. Jax brought her the receipt from the money order, but it was a bogus money order for one dollar. Pamela never thought anything about the money order until the car people called her to tell her they never received her car payment.

She mentioned this to Jax, and he claimed he paid the car note and sent the note in. Pamela took him at his word until she asked Jax for the third time.

This was three weeks later when she let him know she called the money order company, and they told her the money order she received was for one dollar. So Jax lied once again. Pamela told Jax, "I paid my note over the phone. When you get paid on Friday, you're going to pay me back." Jax said, "Okay." Pamela asked Jax, "What did you do with the money?" Jax told Pamela, "I took the money and bought some clothes." When Friday came, he didn't have the money to pay Pamela back. It took him three pay periods before he finally paid Pamela. After that, Pamela never trusted Jax with any of her money. Pamela would never lay her purse down in Jax's house. She always kept her purse with her. Then one night, Pamela went to visit Jax, but before she got out of her vehicle, she put her money in the side compartment of her car somehow, Jax found her money in the side compartment and took it. By then, Pamela had enough of him and his lies. She was very much glad that Jax broke it off with her. All the money, Jax kept taking from her. He bought him a car. How real was that. Jax saw an opportunity to get over and use his street smarts to get over on Pamela. Through all the games, Jax ran on her. Pamela wasn't dumb to what he was doing, but she longed for his companionship. Pamela truly treasured disappointment. When you look at this relationship, Pamela was very understanding with him, and she'd accept Jax as he was. She wasn't trying to change him. She just wanted him to be honest with her and himself. We need to learn from the fact if you tell a lie, that lie will catch up with you in the end. A lie can harm a relationship with a good woman.

A good woman is hard to find. Pamela caught Jax in so many lies, then he told her out of the blue he wasn't ready for her. This helped Pamela to walk away and take Jax at face value at his word because she had enough of his lies and stealing from her. Pamela never contacted him or saw Jax again. Something we need to do as individuals when someone says they're not ready for you. You need to leave the person alone and move on because if a person is meant for you. He is going to be with you. It's up to you to accept him with all his flaws. No person is perfect, only Jesus Christ. When you want a person in your life, see if he possess some qualities within himself, you can live with or endure with him.

Pamela went to this club on a Friday night. At the club, a bridal shower was given for her friend. Everyone at the club was dressed in red blouses and black pants. —the bride to be is going to marry her high school sweetheart.

Pamela saw people at the bridal shower she hadn't seen in years. The bridal shower was also like a reunion. Pamela and everybody had so much fun by drinking, dancing, and catching up on how everybody had been doing. When one o'clock came, everyone started leaving the club going home. As the party left, Pamela stayed at the club dancing and drinking. Pamela went into another room of the club where they were having another party. This was when Pamela's hand was grabbed by this man. This man was a heavyset man with a lot of gray hair.

When Pamela looked at him, he reminded her of a man she used to date who dumped her for a light skin lady with a manager career. This man introduced himself to Pamela as Justin. Pamela introduced herself to Justin as Pamela. Justin told Pamela that he was watching her the entire night. Then he disappeared, but as Pamela was leaving the club, he followed Pamela out of the club to her car. When Pamela turned around, he was right there. This kind of scared her, then Justin asked Pamela if he could go home with her. Pamela told him no because she just met him.

So, Justin asked her out for breakfast at the Kettle restaurant. Pamela said, okay. Justin told Pamela to follow him, and Pamela did just that followed him, she didn't know how to get there. Once they arrived at Kettle's restaurant, Justin ordered for Pamela. Pamela thought he should have asked her what she wanted to eat. Then Pamela was okay with what he ordered for her. Justin and Pamela talked and ate. Justin told Pamela he was a manager at Johnson Space Center. He had been on his job for eighteen years. He was a single man and had one daughter he was raising alone. His daughter was in the eighth grade. His daughter's mother was a crack head on drugs since his daughter weas twelve years old. He had to fight for custody of his daughter, and he won. So, Justin told Pamela, "my daughter goes to school in the area where my mother lives." Justin turned to the side of Pamela's left ear and said, "You are a very sexy woman, can you go to the motel with me?" Pamela backed away from him and told Justin, "I can't sleep with him because I don't know you." Pamela said, " I need to get to know you before I sleep with you." "When can I feel you," replied Justin. Pamela replied, "Maybe a month from now because I don't want to be a booty call."

Pamela and Justin Finished their breakfast, and they both left the restaurant. Pamela got into her car and went home. Justin got in his car and went the other way. From then on, Justin called Pamela every day, wanting to have sex with her, which was the whole conversation. After a month and a half went by, Pamela decided in her mind that she would sleep with Justin if he asked her again. Justin called her one Friday night and asked Pamela to come over to his house for some drinks. Pamela said, okay. Justin gave Pamela directions to get to his house, which took Pamela forty-five minutes to arrive. When Pamela arrived at his house, he pushed the button to raise his garage door. Pamela went through the garage into his house. Justin had a big house. Justin had a three-bedroom house with a den, formal living, formal dining room area, and kitchen area where a kitchen table was in the kitchen.

Pamela was very impressed with Justin. After a couple of drinks, Pamela was very tipsy, and Justin came over, filling and kissing on her. Justin definitely was getting Pamela hot below. Justin took Pamela in his bedroom, but before they could reach the room, he started taking Pamela's clothes off. Pamela asked him if he had a condom. Justin said he has one right on the nightstand. Pamela said, "That's good. So, you practice safe sex." Pamela went onto say, "I like that." Pamela took off her clothes, and Justin took off his. They were in bed having sex. He asked Pamela to get on top and work it for him. Pamela said, okay. She gave Justin a good workout. Justin was pleased. Pamela asked him for some gas money and some money to get her something to eat. Justin gave Pamela fifty dollars.

Every time Pamela would see Justin, they would drink, kiss, and have sex. Pamela would get up out of bed, wash up, and Justin would give her money before she left to go home. One particular evening, when Justin and Pamela hooked up and after the sex was over, Pamela just lay in bed. Justin was rolling over kissing Pamela. Then all of a sudden, he began talking about the woman he was in love with. Justin told Pamela, he was in love with this lawyer, and she had two kids. She was still talking and sleeping with her children's father. Justin wanted to marry her someday. He told Pamela he could never love her because she was not his kind of woman. For her not to fall in love with him because he would never love her back. All he wanted from Pamela was the brain. Pamela said, okay because she loved his company. Justin would see Pamela every Friday. All he wanted was the brain, and he talked about his girlfriend and his best friend business about his girlfriend he was dating.

Justin would always ask Pamela for her advice. He would follow her suggestion and the advice she would give him. He loved his lawyer friend. She would be at his house every weekend. Pamela would not see Justin until she went out of town. This was still okay with Pamela because every time she saw Justin, he would give her money and gas up her car. She knew her boundaries. One Friday evening, she saw Justin, and he showed Pamela an engagement ring he got for his lawyer friend. The ring was two carats. It was very beautiful, and the diamond was clear. Pamela wished it was her, he was putting the ring on her finger, but it was not. Pamela told him to think about it before he put the ring on her finger because she was still seeing her children's father. Justin replied, "We will work the situation out in time." They had sex, and Pamela got her money and left. Pamela didn't see Justin for a while because he was playing house with his fiancée. She had moved in with him. Then his daughter and hers were having conflicts. Then she and Justin would get into it. One weekend his fiancée left to go out of town. She stayed gone for two weeks, and Justin wasn't feeling right about the situation, so he called Pamela and discuss the situation to her. Pamela suggested he surprise her where she was to put his wandering mind to rest. He flew out there where his fiancée was but didn't tell her he was coming. He found another man there. Justin was hurt, of course, he left the same day and came back home. Justin fiancée flew back home right behind him.

They had this huge fight. Justin told her to pack her things and get out of his house. She busted a hole in his wall. Justin had to call the police to get her out of his house. After the incident, Justin mentioned that he would never let another woman near his daughter until she finishes school.

He never brought another woman near his daughter. This incident happened between his fiancée and his daughter had his daughter's grades slipping. Justin had to make sure his daughter wasn't tense and shaken up behind his fiancée's actions. Justin told Pamela he would not marry any woman until his daughter went off to college. Because he does not want her feeling any competition with the other woman or have any disagreements would affect her mentally. This is what Pamela loved about Justin because he truly was a father to his daughter. He would also take his daughter to PTA meetings to the George R Brown for school circulant and the different organizations she was in.

Justin would get up early in the morning on Saturdays and take his daughter to any school activity the school was having. He wanted his daughter to know how to converse with others, connect with others, and how to mingle in with other people. Justin felt like this would get her out of her shyness. When she gets ready to go to college, he wouldn't have to worry about her being afraid of anything. Justin would be confident his daughter could hold her own. Justin started this once his daughter went to high school. When his daughter's birthday came around, Justin would always take her friends out with them and pay for everything. When she wanted to go to the movies, he'll take his daughter and her first cousin to the movies all the time.

Then every other Saturday, Justin would take his daughter to the beauty shop to get her hair done and sit right there until his daughter's hair was done. Justin is a fine example of raising his daughter alone as a single father without her mother. This is what Pamela loved about him was he was there for his daughter in every way she needed him to be. His daughter's mother got hooked on crack cocaine when she was twelve years old. Her mother started running around with a different type of crowd, eventually got her caught up in drugs. Justin ended up getting custody of his daughter. Pamela loved the fact Justin was a good father. Justin was a hard worker in his job. He was also complacent with his job but smarter enough to climb higher up the ladder if he wanted to do.

Justin was a well-dressed man. Pamela always saw him in nice slacks, collar shirt with a tie or a sweater. When Justin wore jeans with a jersey, for a big guy, he had nice physic. Justin was also a church-going man, and his family was a family of pastors. His family was very active in the church. Justin was in a fraternity since he was in college. He still loves to drink and party at the fraternity parties given. He would be the bartender at these fraternity parties. He also a mason too. Justin never took Pamela in public places with him or around his family. Justin only took Pamela to the motel for sex, the only place he would be seen with her. After Justin got over the hurt of his fiancée, Pamela and Justin started up having sex again. This time, Justin brought his different flavor condoms and peppermint to the motel room, Pamela would suck his brain with the flavored condom on with peppermint in her mouth. Justin would bring different flavor condoms with him, such as orange, banana, vanilla, and strawberry. Pamela would just take her pick of what flavor she wanted to suck on his brain. Justin loved Pamela to go down on his brain sometimes for a whole hour just depending on Justin's mood, especially if Justin was stressed on his job. Pamela had no problem with Justin because he paid Pamela very well to take care of his sexual pleasure. It was whatever Justin wanted Pamela to do to him. Pamela just wanted to please him the best way she could.

She did love Justin, but she had to keep her feelings locked inside of her. Pamela loved Justin's kisses and how he held her close to his body tight in his arms after the sex was over. Justin made her feel like she was all that matter to him. When Pamela was with him, he made her feel loved even though he didn't tell Pamela he loved her. Justin always talked about situations his friends were in with their girlfriends and always sought for Pamela's advice. Justin would go back to his friends and give the advice he had received from Pamela. Pamela was the type of person who gave neutral advice. Pamela may have loved Justin, but she was not going to let her feelings get into the way of her advice to him. Justin always told Pamela constantly that she should have been a psychiatrist. Justin would always laugh at her and jump all over her playfully.

Pamela would listen attentively to what a person would be saying if they had problems and would advise accordingly to the problem being address to her. Pamela would always listen closely to whatever Justin's conversation was to help him to deal with whatever he was going through. When Pamela would be with Justin, he made all the decisions while they were together. For as what they ate in the room, how he wanted to be loved, and what type of wine she was going to drink. If it was something she didn't like that he got for her, Justin would always look at her facial expressions and know she didn't like it. Pamela would never say she didn't like it. She never wanted to disappoint him in anyway Pamela treasure love with Justin, and Pamela did not treasure disappointment.

Pamela accepted the fact that he didn't look at her as someone to be in his life permanent, but he just wanted Pamela to stay between his legs, giving him a brain. Justin was the type of man, made it happen for himself, making sure he had longevity on his job and taking a portion of his payroll check setting aside for his 401k for his future. Pamela admired Justin's way of thinking about the layout of his future plans for his life. The that thing stood out the most with Justin was he would make Pamela feel like she's the only person who exists with him. Pamela loved Justin's kisses, tight hugs, and how he always complimented her in every way. In reality, Pamela was just Justin's garden tool. She would never be a person he would let share his intimate life with or be by his side, one to cherish love and support him in his life. Pamela knew she had to close the chapter on Justin. One night, a phone call helped Pamela to realize just where she really stood in Justin's life, and his lies caught up with him. Pamela did not know he was seeing anybody.

Pamela's phone kept ringing around twelve o'clock in the morning until four o'clock in the morning. Pamela had to get up and go to work. Pamela finally answered the phone and said, "Ido not know who's calling, and if you want to talk please do. I'm listening." This woman asked her, "Are you seeing my man? We just came back from vacation, and I noticed your phone number on his cellphone." Pamela asked her, "Who is your man?" She said, "Justin." Pamela said, "What?" "I've been seeing Justin for three years," she told Pamela. Then she added, "I'm Justin's fiancée. We are going to get married, and I saw your number on his cellphone all the time. So, I decided it was time to call you." She felt Pamela had Justin heart. Pamela told her, "I love Justin.

She should not have gone through his cellphone. Pamela asked her, "Are you the lawyer fiancée with the two kids? She said, "Yes. You know about me, right." Pamela said, "Yes, I do." Pamela told her, "I know Justin truly loves you. All I'm doing was giving him brain, something you should have been doing with your fiancée so he will not cheat on you and fall in love with another woman." Pamela told her, "You need to give him a brain, and you'll keep your man. You won't have to call another woman and tell her to leave your man alone because of your insecurities. I'm just Justin garden tool, but he loves you, not me." She asked Pamela to promise her, she will never see Justin again. Pamela told her she must be a threat to her relationship with Justin for her to call her so much in one night.

Pamela told her if she promised to leave him alone for good, she has to make sure she gives him brain because that's what he likes in sex. Then she'll promise to leave him alone for good. She agreed to take care of him sexually like he wants it so he won't cheat on her. Pamela agreed to leave him alone for good. She told Pamela by her conversation that she knows she's a woman of virtue and morals. After the conversation, she never saw or talked to Justin again. Because if someone asks Pamela to promise them something, Pamela is a woman of her word, and she will keep her promise. So yes, Pamela treasure disappointment. she was just fooling herself with Justin. This man had the money, profession, house, and the love she always dreamed of having, but he didn't return the heartfelt feelings Pamela had for him. Only the sex was returned.

Jarvis was a dark skin man, tall, and he worked for a cable company. Pamela met Jarvis when he was putting the cable in her apartment. Jarvis asked Pamela, "Are you single?" He put his hand up in the air and turn his hand around. Pamela asked Jarvis, "Why are you doing that?" Jarvis said, "Because I'm single. I have no ring on my finger." Jarvis asked Pamela for her telephone number, and Pamela gave her telephone number to him. Jarvis called Pamela within a week. Both of them began talking on and off. Pamela was not interested in Jarvis because she was talking to a married man.

One particular night Jarvis came to Pamela's house at midnight with his clothes to move in with her. Pamela let him know he could not move in with her because she was dating a married man, and he comes over a whole lot. Pamela asked him that if he could deal with that, then it's okay. Jarvis said, "Yes, I could deal with it because I'm going to be evicted from my apartment." Pamela asked him, "Why are you going to be evicted?" Jarvis replied to Pamela by saying, "I stay in an apartment for three months without paying any rent, and then I move. I always move in when there's a special going on with the apartment complex until the constable tells me to leave."

Pamela also let him know, "If you stay here, you would have to pay half the rent, and this would be three hundred and fifty dollars." Pamela asked, "Jarvis, could he handle this?" Jarvis said, "Yes, I could." Pamela let Jarvis move into her apartments and gave him a key. That particular night they had sex, and as Pamela was on top of him. She saw an eye on his forehead, looking at her. Pamela screamed and told Jarvis what she saw, but he continued having sex with her as if he didn't hear her, then the eye had disappeared from his forehead. After they had finished having sex, Pamela put her head on his chest, closed her eyes, and saw a head full of snakes in a vision. This woke up Pamela only for her to see a black cloud moving over to Jarvis' side of the bed.

Then Pamela got scared, so she started praying, but the black cloud stayed over on Jarvis' side of the bed, and Pamela's side of the bed was light shaded. Pamela knew from then on, the Devil had possessed his soul. Pamela fell asleep, and when she awoke the next morning, the dark cloud was gone. Pamela kept praying for Jarvis every day because she knew the Devil was real, and he possessed Jarvis' body. Christ was in Pamela's life. She knew Christ was her shield and protection. On Sunday, Pamela went to church with Jarvis, and he introduced Pamela to all his church friends he knew. Jarvis also introduced Pamela to his Pastor and the Pastor's wife. Then Jarvis introduced Pamela to his best friend, and he kissed Pamela on the cheekbone.

Then Jarvis introduced Pamela to this particular man. Once the church was over, this particular man came up to Pamela and told her Jarvis was no good to watch out for him. Pamela just told the man, okay. Then this church woman came up to Pamela and told her not to do anything for Jarvis because he was no good. Pamela told her, okay. From all of this, Pamela wonder in the back of her mind, what type of man was she getting involved with. Jarvis grew up in this church as a little boy. Then Jarvis took Pamela to meet his family. His family welcomed Pamela. Jarvis broke the relationship down to his brother, and they were just roommates. After six months of Jarvis and Pamela being together, Jarvis ran the old married man down the street, chasing him in his vehicle for him to never come around again. Pamela asked him, "Are you crazy? Jarvis, don't answer, I already know what you're going to say. Jarvis said, "No, you don't. I'm not going to come around anymore because if I do, I'm going to let my wife know what's going on between us." Pamela said, how are you going to do that because you don't have his address or phone number. Jarvis said, yes, he does because he followed him home one day, and he got his number off her cell phone. Pamela said to Jarvis, you've been a very busy man.

Jarvis drove a small vehicle. The inspection and registration sticker had expired on his car. Pamela mentioned to Jarvis if the cops stop him, he would get a ticket. If he had any other outstanding tickets, he would go to jail. Then one day, this happened. Jarvis called Pamela from his cell phone. Jarvis told Pamela, he was in a police car, and the officer let him call her. Jarvis gave instructions for Pamela to have his car toll to the apartments. His car was at the stop-n-go store. Pamela met a toll driver at the stop-n-go store, getting gas. He had toll Jarvis' vehicle to the apartments, free of charge. Pamela thanked the man because she didn't have any money, then Jarvis stayed in jail for three days. He came home in a cab. He had no shoes on his feet, smelling stinky. Pamela told him to get into the shower so he could smell better. Jarvis told Pamela, he hoped he didn't lose his job.

The next day Jarvis went to work and told his boss man what had happened to him and asked him if he still had a job. His boss man told him yes, he still had his job. Pamela was very happy for Jarvis when he shared the news with her. Sunday, he gave the car back to his ex-wife, whom he took the car from. He had Pamela drive him to Beaumont, where he picked up this raggedy truck, which you could hear a mile away. When Jarvis would come home from work, you could hear his truck a mile away. His truck would make a loud noise. Jarvis didn't have any money to buy him a better vehicle. The next weekend, both of them went to his church in Beaumont. He wore jeans and a see-through shirt on like he would wear in a night club. Pamela said to Jarvis, "Don't you have some church clothes?"

He told Pamela, "No. Because I lost so much weight, I couldn't fit my clothes anymore." So, Pamela bought him a suit, shirt to match, shoes, and socks each time she would get paid until he had seven suits with a shirt and tie to match with shoes to go with his outfit. Pamela helped Jarvis get on his feet, and he helped Pamela get on her feet also by being her roommate.

Jarvis started taking up photography, taking pictures for churches. Pamela and Jarvis would travel to Texas City a lot for churche anniversary or some kind of church activity they were having for Jarvis to take pictures. He made money at those picture shoots, and the pastors loved him. They took very well to Pamela also. Then when Pamela leased were up.

She no longer wanted Jarvis in her life anymore. She felt he was on his feet, and she was too. That morning, she had sex with Jarvis. When he went to take a shower, Pamela took her key off his key ring and replaced it with a similar key. She cooked him breakfast and kissed him goodbye. Little to his knowledge, he wouldn't be able to get back into the house. Pamela was moving the same day that she took her key off his key ring. The movers came about nine o'clock that morning, and everything was moved out of the apartment by twelve o'clock. Pamela left Jarvis' clothes and the rest of his things in the apartment so he could get his things out also. Jarvis called Pamela and told her he tip his hat off to her for how she did it.

He asked Pamela if he could get his things out of the apartment. Pamela told him to meet her at the apartment at six o'clock that evening. Pamela came with her daughter, who let Jarvis into the apartment to get his things. Pamela and her daughter left and went back to her new place. Pamela moved into a nice one-bedroom apartment about seven hundred forty-seven square feet versus her six hundred twenty-four square feet apartment she moved from. It took Jarvis about two weeks before he called Pamela ranting and raving. He told Pamela that she was a cold-bloodedfemale dog. Then he told Pamela he was staying with his first cousin and he wanted to come home. Pamela asked him why he wanted to be with her after she did what she did to him.

Jarvis told Pamela, "I missed you, and regardless of what you did, I still love you. Pamela said, "I missed you, too. Sure, you can come home. What about the weekend?" Jarvis said, "Okay." Jarvis came home, and everything was fine between him and Pamela. They were no longer roommates but became lovers in a relationship. Jarvis bought himself a new vehicle. The vehicle wasn't noisy, but quiet and new. He bought him a new SUV. Pamela just had to vouch for his address, and he drove the vehicle off the car lot. Jarvis and Pamela's relationship was good. The relationship was everything Pamela looked for in a relationship. Then it came upon the third year Jarvis and Pamela had been together, and things started to change in the relationship. Pamela got up one Sunday morning, early around five o'clock in the morning going to church.

Jarvis worked two shifts at church, running the video and sound system at church. At the eight o'clock service, Pamela fell asleep at church, snoring and dropping everything in her lap onto the floor. Jarvis was really mad at her for falling asleep in church. After this, he never took Pamela to church with him anymore. The next Sunday, Pamela came back to church. This was valentine's day. Pamela noticed that Jarvis kept rubbing on a seventeen-year-old back in the video center. Then one of the ladies put his suit coat jacket on the back of the chair he was sitting in. Then he got up and was gone for ten minutes. The assistant pastor asked her if she knew where he was. Pamela said, no. Then Pamela got up from her seat to go look for Jarvis.

She looked for him in the lobby of the church but did not find him. When she looked in the parking lot where he was kissing on another woman and her two daughters, Pamela asked him, "What the hell is going on here?" Jarvis said this was his goddaughters. Pamela said, "It seems like more to me compared to the way he treats her at home." They both went back into the church. The Pastor brought all of this out in his sermon. Jarvis and Pamela argued in the church house and took it outside in the parking lot once the church was over. All Pamela was trying to do is surprise him on Valentine's Day and take him out to brunch, but she was shocked behind what she saw him doing at the church house. Pamela felt God was bringing out what he was doing in the dark to the light. Pamela told Jarvis that God was fixing to unravel things he has secretly been hiding. Once something is revealed, then there will be other deep dark secrets to come out. Two weeks after this happen, Jarvis came home and took a bubble bath. Jarvis laid his cell phone on the countertop. Pamela looked at his cell phone because he got a text. This text consisted of a big fat naked woman bending over, showing him her fat butt. When he got into bed, Pamela asked him, "What was this?" Pamela cursed him out. As she was cursing Jarvis out, Jarvis dialed his Pastor's number while Pamela was cursing him.

His Pastor asked Jarvis why he was with Pamela? Then the next week, he got another text from his son. This time, he called Pamela into the room to see a baseball bat being stuck up in a child butt. Pamela said to Jarvis as she was washing dishes, "Why did you call me in the room to see this text. This is disgusting! As a Christian man, you shouldn't even be looking at something like this. You need to tell your son not to send you this kind of stuff on your cell phone." Pamela went back into the kitchen to finish washing her dishes. Then Pamela snapped, went back into the bedroom, and called Jarvis a sick person. She did not know Jarvis was on the telephone with another pastor. Now it makes two pastors now have heard Pamela cursing Jarvis out. Every time Jarvis and Pamela got into it by him looking at porn or another woman calling him on his cell phone, or when she would curse him out, he was always talking to a pastor. The pastors would always take Jarvis' side if he told the pastors he was up all night having an argument with Pamela. Jarvis would always come home and tell Pamela what they said. Pamela would tell him they just don't know what he's done to make her go off. Pamela told Jarvis, "I could not believe you hold this big position in the church and how you act when you're at home, and it surely not Godly." Jarvis called Pamela a red-headed devilish winch, and if not this, then he called her a cockeyed female dog. Sometimes he'll tell Pamela that she's just a silly ass woman. Pamela dated a married man, and he would always throw up in her face, "You can't take a whore out of a whore."

Pamela would always ask Jarvis, "are you talking about yourself? He would say, "No. I'm talking about you, Pamela." Then, their relationship went downhill. One weekend, they drove out of town to see his son. Pamela never met his son's mother, but that day she did. As she met her, Jarvis and his baby mama were carrying on a conversation like they were still married. Her husband went outside because he knew how they act when they get together. Jarvis and his baby mama talked about Jarvis' boys, her children and then brought out their wedding album. Pamela asked her, "Why did you divorce? It seems to me that you both seem to be still in love with one another." His baby mama told Pamela, "We had a child together.

We were young when we got married and made a lot of mistakes that we can't change." When she sees Jarvis, she would always catch up on the family, and she keeps him in tune with his son. The next day, they all went to dinner at a cafeteria. As they began to eat, Jarvis and his baby mama were talking to one another as if Pamela and her husband weren't even at the table with them at all. Her husband got angry and left out of the cafeteria to take him a smoke. Pamela got up from the table went outside where he was. She asked him, "They act like they still married, don't they?" Her husband said, "Yes, but once he leaves, she goes back home with me." Pamela said, "Sure, you're right. Tut one day, it seems to me that they will find the way back to each other." Her husband said, "They might." Pamela and Jarvis left headed back home.

While they were in the car, Pamela was quiet as a mouse. She said nothing to Jarvis. Jarvis didn't say anything to Pamela also. Once they arrived back home, Jarvis made love to Pamela, stating she's the only one he cares about and loves. Pamela said to Jarvis, "I hope so." Pamela fell asleep in Jarvis' arms. A couple of weeks after that trip, Jarvis started coming in late from work every night. Then he started leaving on a Friday night and not returning until on Monday evenings. Jarvis would always tell Pamela that the church was having some sort of event going on, which requires him to set up the sound system. Then he started working out of town on his job. Jarvis would be gone for about three months at a time. When he was out of town on his job assignment, Jarvis would call Pamela and let her know what hotel he was staying at, his room number, and the hotel's telephone number. Pamela was okay with this.

One night he called Pamela and told Pamela he was in the Hotel Lobby. Pamela asked him, "Why are you not in your room? Jarvis told Pamela, "The hotel got a prostitute to have sex with all the men whom he worked with to relieve them of their pressure." Pamela told Jarvis, "You better not be sleeping with a prostitute because you could get AIDS." Jarvis told Pamela, "I'm not sleeping with anybody. That's why I'm in the Hotel Lobby until she comes out of the room, which I was sharing with my co-worker. The prostitute is going from room to room, sleeping with the cable men." Pamela told Jarvis, "What about their wives? They're being unfaithful. If they're not using protection, their wives could get AIDS, some sexually transmitted diseases, or become HIV.

Jarvis said, "That's not my problem because I'm doing nothing but behaving." Once the assignment was up, Jarvis came home. Jarvis and Pamela made passionate love, and she fell asleep. Pamela really missed Jarvis. She cooked for him every day. She made ice tea for him. She cleaned up behind him every day when he came in from work. Jarvis was a very trifling man. Jarvis never picked up behind himself. He left the toilet a mess, and Pamela had to keep the toilet clean every day. Jarvis would never clean out the tub. Jarvis would eat in the bed all the time, and crumbs would be everywhere in the bed. He would throw his trash on the floor. Pamela would always have to pick up behind him. Pamela was in love with him because she may complain, but she kept cleaning behind him.

Jarvis worked outside, installing cable but would never take a bath or a shower when he came home. He would get straight in the bed filthy and smelly. One night, he was eating in the bed, Pamela told him, "If you keep eating in the bed, this will bring roaches." So, Jarvis laid down to go to sleep. When he got up to go to the bathroom, two roaches were under him. Pamela screamed and jumped out of bed and turned on the light for

Jarvis to see the roaches in bed. Jarvis killed them, and Pamela said, "Please stop eating in the bed." But Jarvis didn't stop eating in bed. He continued. Pamela was a good person, but Jarvis wanted all his friends to think that she was a bad person raising hell all the time.

When Pamela tried talking to Jarvis about what problems they were having between them, he would always tell Pamela to shut up until he feels like talking to her. Pamela was the type of person that wanted to work out any kinks in a relationship to make it better. Jarvis told Pamela one day, "I would never marry you because you're not the type of woman I was looking for to be my wife." Pamela was hurt by this. So, Pamela asked Jarvis, "Why are you with me?" He said, "I'm just trying to save my money and pay off my bills." Then he said that one day he was going to move on. Jarvis asked Pamela, "Why are you with me?" Pamela said, "I'm with you because I love you. I needed to buy a wardrobe of clothes and get out of debt." Jarvis said, "No, you're not.

You're with me because I pay the rent." Pamela said, "True, but I do love you." She said to Jarvis, "I would not have been with you this long if I don't love you. Pamela said, "If she had to, I could pay my rent somehow. It might be tight, but I'll be able to manage." One night when Jarvis came home, he put three dollars on the nightstand. Pamela picked it up. As she was about to put it back, Jarvis pushed Pamela against the wall like he wanted to beat Pamela up, but instead, he bent Pamela's finger back, almost breaking her finger. Then Pamela realized he didn't love her because he was trying to hurt her for nothing. She also realized Jarvis had a hot temper. Pamela asked Jarvis, "How can a Christian man like yourself hold a position in the church and act like a heathen at home?"

Jarvis didn't respond to Pamela at all. The next day, Jarvis told Pamela he'll be late coming home from work because he will be working a double shift. Jarvis did not come home until the next day at eight-thirty that morning. He said his job had them putting in cable for this fitness center. Pamela felt Jarvis was lying. She decided since Jarvis wanted to stay out all night, she was not going to answer any of his calls or open the door to him until she woke up. Jarvis stayed outside until Pamela woke up that morning. Jarvis and Pamela kept having problems one behind another, arguing and fussing. Even accusing one another of cheating but Pamela wasn't doing anything but going to work, church, back home, and making sure Jarvis had his dinner ready when he walked in the door.

When Jarvis would get home, he'll get on his cell phone and begin to talk to his friends about Pamela being really bad in order to justify what he wanted to do because when Friday would come, Pamela wouldn't see Jarvis until Monday evening. When he comes through the door, he would always tell Pamela, "No questions." Then he would ask her, what they are going to eat tonight, or how long will it take for dinner to be ready. Jarvis got up one Saturday morning and told Pamela, he was leaving going to Brownsville with his cable job, and he won't be back until next Tuesday. Jarvis told Pamela he was driving his own vehicle. The cable company was going to pay him twenty-three cents a mile. Pamela found this story to be odd since this cable company had its own company vans. Pamela did not believe this story that he was going out of the market with his job, but she went along with it to see how this lie was going to play out. When Jarvis would go out of town, he usually would give Pamela the name of the hotel and the hotel number, but this time, he didn't. Pamela called Jarvis on his cell phone, but he didn't answer. Jarvis waited thirty-five minutes before he called her back. Pamela answer her cell phone, he told her there was a bad connection, and he couldn't hear her. Jarvis told Pamela that he would call her back, but he never did. Pamela did not see Jarvis until Jarvis walked into the door on Tuesday. Jarvis greeted Pamela a good evening. Jarvis did not come into the house with no clothes to hang up in the closet, only his laptop. Jarvis went into the bedroom and got into bed.

Jarvis and Pamela argue for one hour about him being gone for the weekend and not picking up the telephone to call her. Pamela felt he was on vacation with another woman. Pamela was so mad and upset. She told Jarvis to get out of her house because she was not going to let him disrespect her like that. Pamela also went onto say to Jarvis, "I'm not going to allow you to cheat on me in my face." Pamela told Jarvis that she just wanted him out of her house. When Pamela went to bed, Jarvis told Pamela he was just tired of the bullshit. Pamela could tell by Jarvis' eyes when she looked up at him that he was serious, but Pamela fell asleep and did not discuss it any further. Then the next day, Pamela realized she needed to make some drastic changes within herself. Pamela texted Jarvis and asked him not to leave her, and she loved him. She didn't mean any of those words she said to him last night. Pamela actually was begging Jarvis not to leave her. She told Jarvis she would not fuss anymore. She promised no more questions about his whereabouts. When Jarvis arrived home, Pamela didn't say a word. She cooked Jarvis some spaghetti and told Jarvis that he could eat. Pamela and Jarvis both took baths right behind one another. Pamela asked Jarvis if he got her text. Jarvis replied, no. Pamela resent the text while Jarvis was standing right there by her. Pamela asked Jarvis to check his cell phone for her text she just sent him. Jarvis said that he would read the text tomorrow. Pamela got into bed to go to sleep. Jarvis started feeling on her. This was his way of wanting sex with Pamela. Pamela asked Jarvis would he go down on her.

Jarvis said yes because we only have a short time. Pamela did not catch onto what Jarvis was saying until the sex was over. Then Jarvis told Pamela, "my boss man let me go home early because I looked like crap." Pamela asked Jarvis, "Why did you look like crap at work?" Jarvis told Pamela, "I told my boss man I was up all night long because of our arguing. He couldn't sleep. My boss man told me to go home and get some rest." Jarvis actually lied to his boss man because he and Pamela argue for one minute, and Pamela fell fast asleep, and afterward, so did he. The next day Jarvis came home, and he was kissing all on Pamela. Then one thing led to another, and they ended up in bed having sex. Once they finished having sex and they both cleaned up. Both of them got back into bed. Jarvis told Pamela, "I put some money on an apartment, and I'll be moving out by the first of the month."

Then he told Pamela, "I talked this over with one of my sons and a pastor." Pamela said, "What? You're leaving me? Why?" Jarvis told Pamela, "You're always accusing him of being with another woman. When the only thing I know was not doing anything but working my butt off." Jarvis also told Pamela she's always raising hand with him for no reason at all. He also said, "When I came home from work, all I wanted want was some peace and quiet." Pamela said, "It sounds like you made up your mind to leave. When you leave, Jarvis, you can't come back once you walk out that door." Pamela said to Jarvis, "Please take everything that's yours in this house with you." Jarvis told Pamela, "I was just going to take a few things with me and leave his barbeque pit." Then Jarvis told Pamela that while he was at work, he listened to every voice message she ever left him. Pamela told Jarvis, you saved all those voice messages all that time, and your cell phone doesn't erase them automatically.

Pamela said, "my cell phone erases my messages automatically. Okay, Jarvis, why do I feel like you're lying?" Jarvis replied, "I'm not." Pamela said, "Yeah, right. You think my willy foo foo." Pamela told Jarvis, "It seems like you had this planned for some time to leave me. I felt you didn't think about discussing your decision with me, and you were trying to make me be the bad guy here." Pamela kept on talking to Jarvis, saying, "While we have been together, you never ever wanted to talk to me. When I try to talk to you, you always tell me to shut up." Pamela goes on to say, "When you're in the bedroom, I can't watch anything on TV because you're watching all your favorite shows." Pamela said to Jarvis, "Besides, I have to sit at the table and watch TV until I fell asleep at the table. Then if I'm in bed with you, I bet not rub against you or touch you without you coping an attitude with me." Then she went onto say, "If your family is giving any parties or get-togethers, you didn't invite me to come along. You go by yourself, never including me in any aspect of your life." Pamela went onto say, "You had even told me that you would never marry me. Everything makes sense now." She told Jarvis again, "You've been planning to leave me for a while. You know I'm a good woman. You're not going to ever find a woman like me." She even mentioned to him that the grass is not greener on the other side. It might seem like it is, but when you get over there to know her. She might process flaws you may not be ready for. Pamela ask Jarvis, "Did anybody told you to leave me?"

Jarvis said, "No." "Then what happened for you to come to this decision?" Pamela snapped. Pamela told, Jarvis once again, "I love you, please don't leave me." Jarvis told Pamela, "I want to leave for six months and within six months, if we still have feelings for one another, we will find our way back to each other." Pamela told Jarvis, "You just want to see other women and have your cake and eat it too, but I'm not going to let you degrade me like that." Pamela asked Jarvis, "Why you're telling me just now that we have a problem? Jarvis, why you can't stay, and we will work out whatever problems we have? If you walk out that door trust, and communication will be lost and thrown outside the door."

Pamela laid on down in the bed, and she started crying. Her heart started hurting inside because she loved Jarvis. Jarvis turned over for the first time in three and a half years and hugged Pamela. That hug of his gave Pamela the confirmation that he really was going to leave her. The next morning, Pamela called Jarvis on the telephone and said she saw his mind was made up. He didn't care and didn't care about Pamela's feelings. He was so bold, conniver, and a schemer. Pamela never thought in a million years that he would leave her. He treated the relationship like it was nothing to salvage, or nothing could be worked out. Pamela said to Jarvis, "But, what about this, can you stay here until the lease is up? This is just three months away."

Pamela suggested to Jarvis, "Can you pay the rent for next month? The next two months, we both can come up with half the rent. In this way, you can save money, and I can, too." Pamela also mentioned to him, "You can come and go as you please." Pamela also said, "I will not say anything about your comings, goings, or question your whereabouts at all." Pamela told Jarvis that he owes her too, at least, show her this common courtesy before he walks away from her because she has been nothing but good to him. Pamela also told Jarvis, she'll be caught up and can pay her rent with no problems and he'll be able to save some money and his pocket book won't be tight. Jarvis told Pamela that he'll let her know tonight. Pamela said, okay. Pamela told Jarvis, "In this way, I can mend my broken heart."

Pamela hung up the cell phone. Jarvis' mind was made up about leaving, but he'll give her two hundred dollars at the end of the month to help pay her rent. When Jarvis told Pamela he was moving out and the way he did it, Pamela wanted to kill him, but God kept her from doing this because his Holy Angels put her in a deep sleep so she would not think about killing him and spending the rest of her life in prison. Pamela was in a messed-up state of mind. She didn't know the both of them had any problems because he truly never spoke to her about anything, and every time she wanted to talk to him, he would always tell her to shut up. Pamela wanted so bad to put Jarvis out of her apartment when he told her he was leaving her, but she couldn't because he paid rent on the first of the month. Jarvis had made sure his name was shown on the check made out to the apartment people. In this way, Pamela could not put him out.

If she changed the locks on the door, the apartment people would have to let him in. That Sunday morning, Jarvis got up to get ready for church. His cell phone rang at six o'clock in the morning. Jarvis answered his cell phone, and the caller asked him on the other end of the phone if he was on his way to pick her up. Jarvis told her, "I'm on my way," paused and said, man. He was trying to pretend he was talking to a man on the phone, but in reality, it was a woman. Pamela guessed that he was taking her to his church to introduce her to everyone like he did Pamela. Jarvis did not return home until eight o'clock that evening. Pamela did not go ballistic or curse him out for being inconsiderate toward her because she knew he was leaving her and she had to suck it up. Pamela still cooked for Jarvis every day when he came home from work.

If Pamela didn't have Christ in her life, it would have been hard for her to deal with Jarvis leaving. The Heavenly Father kept Pamela and gave her the peace inside, not to blame herself because she didn't do anything wrong. The Heavenly Father gave Pamela grace to know he didn't deserve her because he left her for someone else. The Heavenly Father gave Pamela mercy to forgive him and enough strength to let him go. Before he left, Pamela gave Jarvis the bedspread on the bed, a set of sheets, plates, silverware, glasses, bowls, towels, and pillowcases. Pamela packed it all up in a box for Jarvis. Pamela just wanted Jarvis to be happy and in love. Jarvis was a good liar, very selfish, and a cold-blooded man, not compassionate or considerate toward Pamela's feelings.

Through it all, Pamela was very stunned and surprised by his deceptiveness because she never saw this coming. Jarvis told Pamela that he was leaving her for her insecurities, and since he was on his feet, he wanted someone educated like himself with a degree or have an executive position and more on his level. Jarvis told Pamela that she was stupid and crazy. Pamela recalled a conversation, one of Jarvis' church members told her that Jarvis was no good. Instead of her listening to that person, Pamela had dismissed that conversation all together until now. See, Pamela did not want a man that didn't want her. Pamela realized she needed a man to love her, caress her, talk to her, have sex with her, listen to her, lift her up and not put her down, keeping it real with her. She needed a man she could lean on and have her back for a change, especially when she falls.

The last day at Pamela's house, Jarvis was moving his things out. He asked Pamela to help him get his things out, and if she refused, she would not get her house key, gate key, and the two hundred dollars she needed for rent. So, Pamela had to help him pack his stuff to his car. As both of them moved the last item, he gave her a hug around her waist, a kiss on her cheek, and told her he still loved her. Pamela said, "Yeah, right," and went back into her house. Pamela was very devastated when Jarvis left. She cried in her sleep, and she thought she was sleeping, but she wasn't. Pamela looked a hot mess with teary eyes and a swollen face. Pamela could not even eat. If she ate anything, it was a spoonful of food.

Pamela's heart was hurting deep inside. Pamela never did breakdown and call him, but the pain was there, and the pain would not go away. Jarvis was an opportunist. He was the type of man that looked for the next woman to advance up. Pamela was told this by one of his closest friends. But Pamela still wished him love in his life because eventually, he would have to settle down sooner or later before he ends up with nobody in his life. When a person doesn't communicate with you or wants to talk to you. you know you don't have anything in common anymore, especially if he treats you cold. But will smile, laugh when his brother, pastor cousins, and anybody in the video ministry, but when it comes to talking to you,

he frowns up, puts an ugly face on, or tell her not to talk to him or tell her to shut up. He never even tried to hold her or kiss her. So, she knew it was over. She just needed to come to this realization. She just needed to make that adjustment of him not being with her anymore, no matter how it might hurt inside. Believe it or not, she got feelings. Pamela knew if she goes looking for something, she'll find it. She might be shocked and hurt about what she found out because Jarvis had a whole lot to hide. Pamela knew he was leaving her for another woman. Pamela felt Jarvis try to intentionally do her in. He tried to bring Pamela down because when Jarvis left her, Pamela had to pawn all of her jewelry to pay her car note, rent, and utility bills. She had to get payday loans just to survive.

All of the major credit card bills got behind her, and the credit went downhill. Pamela didn't lose a thing behind him. The Lord didn't let that happen. God kept her and made sure she didn't lose a thing. Everything was rough and tough for Pamela, but she eventually got out of debt, but she never gave him an ounce of thought in any form of reconciliation. Jarvis had Pamela going to his church every Sunday, leaving her to turn her back on her own church, so when he left her, she did not have a leg to stand on without her church family, who kept her strong and equipped in God's Word the Bible. When you're an older man, and you leave a good woman for something you think is better on the other side than her, it might not really be for you once you go to the other side where she is. So, what you have right in front of you is really for you and nobody else. Some people throw this all away for not a sure thing.

Pamela treasured disappointment with Jarvis, but she believed Jarvis was blocking her blessing. The Lord moved him out of the way so she could receive her blessing that the Lord has in store for her. Pamela believed if God brought her to it, God was going to bring her through it. Pamela could never imagine her life without him, but she was better off. She did not realize it now, but she realized it later.

She knew Jarvis would never love her. She knew he would never show a woman love because of something that happened to him in his childhood life. He treated Pamela dirty, and he was cold toward her. Although Jarvis had a good job, made good money, and grew up in the church house and knew God's Word like the back of his hand, his spirit and ways were wicked to the core. Throughout everything, Pamela maintained her calmness and coolness when Jarvis decided to leave her. She realized she was not the same person she used to be because Christ was in her life, and she knew somebody had to get hurt in this situation, and she guessed it was going to be her.

After Jarvis, Pamela began to heal her soul within because she been in many relationships, one after another, and it didn't work out. She was always the one that lost out on everything she put into a relationship. She wished Jarvis loved her, liked she loved him. Pamela wrote a poem about Jarvis, a love she thought she had, and it goes like this. "She had a love that did not want her. She had a love that walked out on her. She had a love that didn't want to be with her. She had a love that eyes didn't love her. She had a love that wouldn't hold her at night. She had a love that didn't pray with her. She had a love that did not want to take her to church with him. She had a love that screwed her and told her he was leaving her all in the same night. She had a love that never told her he loved her back. All a difference a day would have made if she had a real love that truly loved her." Boy, he hurt Pamela real bad. Do you think she'll be able to get past this? Love definitely hurts. Pamela will be just fine as long as she keeps relying on Christ to give her strength. After Jarvis was gone, Pamela found out just what really went wrong in the relationship and why he left her from him and his baby mama. Pamela found out all the time he said he was traveling on his jobs, he was seeing his baby mama. They were rekindling their old flame. They would meet at different hotels with their son out of town.

They were planning to be with one another, even if this meant hurting the persons they were with. The baby momma was still in love with her baby's father. They had divorced and lived separate lives until one day, the baby momma mentioned to the baby's father his son needed a man figure in his life because his son started lying and getting into trouble at school. So one day, they started preplanning their move together. They just up and left the persons they were with no matter who got hurt and was devastated behind their actions. The baby daddy left, thinking the grass was greener on the other side because she was a nurse, nnly to find out she lied. She was trying to go to school to be a nurse. She did not have a job. She couldn't have sex with him because she needed surgery on her kitty cat.

She knew he had insurance. She knew she had the baby daddy's heart, so she played with it however she wanted to do with his heart as she pleased. He loved her dearly, but she did not love him. She had other plans for him, and there are things she needed to get done for herself. She needed his insurance to have surgery. She divorced her ex-husband and changed her last name back to the baby's daddy, the last name to use his insurance. Jarvis was just bragging to his friends that his baby was back, and she wasn't going anywhere. She was sitting there laughing to herself inside because she knew she was not going to stay with him.

In the end, Pamela was blessed with everything she prayed to the Lord, for it was staring her right in the face, her happiness. God blessed her with the five-bedroom house with the three-car garage, fine furniture, the Mercedes, Jaguar, and a Godly Jamaica man that truly loved her unconditionally. Pamela did not want to date an African American Black man anymore. She became fed up because they cheat too much on other women. This is just what she experienced with them. They do not know how to be happy and in love with just one woman. Then when the men get caught, they act like they didn't do anything wrong. It's like you are over exaggerating and taking their wrongdoing out of proportion. After Jarvis has seen that the grass wasn't greener on the other side with his baby mama, he started calling Pamela to get back with her. He even took Pamela out on her birthday at Pappadeaux while he was with his baby mama. The old saying, if a man cheats on you with another woman, he will cheat on the woman he left you for. Check this out, he even got a hotel room and had sex with Pamela and went downtown on her. He didn't even want to come up for air. Four months passed until Pamela heard from Jarvis again. He needed to borrow twenty dollars from Pamela for some gas to put in his truck. Jarvis looked like a hot mess.

His hair was raggedy looking. He used to get his hair cut on a regular basis and buy him suits every month. All of this came to a stop when he and his baby mama got back together. After two years went by, both of them started arguing, fussing and fighting. Both of them decided to part because it was not working out as she thought. The baby mama realized they did not have anything in common, and he couldn't satisfy her sexually. He came down too quickly, and he wasn't gentle in sex. See, when you divorce one another you, divorce for the reason that you could not resolve.

She said that she did not know they still had those same issues they had when they were together. She even told Jarvis that she did not love him. She only used him to get to Houston and to go to school to get a nursing certificate. Also, she only used him to get what she wanted from him because she knew he was still in love with her. She even told Jarvis while they were arguing, he should have never left a good woman for a no sure thing. Everything Pamela went through with him, she started going through the same thing Pamela went through with him, but the only exception she did not want him from the beginning. Soon, both of them started sleeping in separate bedrooms.

One night, Pamela and the Jamaican man were arguing because when he gets drunk, he likes to talk and argue all night long. This particular night, Pamela received a text from Jarvis' baby mama stating that Jarvis needs a friend right about now. So Pamela called her to see what was going on. Pamela told his baby mama she thought they were happy since he left Pamela for her. She told Pamela that she still loved her ex-husband, and she had not had sex with Jarvis because he comes down too quickly, and he could not satisfy her like her ex-husband can. Pamela let her be truthful here, and she was wrong to take her man from her. She just had her own selfish reasons. She knew she's going to pay for the wrongdoing she had done.

This is why she's going to give him back to her. Jarvis baby mama went onto say that she had remarried her ex-husband, and she needed Jarvis out of her apartment by the end of the month because her husband was coming home. Pamela said, "You did what? Jarvis is still in the house while you re-married your ex-husband." Pamela told her, "You are bold. Did Jarvis knew anything about this? She said, "No." Pamela said, "He's going to kill your butt." So, Pamela told her that she'll call Jarvis and tell him for her. This is what Pamela did. When Pamela told Jarvis, he did not seem shocked. Jarvis just stated, she was going to reap what she sowed one day. He told Pamela he learned the grass is never greener on the other side. It just smells pretty but feels nasty. Jarvis told Pamela that he would never leave her again because he learned his lesson. He asked Pamela, "Can we re-kindled what we had before?" Pamela replied, "I'm no longer that person when I was with you before." She was a woman scorned by him. She could be very revengeful. Pamela asked him if he could deal with that if this happens. He said yes. Pamela said, "Let me think about it because I'm going through some things with the man I'm with. I will let him know." Pamela called the baby mama and told her she let Jarvis know what was going on with her. Jarvis baby mama then said, "Now all of us can be happy. You will be back with Jarvis whom you love, and I'll be back with my husband, whom I should have never left." Pamela asked her, "Why did you leave him?"

She replied, "He did not make enough money to support me. He could not read or write. He was pedophile, and he molested my twelve-year-old niece. I will now accept the little he has and move on with my life with him because he truly has my heart. I truly love him." Pamela asked her, "Why would you want to be with a pedophile, and you have a son? What if he molests your son?" Jarvis' baby mama said he won't. Pamela replied, "You know if something were to happen, Jarvis would kill you both." She said she knows. Pamela told her, "This is going to catch up with you. If you ever take Jarvis to court for an increase in child support, I'll make sure Jarvis and I will be raising your son. I will be the one paying him child support."

Pamela went back to Jarvis after the Jamaican man threw her down the stairs and left her for dead. Once she fell down the stairs, he picked her up and put her on the couch. He did not even call the Paramedics. Pamela did not wake up until the next day. Pamela felt she could have died all because he was on his drunken binge for the weekend. He was always jugging a knife at Pamela like he wanted to stab her to death. Pamela told Jarvis about this. He seemed pretty concerned about her welfare. He mentioned to Pamela that they should get an apartment together until both of them get on their feet. Pamela was laid off her job, trying to find a permanent job, and she was receiving unemployment.

No apartment complex would let her get an apartment in her name because she had no permanent job. Jarvis had just found a job and said he needed help in paying the rent because he was in debt. He asked, Pamela to find them an apartment, and Pamela did just that and found an apartment. They moved back together. They became roommates paying half the bills until they both get on their feet financially with having sex occasionally. As Pamela was with him the second time around, her eyes became open. She noticed he still didn't take baths. His cell phone was ringing off the hook, and he was still talking to other women. He would still eat in the bed. He would still mess on the commode, leaving Pamela to clean up behind him.

He would still put on clean clothes over a dirty body. He still would not wash his face and brush his teeth when he wakes up in the morning. He still would leave Pamela at home when he would go somewhere. He still didn't do anything with Pamela or take her anywhere with him. He was still not holding a conversation with Pamela. When she would try to talk to him, he would tell her to shut up. The only time he would talk to her when he wanted to talk about his daily activities on his job. He was still not managing his money right because every time a bill needed to be paid, Pamela had to pay the bill herself first, and then he would give her the money when he got paid.

Pamela did not make enough money to pay the bills because she was only getting unemployment. He was the only one in the household with a steady job. Then he would have an attitude when it comes to paying bills. Pamela just got fed up with his attitude and begging him for the bill money in the house. Pamela believed if you can't pay the necessary bills in life, how will you move forward in life and save money to get where you need to be or have something in life.

He wasn't trying to hold Pamela up spiritually, like have Bible discussions or read the Bible together with Pamela. Pamela wanted to grow spiritually with Jarvis, but he didn't feel the same way. When he talked to Pamela, his voice would always be high pitch like he was screaming at her. Jarvis told her one night that he still loved his baby mama even after all she did to him. He would never marry Pamela still because he didn't and couldn't ever love her even though she was a good woman. When the lease was up at the apartment complex, Pamela and Jarvis went their separate ways. Pamela never had any regrets or even thought twice about being with him or missing him. She knew she could close the book on him and never look back.

Pamela was sitting on the steps of her apartments when she heard this man in the background, talking on the telephone. He was talking loud on his cell phone. He was going to his eighteen-wheeler truck to get something out. He noticed Pamela on the stairs. He asked Pamela if she was single, and Pamela said yes. He asked Pamela what her name was. She said that her name is Pamela and he introduced himself that his name is Jermaine. He just came in from out of town on a Friday night from driving on the road. Pamela was going to the dumpster to empty the trash. He told Pamela how to get to his apartment, and he gave her his apartment number for her to come and see him tonight.

Pamela turned around and went to his apartment. She knocked on the door and stood on the other side of the door. He was shocked to see Pamela because he jumped. Jermaine looked up at Pamela said, he thought she was one of those kids. He told her, "Come on in, girl, you are in a danger zone." Pamela did not catch on to what he was saying. He told Pamela that when he came home, his refrigerator was left open all his food had spoiled, and the blood from the meat spilled all in the fridge. He had bleach on the countertop to remove the bloodstain from the meat. Pamela was standing by the countertop. He came over there, screwing Pamela with his clothes on. Telling her once again, she was in the danger zone because he came off the road, and now he wants some sex.

Pamela said, "I can't help you because I'm bleeding." He said, "What?" Pamela said, "I'm on my cycle." She asked him, "Don't truck drivers get sex on the road traveling to different states?" He said, "Some of us do, but not me. He said, "I do not know what those women have and what motive they could have." I'm not trying to get in trouble or go to jail out there on the road." Pamela asked him if she could take a look around his apartment. He said yes. Pamela looked in his living room. He had a brown sofa & loveseat. He had a sixty-inch big screen TV. She went to his guest bathroom. It was white. He had a white shower curtain with white & beige rugs on the bathroom floor.

His bathroom had a brown shower curtain with a white and beige rug on the bathroom floor. In his bedroom, he had a big, soft, comfortable queen size poster bed with a fifty-two-inch screen TV in front of his bed. He also had some big fluffy pillows and a nice bedspread. So, Pamela left out of his bedroom and back into the living room. But she stopped at this door that was shut. She asked, "Jermaine, what's in there?" Pamela opened it up really quick. She noticed some papers and a blanket on the floor. She asked him, "Who lives in this bedroom?" He said, "Nobody. I need to put a bed in there. Shut that door." So, Pamela did. He was standing by the sink and Pamela was standing by the countertop.

She asked him if she could move to the second bedroom? He said, "No. I do not want a roommate." Pamela said, "Let's get married." Jermaine said, "Oh no, I'm never getting married." Pamela asked him why. He said, "Because I've been dating this woman on and off for two years." Pamela asked him if he thought she has another man. He said, "No. Even if she did, I wouldn't expect her to be faithful to me because I'm on the road all the time. I'm living in a one-bedroom apartment in the front until she said she was going to leave her husband, so I got this two-bedroom apartment, thinking she was going to move in, but she didn't. Pamela, you need to call me before you come over." Pamela said to him, "Is this because you're seeing other women?" He said, "Yes I am. He tells a woman up front they need to call before they come over because another woman might be here. If you call before you come over, this will keep down confusion. Pamela said, "Don't think I wouldn't be prepared. I would say I'm looking for Georgia, and I'm sorry that I got the wrong apartment number." Jermaine said, "You're sharp." Pamela said, "I know how to handle different situations I get myself into." Jermaine said, "That's good. Would you like a drink?" Pamela said, "What do you have?" He said, "I just have some crown royal." Pamela told him, "My man just broke up with me. He's calling my phone every hour on the hour now. All he wants is some sex, and for me to go down on him." "Why didn't you say this early? You give brain! Give him some brain" Jermaine said. He came from the kitchen and sat on the couch with his legs open. Then he jumped up and went into his bedroom and got some trojan condoms. He came back into the living room and sat on the couch.

Pamela was sitting down on the other end of the couch, sipping her drink. He fixed her. She asked him what was that scar on the side of his leg. He told her that he got stabbed there from fighting. Then she saw another scar on his knee. He told her that it was from his surgery. Jermaine said, "Damn, girl, what else do you want to know." Pamela asked, "What's that mark on your arm?" He said that he got burned on the barbeque grill. Then Jermaine said, out of the blue, that he had his neighbors' kids in his house giving candy to them. Then he thought about what he said. He said to himself, "They may think I'm a pedophile." Pamela said, "Are you?" He said, "Heck no." Pamela told Jermaine, "You can't do that being a man because what if you get accused of trying to mess with one of those kids.

You can't let those kids in your house anymore and give them candy because you could get yourself in a world of trouble." Then all of a sudden, the neighbor kids who were boys kept knocking at his door. He just stood there and kept opening, telling them to stop knocking. Then they finally did. Then, he sat back down on the couch and asked Pamela to give him some brain. Pamela did just that. While Pamela was sucking his brain, his eyes were rolling behind his head when Pamela looked up at Jermaine. He was enjoying the brain she was giving him. As Jermaine was about to cum, he took his hand and put his hand on top of Pamela's head to control her strokes on his brain. Then once Jermaine cum, Pamela threw up all the cum back on his brain. She started gagging. She went into the bathroom to washed out her mouth and washed her hands.

Jermaine asked, "Pamela, are you okay?" Pamela said, "Yes, but don't ever put your hand on my head. I couldn't stand for a man to do that. Jermaine, please always let me know if you're gonna cum. So you won't cum in my mouth. You should have had that condom on. I'm not a whore." Jermaine said, "You give good brain." Then Jermaine said, "You know, two to three percent of women have AIDS," just out of the blue. Pamela said, "Women have a higher percentage than two to three percent with AIDS. The majority of the women that's drug users are not gonna tell you if they are HIV or have full-blown AIDS. Some of these women are gorgeous, women with beautiful skin."

Pamela told him, "Looking at a woman from the outside doesn't mean a thing you're never know if a woman has AIDS or is HIV positive from the outside." Pamela gave Jermaine some advice, being a truck driver watch who you sleep without there because you never know one day you can wake up to the world of the unknown AIDS. Some women pass it around and don't have the courtesy of letting the person know whom they are sleeping with, Pamela told Jermaine. She knows you get lonely on the road. Just make sure you're careful and use plenty of condoms. Pamela got her purse and told Jermaine she enjoyed her time with him. Pamela said, let her see his tongue. He's crazy, and he stuck out his tongue.

Pamela said, "Your tongue got a pretty pink color and no marks on it." Jermaine said, "What does that mean, Pamela?" Pamela said, "It means you would have some type of sexually transmitted disease." Jermaine said, "I have learned a lot with you today. You checked me over with a fine teeth comb with all your questions and inspecting my body. Yes, I have a hairy chest, too." Pamela said, "Let me see your chest." She said, "Yes, it's hairy. I like a hairy chest on a man." Pamela told Jermaine goodbye. Pamela left and went on some errands. Pamela could not get out of her head about him bringing those young boys in his house and giving those boys candy. This truly disturbed Pamela. When she opened the door to his second bedroom, there was a blanket and pillow on the floor. She wandered in the back of her mind if he was messing with one of his neighbor's boys and if he were a pedophile.

Then one Saturday night, he came home because when Pamela got ready to go to church. She was going to her car. She saw his truck parked. As she was coming around the way before, she was exiting the gate. She saw Jermaine washing his car. Pamela stopped and rolled down the window to her car. The first thing came out of Jermaine's mouth, "girl, you make me want to molest you." Right then, there was confirmation he could be a pedophile. See, we need to be careful to listen to what comes out of a person's mouth. That will tell you about him. So, when Pamela got out of the church, she went to Jermaine's apartment. He told her, "I had a few errands to run, so let's ride, Pamela." Pamela came to his house without calling. He told Pamela to promise him that she will call him before she comes over because he's seeing other woman he doesn't want any drama.

They both left the apartment, and Pamela got into his vehicle. He stopped at the Post Office to get the mail out of his P O Box. Pamela asked him why he had a P O Box when he lives in an apartment and automatically has a mailbox. He evaded the question and did not answer. So then he stopped at the store and got him some beer. Then they went back to his apartment. He continued washing dishes, washing clothes, and he was dusting. So, Pamela said that she will see him the next time he comes to town. Pamela left and went to get her something to eat. Pamela hadn't heard from Jermaine for months. Then out of the blue, she got a call from him stating he needed some sex and brain. He told Pamela that he's in town and he'll call her in an hour. Jermaine told Pamela to come to his apartment with a robe and nothing underneath it. Pamela did.

As she arrived to his apartment and was about to knock on the door, he shouted from the inside and said the door was open. Pamela came on in. He fixed Pamela a glass of wine. After he saw Pamela was tipsy, he was ready to bone her. When Jermaine started boning Pamela, he had to have all the lights on. He wanted it from behind, slapping her butt cheeks with both his hands real hard got him off. Pamela would always look at him to see what effect her pernana had on him. His eyes would be rolling behind his head. Pamela was not feeling this at all. She felt like she was in some type of porno flick. Pamela treasured disappointment with Jermaine.

She thought she found her, man but she didn't. Then Pamela also felt he was still in love with the woman he was with for two years. They had one of those on and off relationship again. Jermaine was seeing other women too. Pamela also felt he was a pedophile probably on the run from another state, or his name was not his real name. Pamela felt he was not the man for her, and he didn't seem the settling type. So, Pamela never called him again or came by his apartment again. She never answered his telephone calls. She did not regret giving him some brain that he did not deserve. After finding out about him upfront by asking him all those questions about him, which gave her the decision to walk away from him early before a relationship got started and got serious, sometimes we got to do this just walk away from a man that's not for you.

THE OTHER MEN

THE OTHER MEN THAT YOU WILL BE READING ABOUT IS MEN that Pamela was only with for a short period of time. The other men were very interesting, and each acquaintance was different. After Pamela's marriage ended, Pamela's eyes became wide open to a whole new world. She was not trying to find another man to settle down with or get married again. Instead, she was trying to live the life that she missed out on. She just wanted to have some fun for a change. She didn't know what it was like to go clubbing, dancing, having sex for fun without the ring thing. She began to enjoy going to movies around ten o'clock at night, fine restaurants, which included ordering the most expensive food on the menu, dating other men, visiting her girlfriend until wee hours of the night, going shopping, wearing tight and revealing clothes showing her cleavage. She loved wearing her mini dresses, miniskirts, and showing her sexy million-dollar legs. Pamela was partying like it was nineteen ninety-nine. No man would hold her down. She looked to the other men as a friend, booty call, sugar daddy, or somebody there for her until she got over the hurt and pain from a previous marriage or relationship. The other men are men you can never commit too or fall in love with. The other men are also like a flyby acquaintance, which means a meaningless relationship going nowhere. There's no expectation to be met. You're not putting anything into the relationship to receive anything back. It's like hit it and quit it with no emotions developing. It's like once it's over, it's over, and you both can go your separate ways because there are no levels to reach with the other men. The acquaintance never got serious because he's going to fly right by you with no admiration for you nor stopping to give you the time of day or a shot with him. The other men are like a ghost acquaintance who is gone or disappeared out of your life with no heart feelings involved. You may not ever remember him again or no lasting effect on your mind or heart. The other men you meet just might think of you in the same manner. He just might only want you for sex or to help him with his bills, and that's it. The other men could also be a friend with just fringe benefits. Someone you can go out with every now and then, no commitment, no kissing, no holding you in his arms, no giving you money to help you like some men do in a relationship or marriage to pay your bills or for you to pamper yourself with a manicure, pedicure, eyebrows arch, hair removal from face and armpits, getting your hair done and buying gas for your car. The other men can be an acquaintance to just listen to your woes you're going through due to some unforeseen circumstances that happen with you. The other men can also be an acquaintance who will take you to dinner, club movie, or take a trip with you so you will not go alone. If you happen to fall in love by chance, which is a no-no with other men, then he might walk away from you, ending whatever friend you may have become to him. The other men may come and go in your life, so you need to ask questions so you won't be getting hurt. If there's some physical attraction for him, you need to sit down and talk about the matter at hand. Are both of you involved with someone? What boundaries do you need to set with the other men? What's your expectation of him? You want to keep in mind when you with the other men, there's always going to be doubt creeping in the situation. The other men are not a sure thing you can bank on. The other men do not want to take the acquaintance further to the next level because you're not what he wants when it comes to spending his life with. Sometimes we, as women, need to recognize this so we don't get hurt inside our hearts because once we began to care and have a love for the other men, this is when the trouble will start. You've heard the old phrase, nothing from nothing leaves nothing. The other men will never amount to anything with you if you're not in a personal relationship with him and if he doesn't commit to you.

DAVID

Pamela met David at a grocery store because he was a stocker. He was medium height, medium skin tone, a slim man, and he had two boys. He was a very strict father, David lived on the same street as her father. He was a gentleman. He asked Pamela's father permission to date her. Her father said yes. Pamela liked David a whole lot, but David was dating a young lady with two daughters, and he was smitten with her. He wanted her to be his wife. Pamela knew she didn't stand a chance, but she liked David. She dated him anyway. Pamela and her two daughters and his two sons, along with them, went to Astroworld. Both of them and the children had so much fun. Pamela and David liked the idea of the children was getting along. Pamela and David, one night, had unprotected sex. He called Pamela on her job and told her to make a doctor's appointment because she gave him VD. Pamela went to the doctor that afternoon and called him back and told him she didn't have any venereal disease. David has sworn up and down that Pamela gave it to him. Both of them got into a big argument, and Pamela pointed out to David, "Are you sure your fiancée didn't give you this disease?" David said, "No." Pamela said, "I did not give it to you. Here's the doctor's number, and he'll tell you what the results are since you do not believe me." From then on, Pamela stopped talking to David. She never saw David until he located her and came by her apartment. Pamela asked him how did he found her. He said her father gave him the address. When Pamela answered the door, her hair was all over her head. Pamela was embarrassed for him to see her like that. Pamela invited him in. She let David know she was married and to call her at work. Then he left and called Pamela the next day at work. David said to Pamela, "You were right. My fiancée whom I married, gave me VD. She got hooked on drugs." Pamela asked him, "How did she get hooked on drugs?" David told Pamela, "I sold drugs, and now I own and drives an eighteen-wheeler." Pamela said, "So, you moved up in the world." He said, "My wife wrote checks on me and signed my signature to my checks." David said, "She had to go then but I loved those girls and it was the hardest thing for me to do." He said, "I divorced her." Pamela said he should have married her but Pamela guess, she was not his type. David told Pamela that he always liked her. Pamela said she knew. After that, Pamela didn't see David until fifteen years later. It was on Mother's Day when Pamela went to the neighborhood to visit her stepmother. Once she left her house, she went down the street to David's house. When she came upon his house, she got out of the vehicle and rang the doorbell, but she did not know if it was his house. As she was about to leave because no one came to the door, this old man who had plenty of gray hair, gained weight, big stomach, and very bald-headed. He asked Pamela, "How could I help you? Pamela said, "I'm looking for a man, named David." He said, "I'm David." Pamela said, "What happened to you?" He said, "Come in, Pamela." both of them went thru the garage. When Pamela walked into the house, it was a disaster because David was remodeling his house. He said, "Hurricane

Ike had damaged my house, and I'm just remodeling my home. The ceiling and roof had caved in. There was no air conditioning on, I'm sleeping on the couch in the living room, my bedroom didn't have a floor or wall, no running water, the ceiling was not up at the top in the living room and the kitchen was completely tore up." Pamela asked, "David, what's been going on with you? Something must have to happen to you because the David I knew was very organized, clean, and tidy." Something had to happen to him. This could be the reason she's here because the Lord lead her to his house after all these years. "So, David, tell me what's troubling you. Everything up in your house is completely out of order." David told Pamela his son had passed away in 2006. It seems like his life just came to a stop. Pamela asked, "What happen to your son?" David told Pamela his son had a barbershop, and it was just a front for him selling drugs to hide his drug money.

He said his son was driving home with a friend. His friend shot his son in the head and fled the scene. Some people saw the SUV run off the road, but the people didn't see anybody in the car because the windows were a very dark tint. The people did not see his son in the car. Pamela said she was very sorry for his loss, and he had her condolences. She asked him which son was this. David said his oldest son is a minister, so, the son that got killed was his youngest son. Pamela said, "Do you think he followed you in your footsteps of selling drugs?" David said, "Possible." Pamela said, "You were very strict on your boys. How did your son get into that lifestyle?" He said, "When he turned eighteen, he just started running around with the wrong crowd, just doing his own thing, nobody could tell him anything. The Police never did find the person that shot him." Pamela said to David, "You got to get out of this mode, snap out of it, and start taking care of your business in this house. Now, have you paid the bills in the house.?" David said, no. Pamela said, "Let's pay them now." Both of them were going through all the bills that needed to be paid and throwing away papers that were old. Pamela stayed the night and slept in the recliner. It was very hot in his house, but Pamela endured. David cooked breakfast the next morning, and afterward, Pamela left to go home. Then the next two weeks, David started calling contractors out doing work to his house and calling Pamela to come over for her approval. David decorated his house like the home magazines he bought. Pamela was very impressed with David's color coordination in his house. She loved his home the way it was decorated inside. Pamela and David went out to a club one Friday night. Pamela met him there. Pamela walked in, but she didn't see him.

He called her on his cell phone to let her know where he was sitting. David went to the bar and ordered her a drink and told Pamela that the bartender knows what he drinks because he is in the club every Friday. As Pamela was sitting by David, he told this woman next to him to stick around because he wanted to take her home with him. Pamela told David, "You got some nerves to invite me out and leave with another woman. Why, David, are we like two ships sailing, always passing one another but never stopping or tooting our horns to each other and never stopping to get acquainted?" Pamela told David goodbye and kiss him on his lips. Three months later, David called Pamela to come over to visit her. Pamela gave him directions to her house. David let Pamela know he was going to South Padre Island for a vacation with his buddy. Pamela told David you must have some kind of attraction for her, but maybe you don't want to admit it to yourself. Pamela told David, "Here's the deal. Let me tell you what I'm looking for in a man." Pamela said, "I wanted marriage. I wanted life insurance policies for both of us. I wanted them to buy a home together or for you to put my name on your house deed. I wanted to be on your 401K." She said, "I didn't want anything prior before me because I knew you left everything to your son. I don't have time for games and deceit because I'm getting older." She told David, "If you want me, you know how to find me." Pamela fed David something to eat, and then he left. Pamela didn't expect anything from David, but a goodbye. This all she always got from him because nothing never got off the ground between them. Pamela liked him a lot. He was a good dresser from head to toe. He drove a fine car. He was financially stable. He ate his chicken, shrimp, and fish with a folk. Pamela ate with her fingers. Both of them could communicate with one another very well. Both of them could tell each other anything. Somehow the both of them could never connect. They were like two ships sailing in the ocean sailing alongside one another ,just passing each other by again and again.

DAMON

Damon was a suave kind of man. He was tall, dark skin tone, very well dressed from head to toe, and always smelling good. Pamela met him through a co-worker who introduced her to him in an effect to get over a breakup of another man. The one thing about this suave man is that he loved his weed. He smoked weed when he got up in the morning until he went to bed at night. If he was high, he loved to go down on Pamela and eat her very well. His polo stick was little but alright because Pamela knew how to work with it. Damon loved going out to the clubs. Both of them would go out every weekend partying and smoking weed because, after that, the sex was better than good. Pamela thought of Damon as her good-time-man. Nobody to be serious about, just to have a good time with. When Damon and Pamela be up in the club partying, he will not dance with Pamela because he didn't want to get sweaty. He'll let Pamela dance with other men in the clubs. He wasn't the jealous kind like most men today because he knew Pamela was going home with him. Damon and Pamela stayed together for about eight months. During the time, Damon lived in the past. His whole conversations with Pamela was about his ex-wife and kids. Damon would talk about how they used to live, how much he loved her, how his kids had everything, how much money he made cooking on the ship, how he hurt his back, and retired from the job collecting disability. He would talk about the same thing every day, like a scratch record. He loved his porno flicks. He watched his porno flicks for amusement like the porno movies were his way of life Damon loved to cook. He would prepare dinner for Pamela every night when she would get home from work. Pamela eventually grew tired of Damon living his life in the past instead of living in the future. So, Pamela let Damon go. Pamela didn't see Damon until five years later. Pamela had just moved back from Austin and needed a place to stay. Pamela went to the church where his family worship on a Sunday morning. His family automatically gave Pamela his number with no problem. She called Damon and asked him if she could stay with him for a while. He told Pamela to come on and gave Pamela directions to his townhouse. Once she arrived at his home, he welcomed her with open arms. Damon was so sweet to her. He was cooking for her. He loved her from her head to her toe. He would run her bubble bathwater. Then two months after Pamela been living there, he told Pamela he was behind on his taxes, light bill, cable, and the telephone bill. Damon asked Pamela to help him get all his bills caught up. Pamela said, okay. Pamela knew the importance of paying bills and staying afloat. After Pamela helped him to catch up on all his bills, Damon's personality started to change. He began to be mean to Pamela. Pamela had never seen this side of Damon. He kept that mean side well hidden. Pamela could never watch any of her shows she liked on TV. Damon was always watching his favorite shows but very inconsiderate toward Pamela. Then both of them would argue all the time. The arguments would always be about money. Damon started not paying the bills in the house. He would take his money from disability and do other things with his money. He started lying to Pamela about this and that. Saying his medicine was expensive or he had to buy his mom's medicine. Pamela accepted what his reason was, but deep inside, she did not believe him. Every month for about four months, Damon stopped paying any bills in the house. Every time Pamela would come home, the lights would be cut off; the phone would be cut off; the cable would be cut off. Pamela had to get everything cut back on. Pamela would end up paying all the bills in the house. She could never see herself catching up on the bills that she needed to pay. Pamela grew tired of this ordeal. So, one day when Damon left to go to the doctor, Pamela started moving her clothes. She had enough of what he was doing. When Damon came back home and saw Pamela moving out, he was surprised. He picked up the phone and called his sister to try and stop Pamela from leaving. Instead, Pamela turned around and asked Damon's to help her move. She let Damon know she was moving because she couldn't pay all the bills in the house and he do whatever he wanted to do with his money. Then she let him know she had to put up with him being mean to her. She has been nothing but good to him. After that, she never saw Damon again. Pamela wanted a relationship with Damon, but that never happened because he just wanted someone to pay his bills. Pamela thought both of them had a good thing going on. She found out different in the end. Damon was just mean, selfish, and all about him. Pamela knew he smoked weed, but she didn't know if he did more than that. If he did, he kept it on the down-low. Pamela was stupid to have moved in with Damon because when you been apart from someone that long the person doesn't stay the same. Pamela probably saw this coming but stay to see the outcome. Pamela knew he had a drug habit of smoking weed but knew it probably escalated to crack. Just maybe Pamela did not want to accept that about him. But she was smart enough to leave before his world succumbed to her. Pamela was smart enough to follow her first mind, which had never misled her like her second mind always did.

DENNIS

After one of Pamela's marriages, she met this man down the street from her father. Pamela was staying with her father while her divorce was being finalized. Dennis was an older man like Pamela's dad. He was short, his beard was gray, his hair on top of his head was full of gray, and his mustache was also gray, which was curled of each side of his mustache. He was also on the heavyset side. Dennis had a daughter, but she was away at college. Dennis would always take Pamela clubbing because this is what he loved to do is dance. Pamela loved to drink that she ended up drinking four glasses of alcohol. By that time the club closed, she was drunk. Alcohol tasted good to Pamela because this was the first time Pamela ever drank alcohol. After both of them dance, both of them went back to his house and had great sex. The sex was just up and down sex. Dennis worked for the Post office. He loved to smoke weed with embodied fluid mixed inside. Dennis always wanted Pamela to join in with him, but she wouldn't because she grew up in a family of drug addicts. Pamela knew how to say no with no problem. Pamela knew that drugs could put you out of your mind. Pamela wanted to stay in control of herself. Pamela would just watch him get high. After he finished getting high, sex was on like donkey-kong. Pamela would always ride him to put him under her spell. Pamela knew sex is some men's weakness if a woman knew how to throw it right. Once Pamela's divorce was finalized, she wanted her own apartment. Dennis got Pamela's first apartment for her being on her own for the first time. Dennis became a very possessive man. Dennis tried to keep up with her every move. Dennis paid her rent every first of the month in the office. He bought her groceries to her apartment. If there was anything that Pamela wanted, he got it for her with no questions asked. Dennis became Pamela's little puppet on a string. Pamela called him, and he came running. The only thing Dennis and Pamela had in common was partying in the clubs and sex. Dennis was a good guy. When he loved, he loved hard. As time went on, Dennis and Pamela drifted apart. Pamela wasn't ready for marriage, and Dennis was. Pamela told Dennis she still wanted to explore her world. Both of them stopped seeing each other gradually. Six months later, Dennis died of a heart attack. Pamela always remembered the good times and fun she and Dennis had. She never led Dennis on or made any promises to him that she couldn't keep. There were no heart feelings between them when both of them said goodbye to each other. He kissed Pamela on the cheek and said, he will always love her.

DALE

Pamela was introduced to Dale by her play brother, but Dale was a drunk. Pamela knew nothing could ever be between them. She met Dale at Pappadeaux, and he was drunk. He smelled like booze. His breath smelled like alcohol. When he got up to go to the restroom, he was stumbling all over the place. Pamela was flat out embarrassed by him. Dale's clothes were also fallen off of him. His clothes were too big. Dale was dressed like he was a homeless man. All Pamela could do was laugh at herself for going out on a blind date. She said to herself she will never go on a blind date ever again in her life. She was going to kill her play brother when she saw him. When Dale was talking to Pamela, spit was flying all in Pamela's face. In the end, Dale and Pamela became best friends. Because when he was sober, he was a good person. Dale was medium height, medium skin tone, and not too thin of a person. Dale was a security officer. Pamela asked, "Dale, what led you to drink?" He told Pamela, "One day, I had it all, jewelry, cars, houses, money, and women. The next day, I had nothing, and I lost my wife, whom he loved wholeheartedly. When I lost her, nothing seemed to matter to me anymore, but alcohol. The alcohol became my best friend." Dale became Pamela's best friend like a real brother she could count on.

DANIEL

Pamela met Daniel in a department store. Daniel just came up to Pamela and asked her for her telephone number. He told her how gorgeous she was. Pamela gave Daniel her telephone number. He called her, and both of them talked every day. Daniel was short, medium-dark skin tone, very muscle tone, and had a hairy chest. He worked in communication where he could hear whatever you're saying in your household. Daniel worked out of town for the most part of his life. Pamela didn't see him as much as she wanted too. Pamela saw him at her company Christmas party. He picked her up in his red Ford F150 pickup truck. He took her to his apartment. His apartment was laid. All the colors matched in his apartment with his furniture. The kitchen table was set with plates, water glasses, wine glasses, silverware, and napkins. Daniel had expensive wine that cost a hundred dollars a bottle. Daniel's bedroom was black and red. The sheets were black satin. Daniel had a black and leather sectional sofa with red whatnots. Then Daniel and Pamela went out to eat at her favorite seafood restaurant, which was Pappadeaux. After both of them finished eating, they went back to his apartment. While she was in the vehicle, he was telling her how pretty she is not her clothes because clothes don't make a person. Daniel was letting her know she a pretty lady and let that speak for you. This sort of brought Pamela her self-confidence back by hearing those encouraging words. When Pamela looked at Daniel, she knew he was the kind of man, and she would like to be part of her life. Pamela was very impressed that she met a man that over one hundred thousand dollars a year. Both of them boned that night. The next day, Daniel took Pamela home. Both of them got to know one another very well. From the conversation, both of them had with each other. Pamela knew both of them had a lot in common. She hoped that just maybe he would be the one she was looking for all her life like the man of her dreams. The sex was great between them. Daniel always gave Pamela good advice as to her career and she definitely took it to heart and made her career, happen for herself. Pamela knew deep inside that Daniel was some type of successful man. She respected him and never asked him who he really was. But she did notice when he took her out to eat. The waitress did not stop coming back to the table, waiting on them or asking if everything was to his satisfaction, and the people in the restaurant kept staring at them. By that, Pamela knew he was an important figure. Pamela just adored him. Pamela always had to call him. Daniel never called Pamela. By this, Pamela felt like he was probably married. Both of them had chemistry. The last time she saw Daniel was at a motel. He thanked her for her body and the lace underwear she wore. Daniel kissed Pamela and told her she could make her career happen. To believe in herself and God above, the Lord can make it happen for you and guide you. Pamela appreciated his good advice and the love he shared with her for a short time.

DOMINIQUE

Pamela met Dominique at a fast-food restaurant. Dominique grabbed Pamela's hand as she was about to leave and asked her for her telephone number. Pamela gave him her number. Pamela was at the fast-food restaurant with her girlfriend. Pamela's girlfriend noticed Dominique staring at her the whole time. Even when Dominique got up to order him some more food. Pamela looked a hot mess for a man trying to get her telephone number. Pamela had no makeup on. She had a big oh mama dress on and flipflops. Dominique was probably attracted to that sexy walk of hers. Dominique called Pamela the next day and took Pamela out. Pamela hadn't been out in months with a man. Dominique picked up Pamela and took her out to a club. Both of them danced the night away and talked the whole night while both of them were at the club. When both of them left the club, Dominique let Pamela drive his Cadillac car. The next day, Dominique picked Pamela up and took her to his church. Pamela had on a lavender suit. Both of them arrived at church late, and Dominique had to find a parking spot to park his car. When Dominique got out of the car, he had on a super fly suit. His suit was purple with a long train. Pamela smiled and walked in the church with Dominique with her head up, not being embarrassed or ashamed of the way he was dressed. After church service, both of them went to Luby's to eat. Then he took Pamela home. When the evening came, he picked her up again to take her to dinner for seafood at Pappadeaux. Then he drove her around his neighborhood for her to see how he grew up. Then he took her to a yard where there were fifteen eighteen-wheelers. Dominique owned his own trucking company. Pamela met his cousin, who was the company's mechanic. Dominique took Pamela to the bar for drinks again. Once the both of them left the bar, he took her to meet his sister, but she wasn't home. Then he took Pamela to his home, but she didn't go in. Then both of them left there and went to a club. Pamela danced so much. She really enjoyed herself. This was the first time Pamela ever wore jeans to a club. Pamela drank so many drinks, and she was drunk as a skunk but kept her composure. She was not fallen over anything or wobbling. Then both of them left the club. Pamela was drinking because Pamela was drunk. He took Pamela home and asked her if he could spend the night Pamela said, yes, of course. Both of them made love. Pamela really enjoyed being in his arms. Pamela started talking ugly to him. She told Dominique after both of them had sex, if he couldn't eat her below, she would drop him like a hot potato. She also mentioned since his wife had passed when and if both of them became serious, she couldn't live in her house because that's what they had together, not them. Pamela told him she preferred him to give the house to his son because that's his inheritance. She also preferred him to buy her a house or a townhouse, something both of them can have together. Pamela didn't mean this like it was coming out of her mouth. Pamela felt like it was the alcohol talking. When he left the next morning, he told Pamela she would never have to want for anything in her life ever. Dominique left Pamela a hundred dollars on her dresser. This made Pamela feel like she was a whore for him to leave her money on the dresser. Here's the catch twenty-two. He made Pamela so many promises to take care of her. He didn't do anything he said he would do. Just maybe Pamela said too much after both of them made love from drinking too much alcohol, which caused her to lose him. As matter of fact, when Pamela tried to call Dominique had changed his cell phone number so Pamela couldn't call him. What he didn't know is that Pamela fell in love with him. He swept Pamela off her feet. This was due to the time he spent with Pamela and the weekend he spent with her also. Dominique had Pamela's heart and didn't even know it. Months went by, and Pamela would just cry herself to sleep many nights. One day her cousin was tired of Pamela's looking sad and crying her heart out. Her cousin asked Pamela, "Do you remember where he lives?" Pamela said, "I think so." Her cousin said, "You only live once. Let's go find him." Pamela got up and both of them left and found the house after getting lost several times. Pamela knocked on the door, and a young man came out of his house, which was his son. Pamela introduced herself to his son. His son said to Pamela, So, you're the young lady my dad took to church since my mom passed away." He told Pamela that she had just missed his dad. His son was blushing because he told Pamela she was a very beautiful woman. He was going to make sure his dad get this phone number even though he didn't call Pamela. Dominique will always have a place in Pamela's heart. Pamela found closure with him. She felt that Dominique missed out on his true happiness and love. After Dominique, Pamela became a little bitter and mad at herself for letting the alcohol take over. She taught herself when you're drunk, just be quiet and never let the alcohol talk for her. After Dominique, she knew what type of man she wanted in her life. She wasn't going to settle for anyone less.

DEREK

Pamela met Derek in a club. As Pamela was walking, Derek grabbed Pamela's hand. He talked to Pamela all night, buying her drinks all night. Derek wanted Pamela to go home with him. Pamela liked that, but she could not go home with him because of her last experience of meeting a man in a club. Pamela talked to Derek for a whole month on the telephone before she went to his house. As Pamela was talking to Derek, she found out he was a truck driver. He had one daughter living in Chicago. Derek would see his daughter during the summer. Derek and Pamela became a couple. Derek started paying Pamela bills. Both of them spent time with one another at each of their apartment. Pamela sensed something was wrong with Derek. Pamela noticed if she stopped by his house unannounced, Pamela would have to wait at the door for a long time before he would answer the door. This really made Pamela mad, but she wouldn't let him see her mad about it. When Pamela would walk in the house, the house would have a bad odor like a shit smell. When she would come over, and he was expecting her, his house would smell fresh. He loved to have sex from behind. This is something Derek told her. Pamela let him know, she would never let him do it to her like that way because both of them would have to be husband and wife. Pamela wasn't stupid. She knew if he wasn't getting from her, he was getting it from someone else if she was not accommodating his sexual desire. Then one Saturday, she went to his house unannounced only to meet another woman coming up his stairs the same time she was. The woman looked at Pamela. Pamela looked at the woman. Both of them knocked at the door at the same time. When Derek open the door, he looked dumbfounded. Pamela being the lady she was, she left first. Derek was calling her all that day. Pamela never answered her telephone because she knew it was him. Derek and Pamela drifted apart because Pamela hated a cheat. She believed in dating one man at a time. Then one year later, she ran into Derek at a food store only to learn his mom had passed away, and he was on crack. He told Pamela he was trying to piece his life together, but he was still driving trucks. Pamela told him he had her condolences. She told Derek he could kick his crack habit if he wanted to stop on his own, and prayer would be his helper. Pamela told him goodbye and went on her merry way. She never saw Derek again but always kept him in her prayers in the hope of him getting off of crack. Pamela realized the smell she always smelled in her apartment was the crack. She also realized he was on crack for a long time. Pamela always prayed for Derek because a crack habit is a man's downfall and could cause his life to be in a world spin causing him to lose everything that he worked so hard for. Pamela realized if he could look himself in the mirror and find out the reason he got on crack in the first place, he could move on with his life.

DARRELL

Pamela met Darrell at a club at a happy hour. He was surrounded by a beautiful woman that had their figures well put together. He was dressed to kill with his amanti suit, alligator shoes, and the bling-bling on his fingers and wrist. Pamela just looked at him with her beautiful sexy eyes. At this time in Pamela's life, she was a little heavy. She danced with him one time on the dance floor. Pamela was with a girlfriend who was just laughing at her. Pamela had a man came by, sat down with Pamela buying her drinks all night long, but Pamela was not interested in him. When the man got ready to leave, Pamela did not give the man her telephone number. Darrell gave Pamela his telephone number before he left the club, and Pamela took it. The woman was looking at her in despise. Like they wanted his number, but he gave it to her. She's a lucky female dog! The next day, Pamela could not wait until she called this man. When she called him, he picked up the telephone and he said, "Hi, Pamela." Pamela was shocked, he remembered her name. Darrell set up a date with Pamela. Pamela arranged for Darrell to pick her up at her mom's house because she knew nothing about this man. Darrell picked her up at her mom's house in his truck. He took her to this bar where nothing but firemen hung out. Pamela didn't know he was a fireman. The bartender knew him like he was a regular. He ordered Pamela a long island ice tea drink. Pamela never had one of these drinks. She drank that drink like it was water. Darrell told Pamela the long island ice tea had seven alcohol mixed in it. Pamela started on her second drink. She took her time drinking this drink. Pamela's bladder got full, so she had to go to the restroom. When Pamela came back, she finished her drink. Then all of sudden Pamela blackout she thought Darrell had her best interest at heart, but to her dismay, he didn't. She remembered Darrell helping her to his truck. Then she started throwing up all in his truck. She remembers also waking up in a motel room with him screwing her in the butt. Pamela was so defenseless because she realized, oh yes! That he put something in her drink. After he finished sexually abusing her from the front to the back, he dressed her up with her clothes backward with no underwear on. Then he dropped her at her mother's house unconsciously. Her mother was in a state of shock. Her mother did not know what to do. Pamela came through about four o'clock in the morning. Her mother was right by her side. Her mom asked Pamela if she wanted her to call the police. Pamela told her mom, "Nno, because he was a firefighter, and that would ruin his career." Pamela said, "I couldn't do that to him." Her mom replied, "Look what he had done to you." Pamela's mom told her she looked in her purse and found that he bought her panties from Victoria Secret. Her mom asked, "Pamela, when did he find time to buy you panties?" Pamela said maybe he did that before he picked her up. Mom told Pamela, "He's crazy, Pamela. He has a sick illness." Pamela told her mom she's right. Pamela got up took a shower because she had to go to work the same day. When she arrived to work, the ladies asked about the date. Pamela told her co-workers exactly what happen leaving nothing out. Her manager told her she can still file charges against him. Pamela told her manager, "I'm was going to call him and talk to him first, before I make a decision to file charges." Pamela called Darrell, talked to him and asked him why did he do those things to her sexually, And what did he put in her drink. Pamela told him to be honest. Darrell told Pamela, "You're the first woman who ever confronted me." He said, "All the other women never remember anything when they woke up." Pamela asked him, :So, what did you put in my drink, and how did you get this drug?" Darrell replied, "I'm also a paramedic, and that's how I got my hands on the drugs." Pamela asked him another question, "So, what happened to you in your childhood that would make you put a mickey in a women's drink just to sleep with me because you're a very attractive man." He could have any women he wanted. She told him he doesn't have to do this. Darrell told Pamela, "I was raped by my father. I felt like I had to take it from a woman when I was helpless because my father would take it from me when I was asleep in bed at night." He said, "I could not cry out or make a sound." Pamela became Darrell's psychiatrist. She realized he needed to talk about what happen in his childhood life so he could move on with his life and get the best out of his life to be happy. Darrell talked to Pamela openly and freely. Believe it or not, after him talking about what happened to him, he was able to moved on with his life. Pamela and Derek remained the best of friends. Pamela learned something from this ordeal. Because a man can be dressed from head to toe in amanti suits and alligator shoes, what looks good on the outside may not be good on the inside, You can't judge a book by its cover. What Pamela found in the club could have cost Pamela her life if he was a serial killer. There was no way for Pamela to distinguish what type of man he was because he had a good profession as a firefighter and a very well-dressed man, Pamela realize she had the Lord with her that particular night.

DARNELL

Darnell was a Jamaican man. Pamela's car broke down across the street from his mechanic shop. Darnell had one of his workers to push her car to his shop. Darnell worked on Pamela's car but didn't charge her. Instead, he asked Pamela for her telephone number. Pamela gave him her telephone number. Darnell would only call her from his shop. Pamela asked him if he was married. Darnell said no, he was not married. Darnell let Pamela know his wife left him because he cheated on her with another woman.

Treasure Love, Treasure Disappointment

Darnell told Pamela he had two daughters and one son he never met living in Jamaica whom he had never seen. Then one day, Darnell asked Pamela what she'll be doing this evening. Pamela said, nothing. Darnell asked Pamela for her address. He said to Pamela he would be by to pick her up at six o'clock when he closed the shop for the weekend. When she arrived at his house to Pamela's surprise, Darnell's house was a big mansion. Pamela saw a jaguar in his garage. His house had five bedrooms, living room, a basement under the floor, four bathrooms, kitchen with a breakfast room, three stair ways on different sides, and a huge game room with everything you could desire, for instance, there was a stereo, exercise equipment, bar with liquor and wine glasses, pool table with living room with furniture. Darnell's house was everything Pamela dreamed of having in her life. Both of them dated for almost a year. During this time Pamela notice he was controlling. He always belittled her, trying to bring her self-esteem down. He loved to fight her every weekend even to the point of whooping her with a belt, like she was some child or something. Pamela hated to change her eating habits. She had to drink Jamaican drinks and eat Jamaican food. Pamela could still eat her candy, potato chips and cookies. She only ate American food when both of them would go out to eat on a Sunday at any restaurant of Pamela's choice. Darnell would always do the cooking. Pamela washed the clothes, clean the house, and wash the dishes. Darnell was a well-dressed man he loved for a woman to compliment all the time. She could not disagree with him on anything he said or spoke about. He basically wanted a yes-woman. If you did not agree with Darnell, you would not be his woman. Pamela knew this and accepted whatever Darnell wanted. She wanted to be his woman, live in the big fine house with all the amenities. All Darnell kept on doing was downgrading Pamela all the time. He was always picking on her all the time like she couldn't do this right or that right. Pamela had to answer Darnell anytime he was talking to her. One Sunday, both of them had been arguing and fighting all that day. He never cared about how Pamela felt. Darnell took her to dinner that evening. He automatically ordered her food and didn't ask her what she wanted to eat. When the waitress brought the food. Pamela threw her food on the floor. Darnell slapped her in the face in front of everyone at the restaurant. Darnell asked the waitress for the menu again. Then he let Pamela order what she wanted to eat. While Pamela was eating, Darnell busted out laughing. He told Pamela, "You're crazy, you know that." Pamela told Darnell, "No, you're the one who's crazy." Darnell loved Pamela. Pamela understood his crazy self. When Darnell would act crazy with Pamela, then he wanted to make love. This is the part Pamela didn't like about him was his sexual pleasure. Darnell only had sex when he had the urge and wanted sex the way he liked it. He had sex once his food digest. Then he would take a nap for an hour or two. Then he would come to bed about one or two in the morning by this time Pamela would be sleep. This makes it hard for Pamela to get into sex when he wakes her up from her sleep. Then he would get on top of Pamela and do his business, which took four minutes, then he would roll over and go to sleep. Once Pamela would wake up in the morning, she would get on top of him so she could be satisfied sexually too, but he would push her off of him and would tell her to get off of him, you, crazy woman. As time went on in the relationship, Darnell began to grow tired of Pamela. He started seeing another woman. She was a school teacher. She was really ugly, nothing to compare her with Pamela. But looks aren't everything beauty is only skin deep. Darnell told Pamela he enjoyed her company, but he didn't like her as a person. He mentioned to her the other woman had more to offer him than she could. Darnell wanted to build his own mechanic shop where he wanted a fast food restaurant and detail shop. The bank had approved his loan, but he lacked fifty-thousand dollars. This school teacher had what he needed to make his dream come true, so he dumped Pamela. Pamela accepted the decision he made. She packed up her little clothes and left his bid mansion of a house. Both of them remained friends.

DETROIT

Detroit worked at an insurance company. Every time he would see Pamela, she had on sexy tight clothes that would show her figure. Pamela took insurance classes but could never pass the test. She would always ride on the elevator with this man. He would always say "hello" to her. Then one day, Detroit introduced himself to Pamela. Detroit told Pamela he worked on the sixth floor. Detroit asked Pamela if he could meet her somewhere for lunch. When lunch came, Detroit met Pamela at a park near the job. All Detroit started doing was touching Pamela all over her body and kissing her. Then she would return to work like the both of them didn't know one another until lunch came again. Both of them would kiss and touch one another every day for two weeks. Detroit was a devoted father, and husband to his family. This is the way Pamela wanted this relationship to be, "no getting serious". Detroit would take Pamela to lunch all the time.

Then finally both of them had sex because all the kissing and touching made Pamela hot as a firecracker and him too. She did it with him at the park in his car. Only to be let down because he had a little wiener. Pamela liked those men with big polo sticks. She kept seeing him and let him feel on her and stuff, but she didn't have sex with him again. He didn't have the meat to satisfy her. Detroit was an insurance adjuster. Detroit started taking insurance classes to open up his own insurance agency. Pamela stayed within her boundaries because he was a devoted father and husband and she was not trying to break up his happy home. Because she respected him and his position at home. The both of them remained friends.

DEMPSEY

Dempsey was a businessman. He was in the food chain. In other words, he was a restaurant owner. He had a wife and several grown kids. Dempsey was in his late sixties. It seems he was very happy in his marriage. Dempsey loved beautiful young women. Dempsey was mesmerized my Pamela beautiful brown eyes. Because once Pamela put those eyes on you, a man couldn't help but come under Pamela's spell. Pamela met Dempsey one day at his restaurant. Pamela had on a low-cut blouse and a sexy mini skirt that fit tight to her waist. Dempsey couldn't keep his eyes off of her. Dempsey told the cashier that her lunch was free. By the way, his wife was there, noticing her husband could not keep his eyes off of Pamela. Once Pamela got threw eating, she left the restaurant to go catch the bus at the bus stop. Low and behold Dempsey told her to get in the vehicle, Pamela did. Dempsey took her to pick up her kids at the babysitter, and then he took them home. Both of them talked for hours. Dempsey told her if she dates him, he would pay half her rent, buy her groceries, and pay her light bill. Pamela agreed to it and said she would love to date him. When Pamela got out of his vehicle, he gave Pamela his business card. Dempsey was a short man, small built frame, medium skin tone, and no hair in the middle of his head. Pamela called him one afternoon, both of them talked for hours. Dempsey told Pamela all about his wife and kids. He asked Pamela if he could spend some time with her, Pamela said, yes. He met Pamela at this fabulous hotel where both of them had sex. Dempsey satisfied Pamela completely to be in his late sixties. He had a big polo stick. Pamela and Dempsey carried on for years. Dempsey even gave Pamela a down payment for a vehicle. Even though Dempsey was married, he was very faithful to his wife. A man can be faithful and cheat on his wife without her knowing because he was always home on time, at work on time and home for dinner on time. He saw Pamela when he ran his errands and took care of his restaurant business. Pamela didn't care about him being married; she just wanted to have fun with him. Dempsey helped to take the pressure off of Pamela by paying her bills off. She could get her children the things that would make them happy, like lots of toys, clothes, going to Luther's Barbeque, McDonald's, Pizza, Church's Chicken, and Frenchy's Chicken. One day in the afternoon, he called Pamela and told her to meet him at his brother's house. This is where Pamela and Dempsey had sex at his brother's house. His brother would watch Pamela and Dempsey have sex. He would just pull up a chair and watch Pamela get on top of Dempsey having sex doggy style, up and down, side to side, and giving him brain. His brother watched Pamela putting her stuff on his brother. Dempsey made it a habit of Pamela meeting him at his brother's house to have sex with him. This was Dempsey excused to his wife that he was going to his brother's house. His wife didn't suspect a thing. Dempsey's brother would watch every time him and Pamela would have sex. His brother had a girlfriend he had been with for twenty years. She would always be in the other room, knowing her man was watching Pamela naked. One day, Pamela came over his brother's house waiting for Dempsey. Dempsey brother told Pamela, "My brother won't be able to make it tonight." His brother told Pamela to stay with him tonight and keep him company. Dempsey brother started feeling all over Pamela's body. He was kissing her, and started taking her clothes off Pamela got hot as a firecracker. His brother's girlfriend was there in the house knowing what the both of them were doing. Somewhere down the line, Pamela lost her morals. Pamela was screwing both brothers. Then one day she was waiting for Dempsey, he was late showing up. His brother starts sexing her up all over her body. Pamela ended up in bed with her. Then Dempsey arrived. He saw both of them in bed and got in bed with them. Then Pamela had sex with him also. Pamela had fun having sex with both brothers. Both brothers enjoyed Pamela, and was fully satisfied sexually. Pamela was exhausted afterward and fell asleep. When she woke up the next morning, the brothers were gone. She was left in the house with Dempsey's brother's girlfriend. Pamela got up and took a shower. Pamela got dressed, and when she came into the living room, Dempsey's brother's girlfriend told Pamela she fixed her some breakfast. Pamela ate and told her, thank you. She told Pamela that her friend wanted her to come to her club tonight. Pamela asked her where was his club located.

She gave Pamela the name of the club and the address. Pamela went to the club named "Mister B's" that night. She went into the club, and the club was popping. Disco lights were everywhere. Before Pamela could get to the bar, some man grabbed her arm and led her to the dance floor. Pamela started dancing and shaking her booty and dancing very sexy. Then Dempsey's brother interrupted that dance. He started dancing with Pamela. Pamela started dancing her sexy dance with him. She was going down to the dance floor, she was opening and closing her legs and shaking her booty all in front and back of him. He was just a smiling from one cheek to the next. When Pamela got tired, she went to the bar and had a seat. Men was all over the bar looking all in Pamela skirt and buying her drinks. Pamela had drinks lined up at the bar. As Pamela was drinking some of her drinks, Pamela noticed the woman that cooked her breakfast was sitting next to her. She told Pamela, "My man is fascinated with you and your body. Please don't take him from me." Pamela told her, "I do not want your man. I was just having fun, that's all." Dempsey's brother's girlfriends said, "Okay. Thank you." She told Pamela, "You are definitely very attractive." Pamela got sloppy drunk. Dempsey's brother took her home with him. His woman was in the room watching. Pamela didn't care. The next morning, Dempsey came over and got in the bed with her and his brother. Pamela was doing both brothers. Pamela got up the next morning, took her a shower, and put her clothes on. His brother's longtime girlfriend cooked her breakfast. Pamela ate and left. Pamela never came back to Dempsey's brother's house or his club. Pamela could tell Dempsey's brother was getting attached to her. His brother was calling her every hour on the hour. Pamela had to ended up blocking his number from her cell phone to stop his obsessive calling. Pamela remembered what his woman had asked of her. Pamela respected that. Dempsey called Pamela and asked her to meet him at the restaurant. Pamela did meet him there. She ate lunch with him, Dempsey told Pamela, "It's okay with what happened in bed with me and my brother. Here's some money to help pay your bills. This is from me and my brother also." Now, she must say goodbye. Thanks for the ride period. Dempsey told Pamela, "If you ever need anything, don't hesitate to call me." Pamela replied, "I won't." Pamela never felt ashamed of sleeping with two brothers. She always wanted to experience what it was like sleeping with two brothers. Pamela heard of her girlfriend's doing it, and the opportunity knocked her way.

DONNIE

Pamela met Donnie at a Zydeco club. In Pamela's mind, men you meet in a club that's where you end up finding them when you began looking for them. In a club! Donnie was a tall man. He was medium built and a medium complexion. He had the cutest little dimples in his cheeks. Donnie drove a bus for the metro. He had a lot of class about himself. Donnie always wanted to be the center of attention. This is what attracted Pamela to him. Everything Pamela did with him was for his attention, not hers. Both of them went to a house party where one of Donnie's friend was giving. Pamela and Donnie's friend's girlfriend were getting dress in a room, putting on their swimsuits to go swimming. The men came into the room while they were naked, putting on their swimwear just watching them. Donnie came up to Pamela feeling on Pamela's naked butt. Donnie told Pamela her butt was very soft like jelly. Donnie felt Pamela was too slow putting on her swimsuit. He helped Pamela put on her swimsuit touching, all on her private body parts. Pamela had that long curly weave where when she gets in the water, Pamela's hair will not nappy up. Her hair would be wet and wavy. As everybody got into the pool, all of them began to swim. Pamela did not know how to swim. She stayed in the shallow part of the water where she can stand in the water. Donnie's friend's girlfriends were kissing on their man. Donnie wanted Pamela to kiss him too. Donnie told Pamela to make the kiss long and let it be a juicy kiss where he can have slobber all over her. So, Pamela did what he wanted. Everyone was looking at them. One of the girlfriends told Pamela, "Quit. You just met him." Donnie seemed to like that remark, and started laughing and smiling. Pamela stopped kissing him. She told Donnie she was hungry and going in the house to get her some food. Donnie said, "Fix me a plate, too." Pamela brought two plates to the swimming pool area. Then as Pamela was eating, Donnie asked Pamela to feed him. Pamela said, "Are you crazy?" Pamela said, "You can feed yourself. you're a big overgrown man." Donnie said, "Please." He said, "It's been a long time since I had a woman in my life." He said, "I love attention from you, Pamela." Donnie said, "Do you hear me?" Pamela said, "Yes, I heard you." Donnie told Pamela, "Come over here and dance for me." Then Donnie told Pamela, "You dance sexy. You're little sexy thang." Donnie said he like that dance. When it came to night time, he wanted Pamela to stay the night with his friends that were throwing the party. So, Pamela agreed to stay. Pamela slept on the floor with Donnie. Both of them didn't have sex. Donnie wanted Pamela to holla out loud so all his friends could think both of them were having great sex. Pamela found this game to be cool. Donnie wanted his friends to tease him about it and let Donnie know he really put it down last night. Pamela was moaning out loud so his friends could hear. Donnie loved that. Pamela always got a big laugh out of the ordeals she did for Donnie. Donnie wasn't good in bed. He was a one-to-two-minute man. Pamela was never turned on sexually by Donnie. Donnie loved for Pamela to go down on him and give him brain. This was Pamela's specialty. Donnie took care of Pamela financially. Come Friday, Saturday, and Sunday, both of them would party hard at his friend's house. It was a house party always at one of his friend's home. Pamela was young and just loved to have fun. Donnie also loved Pamela's cooking. He would come over every day to eat. One Friday night, it was Pamela's birthday. Donnie and his friends took Pamela out to a Zydeco club for her birthday. Pamela started drinking and dancing. Donnie asked Pamela to dance for him. Pamela said, "What are you, crazy? Donnie, you want me to dance in front of all these people in this Zydeco club." Donnie said, "Please do it for me. Pamela said, "Everybody will be looking." He said, "I love the attention it will bring to me." Donnie said, "I can let everybody know that's my woman." So, Pamela got up from her chair moving slowly to the music. She was moving from her waist then she started moving her body like Shakira. Believe it, eyes were definitely on her. Donnie was just smiling from one ear to the next ear. Pamela worked her performance on top of the table. Everybody in the club turned their attention to Pamela dancing on the table. Yes, they were throwing her money. She did pick it up because after all, it was her birthday. She was game for anything. The club owner gave Pamela her drinks free for the rest of the night. All of Donnie's friends told him he got a wild one. "Man, does she dance for you like that every night?" Donnie said, "Yes." Just lying through his teeth. Pamela realized Donnie loves to stand out in the crowd. The relationship between the two got serious. If his friends give a house party, he would always ask Pamela to cook a dish. Pamela indeed was a great cook. Anything Pamela cook, his friends would love her dish. Donnie loved for his friends to tell him she cooks well like her mother or grandmother. "Man, you better hold on to her." One day during the week, Pamela had to pick up Donnie on the highway because his car broke down on the side of the road. This was the day she met his mother and father. His parents were up in age. Pamela loved their house. The house had so many rooms. The garage was made into his room. Donnie lived in

Pleasantville, a little town on the outskirts of Houston. It was a long ride to get to his house. Pamela noticed something about Donnie that she never noticed before. Donnie was very jittery. He couldn't sit still. After Pamela was in his parents' house for an hour, Donnie asked Pamela to take him to the park. When both of them arrived at the park, this man came up to Donnie and handed him a package. Pamela didn't say anything. Donnie got in the car and asked Pamela to drive him home. Pamela did just that. Pamela dropped Donnie off at his home. She went home herself. As she was driving home, she thought to herself, does Donnie do drugs? Is he a crack head, but he got a good job. He takes me out every weekend? Both of them have fun together. Pamela realized her relationship is not going to work with him if he does drugs. Donnie was coming to the house on a regular basis. Pamela started noticing her money would be missing in her purse. Her jewelry in her jewelry box wasn't there. Pamela stopped accepting his emails and his telephone calls. She stopped opening her door to him. She just watched Donnie through the blind, standing outside, knocking, and knocking on the door. This went on for a week until he got the picture. It was over. Pamela did not regret doing this because she did not want to with a crack head. Pamela grew up around addicts and family members on drugs. She knew you could try crack for the very first time and become hooked because you're trying to reach the same level of high you felt the first time you tried crack. How her friend tried crack for the very first time at the sweet age of sixteen and died of a heart attack. Pamela was fond of Donnie. Letting Donnie go was the hardest thing Pamela ever had to do.

DONALD

One day Pamela went into Shipley's donut shop to buy her some donuts. There was a high yellow Frenchmen with curly black hair. He was short, dress in a white uniform, making donuts. As Pamela was ordering, he asked her how many glazed donuts she wanted. He brought the donuts to her that he had just made. Pamela asked him his name. He told Pamela his name was Donald. Pamela's donuts were free, with the exception of her calling him. Pamela said, okay. Donald gave Pamela his telephone number to call him. Pamela let two weeks go by before she called Donald. Then she went back to the donut shop, ordered her some donuts from Donald, whom he took her order. Donald asked Pamela why she hadn't called him? Pamela said she would. The next day Pamela called Donald and talked to him for hours almost until the next morning. Then one day, Donald decided to come over to Pamela's house. Both of them chatted a bit. Then Pamela's children came home after spending the weekend with their Dad. So, Donald met her children. He told Pamela when he comes back to visit her, and he'll bring his children. During her conversation with Donald, he told Pamela he was divorced and had four kids. Donald said he was looking for a special lady to spend his time with. Pamela started blushing. Donald said he wanted to start off just friends. The next week, Donald called Pamela to take her dancing. Both of them went dancing. Both of them dancing on the dance floor with Pamela' long hair bouncing from left to right. Pamela had her long hair working and the body that made a man hollow. Pamela felt free, happy, and loose. Pamela and Donald dated for months, went to a lot of parties given by his and Pamela friends, went dancing at clubs until the club closed, and both of them drove out at the most expensive restaurants. It was like the fun of the century for Pamela. When both of them made love, it was until the wee hours of the next morning. By Pamela spending a lot of time with Donald, she wanted that love in her life, and she wanted his love. Pamela asked Donald if both of them could go to the next level. Donald said, yes, but guess what he had a dark secret that Pamela didn't know about. One Saturday, Donald told Pamela, he was going to come by to see her. He wanted Pamela to fix him some breakfast. Donald didn't show up, and neither did he call Pamela to let her know he wasn't coming. Pamela was mad as hell. Pamela had cooked a big breakfast, which included grits, a slab of bacon, eggs, sausage, pancakes, biscuits, orange juice, and coffee. Pamela started hearing from Donald less and less. Donald showed Pamela where he lived, but she never came to his house. Then one Saturday, Donald popped up at Pamela's house with his son for breakfast. Pamela's kids were not there. Pamela cooked breakfast within thirty minutes. She cooked grits with lots of butter, bacon, eggs, toast, and orange juice. After breakfast, Pamela and Donald shared a kiss. Then five minutes later, both of them made mad passionate love. His son was playing a game in her kids' room. After that, Pamela didn't see Donald for weeks. Pamela was just calling Donald on his job all the time, but he would tell someone to tell Pamela he wasn't there. Pamela was strung out, running behind him. Since Donald was not returning her calls, Pamela was going crazy wondering what did she do wrong. She was just freaking her mind out, going over and over in her mind what did she do wrong. Then she snapped, she didn't do a thing to mess up the relationship. One night she went to Donald's house. A woman came to the door. Pamela asked her who she was and what was her relationship with Donald. She told Pamela that she was his wife. Pamela was the bold type of woman. If it's something she wants to find out, she will research it or find out for herself what's going on to put her mind at ease. Pamela told his wife she was his girlfriend. Pamela asked her, "Where's Donald?" She said, "He had to work late." His wife told Pamela he cheats on her all the time but she loves her husband. Donald's wife told Pamela she couldn't take care of six kids on her own so she put up with his cheating behavior. His wife told Pamela that he told me about you. "Please do not see him again." She said, "I know it may be hard for you. You looked to be a good person and can respect me and my children. Please let us be." Pamela got into her car and drove off never to see Donald ever again. Donald was a very deceitful, and a person lying about himself being married. Pamela realized both of them had so much fun but it was all for nothing. Pamela knew that if you are a liar, that's what your relationship will be about lies. See a liar never know how to tell the truth because the truth is not in a liar. If you can't trust a person to be honest with you, how can he be honest with himself?

DEVON

Pamela met Devon through her auntie. Pamela didn't know much about Devon that he was a drug dealer. He made big bucks dealing drugs. Pamela would help him to make some extra money. She would watch Devon cook crack over the stove and mix it with bacon soda. Devon would take the crack to his clientele's house. Pamela was amazed as to the professional people that did crack. Pamela learned a lot about the drug world and the people in it. Devon lived with his big-time drug dealer that ruled him. He was a runner. Devon and the big drug dealer lived in a beautiful rich looking townhouse. The townhouse was well design and custom decorated. Devon and Pamela had sex in one of the bedrooms that had a round bed with a custom-made headboard. The bedroom's color in it was black and white. Devon had a big polo stick that truly satisfied Pamela. Devon and Pamela were seeing one another for quite some time. The relationship was about sex and making money. Pamela was always wondering as to how Devon got into the drug game? So she asked Devon what happen to him that led him to sell drugs? Devon told Pamela, he used to be a prison guard and that's where he met his friend. He got hooked on crack and ended up in this game ever since. He told Pamela to promise him, she'll never try or do this stuff, because you will get hooked. Pamela swore to him, she will never try or do crack. He told Pamela, they travel from city to city bringing in crack to the neighborhood. Pamela was a strong willed woman because she didn't do drugs. She could watch you do drugs and never partake. Devon told Pamela you don't meet very many strong willed women like yourself that don't want to try crack. Once you try crack, yes you're hooked then because you trying to reach that first high. You keep doing and doing never getting to the first time that you tried crack. Crack is like the devil riding your back leading you down the wicked pathway to get crack anyway you can. Pamela told Devon, she did all kind of drugs in high school and drugs never turned her on. Pamela and Devon stayed together for a long time until he left to move to a small town to sell drugs. Devon taught Pamela about the drug world and how to survive and not to trust too many people but always rely on her own instincts because that will take her far in her life.

DEMETRIUS

One particular night, Pamela and her girlfriend Sabrina went out clubbing. The both of them got wild and crazy on the dance floor. Both of them were shaking there booties, waving their hands all in the air, waving them from side to side and dancing with every man both of them could on the dance floor. Both of them was not drunk, but just loved to dance. Pamela and Sabrina wore themselves out dancing. So, Pamela suggested to Sabrina for them to go to Denny's and get something to eat. Pamela was hungry and thirsty. So, Pamela and Sabrina left the club and went to Denny's to get something to eat. When both of them arrived there, both of them had to stand in a long line. When the waitress got the menus, she led them to a table right across from this attractive man with two women sitting at his table. This man could not keep his eyes off of Pamela. Pamela had this red tight skirt and blouse on with her long black hair. When Pamela and Sabrina were about to order, Pamela looked up and the attractive man was standing right in front of Pamela's face. He introduced himself as Demetrius. Demetrius asked Pamela if he could join her table, and Pamela replied, "What about the women you were sitting with." He told Pamela, "I'll be right back." He told Pamela, "I gave the ladies money to get a cab home." He sat beside Pamela, and they all ordered them breakfast food to eat. Demetrius paid for their breakfast. He sent Sabrina away in a cab.

Demetrius was very clean from head to toe. Demetrius told Pamela, "You're a very gorgeous and beautiful woman. This is the kind of women I date." He asked Pamela, "Is there anything you needed?" Pamela replied, "No, there's nothing I needed because I didn't know anything about you." After Pamela and Demetrius talked about everything and their ham sandwiches, both of them left the restaurant. He followed Pamela home. He drove a white corvette. Pamela drove a Jalopy, a big huge burgundy car. Pamela drove into her apartment complex. Demetrius got out of his car. Pamela walked side by side walking sexy as can be. When both of them went inside Pamela's home, she fixed him a glass of wine. Demetrius was kissing all over Pamela. He was trying to woo her out of her panties, but Pamela stood her ground. She said to Demetrius, "I might look sexy, gorgeous, probably drunk, and horny, but Ijust couldn't sleep with you because I just met you." Pamela let him know she does have morals. Demetrius told Pamela he fell in love with her at first site. Then he asked Pamela, "Would you like to move in with me in my condo?" just out of the blew. Pamela said, "I could not move in with you because I have two daughters. I did not know how you live your life." She let Demetrius know she could not put her children in any type of environment that may not be good for them. He said, he just wanted her and not the children. Pamela kissed Demetrius on his mouth she gave him a big, and juicy kiss. She told Demetrius she really enjoyed her late-night brunch with him. Demetrius told Pamela it was definitely his pleasure. Demetrius kissed Pamela and put his hand on her, but squeezing it. He said, "Got damn you're gorgeous and fine, damn, I wish you could be mine." He said, "Goodnight, Pamela" and he left. Pamela was shocked that a man was mesmerized with her at a stare. Pamela was young and immature, but she made a wise decision in the best interest of her children. Pamela's grandmother always told her, "You cannot believe everything that comes out a man's mouth that you do not know."

DARWIN

Pamela started going to clubs. She just loved to dance. She loved to dance at this club called "Hot Spot." The bartender would always serve her drinks and sometimes would let her have her drinks free. Pamela always walked in the club with a mini skirt and a low-cut shimmery blouse showing her boobs. She would show her pretty light skin legs. No man resist looking at Pamela. Pamela knew all eyes were on her, and she loved being the center of attention as she walked into the club. Pamela loved dancing on that dance floor. Once she got off the dance floor, she would head straight for the bar. The men would have her drinks lined up at the bar as she sat down. Pamela would just throw her long black weave hair around. When Pamela caught her breath, a man would ask her to dance. She would get up walking with a twist, which was her normal walk. The way Pamela would dance was very provocative. Men couldn't keep their eyes off of Pamela, especially Darwin. Darwin was one of those bodybuilders. He had those muscles working. He was just well built, which Pamela couldn't keep her eyes off him too. Then one night out of the blue, he asked Pamela to give him a ride home because his car broke down. Pamela, of course, said yes and took him home. That's when it all began. Both of them sexed one another up all night long until the next morning, knowing both of them had to go to work the next day. Every Friday and Saturday night, that's when the fun would begin. As soon as she would walk in the club, the waitress would come over and ask her what she likes to drink because the man over the way would be buying. Pamela's favorite drink was Crown and coke mixed together. Pamela never went home drunk or tipsy from the Hot Spot. If Pamela would drink water or hard candy, her drink would come down before she left the club. While Pamela was drinking, she would dance on the dance floor with any man that asked her to dance. She didn't believe in turning a dance down because her whole focus in the club was to have fun. Pamela was laughing and talking to people she didn't even know at the Hot Spot. When you're at the club, it should be all about fun, and that's exactly what she did party with her club acquaintants. So, the Hot Spot was Pamela hang out on Friday's and Saturday's when she walked into the club, she was familiar with faces and people's names being a regular at the club. Pamela always believed what the wise ones would always say when you find a man in the club. That's where he'll always be when you need him. One particular night, Darwin and Pamela were at the club. Darwin was bar tendering telling Pamela no alcohol for her tonight, only wine tonight because she's fine as the glass of wine she's drinking. Don't get it twisted Pamela was conceded on herself. Her mom taught her if you don't love, you don't expect to get love from someone else. Darwin was a heavy-set bartender, he was a medium tone skin man. He was a weightlifter. He was an eye taker. He wore a tight white shirt on where you could see every inch of his muscles with black pants on. He was making those drinks fast and serving those customers and refilling those drinks once the customers finish quickly. This particular night, Pamela stayed sitting at the bar until his shift came to an end. Darwin was not a jealous man. He didn't care who Pamela dance with. He knew when the club closed, Pamela was coming home with him. Darwin was hot, but when both of them would have sex, the sex was better than good. Both of them didn't have sex every time they saw one another. Instead, sometimes both of them would go walking or both of them would walk home from the club, holding hands, laughing, and talking about everything. Both of them would walk make wishes upon the stars in the sky. The relationship between Pamela and Darwin was a delightful one. One you can cherish and remember with love. One night when Darwin got off from work, Pamela and him went to his apartment and laid down on the floor and listened to his old records. His favorite artist was Tina Turner. He knew every song that Tina Turner sang. Now, when Darwin was not working as a bartender, he was a librarian in the daytime. So, Darwin loved to read and so did Pamela. Some days, Pamela and Darwin would go to the library and read books for hours. Darwin had a dream of becoming a school teacher. As he worked as a bartender on the side, he was saving his money to go back to school. Pamela could appreciate a person pursuing their dreams. One Friday night, Darwin and Pamela went to the Galleria when he was not working. Both of them would walk around and sit by the waterfalls because the waterfall would light up at night and the waterfall was so beautiful. Both of them would splash water on one another. Pamela and Darwin laughed about everything. The both of them told corny jokes to each other. Both of them talked about how they had a good relationship, and they knew the relationship would end one day and how both of them was just filling a void in one another's life for the moment. Pamela told Darwin, "It's always good in life to have a good wholesome friend besides being sexual partners where both of us could reach out to one another in whatever situation one of us or both of us could be going through." On a Monday night, Darwin came over to Pamela's apartment, kissed Pamela on the forehead, and told her he was accepted into college with a full scholarship. Darwin also told Pamela he would be leaving in two weeks. Pamela was happy for him. She grabbed and kissed him. Darwin picked Pamela up with those big strong muscles of his with one arm and started turning and turning her around. Darwin was very happy. Both of them went out and celebrated his education with dinner. Then both of them went back to his house, had drinks, made love, and wrapped up in each other's arms, and fell asleep. Both of them spent every moment and everyday together until he left for school. Darwin kissed Pamela as he left for college and told Pamela goodbye. This was the last time both of them ever saw one another. Pamela held on to every moment both of them shared together. Pamela always hoped he'd become the school teacher in life he dreamed of being. Pamela did not stand in his way. Pamela knew all she had to say was, please don't leave me. He wouldn't have left her. Pamela could not do, and she wished Darwin well. She knew you only get one chance at life to follow your dreams. If you can better your education, you should go for it. Pamela knew, in life, you don't get many destinations to fulfill your dream. Pamela never ran into Darwin through her course of life or heard from him ever again. Pamela remembered a happy time with Darwin filled with no grief, sadness or tears.

DASHAUN

Pamela hadn't been out for a long time since she was really hurt by her last relationship. Pamela was sitting at her desk doing her work when her co-workers came up to her, letting her know it is time for her to get out and mingle with other people. Her co-workers said to her that it's been a year now, and stop feeling depressed and feeling sorry for herself. This is Wednesday night at the club, ladies' night. Pamela said, "Okay. What do you all want me to do?" They all said, "Go out to the club." Pamela said, "I do not have any money to get in or buy a drink." Her co-workers gave Pamela five dollars to buy her a drink. They told her to go the Octavia Club off Martin Luther King street. Pamela went to the club. Pamela had to stop and get her oil change in her car. Then she went to the club. Pamela stood by the bar and paid for one drink. Pamela was not a drinker. She barely drunk the drink she bought, then she got up from the bar and went to the restroom, unaware that a man was checking her out from the time she walked in. When she came out of the restroom, she went back to the bar and sat down. The woman next to her told her how beautiful she was. Then all of a sudden, this man came up to her. He said, my name is Dashaun. He's retired, and he would come to Octavia Club every Wednesday night. He has a home at Love Field, TX. He has worked for the police department for thirty-five years. He asked Pamela, "Do you have a job? Are you single? Do you have a car? Why are you in the club tonight?" After Pamela answered all his questions to his satisfaction, he asked Pamela for a dance. While they were dancing this man said, he was going to ask Pamela to come home with him, because it was his birthday. Dashaun said,

"You lost out you're with me, man." Pamela and Dashaun kept dancing on the dance floor. When Pamela came back to her seat, the woman next to her said she knew she would be picked up by someone. Once ten o'clock, Pamela left the club with Dashaun. They talked until eleven o'clock in Pamela's car about his children, his divorce, his job he retired from, how he travels, how well off he was, how he owns his house on four acres of land and how he's looking for a good woman. Pamela asked him, "What's your definition of a good woman?" Dashaun said, "She has to cook me a meal which includes, breakfast, lunch, and dinner. She has to clean my house and wash clothes. She has to pay half the bills in the house. She has to be understanding to his sexual needs. She definitely has to go down on me. She has to watch all my old movies with me There will be no eating of fried foods in the house. She has to go where ever I go. She has to be loving, affectionate and cuddly. She has to attend church with me and be ready to leave at one o'clock even if the preacher is not done with his sermon for the day." Pamela said, okay. Pamela and Dashaun parted ways that night. Pamela went home and went to bed so she can get ready for work the next day. Pamela's co-workers asked her how was the club, and if she met a man. Pamela response, "I love the band. The band sung all the songs I loved to here. I met this wonderful man. I'm having lunch with him this afternoon." Dashaun picked Pamela up from work. Both of them went to eat at Soup and Salad, and he loved their gingerbread. Pamela fixed her a salad with everything on it. He had a salad, soup, gingerbread, taco, and nachos. Dashaun was a very small guy, he was short, medium complexion, and walked with a little twist, but he was all man and not gay. Both of them left the restaurant, and Dashaun took her back to work. When Pamela got off work, she went to her second job at J C Penny. When it was time for her to get off of work, he texted her to come to his house in Love, TX. Pamela texted him and let him know she didn't remember how to get to his house. Dashaun met Pamela halfway to his house by the beltway eight. Dashaun lived back alongside a country road. The scenery was pitch black. It was a two-hour drive. You drove a long way before you saw a street light. There were plenty of trees alongside the highway. As Pamela was following him, she saw deers trying to cross the streets. Pamela was scared because if the deer's crossed the street, she wouldn't know how to stop. She definitely didn't want her car bent and damaged by one of those deer's. Pamela kept up with Dashaun because he drove fast. As they were approaching his home, he turned off a dirt and rocky street where it was no lights or street signs, but Pamela kept up with him. Dashaun was in an area where it was kind of scary. The roads were long and rocky. There were trailer homes and homes surrounded by lots of trees. Some homes were space between one another. Dashaun's home was on four TV acres of land. He built his home room by room. His home was a green and white wood frame house with two portraits. He had an outhouse where he stored all his food. He would buy food in quarters and buy food twice a year. His home was a three-bedroom house, and the rooms in his home were huge. In each of his rooms, he had TVs. His living room had an eighty-inch TV, and his bedroom had a fifty-inch TV. His third bedroom had a forty-two-inch TV. Dashaun had gorgeous furniture in his home. He had so many old movies he would set up and watch all night long. First, he would watch the Johnny Carson show at ten P.M every night. Dashaun was a religious man. He knew about the Lord. You better make sure you equip in the word because he's the type of man that would bring up doubt in your worship with the Lord if you did not have a strong belief. Pamela came in from work one night, and she sat at the table, reading a scripture verse before she took a shower. He asked Pamela did she know God and did she have a relationship with God. Pamela said, yes. "So how you know God is real? If you know God is real why is people unemployed? Why God let their lights get cut off? Why are people homeless? Why God let some women get killed and beat up by some men?" Pamela was very well equipped in her scriptures. She answered every question. He asked her never wavering or trying to think about what to say. He mentioned to Pamela that he was in a secret society religion. He has read every book of the Bible and every language and religion. He told Pamela what each denomination believes in and how they worship. Dashaun told Pamela all about the women he met in his life. "You're the first woman I know that's really true to God. God has you traveling this road for a reason." Dashaun told Pamela, he looked at her and could tell she loved the Lord and, you are very knowledgeable when it comes to the word. Pamela told Dashaun, the only thing that she wished she could do when it comes to God's word is remembering the scripture verses she needs to know. She does remember the books of the Bible, she needs to know to get her point across. Dashaun told Pamela, "At least she can go toe to toe with me, and talking religion never wavering in your faith." Pamela told Dashaun, "You make me feel like you're an atheist." Dashaun told Pamela, "I believe in God. When I go to church, I'm not going to give all my money to the church house because I used to be a Deccan. I gave money for this and that until I didn't have enough money to pay my rent, light bill, water bill, and buy food. I know God does not want you giving all your money to the church house and you can't keep a roof over your head." Pamela said to him, "I hear you." If the pastor had not finished his sermon at one o'clock, he's getting up leaving and going home or get him a bite to eat. This is a daily regimen on a Sunday. Pamela said, "You do not wait for the pastor to dismiss you." He said, "No." Pamela replied, "I thought that was disrespectful." After Pamela and Dashaun finish their conversation, he started cooking. He cooked some chicken breast, rice, and green beans and rolls. Dashaun believed in a woman eating with him at all times. There's was no eating by yourself. The both of them ate together. After they ate, they watched some TV. Then once Johnny Carson went off, they went to bed and made passionate love and fell asleep. Dashaun was the perfect fit inside Pamela. What Pamela like most about the sex is just wasn't having sex with one another, it was actually lovemaking feeling passionate explosions built up inside for one another. When Dashaun kiss Pamela she would always melt inside her soul. She knew Dashaun was the one for her. They talked every day and every night. She would visit Dashaun at his house at least three days out of the week. Dashaun would always pick up Pamela for lunch and take her back to work. One day, Dashaun told Pamela, he never thought he would meet the woman of his dreams in a club, because most women in a club, have no job, no car, no money for a drink, they live with a man, or they are married, and they come dressed to kill with their sexy outfit. He also mentioned his best friend met his wife at a club. Both of them have been married for three years and still going strong. He kissed Pamela, hugged her, squeezed her, and she laid comfortable in his lap. He told Pamela, he's going to have to tell his children about her. Then the next week, his daughter had a baby. He was flying out to Atlanta, and he would be gone for two weeks. Pamela said, "Okay. I'll see you when you get back." Pamela called Dashaun to see if he made it okay. He said, yes. He was standing out on the balcony in his underwear, he said, "The baby was a girl and she was beautiful but I'm not going to change a boo boo diaper." He said, "All she does is sleep and cry." Pamela said, "I'm was so happy for you." She called him grandpa. Dashaun said, "She's going to have everything her heart desired but first, I'm going to put three-hundred dollars in a savings fund for my baby girl." While he was in Atlanta, his daughter told him their mom was dying of cancer. He told them he met a young lady back home, and he wanted to marry her. He also wanted everybody to welcome her into the family. His daughter said, "You can't marry her because mom is sick. You need to be there for her until she's not here anymore. This would be the right thing to do." Dashaun called Pamela, left a message on her cell phone, telling her he wanted to talk to her. He would call her about eight o'clock tonight. When Pamela, listened to his call, she got this quiche feeling in her stomach that he was going to breakup with her. Pamela felt her relationship with him was the ideal relationship she always longed for. She loved the fact his house sat on those acres of land. It was so quiet where he lived. You could hear the roosters crowing in the morning. You could sit on the porch in your nighties without a worry in the world. Pamela answered Dashaun's call. He said, "Hey baby. What you doing?" Pamela replied, "You're not trying to breakup with me." He told Pamela, "I loves you and you are a good woman. You know if it's coming from me, it's true. My ex-wife is dying of cancer that's why when we divorced, she didn't take anything. She let me have the 401K, money in the bank, house, land and cd's. So, I needed to be there for her." Pamela said, "Are you crying?" Dashaun said, "Yes. Pamela, I love you." Pamela told Dashaun, "You don't need to say more. I understand. You have to be there for her because if you didn't, you would never forgive yourself." "Pamela, thank you for being so understanding to my situation. The next man you'll meet is going to be the one. You will not have to look any further. When I return to Houston, I want to take you to lunch because I wants to see Pamela one last time." Pamela said, okay. Once Dashaun got back, he called Pamela and told her he will meet her at Luby's for twelve o'clock noon. When lunch time came, Pamela was at Luby's for twelve o'clock noon. Pamela got her chicken fried steak with brown gravy, navy beans, macaroni and cheese, and a roll. Dashaun ordered Tilapia fish, navy beans, salad, and a roll. Both of them set at a booth table. Dashaun looked into Pamela's eyes and started crying. Pamela said, "Please don't cry, everything is okay." Pamela replied, "I'm okay with it. You have to do this and once she passed away, whenever that may be, because you know she can beat her cancer and survive with the right treatment. Anyway, all I wanted is for your happiness. Let me ask you this, do you still love her?" Dashaun replied, "Yes. My wife never cheated on me. She just stopped having sex with me. Now, I know the reason why." Pamela said, "There's your answer. Just be happy and love her until the day she passes and make her life as comfortable as you can while she's still here. In this way, your conscious will be free from guilt." Pamela told him, "I will never forget you as long as I live because, in reality, you were the one and only true man I ever longed for my life." The both of them finished eating their lunch. They went to his car to get the rest of her clothing she left at his house. Once he put her clothing in her car. He kissed Pamela on her left cheek, and the both of them said goodbye. Pamela got into her car and started her car up. Dashaun got into his car and started his car up. The both of them left and never talked to one another again.

DUANE

Pamela was bored this day. She wanted to do something and have a little fun and get her to drink on. Pamela realized this was Wednesday, ladies' night and drinks are two-dollar until eight o'clock at night. Pamela decided to go to the club for happy hour, sit down and listen to the band play a little jazz and rhythm and blues music. As she arrived and stood by the bar, Pamela had on some tight pants, boots, and a sexy blouse on her body. The men were walking by and speaking to her and looking down her blouse. As Pamela was ordering her a drink and about to pay for her drink. A man reached over her and paid for her drink. He had on a Felt Tip hat, boots, jeans, and a shirt. He had a diamond Rolex watch on his wrist and a big gold necklace around his neck. There was no ring on his married finger, and Pamela knew he had money and a well to do man. He introduced himself as Duane. They drunk alcohol and danced the night away, as they were about to leave the club, both of them exchanged telephone numbers. Duane called Pamela the next day, and the both of them talked for hours. Pamela fell asleep on the telephone with him. When she woke up the next morning, her telephone had this loud noise for her to hang up her telephone. Pamela took a shower and got ready for work. When she got off of work, Duane called her at five o'clock exactly. He called her for two weeks straight at the same time every day at five o'clock. Pamela found during her conversation, he was a blues singer and traveled all around the country. He has two girls and two boys. His older son takes care of all his affairs, business, women, and his money. When he comes to Houston, he visits his older son. Then he goes to Louisiana to visit his other children who write his music and make his background music. A month went by, and Duane decided to come back to Houston. He called Pamela from work and asked her to meet him at this club. When Pamela was off from work, she went home and put on her sexy clothes to impress him. It was a Friday night, and she was ready for whatever. She had on a black halter dress and some boots up to her knees. She had her makeup working on her face. Her lips were ruby red. She arrived at the club, but Pamela could not remember what he looked like. She hadn't seen him since the time she first met him in the club. His son noticed her when she walked in. He brought her to his father at the bar. Duane kissed Pamela on her cheek. He asked her what she's drinking. She said, Apple Martini. After Pamela had a couple of drinks, she started dancing in front of him and moving her body all around him. Definitely, this was turning him on. Pamela liked that. As they were in the club, other women were talking to him. Pamela didn't mind because she knew they were leaving together. Men were talking and dancing with Pamela also. After Pamela had a couple more drinks, Duane was ready to leave the club. His son asked Pamela was his dad riding with her. Pamela said, "Yes. We're going to the motel and spend the night. He'll call you to pick him up." Once both of them arrived at the motel, Duane went and got a room for both of them. Once they went into the room, he rolled him up a joint. Pamela poured her a drink. Pamela turned around him and asked him, "Don't you think you're too old to be smoking weed because Duane, you just turned 68 years old." Pamela said, "Are you not scared of having a heart attack? I definitely don't want you to have a heart attack on top of me. I definitely don't know CPR." Pamela started taking off her clothes. Duane starts taking off his clothes. He cut off the lights as Pamela was getting into the bed. Duane was on top of Pamela, making love to her. He asked her when was the last time she been with someone. Pamela said, some months. He said, "I can tell. I need to get some Vaseline so it won't be so tight." From then on, Duane said, "You're a good woman Pamela, I can tell. You have morals and integrity. I need a woman in my life like you." Pamela told him, "Men just want me for sex and that's it. They don't want me to share in their world." He asked Pamela if she would travel to the different counties to hear him sing. He would get her a ticket so she can travel to hear him. He also told Pamela, "Women be surrounded around me, but you don't have to be jealous because I'm going home with you. This is my lifestyle." After he told Pamela this, she got to thinking if he had a woman in every state, Pamela knew if this is the case, this is not the man for her. After the sex was over, both of them fell asleep. When the next morning came, he wanted to have sex again, but he couldn't get it up again. Pamela said, "It's okay. If you travel like you have done and screwed a lot of women, you did not take care of your body and that's probably why you're losing your potency as a man." Duane admitted to Pamela that he had a lot of women in his life. The woman he had just used him and left him with practically with nothing. He was smart enough to put a nest egg away. Pamela said,

"Good for you because there are gold-diggers out there who will tell you they love you, and all they want is your money. But when the money runs out, they're going to leave you." Duane said, "You are absolutely correct." Duane said to Pamela, "I wished I have met her sooner, and I would have given you everything your heart desired because I knew you would have stayed by my side." Pamela said, "Yes, I would have." The telephone rang, and that was the receptionist telling them time was up. So both of them packed up their belongings. Pamela took him to his son's house. Pamela had no sense of direction and she got lost. So, his son met Pamela in the middle, and she followed him to his house. His dad told Pamela to get out of the car because he wanted to introduce her to his daughter-in-law and grandchildren. Pamela met his family, and they made her feel right at home. Pamela stayed there a good hour and then she left. She kissed Duane on his cheeks and told him she had a great time with him. He told Pamela he was going to stop in Galveston to visit an old flame, then after he was headed back to Louisiana. He would call her once he arrived in Louisiana. Pamela told him she was going to write him a blues song and email it to him. He said, "Here's my email address and my business card." Pamela took it and put it in her purse. It was weeks and weeks before she heard from Duane. So, Pamela drew her own conclusion. When she heard from Duane, he was in Louisiana visiting his other son, cousins, sisters, and brothers. Pamela talked to him for so many hours. Duane told Pamela he was going to stay in Louisiana for a month before he goes back home to New York. Pamela said to Duane to continue to call her until he leaves for New York. Each time Pamela spoke to him, she found out things about Duane she didn't like. She found out he was an alcoholic, he had no driver's license, he had no money to get back home to New York, and he was still involved with his ex-wife. They were still living together, even though they were divorced. This was when Pamela told Duane she liked him, but she's going to have to end their relationship because he was living with his ex. This was like he was married to Pamela she doesn't want to get in that triangle. This would be too much drama for her. He told Pamela he was thinking about moving to Houston. He was going to have his son look for them a house. This did not sway Pamela's mind. The next week she went to the club and met another man in the club and his son was there. He went back and told his father he saw her talking to another man. Even though Pamela broke it off with Duane, Duane, in turn, called Pamela and broke it off with her. Pamela just laughed to herself when she hung up the phone with him. So, Pamela started writing that blues song she told him she would write. The name of the song is "Brown Sugar" and goes like this. "I met this lady in Houston, TX, she was one of those red chick gals. Her skin color was medium-tone. I named her brown sugar. When she kissed me, I felt brown sugar melting all over my lips. She dressed like a million dollars ain't got a dime. She'd been through some things you couldn't tell by looking at her. Every man took her for granted. No man to love her like she need to be loved. They just wanted her to sex them up. Brown sugar, Brown sugar, sug sug gar oou oou sugar oou oou sugar brown sugar melting all over my body like hot butter syrup melting brown sugar turn you on with those sexy eyes. Just what I need to take my mind off thangs. When you get a taste of brown sugar over your body you not going to want anyone else. Brown sugar sugar gar gar oou oou melting over my body like hot butter syrup melting oou oou sug sug. Men mistreated brown sugar all the time as I watched the rain pouring down her face, it hurt me too —all she ever wanted was a love to be true. Any man would answer to Brown sugar beck and call. Brown sugar Brown sugar sug sug gar oou oou sug gar oou oou sugar Brown sugar."

Pamela never saw him or talked to him to give him this song she had written for him. He always stayed in her heart.

DEACON

After Pamela's last relationship, Pamela stopped going to clubs. She just started going to church every Wednesday night Bible school, Sunday morning worship, and Sunday school. She wished maybe the Lord would send her a man in the church house. Send one that loves the Lord like she did. Pamela was at work one day one of her co-workers mentioned to her she was having a birthday party at the Octavia club at seven p.m. She mentioned its happy hour and drinks are two dollars, so please come. Pamela mentioned to her that she might be late because she has to change her oil in her car. Pamela finally arrived at the club. She didn't have on any hootchie mama clothes. Pamela wore some Capri pants and a shirt that covered everything up at the top. On her feet, she wore flip flops. Once Pamela sat at a table, she had drinks coming all night long. Pamela could not understand because she was not dressed sexy like the other women. Pamela stayed on the dance floor dancing all night long. She also decided she was not going with any man in the club or going to give out her phone number to any man in the club. The men in this club were not about anything but a bunch of lies. This is how Pamela felt after listening to music and having enough alcohol in her system. She was ready to leave, but first, she needed to go to the restroom and let her bladder out. On the way out, this man grabbed Pamela's hand, asking for her telephone number. Pamela snatched her hand back from and told him she was on her way home. He kept grabbing her hand every time she was walking toward the exit door. Then Pamela gave him her telephone number so she can go home. Pamela did notice he had on expensive shoes, a nice expensive belt to match his expensive shoes, and his nails were cleaned. The next following Monday, he called Pamela. Pamela asked him for his name and he said everybody called him Deacon. He was 54 years old. He told Pamela that she was a nice-looking woman and she looked thirty-two years old. Pamela didn't tell him anything different concerning her age. Deacon and Pamela talked for two weeks before he invited her to his place. She came over on a Friday night. He had just got off of work. He stopped by the grocery store before he came home. Deacon said he needed to take a shower and if she would fry the fish and shrimp he bought from the store. Pamela said, okay. When she walked into the kitchen, it was a mess. There were dirty dishes everywhere. Pamela had to wash dishes before she could cook in a kitchen. Then Pamela had to clean and peel the shrimp he bought before she could buy it. Both of them did not eat until 11:30 p.m. After that, Pamela told him goodnight and went home. Then both of them talked for another two weeks. She found out his mother was a prophetess and a pastor. She found out his sister was an usher at his mother's church. She found out the Deacon spent ten years in prison for selling drugs. She found out he is an overseeing Pastor in the church, but he preferred to work for material possessions than except his calling to preach God's word and Shepard, the flock at church. She also found out he had two children. Deacon's kids don't have anything to do with him, but only when the both of them need money. This is when he hears from his children. After Pamela and Deacon hung up the phone, Pamela thought long and hard if she wanted to start up a relationship with him. After a month went by, Deacon invited Pamela to come and spend the weekend with him. She did, without any hesitation. She watched a movie with him; cuddle up on the couch with him. He loved to watch the action and scary movies. Then after both of them finished the movie, they went out to eat. As he was driving, he told Pamela he didn't have any money to pay for dinner. Pamela said, "What?" Deacon drove to this seafood restaurant where he wanted to eat. So, Pamela got out of the car and went into the restaurant. Both of them order the seafood platter and ice tea. He talked about where he worked, which was a tire manufacturing company where they hire men with felonies where he been there for two years. He also talked about the different restaurants he ate at in the area. Pamela ended up paying for the meal on their first date out. They got back to his apartment, made passionate love, and fell asleep. Everything clicked together with them in bed. From then on, Pamela started calling him Big Daddy. The next day was Sunday, and both of them were lying in bed as they woke up. Pamela asked him about faith, what was the definition of faith, so that she could comprehend. But before she knew it, he gave her a sermon on Faith. This was when Pamela knew he had a calling with the Lord. She thought she was at church, but she hadn't put any money in the collection plate to hear this sermon. Then after the sermon, he got up to take a shower and get ready for church. It was the third Sunday, and this is the youth Sunday, and Deacon was over the service. He turned on the TV, and every church service he turned to were talking about Faith. Pamela was saying to herself, "wow". She felt the Holy Spirit in him as he was giving his sermon. Big Daddy left for church, and Pamela got all her belongings from his apartment and went home. The next time Pamela visit Big Daddy, it was on a Saturday after she got off of work. Both of them talked all night. Pamela was asking him questions about the Bible. Then she asked him when she goes to church, she felt everybody be staring at her. She asked Deacon why. He told Pamela that she wore her makeup to heavy. What she needed to do was to tone her makeup down. He suggested that she wear her makeup light and her lipstick not too heavy or too much on her lips. Pamela tried this out. She wore her makeup light. She was the type of person to take constructive criticism very well. Deacon also told Pamela a woman should do what she's told by a man or get in the hole for being disobedient. Pamela said, "this is your prison talk." He also said, "When I would get into a fight with someone on the yard, I would have to go to the hole." Pamela told him, "You got mental problems, too." The next day was Sunday, Pamela got ready for church and Deacon got ready for work. Pamela watched the Pastor go up to the people in the church, pray for them, and put her hands on them. So the evil spirit that's processing their soul causes them to sin to leave. Pamela did not know she was his mother until they introduce the Pastor of the church and let you know what her sermon she would be taking on. This was the same lady that invited her in the church when she had fast arrived. Pamela smiled. As the Pastor got up to give her sermon, everybody rose to their feet and turn their Bible to the scripture in contrast with her sermon. Pamela enjoyed her sermon and could relate the sermon to her life. After the church service was over, his mom asked Pamela how did she come to know Deacon. She told Pamela all about him. How many brothers and sisters he has and where they lived. The fact he had been incarcerated, and the fact his kids do not come to visit him. Pamela told his sister that she looked just like her brother but better looking than him. Pamela liked his sister. Pamela started coming to his church without him because he always had to work on Sunday's. One Sunday, when she went to church, the Pastor revealed to her why she was at her church. She also revealed to Pamela that she had her own special relationship with the Lord. The Lord revealed to Pamela why she was at her church, and that was to grab her blessing from the spiritual realm to the natural. This was reaching her hand to the heavens and grab her blessing down with a closed fist to the material. Once Pamela started doing this, her life started changing for the better. Pamela realized Deacon wasn't right within. She called Deacon when she got off of work at nine o'clock and asked him if she could come by and spend the night. He said he'll call her back and let her know. Deacon was the kind of guy she always wanted Pamela to buy food to bring to his house or treat him to dinner. Pamela heard from Deacon at twelve o'clock at night to come over, and Pamela went. Both of them watched a movie and had sex together. Pamela noticed that the sex was different like he wasn't off into her. She noticed his phone started ringing around one o'clock in the morning and didn't stop until three o'clock in the morning. Pamela realized he called her on the rebound. The woman he truly wanted to be with didn't come through for him. Pamela was the next best thing, but Pamela didn't say anything about the situation. As they were lying in bed, Deacon told Pamela he would have never talked to a woman like her because his grandfather always told him to talk to or marry an ugly woman. Pamela said, "What?" Deacon said, "Ugly woman doesn't cheat, leave you for another man or use you like a pretty woman would. They are just grateful that a man wanted to talk to them and be with them because they're not pretty." Pamela said to Deacon that his way of thinking is wrong. A man should never judge a woman from the outside appearance. A man should look at a woman's inner beauty, her mind in the way she thinks and carry herself, because if a man judged a woman by her appearance, he could miss out on a good woman. She continued to say, "There are some pretty women with some good moral standards. There are pretty women that love Christ and try to live their lives according to Bible's principles and examples of virtuous women to set forth in the Bible." Pamela always said that pretty women know how to treat a man and love him like he wants to be love given a chance. The next time she talked to Deacon, he told her she shouldn't be wearing suits to church because people dress ordinary in church. "What did he say this for?" Pamela got angry and let him have it. Pamela said to him that he should accept her as she is not trying to change her into what he wants her to be because, after all, she accepted him with his prison record. Another thing, she's not his trick chick where he can call her when he can't be with the other chick because she let him down. She also told Deacon, he was just using her and didn't truly care about her. She told Deacon if he doesn't stop running from the Lord and accept his calling as a Pastor whom God discretely gives that title too. He will be lost in the wilderness and will not find his way back for years. Pamela hung up the phone in his face and never called him back. She deleted his telephone number out her cell phone

DUNCAN

Pamela met Duncan on a Sunday on her way to church.

Pamela realized her gas needle was almost on empty. By far, she noticed this Infinity was all beat up. It was pearl white and had some awesome tires on it. This was Pamela's favorite dream car, Infinity QX56. Pamela was all dress up in her Sunday attire. When she got off the car, going into the store, this white man was holding the door for her. Pamela said, thank you. As Pamela was paying for her gas, he said, "You sure is a beautiful woman." Pamela said, thank you. As Pamela were going to her car to pump her gas, Duncan told her he will pump her gas. Pamela told him, "Do you realize you are talking to a black woman? Duncan said, "Why would you say that?" Pamela said, "Well, because you look white." He said, "I'm Creole. I'm a Frenchman and I'm black." Pamela said, "Well you, fooled me." You look white to her. Duncan asked Pamela for her telephone number. Pamela asked him to dial her number and she will save his number into her cell phone. After that, Pamela went onto church, and Duncan called her all that Sunday.

Pamela could not put her telephone down without him calling her. Then after this, Pamela did not hear from him until the weekend. Then he texted Pamela and told her he did not want a relationship because relationship brings about drama, and he did not also want to care for a woman. Duncan stated he just wanted sex, and that's it. When he texted her to be ready and if she did not want this type of relationship, he was moving on. Pamela thought Duncan had flipped the script on her. Let me tell you guys about Duncan. Duncan was a good-looking man. He was short looked just like a white man. When he talked, he talked like a Frenchman and had a cute unique accent. Duncan was a singer/songwriter and producer. He owned commercial buildings, car lot and paint and body shop. He was also into real estate. He was a very wealthy man. He drove a Bentley, Jaguar, and a Maserati. He lived in this huge mansion of a house. When he would see Pamela, it was always in a beat-up car. Pamela decided to see Duncan on his terms because she was sick with cancer, and she was having side effects from the medication, plus Pamela hadn't had sex in three years. She met Duncan at his place of business, and then they went to the motel. First, before we went to the motel, he had to stop at Walgreens to get some baby oil. He was the type of man that Pamela had to walk in front of him, not behind him or side by side but in front of him. So, Pamela saw some perfume she wanted, and he bought it for her. Then they went to the motel. Pamela took off her clothes, and then he started rubbing her down with baby oil and started eating her kitty cat for about forty-five minutes. The baby oil was so cold he was rubbing on her body. Pamela kept flinching. Pamela could not come down because she hadn't been with a man for so long. When she did come down, she let out a loud scream, which he had to laugh himself. Pamela felt so embarrassed, and he told her not to be. "It's okay." He said, and Pamela replied, "But you didn't get satisfied." Duncan said, "It was all about you. It was just a mental thing with me." Duncan was also the type of man that if sex was not on his terms when he wants to see you, he would walk away from you. He only saw Pamela when he was on hard. A month went by, and Pamela hadn't heard from him or saw him. During that time, Pamela was really sick and was having side effects from her medication. She was in no shape to see him or let him sex her up. Then maybe a week later, she received a text from him saying, "Would you like to get eaten today?" Pamela text backed and said, sure. He told her to go get a room at the motel. The room cost twenty-five dollars for two hours, and he will give her the money back. Pamela purchased the room. He came and got undress. Pamela was already naked. Duncan ate Pamela below. Pamela shocked Duncan by giving him some brain. He told Pamela to get the pillow, kneel down and give him some brain. Duncan processed mannerisms when it came to him coming down. When he would eat Pamela, he swallowed it and didn't spit it out. Pamela would go get a towel and wash his lips. When he would come down, he put the sperm in his hand. They did not have a rubber because he didn't have time to stop and get one. Then after that time went by again, probably another month, Pamela stopped by his shop when she got off of work. She got out of her car, and she went into his place of business. He had company. Duncan was taking care of business with his client. He asked Pamela to go somewhere for twenty minutes, and he will text her when he's done.

Pamela said, okay. While Pamela was at his place of business, she looked him in his eyes and she realized he had been lying to her. So, she left and went down the streets to Popeye's to get her ninety-nine cents chicken. Duncan texted her and told her he would only be able to spend twenty minutes with her.

Pamela called him back and told him that she was not any twenty-minute whore. She wanted to spend two hours with him at least, in the motel. She wanted him to hug her, kiss, and caress her, but he couldn't do it. She went home and later that night she asked him if she could spend the night with him, but he never texted backed. Pamela realize he was married and she does not mess with married men. Pamela decided not to see him or text him again. She didn't see him ever again. With this man, Duncan gave Pamela the sweetest love. He was so gentle and sweet to Pamela. They could talk about everything and anything. Pamela liked that. They just clicked on every level. She wished she had a man like him a little. He processed some good qualities in a man.

WOMEN'S EXPERIENCE

THESE ARE WOMEN'S EXPERIENCES THAT THEY HAD GONE through with men. Some stories are good, and some are bad. In relationships with men, there is no instruction book. You have to learn as you go. This is where the experience comes into play with many relationships trusting in the Lord to give you the strength to deal with the situation you may have to endure by the hands of a man. The majority of the women today just want a man to treat her right, be honest, faithful, good in bed, and someone they can be attracted to and attracted to them. Women go through so much with just being with a man. You have to take into consideration the changes a man puts a woman through can be very devastating sometimes. In reality, women are stronger than men mentally. We, as women, just like men, think between our legs. It's all about how a man makes us feel sexually sometimes instead of how he can provide for us mentally, physically, and spiritually. Once we have sex with him and the sex part is over. Can we communicate with them afterward? Or do we just lay there speechless in silence with nothing to talk about? Or are we all over him to have sex again with our bodies? This is a man we think we may love or want to get to love. Yes, if you have a man, you're going to trip with him in something, about something, and wanting something in your life. There's going to be some issue with the man you're involved in. There's no perfect relationship when a man is involved. There will be some trip mentally somewhere in the relationship. The women mistreated by a man and done wrong by a man is the same woman will have to take care of him when he's sick on his death bed or just can't do anything for himself like he could before. A man is going to have to answer and reap what he sows sooner or later for not treating that woman right. He could very well suffer a stroke, a heart attack, where he couldn't speak, walk, or have sex. In other words, the same woman he did wrong is the same woman that's going to have to take care of him. This woman is going to remember the awful mistreatment at his hands. Payback might be a little hard to handle for the man that mistreated her. A woman scorned in a relationship is a woman to be watchful of. Some women are happy, contented, and bless with the man they are with. These women experience no mistreated by a man. These men respect them and adore them. They do not flaunt their other woman in their face if they have one. Some women do not have the worrying or just thinking about if their man is cheating or not because it's a respect and trust factor with them. I hope as you read these women's experiences with men. You can learn something from their involvement with a man, husband, common-law husband, or just being in a relationship. The games men play can have a damaging effect on a women's mind, one way or the other. This is a couple that married one another for financial stability. This woman had to do everything for this man financially. She even picked him out a car and bought it for him without him being there. Then she decided she wanted a house to live in instead of giving her money away in apartment living. Both of them decided to buy a house together. When she went too close to the house, she said that she cried the whole time because he wasn't there to close with her. She let him know she loved him, but until he paid her back for all she did for him, then their relationship can start fresh again, and both of them can put the debt situation behind them.

A woman spent thirteen years in a marriage with a man. Her husband grew tired of her and left her due to boredom. Because she loved him so much, she understood why he left her. She ended up giving him all the money they accumulated together, full custody of their children, and the house the both of them lived in. She walked away with nothing because she truly loved him, hoping the both of them could patch the problems up. Then, later on, she found out it wasn't her, it was him because he moved on with someone else, she gave him everything.

A woman lived together with a man since she was fifteen years old. He ended up marrying her, and the marriage only lasted for ten years. After the ten years, she left him because he would not buy her panties, bra, clothes for her and his children. He always kept her in a broken-down car. He kept himself dress to kill. He drove the finer vehicle. She said that he kept them living in a nice house but lacked providing for them.

A woman lived with her common-law husband. Every Friday evening, when he gets paid, he comes home drunk —putting his fist in her face leaving her face black and blue under her eye on the right side of her face, always swollen. She said this happens to her numerous times. She just got used to her face looking like that. She said, it's nothing for her to go out in public places with her right side of her face swollen and her eyes blacken.

A woman came home from work early to find her husband in bed with another woman. She said that she wanted to go get the gun and shoot them, both but something held her back from doing this. Instead, she told the woman to get dress and get out of her house. She did not speak to her husband for weeks, and she moved into the other bedroom. She said that she stayed and forgave him for the children's sake of keeping her family together.

This is a woman who dated her husband for five years, and had two children for him. Then his whole attitude changed toward her, even to the point of him leaving the house going around the corner, getting in the car with another woman, and living with her. His wife saw the whole thing from her backyard, and he had the audacity to have this woman drop him off in the driveway of their house. Then the fighting started. He would beat her up in front of the children. Then he started doing drugs, sleeping with more women and booze. She decided to leave and divorce him and never thought about him ever again in her life.

This is about a woman that lived in the country. Every Friday night, her husband would get drunk, sloppy drunk where he couldn't drive himself home. He would always get a woman from the bar to drive him home. She said that she would be sitting on the porch watching him get out of the car. The other woman would leave in his car and bring it back the next day. She said this just made her cold and bitter toward men and her husband. She moved into the other bedroom during their marriage.

A middle-aged woman in a relationship with a man for twelve years, both of them had an on-and-off-again relationship. It was like both of them could not come together with the meeting of the minds. He was trying to rebuild his credit because she made so many bills, she kept up with the Joneses. Whatever he did for her wasn't enough for her. She always argued with him and belittled him, but he was actually the breadwinner. Then she decided to move to another state where she wanted him to pay her rent, buy a car and co-sign for her an apartment, which he did until his bills started getting behind. She told him that she was going to move back home to have surgery, and that said surgery never happened. She's been gone a year, and he has not been with another woman since his wife left. In order for him to get his wife back, he decided to stop paying her bills in another state so she can come back home to him.

This woman married an engineer. She could not have children for him, so, both of them adopted a girl and a boy. They met in high school, and they were high school sweethearts. She only did hair and makeup for a living. He bought her a fine house cost over two hundred thousand dollars. She also drove a BMW, and both of them are very happy, still in love, and raising their children. He never looks in another direction. His eye is always on his wife.

This woman is married to a rich man. He cannot read but been working on his job for twenty-five years. She handles the money and all the paperwork. She is his eyes. She does not cheat on him like his other wives did. She is a God-fearing woman. She's a good woman. When her husband is home from work, she cannot talk on the telephone, or he will listen in on the phone conversation. While he's at work, she can't go anywhere without him getting upset with her. He's a very controlling man and very insecure in his marriage, but they've been together for almost ten years. When it comes to sex, she has to go down on him. He loves sex, and his penis doesn't get hard anymore. He's in his seventies. If she doesn't satisfy him sexually, he'll cut her allowance off.

A woman has been with her husband for twenty-one years. Both of them have a wonderful marriage, because in their marriage, they do everything together. Both of them of cause has their ups and downs, but they never went to bed angry at one another. Both of them would discuss their problems and work them out before the sun would rise the next day. Their marriage is stronger than ever. They are still happy.

A woman has been in her relationship with her husband for thirty-two years. All both of them would do is fuss with one another all day long. The key to their relationship is communication. The left and right hands know what they're doing at all times. In other words, both of them never did anything the other person didn't know about. They did everything together.

This woman was engaged to this man for eight years. Both of them were a loving couple to everybody. On the day of their wedding, he was nowhere to be found. He'd up and left the city to marry another woman in another city, leaving his fiancé of eight years to explain to the guest why it won't be a wedding today. His fiancé did not know he was seeing another woman beside her. She was very devastated by what he did to her, not being able to move on with her life with someone else.

A woman is walking in Wal-Mart having a conversation with her girlfriend, stating the man she's seeing gives her everything she wants and possibly dreams of having in her life. She says just because he rich and famous, and she will not bow down to no man regardless of what he has and what he does for her. He does everything for her as long as she licked his behind and spanked his butt. She says he has a very perverted mind when it comes to sex. She also says she does not love him. She loves what he does for her.

This lady is married to her husband for almost twenty years. The whole time both of them been married, she never knew he was unhappy. During the course of their marriage, he did everything, and she told him she wanted for whatever occasion there was or whatever reason she said it was for. He catered to her every need. Both of them had arguments and disagreements. He never cheated on her. Both of them lived in the same house but slept in separate bedrooms. Both of them had sex twice a month. Now he wanted more attention from her, but she was not ready to give him the kind of attention he wanted. After all these years the both of them had been together.

A young woman in her forties was in love with a married man. She was a good Christian woman that would make a man a fine wife. She would always fall in love with a married man in hoping they would marry her. She was a good house cleaner and a good cook. She targeted men with a football coach career. Her children were grown. Now she would use her nephews to get close to the coach. When she would go home, she would imagine the coach in her house with her, kissing her, caressing her, and even sexing her. Only to find out it was her lived imagination. For some reason or another, she would think that coach would leave his wife for her but only to be heartbroken in the end. She would tell her close friends everything that would go on in their relationship to only find out her friends went back and told him what she said about them. This was for them to break up, which they did that resulted in her trying to commit suicide because she could not have him. After this, not a day went by that she didn't cry herself to sleep. Then one day, she just got up one morning and left her hometown, which she started this same process of dating a coach again with the same results as previous.

This is a young couple who had been with her husband for twelve years. They had three young boys. She has never had a job no longer than two years at the most without getting laid off or fired. Her husband beats her all the time. She's okay with this because of the children and the fact he is the breadwinner. Since she lives in a big house, she feels she can deal with her situation. She definitely loves her husband and can't see herself without him.

This couple was with one another for thirty years. When she met him, she had five children. He helped take care of her children. He never had children of his own. He always wanted children to fill his void in his life. They had a love that lasts a lifetime and very much committed to each other. A kind of love that's hard to find some people wish they had. This couple never had to worry about cheating in their relationship because they were faithful to one another. When her husband got sick, she stayed by his side until she nursed him back to health.

This Christian woman was with her husband for thirty-five years. Her husband sent her through the ringer but she stayed with him and looked the other way. He always was in a relationship with a different woman from the church. He was a deacon of the church. She always knew about the other women he was seeing, but she always looked the other way. When he would tell her about these women, her rule of thumb was to never entertain them in her house. Her right ear always became deaf to him. She was a good wife to him. She would have his breakfast ready lunch and dinner. She made his bed on the couch. This is where he slept for fourteen years of their marriage because of him sleeping with other women. She never thought about having another man on the outside. She just thought about staying true to him. Now he has suffered a heart attack which brought about one stroke after another, which left him not walking or talking. She has to take care of him, not his other women.

This woman sent her husband through hell and high water because she loved the streets. She loved to party, drink, dance, and have sex with other men. She just became dissatisfied with her husband after two years of marriage. She had a good husband. He never went anywhere but stayed in the house. Her husband was just waiting for her to come in from the streets. She realized what she thought was missing was right at home. Now she's with him all the time inside the house. When both of them go anywhere, they go together. Her husband waited for her and didn't leave her because he waited a lifetime to get married. He was just going to stick it out until she got tired of those streets.

Some women today will do anything to keep a man in their lives. This is a women's experience where she sacrificed her children to keep a man with her. She let this man physically and sexually abuse her daughters while they were kids, and as they got older until a tragedy happened. She says as a woman, she lost her self-esteem somewhere as she was growing up. As she was growing up, her father had no presence in her life, but her stepfather would beat her and then have sex with her while her mom watch. So, she thought that was normal in raising her daughters until one night her man beat one of her daughters to death while she was at work. When she got home, she helped him hide the body, thinking nobody will miss her. Now she's sitting in a prison cell, and women beat her up every day like she let that man beat on her children. Now she's one of their sex slaves. Her other daughter will not go to see her in prison or accept any of her phone calls. She really truly understands why. She finally gets it that to never put a man before your children because children will be there for you when a man will not. She knows she can never make up for her mistakes she made with her girls but only wished her loving daughter to be a better mom than she ever was with her, not letting a man harm her children in any form or fashion. She asked herself every night before she goes to bed. 'Was the love of a man worth the welfare and safety of her daughters'?

This woman was involved with a man that loved women. He cheated on her all the time every day of the week. One day she got off work and caught him home in bed with another woman. This was the day when she put her love in her back pocket and walked out on him. His mom always told her she will always be her daughter-in-law. One day she went to a house party one of her friends was given. This is where she met her husband of twenty-two years. Each day of their relationship was like the first time they met. Both of them had a few problems, but nothing big they did not resolve before both of them went to bed. The key to their successful relationship was the fact he was a car salesman that owned his own car lot, which caused him to work long hours. Now he's retired. Both of them are still in love with one another like the first time they ever met.

This is a young woman on crack. She loved her crack it was her whole world. She never had to pay for a habit, because these professional men with good jobs as a basketball player, teacher, welder, bus driver, lawyer, doctor, and mechanic paid for her crack. She said these professional men never wore a condom because they prefer unprotected sex. The one thing she never told these men she slept with that she had AIDS. She had long curly hair, light tone complexion, slim and just plain beautiful. No man could resist her.

This was a church-going woman who attended church with her husband. She and her husband held positions in the church. Both of them started getting along really bad, where both of them would fuss and fight all the time. Both of them been married for fifteen years. One day, he couldn't take it anymore. He moved out and moved in with another woman. After three months went by, she decided to go to the other woman's house and get her husband to come home. She knocked on the door. She waited for someone to open the door. It was the woman that opened the door. The woman decided to close the door real fast, but his wife pushed the door open. She told her husband to get his clothes and come back home. His wife acted a plum fool with the other woman for stealing her husband away from her. Her husband gathered his clothes up and came home with her. He was so ready to come home because when he got in the car, he couldn't stop kissing her. He kept telling her baby why it took her so long to come and get him. He told her there's nothing like being home with his wife. She was a very prime example that if you love your husband, go get what's yours and work the kinks out. Forgive and move on. Both of them are in the marriage ministry in the church.

This is a young woman in love with her husband, but he's not in love with her. The young woman met her husband through a mutual friend. Both of them dated for two years and three months before they got married. Her husband told his mom that he did not love her, but he was going to marry her anyway. His mother told him to break it off with her because if he's not in love with her, the marriage will not last if he doesn't love her. He married her anyway. The young woman had two children for him. He asked her to have these children before she goes to college or takes up a trade to better herself. She became a stay-at-home mom. After their second child, her husband met another woman which he fell in love with. She worked for the railroad. She had a big two-story home, five Mercedes Benz cars, and her master's degree. Then one day a hurricane came, the wife went to stay with her aunt along with the two children. He didn't come where his family was. Instead, he lied and said he was going to go stay with his cousin because he didn't get along with her aunt. Her husband went to go stay with the other woman that he was cheating on her with. When the storm was over, he did not come back home to his wife and two kids. He divorced his wife and married the other woman he said he was in love with.

This is about a young woman twenty-five years old. Her grandmother died and left her two hundred and fifty thousand dollars. She met a man while she was working in a retail shop. She was so excited to know her grandmother left her this money, and she told this to the man she met shopping in the store. He kept coming up to her job, surprising her with gifts and plenty of kisses. No more than six months, he popped the question and asked her to marry him. He put a five-carat round diamond on her finger. Of course, she said yes. Once they exchanged vows and were married, she put his name on her bank account. Once she did, this he left her and took all the money she had in the bank. He left her penniless, causing her to move in with her aunt. She realized that she can't mix romance and finance together. Her money should have been kept in her bank account without his name on it. She stated the both of them could have had the romance and love still going on had she not done this.

This is a young woman who loved her man more than she loved herself. Her and her man argue all day long, even though she would post their dirty laundry on Facebook daily. Then one day, he decided to leave because he had enough of arguing over nothing. She became lonely without him, even to the point of going to a dark place inside of her soul. She wanted to commit suicide because he was not around anymore. She said she had low self-esteem because she did not know how to go about getting a man in her life.

This woman has been in her marriage for eighteen years. She had five kids age ranging from eight to one year old. She looks good for her age. Her marriage was tough. Her husband went in one direction. She went in the other direction. Both of them went to church and studied the Bible together. Her father was a pastor. She was brought up with morals. It took her ten years before she realized she was married. She found herself out there having fun. She wasn't ready to come in from the streets, but once she did, both of them came in together. Both of them are happy they came in together, the love and their affection for one another kept them together. They renewed their marriage vows. Both of them went on a honeymoon to the Bahamas, where she got pregnant. This was definitely not in her plans. She said that if there's one thing that stood out in her marriage was, he was a provider. She never had to buy herself anything. She appreciated her husband buying her gifts like clothes, jewelry, purses, earrings, and diamond bracelets. This lets her know he has deep love and affection for her. This was the one thing that stood out in her marriage that made her go the long howl when both of them hit hard and tough times in their marriage. They stuck it out together.

A young lady is married to a man who beats her every day. Her man sold crack and weed for a living. This young lady had six kids. Three of the kids were hers, and the other three kids were his. He would beat her so much her self-esteem became low. This lady was light tone complexion, a very beautiful heavy-set woman. One day when she came home from work, her husband told her he was going to kill her. She believed him. She decided to jump from the balcony of her two-story apartment, landing on her ankle, which she ended up twisting. She had to go to the emergency room because she could not walk. When she was examined by the doctor, the doctor and nurses saw bruises on her body plus the two black eyes. The policeman asked her if she wanted to press charges against him. She replied, without hesitation, that yes, she would sign the papers to put him in jail. Before the policeman could pick him up, she called him and warned him the policeman was on their way. He got into his car, drove away to avoid any jail time. He stopped at the corner store and got into an altercation with the store clerk. The store clerk pushed the button under the cash register. The police arrived, arrested him, and he went to jail. Her husband stayed in jail for nine months. She was able to get on her feet. She got her an apartment, food stamps, and a car. She paid the light bill and rent on time. She had a job as a receptionist, paying her good money. Her husband got out of jail, and she took him back again. She ended up losing her car, evicted from her apartment, and lights got cut off, no money to buy milk, pampers, or food. The babies were wearing poopy diapers. One day when she went to work, she did not have enough money to pay for a babysitter to watch her kids. She asked her husband to watch them while she was at work. Her husband whipped her two children and sent them to school with bruises. When the two children arrived at school, the teacher saw the bruises and called Child Protective Services. The principal called the mother to get her side of the story. Child Protective Services came to the house to check on the children. Her baby was in a pissy diaper hadn't been changed for hours. Her husband's kids were fine and not a bruise on their skin. All of the children were put in foster care. The husband once again went to jail and stayed there for some years.

 This woman was dating a married man for about fifteen years. This married man was a sheriff who worked in a small substation. He married his wife because she had lots of money in her 401K. Once he got her to put his name on her 401K, he divorced her. The other woman thought he was going to marry her, but instead, he married another woman, her husband had passed away and left her lots of money. Once she put his name on her bank account, he divorced her. The sheriff would never marry the other woman. He kept marrying another woman that had money. It seemed like he could not stay in one relationship long enough. Every time the sheriff did not marry her, she forgave him even though she stayed angry with him. She loved him. She couldn't stay mad at him forever. She said that sometimes when you're in love, love has you accepting certain situations you know you shouldn't accept with a man. She said that every time he married another woman and not her, he made a fool out of her. When he married this last woman and not her, she said that she had enough. She said that she was going her separate way. Low and behold, the Lord sent her a man that loved her. They dated two years before he asked her to marry him. He showered her with love. He bought her clothes, jewelry, car and gave her plenty of love. His mom adored her. This man she was involved with, they did everything together. They went to the grocery store, movies, church, Bible study, clean the house, cooked, and went out to eat together. Both of them had everything in common, like a match made in heaven. As she began her wedding plans, her fiancé died of a massive heart attack leaving her heartbroken. She said she learned the difference in how a woman should be treated by a man. Her sheriff friend called her to try to get back with her once he found out about her fiancé. He told her he married this woman with ovarian cancer until she passed away. The sheriff inherited her fortune, but he was all alone. He wanted her to come back in his life, and he would marry her. She told him no. She told him that now she gets it, that he will never married her because she had no money to offer him. She felt she was a commoner with nothing to offer him was the reason why he passed her up every time in marriage.

An unhappy woman said that to have a relationship, you have to have togetherness in order for your relationship to work. You can't just do what you want to and expect the other person to look the other way just because you got money, power, position, land, and a home. You have to discuss everything you do with the other person showing respect for that someone. If you stay with a man over ten years and things are not working out in the relationship, you need to walk away. What's not working isn't going to work. A strong woman is not going to put up with foolishness from a man. She is going to wait for the man that will show her love and respect. There are men out here that possess love as one of their traits. Sometimes you have to wait on the Lord. It might take a long time but be persistent in prayer. That man will come.

This woman met a man who was not a people person and would just talk about everything and everybody in a negative way. She considered this man to be a loner and not happy. She wanted to find out what made him tick. She realized she could not change this man, but she still wanted to be in a relationship with a man like this. She decided to spend more time with this man so she could get to know him and for him to open up to her. In this way, she felt he would be more positive when speaking of others. She felt this could work between the two.

Low and behold, it did. He started talking positively about others and truly felt love for her.

A woman that loved to party said that a man that can throw down a party could be the life of the party and an alcoholic and been by himself for many years. Then one day, out of the blue, a woman comes into his life, softens him up and make him realize its more to life than being the life of the party or drinking excessively. This man drinks excessively, and he had a dark side to himself but the woman he became involved with. She changed him, understood him, and realize how to deal with him on a one on one relationship with all his faults. She believes that if a man knows what type of person he is and shares with his loved one in a relationship, then this is a relationship of communication and partnership of togetherness.

An unhappy woman was married to a man who gave her everything she wanted or desire in life. She was not happy and in love with him. She loved what he was worth far as money-wise. When she would go somewhere with him, she would always fall asleep in the car as he was driving home.

She did not know how to hold a conversation with him because she really was not into him like a wife should be. She realized she did not want to die of loneliness and being alone. She said that you could have all the money in the world, but if you do not have love, nothing else really matters without love.

One lady said that sometimes relationships could go back to a person's childhood. If she didn't saw her parents fuss and fight, but instead, eat at the table as a family and go to church, then this would have helped her to stay in a relationship instead of staying in a relationship where she's dogged out and abused by her man. Her family household was like a fairy tale, which consists of no arguing, fussing, or fighting but was very peaceful where love was shown on a daily basis. This is what she expected when she became involved with a man but got the opposite.

This is what a married couple said in their relationship. Both of them were scuffling all through their marriage to make ends meet and raised their children. As soon as both of them refinanced their house for sixty thousand dollars, his wife left him. Then the husband threw a birthday party for his son whom he just met him a year ago. Petty stuff to leave a mate you've been married too for years. The wife said she wished she never left him, but sometimes it's the little things that break up a relationship instead of the big things. Sometimes when money comes into a person's life we get the big head like you can take care of yourself now you don't need him now you can leave him now and make it on your own without him.

A man was in a relationship with a woman for three and a half years. Both of them lived together and did everything together. He said she wanted children and wanted to get married. He was not ready for any of this. She constantly nagged him on a daily basis. His desire was to be rich, have a yacht, and be well established financially before he would commit to a marriage and have children. His woman broke up with him and moved out because he did not want what she wanted. He said that he wished he would have given in to her wants. Now he misses her, but she moved on with someone else. He said she was a good woman that he let to slipped away.

One couple stayed together for seventeen years, only to say that what kept them together was the fussing and fighting. This is how both of them got along. One time she wanted to leave because the fussing and fighting got out of hand, it was too much than she could bear, but the love kept her with him. She said in some marriages, different strokes for different couples.

This is a woman who was married to a man for thirty years. Her husband gave her everything a woman could want but she took all this for granted. All he wanted from her is some kids which she never had for him. She loved being one of the Joneses who loved the party life. One day her husband got sick, and her husband passed away. She had nobody to talk to about anything or to fill the void in her life. Her driver's license was taken away from her for driving under the influence of alcohol for two years. Now she's trying to get herself together and get her some transportation instead of riding the bus because of her dilemma she felt a man would not give her a chance in a relationship since she took her previous marriage for granted. She feels karma came back for her.

A woman's husband had been traveling for fifteen years. Now he got laid off his job. He's at home more frequently day and night instead of being home every two weeks or three months. By him being home more often the both of them have to get used to one another's ways. They're like strangers lost in the wind. The arguing and bickering started with the two of them where the husband sleeps on the couch to keep down confusion. The wife works hard and late hours at work to keep everything together for the sake of the children and the number of years they been married.

A Muslim relationship told by a cab driver, that before there's a marriage between man and woman, both person's family will tell them everything about a person from a through z. The parents will tell the person they're marrying what they have done that's bad and what they've done that's good. This is a sort of marriage that is pre-arranged by their parents. If the other party does not want to marry, they can back out of it. In this way, they won't go into the relationship blindsided like they didn't know this person was that way. The reason this is done is to keep down divorces in their culture and to see what the both of them have in common. This way, their love is treasured more.

A woman became an alcoholic. She said the reason she started drinking was because her children became grown and didn't need her anymore. There were no more issues and drama in her life that come with having a husband and children. Her children were her life. Her husband was there in the house with her, but they were like strangers in the wind.

This is a woman been with a man for four years. When she met her man, she had a good job, and so did he. Both of them had a perfect relationship until she got laid off her job. Their relationship started to change since she was no longer working. She wasn't able to find a job right away, and her man seemed to be okay with that. She asked her man if she could go to school. His reply was, "yes." She went to school to get her degree. After two years passed, she still was unemployed but still in school. One day, her man came home upset. He gave her an ultimatum, that if she does not get a job and help him pay the bills, both of them can go their separate ways because he was tired of paying the bills by himself. After they move into their separate apartments, he still wanted to see her and continue their relationship as it was before. She became devastated by what he said to her because she loved him, and he wants to separate. Now she feels, he never loved her at all since she doesn't have a job. His love was not for real. He was the one who gave her the approval to go to school. Now he's ending their relationship.

A young lady has been married for years. During her marriage, she allows her husband to pimp her to his male family members and friends. She only goes along with it because she loves her husband. In his past, every woman he had, he pimped them for money, jewelry, and items such as clothes, shoes, and sports events. She has acknowledged that she has low self-esteem within her. When she decides to go to church, she can't go because she feels ashamed of what she did the night before and how she's living her life. She felt she couldn't get a real man on her own. She says when she was single and used to date, she would give up the cookie the same day or night. The man wouldn't even call her the next day. She always said that once she get a man, she'll do whatever he wants her to do to keep him.

A woman has been with her husband for twenty-two years. This is what she's says to a successful marriage. Both of them do everything together. When he leaves the house, she goes with him everywhere. Both of them would discuss their problems and work them out before the sun would rise the next day. Both of them had their ups and downs, but they never went to bed angry at one another. Their marriage is stronger than ever. They are still happy and married.

A woman who has been in her relationship with her husband for thirty-two years said that both of them would just fuss all day long. You would think both of them hate each other. The left hand knows what the right hand is doing at all times. In other words, both of them never did anything the other person didn't know about because they did everything together. The way they argue, you think both of them were at odds with one another, but they're not.

A young woman is married to this man who is already in his seventies. He's a very rich man. She lives in a different state from him. He paid for her rent and bought her a nice car to drive. She's trying to make her ten years with him so she can be entitled to half his retirement, pension, money, his annuities bank account, alimony, and his house. He's a very controlling and very insecure man in his marriage. He calls her every hour on the hour. If she doesn't answer, he feels she is cheating on him. In other words, he thinks she has another man in her house. Her rent will not get paid. When it comes to sex, she has to go down on him and try to get him off. If she doesn't satisfy him like he wants her to, he'll cut off her allowance. The sad thing about it was he couldn't even get hard.

A young woman was into a long-distance relationship due to a job promotion. She travels back and forth to see him, or he'll come to see her when he gets a chance. She felt that since she got a promotion, he's not on her level anymore. Now she's looking for someone that can offer her more than she makes and have a better career than she does. She has not shared this with her long-distance companion, but she feels he'll get the memo or catch on that she's not into him anymore.

A young woman dated a man who worshipped his house as his God. He lured her into his home by telling her he was going to retire and collect social security and put the house in her name. He was going to change over his beneficiary to her and that he was a Godly man. As she lived with him on a daily basis, he was definitely not the man he approved to be on the outside that she met. He was nice on the outside but had a wicked heart on the inside. You never know a man until you live with him. He owned his own mechanic shop and lived in a three hundred fifty-thousand-dollar house that took up the whole corner. He came home every night like he was high on drugs. He came home in a rage, also like he was angry with the world. He came home, fixing him a full glass of scotch whiskey. Then he'll start talking about God and how he will never perish and how everybody is jealous of what he has. He asked Pamela to marry him, and she accepted. He said she could change the house like she wanted to. When she got ready to paint the house and put the light fixtures in the ceiling, he slapped her in the face and pulled a gun on her. He told her that her paint and light fixtures were niggerish. She was an ignorant, stupid black trash. If she wanted to do anything in his house such as paint, buy furniture or fix his house up. She had to get his approval, but she did get his approval to paint and fix the house he just didn't remember. Then he told her he was not going to let her bring him down to her level. She was afraid for her life. Then the next day, he told her he loved her, and she could paint the room the color she liked. She didn't because he acted like Lucifer, the devil the day before. She left him and never looked back or answer any of his phone calls because she was a good loving, spiritual, God-fearing woman. All he did was put her down like she was nothing.

This is a woman who married her high school sweetheart.

They had two daughters and a son, but he cheated on her all the time. His high school sweetheart was not going to let a woman come up and ruin her marriage. When she got pregnant with her last child, this one woman would not go away. She did not care if she was married. She just wanted her husband and did not care what lengths she would go. She called the man's house and his wife answer the telephone. His wife had a conversation with the woman to let her know she was not going anywhere. The woman asked to meet her, and she did. The woman told her she thought she would look ruched, but she looks good. His wife told her that she and her husband have sex. She has a degree and a good job. They put their money together and pay the bills. She knows he's not giving her any money. His wife told her she must be on welfare and not work because that's why her husband is with her because he does not have to put any money in your house, buy food, or pay bills. The woman let her know that she is on welfare. His wife said she couldn't give her husband sex every day because she works and have kids to take care of. The woman's husband ended up leaving her for the other woman. They ended up divorced. His wife just has anger toward him because he won't take care of his kids or talk to them.

A group of women sat down and said what made their relationship work and marriage work at a table. This is what they said to a long-lasting relationship is to never let the sun set when you have an argument. You need to make up even if it's not your fault. You need to wake up in the morning and tell each other that you love one another, and each time you talk and end your conversation with "I love you." You need to put your money together to pay the bills and have one bank account. You need to have Christ in your lives, praying together before you go to bed and at the dinner table. You need to do everything together, sticking to one another like glue. You need to forgive one another for the sins you make and not throw it your face when someone gets made. Last but not least, stay together, love one another, keep one another close to your hearts, take every issue and problem to Christ to solve, and respect — no cheating, putting hands on each other and cursing each other out, communicating - discussing every detail that involves each other and supporting one another - having each other back no matter what.

PAMELA'S CONCLUSION

PAMELA REALIZED THAT TO TREASURE LOVE, YOU HAVE TO THINK with your mind and not with your heart when it comes to love. We, as women, love men with our hearts, soul, and mind. When love hurts, it can stab you in the heart real hard, take over your mind, and it can make you lose your mind because you do not have a man to share your world. So, when a man may tell us something, we know may not be true whatever lie it maybe. We as woman tend to still believe them because we want a man so bad. Sometimes this can cause us to get hurt, leaving our hearts to bleed to death inside. Leaving us to commit suicide, leaving us to be by ourselves for many years, leaving us to change our sex preference in life. If a man is sending you through changes, let him go women and trust in the Lord.

wholeheartedly. Hold on to the Lords underlying trust and love for you to work it out for you. Don't give up because when you turn around, God already blessed you with your love interest right in front of you. When you love someone, love hurts, but love can heal in the end. If you find love, grab it, hold it, cherish it, and never let it go because that could be your last chance to love and who wants to lose love. Your heart is the only thing bound to be hurt. With your mind, you think about love, logical, and sometimes realistic. Pamela experience many relationships with men, where she loved with her heart. She was always taken for granted, and not one of them cared about her feelings or took her into consideration about anything that would affect her deep within her soul. She was mistreated and misunderstood by them. She just couldn't get a relationship right. She always treasured it in the majority of her relationship's disappointment. No man ever loved her the way she wanted them too. She never had a real, meaningful relationship that would last like she wanted it too. She never found a real meaningful of love in her life with the men she became involved with. Pamela never got lucky in relationships. She experienced just heartache and pain. After all Pamela went through, she decided to go stay with her mom. She was broke and had no place to go. She was glad she went and stayed with her mom because she learned she was keeping a secret from her. Pamela's mother, one night, yelled out to Pamela to come into the living room so she could talk to her at one o'clock in the morning. She told Pamela to sit in the chair and listen to her. Pamela's mom was sloppy drunk. Her mother told her she was going to tell her this when she was on her death bed because she never wanted to see her with any money. Her mom walked up to Pamela and slapped her really hard in her face. Pamela's mom called her a female dog and told her she hated her; that's why she never did anything for her. She told Pamela, "The dad you think is your dad is not your biological father. Your real father was very wealthy. He owned his own food catering company and he died three years ago." Pamela's mom told Pamela his name. Pamela just sat there, angry at her mom for telling her this. Pamela cried. Pamela told her mother, "You must really hate me to keep a secret like this for so long." She told Pamela, "You look just like him." Her mom also said, "I'm telling the truth, if the family wanted to do a DNA test, it would be a match 100%." Her mother repeated, "They are very wealthy." Pamela told her mom, "I do not care about how much money they have because I don't have any money." Her mother said, "I wanted to tell your father about you, but I didn't want to break up his family. He would have left her if he'd known about you." Pamela replied, "You wish in your dreams, mom, he was not going to leave his family for you just because you had a baby out of wedlock. You committed adultery with another man's child robbing her of a chance to know her real father before he passed away." Pamela could not sleep that night. She cried herself to sleep. She was so angry with her mom for lying to her whole life. The next day, Pamela researched on her biological father and family on the internet. After that, she called one of the sisters and left a message on her cell phone. She was her half-sister. Pamela told her what her mom revealed to her. Then two weeks passed, and the family contacted her to meet with her. Pamela met the two sisters. Pamela looked just like the oldest sister. The other sister Pamela had her smile and her body shape. The sisters did embrace Pamela with love. One of the sisters told Pamela sarcastically that her father had passed away if she was looking for a DNA test to get one from her father. Pamela mentioned to her that her father had passed away, and There was no way to find out if they really were related. Pamela had replied, "The only thing we have to go on is our resemblance and characteristics." Pamela walked away, feeling good about the sisters she never met and never knew. Pamela never heard from them again. Pamela knew they were her family because she looked just like them. Pamela just wanted a family to belong because she was a loner and always treated like an outcast by her family. The sisters could not deny her of being related to them. Pamela's life was finally making some sense now. Pamela was able to figure out where she belongs in her life. Why nothing went her way in her life? Why she had it so hard? The pieces in Pamela's life started fitting together like a jigsaw puzzle. Pamela realized she was not the child of the man her mother loved. Pamela's mother never loved her or showed her love. Pamela was treated as an outcast by her mother growing up. She knew she was different from her family members. Her outlook on life was totally different from theirs. She always wanted to be somebody, have a fulfilled and happy life where her family members loved drugs, alcohol, and a good time. Pamela had determination, will power, and her dreams and she realize that came from her father, who kept her moving forward in her life. Pamela realized she developed some good traits from her father. She found out he loved the Lord, and she loved the Lord. He was a hard worker; Pamela was also a hard worker. He had the determination to make it happen for himself; Pamela had the determination to make her dreams come true. He had the strength to endure; she had the strength to endure all her obstacles and pick herself up when she felled. The father Pamela had really was not her main concern here on earth because she had a spiritual father in heaven that loved her and has her best interest at heart. All her needs and wants to be taken into consideration by Lord above. Pamela learned in trying to have a relationship always examine the fruit a person bears just because a person is saved, they may not live a Christian life. Try to find out from friends and family how the person treated their past relationships before you start one with them because you can walk away from them even if it doesn't work. Pamela knew exactly what type of man or husband she wants in her life. Pamela wanted a man that loved her like Christ loved her. Pamela wanted a spiritual man that would help her draw close to God in understanding his word to explain to others. She wanted a caring man that would hug and kiss her. She wanted a loving man to love her sexually with deep feelings that came within his bleeding heart. She wanted a man that wasn't ashamed to be seen with her. She wanted a man to take her places with him. She wanted a man to walk side by side with her, not ahead of her. She wanted a man to say the word "I Love You" once in a while and mean it. She wanted a man to pick her up when she falls. She wanted a man to listen to her and not belittle her. She wanted a man to take out the trash. She wanted a man she could lean on, and he would have her back for a change. She wanted a man to take her to the movies, out to eat, dancing, take her around his family and children. She wanted a man to put her in a beautiful house, and they worked together to get it. She wanted a man where she could put her money together with his, and he wouldn't leave her dry. She wanted a trustworthy man that loved the Lord. She wanted a man that didn't cheat on her. She didn't want a man that slept around with other women and bring her a sexually transmitted disease and lie to her about being in love with her. She wanted a man not to be jealous of his children fell in love with her too. Pamela looked to God for direction in her life. She realized all she had was herself and God above. She knew God could make everything alright in her life if she kept keeping him first and looking to him for guidance and letting him direct her pathway. She knew one day, God would bring a Christian man in her life, and both of them would serve God together obediently. Pamela took a deep look at herself to cleanse her soul within after being let down from failed marriages and relationships with men. Pamela started cleansing her body of all pain, sorrow, and grief she experienced behind her and started a new one with the Lord. She knew the Lord would never let her down. Pamela knew she could not pick her a man because every man she chose for herself did not work out. So, she began to pray to the Lord for him to pick her someone for her to spend her life with. Pamela did not want to live in sin anymore. She only wanted a certain man in her life that loved the Lord like she does and processes the qualities like herself. She was not going to date a single man involved or talking to another woman, a man separated from his wife, a man getting a divorce, a married man, or living with a woman for a number of years, which is considered as a common law marriage. Pamela has grown to believe when you live in sin, you cannot see the sin you living in unless you are removed from the sin. Then you can recognize and come to terms with the wrong you've been doing. When you live in sin, this can damage your close personal relationship with God, which could make him angry with you. You definitely don't want that. Pamela knew she was not blameless from sin. Pamela believed that if you're obedient to the Lord, he'll bless you with the man he wants you to be with. She did not want to damage her close personal relationship with God that she had developed. She was going to wait on the Lord to send her somebody that would love and adore her. Some may say, "Girl you're going to be waiting for a man for a very long time." Life was hard for Pamela, but she did the best she could with the hand she was dealt with. Pamela was a good woman, but being a good woman was not enough for some men. The men Pamela became involved with just wanted sex from Pamela, and that's all they wanted from her but didn't want to offer her the whole package deal with the big house, fancy car, and the love from a man. She did not blame God for any of her mistakes because those were choices, she made by herself. She had faith and believed in God's blessed assurance. She would be okay through his word the Bible at Galatrons 4:25; we are children of a promise as long as we believe and have faith that Christ died for our sins. The only thing Pamela could do would be to straighten up her life. She was tired of those no-good men in her life that did not mean her any good, always trying to pull her down instead of helping her to go up in life. Pamela never had the advantage of having a good man in her life, like most women. She always wonders how other women got so lucky with having a man that put them in a big house, drive a fancy car, wear diamonds and could shop in the department stores and buy what they wanted. Pamela was never lucky like this. She got liars, cheaters, and profess to be a Christian man. She knew one day in her life she could have the whole enchilada or the whole package deal like other women only if she made some changes within her. She had to stop committing fornication. She had to stop cursing. She had to dress modestly. She had to stop being jealous of what someone else has because she doesn't have what they have. She had to stop clubbing every night. She had to practice being patient. She knew she needed to be spiritually involved in God's house of worship and wait on the Lord to send her a good spiritual man. She knew some men in God's house of worship were men in wolf's clothing. Pamela didn't regret any of the choices she made. She appreciated the road she traveled set by the Lord, which made her wiser and smarter. Pamela recognize her mistakes and failures in her life so she could make corrections in order for her life could head in the right direction that it should go. Pamela asked herself why she couldn't keep a man. Why she didn't have a man in her life. Did she let a man be a man when she had one? Did she play her role as a virtuous woman in Proverbs 31st Chapter? Did she complain so much when she had a man? Did she become controlling with her man? Was there a reason why men cheated on her? Did she perform well in bed besides giving head? She was glad she went through the things she went through with the men she was involved with because it taught her to be tough instead of weak behind a man. Now there were things Pamela will not tolerate or put up from a man for what she's been through. This is why Pamela did not want to fall out of the realm of the Holy spirit or damage her close personal relationship with Christ because when she became lonely and had fleshly desires to be with someone sexually. Pamela kept meditating on Christ principals in the Bible, though shall not commit fornication, and this could damage her relationship with God. This kept her from getting into trouble. Pamela never knew what it was to have a good man. She always had men with no good intentions and just rotten to the core. Men say they want something good, but do they know how to keep her? Or do they walk away for a complaining woman or woman that gives up the cookies easy to be in their lives? Pamela was good to the men in her life. She was a yes woman. She would do whatever it took to please her man only to be scar by another woman taking her man. Some women want what another woman has, but how far do another woman go to take your man. How far will a woman disrespect herself to get your man? Will she come into your home get into your bed with your man thinking he's not getting what he needs from you? When another woman takes another woman's man, karma will get you back because what you do to someone else, and it's not right in God's eye, you will reap what you sow some form or fashion. Your life will take the turn for bad instead of good. Things in your life will not work out for you. So be careful how you get someone else's man. So karma won't hit you in the bull's-eye or bite you in the butt. Pamela learned, in life, you have to face your problems head-on. You have to talk about what happened to you and when it did to move forward in your life. So you won't be locked in bondage with those problems that are bothering you. Pamela also learned about a person who hurts you, what the person did to you and how he took something away from you inside which you can't get back whether it was your virginity, self-esteem, your sanity, your dignity or just needed someone to show you love in a wholesome way, where there's no harm. Whatever or however you got hurt, or someone has done something bad to you, You have to keep your hands on the steering wheel and not swerving but gearing the car steadily so you can stay in your lane and focus on what's ahead on the side of you and behind you looking in your rear view mirror at all times. This is what Pamela did, and she found happiness, peace, and the truth in her life. Now Pamela life has a true meaning and making sense. Now, Pamela looks forward to a relationship that will last forever with endurance. She knows there is no perfect relationship or man. She decided to put everything behind her and start a fresh new beginning for what's ahead. Had not Pamela put herself back together with God's help, she would have been like Humpty Dumpty had a big fall, and all the king horsemen could not put Humpty Dumpty back together again. Although Pamela had a past, she thought she never could get rid of until she came toe to toe with Lord. He changed her whole make up. She realized you couldn't start a new relationship until you have gotten rid of the old relationship. Then God can bless you with whom he wants to make you happy with continue to have patience and wait on the Lord. He changed her whole lifestyle of doing things. He made her into a new creature of Christ. Whatever past she had, she was able to put it behind her. She saw something better God had in store for her. No more hurt, let down, and pain she experienced with different men that were going to hold her back from what blessing God had in store for her. She treasured her love with the Lord. She could really and truly say no more drama, no more pain, no more hurt from a man, but only happiness, peace, and serenity are what Pamela received from the Lord above. All that you have read about Pamela in this book. This is considerately Pamela's past life that she had put behind her. Now she has developed a relationship with the Lord that she treasures devotedly. Ladies, if you have a good man or husband in your life, learn to appreciate him and not take him for granted, everybody's not blessed to have something good to share their world with. Pamela's world was once in a world spin, nothing in her life with a man turn out good as you have read. She felt her life was just a mess when it came to a man, but deep within, she knew she couldn't live her life without a man in it. She never let a man find her. She always went looking for a man. This was Pamela's downfall. Pamela's life was a journey, and you know what, love is a journey. Where love leads, you let God guide you. If Pamela had done this first in her life, she would have avoided all those wrong choices she made with men. She would have been able to live a happy, fulfilled life if she would have relied on God to choose her a mate. Remember, God can't bless you with something new if you still dibbling and dabbling with that old stuff. So, let the old go and bring in something new. Then you will rejoice in God's goodness. That's why she wrote this book for you to look to God for guidance and within your soul for a soul mate to be found.

STEPS TO TREASURE LOVE

A RELATIONSHIP IS WHAT YOU MAKE IT AND WHAT IT BECOMES. If it's over, it's over; if it's lovable, it's lovable; if it's dear to your heart, then it's dear to your heart; if it's the drama, then it becomes drama; if it's deceitful, then it's deceitful. If it's full of game, then it's full of game; if it's not truthful, then it's a lie. It is what it is. This is what the relationship becomes. The author wants her newfound readers to improve in their relationships make it last forever not to walk out immediately when it gets tough. A relationship is a give-and-take thing. You have to work things out even when you are upset and don't want too. Relationships take hard work. Something you heard over and over probably from your friends, parents, grandparents, pastors, and it is true. Anything you want to work, you got to work hard at it like you go to work to achieve outstanding performance as an employee. This is the attitude you want to take in a relationship. You may argue with your mate, fuss, and fight, curse one another out but don't leave the person for anything in the world. In relationships need to be in it for the long haul not giving up when there's a minor problem. You need to be trying to work out each obstacle you go through together, not separated. We can definitely say some men do not think like this. A man's line of thinking is so way different than a woman. For instance, it's so easy for some men to leave a woman at a drop of a dime without giving their feelings any consideration at all or that woman. When we first meet a man, the relationship starts off like a fairy tale romance. You fall in love suddenly. You're having sex more and more with one another. He takes you out to eat often, to the movies, and talking with you all the time until the next morning. He makes sure your needs are financially taken care of. But the time you move in with him, things change. Then you began to see the person wasn't the person you thought to be after all. You began to see the person like their real selves, the person they really are. You might have even paid a fortune on the wedding of your dreams. Do not divorce or walk out on your loved one for the way they changed. See, the person never changed. You were just caught up, you saw it, but you dismiss what you did see. Deal with the change you didn't see at first and conform to accepting a person for who they are. Once you are with that person, no two people are the same. Before a marriage, ask the right questions concerning the individual and provoke the person, if necessary, to see if they are violent if you intend to be with someone like that go the long haul and not the short-haul in relationships or marriages. A diamond in the ruff is something to treasure. When you want to be with a person, be there for the right reasons, not the wrong reasons. We look for the inner beauty in a man. We look for love from a man. We never think about what we want from a man. Sometimes we look for sexual intimacy with a man who controls the love that may develop. Sometimes if we are with an older man, he may not be able to get hard during sex. Remember, sex is not everything because if a man cares about you emotionally and physically, has your back, there for you rain, sleet, and snow, listens to you, helps you financially, and has God in his life if he's spiritual. Then this is a good man because as a woman gets older, sex may not be the number one desire in her life too. With a woman, sex does fade gradually in time. That's why it so important to have the right man in your life. A man should love and care for a woman, please them, communicate with them, and provide for them. A woman is very courageous, self-willed, and has plenty of determination to make things happen for themselves and put up with problems arises from a man. A woman has good characteristics and traits about themselves when handling different situations that come up concerning having a man in their lives, being with a man, and what you got through to make the relationship works. God made a woman from the Rib of Adam to compliment, satisfy, be a companion, friend to a man, wife, or an acquaintance. Some women don't have to go through anything because they have a good man, which God bless them with. They only reap happiness and smiles. Woman endures so much often not given any credit for staying regardless of the situation is unbearable sometimes. In a relationship, there are really issues that will cause a person to start having differences or problems in a relationship.

1. Another man or woman on the side
2. Money problems

3. Family too much in your personal business
4. Unemployment

Before the relationship gets out of hand, you need to fix it, make amends, talk about what went wrong, work it out, cough it up or admit to it and do what you say and mean the words you say. If you cannot talk about it. Then you didn't mean the words you say. Though some marriages and relationships, we just need to endure the ups and downs, sometimes you get in a hole being in debt when both of you are working, always borrowing money from others because your finances are messed up, crying because you're heartbroken your mate has cheated on you, no gas to put in your car until you get paid again, can't buy groceries for your household, penny punching bills not enough to pay the full amount and cannot go to the beauty shop to get your hair done because times may be tough for a little while. We need to stick to our relationship like super glue, not trying to rush out of it. A relationship is not based on choices and decisions on who you want to be with. Relationships are based on the right choices and the right decisions of whom you want to be. How do you know if a man loves you? Just cook him a meal, and if he gives you his last bite of food, he loves you. How does a man know a good woman? By the fruits, she bears in the topic of a virtuous woman in this book. What do men look for in a relationship or marriage? Men look for a woman to be lovable, respectable, trustworthy, understanding, have a job, do everything together, and having things in common with one another. What does a woman look for in a man? A woman looks for in a man is love, understanding, for a not to hold back his feelings because he scared of fallen in love with her and getting hurt. Some relationships people are involved in its either for love or lust. Some relationships may leave you distraught, disconnected, and devastated but at the same time can bring you joy, happiness, and peace you so been looking for. Some women want a sense of belonging to a man. Never thinking about if this man is really for them. Some women today will be with a man that does not work, abuse them physically and mentally. This person does not love them at all. Some women want a man to just to fill the void in their lives. A woman wants a man to compliment them. A woman wants a man to tell them they look good. A woman should value themselves and demand respect from these men. A relationship needs the Lord in it as well as trust, respect, love, forgiveness, communication, honesty, understanding, longevity, acceptance, devotion, purification, balancing, and sexiness for it to work. Let's start with the Lord. We need to depend on the Lord for guidance to work out any problem that comes up in a relationship. If God is in your relationship or marriage whenever a problem exists, we need to learn to go to God in prayer. Both of you, when praying, hold hands, kneel on the floor together or sit on the couch together. Prayer is powerful, Prayer will heal any situation in trouble and turn the relationship around for the better. Then after prayer, kiss and hug one another to seal your prayer request. You have to have faith. This defines relationships. Faith helps you both stand-alone together on God's word. You do not have to visualize the Lord's promise. See God's word helps strengthens your faith in your relationship for you to believe in and make it work as long as both your hearts are in it. Persons contemplating a relationship or marriage adhere to the words in 1 Peter 3:1-7 for wives to be in subjection to their husbands and let the man have a pure heart with a meek and quiet spirit within. Husbands should show consideration to their wives being a weaker vessel. Trust is also something a person has to earn, regain sometimes, and have confidence when a person may love you, beat on you and cheat on you. When you trust someone, you do not ever have to wonder what he's doing and what he's not doing or where he's at any time day or night relying wholeheartedly on your loved one without any doubt. When you trust in God and read the scriptures on a daily basis, this brings obedience to God's word, the Bible where you come into the realm of God's plan. By being obedient in your personal walk with God, you are trusting God will bless you and bring you a wonderful mate. Without trust in a relationship, there's no relationship. Respect is knowing your mate is going to cheat on you due to his human urges as a man, but he respects you enough not to bring his infidelity home. Respect is also when you take your mate's opinion into consideration and not just what you think about a circumstance. Just stop, listen, and take notice of what's being discussed from the both of you and make the final decision about your circumstance together. You need to keep in mind respect also comes into play when you come home at a decent hour when hanging out with your friends instead of coming home in the wee hours in the morning when daylight catches you and you show no consideration to call your mate to let them know you are okay, alive and still breathing. Love with your whole heart and put God first, then love the man or woman next. Some mate in a relationship love because the sex is great and nothing else. Love is also something a person wants badly but don't know how to get it or find it. When you find love, you have to hold on tight with every clinch of your claws. Some mate's love is based on the person being a helper in the relationship, which consists of ironing, cooking, cleaning, fixing things around the house that breaks down just being responsible. Love is tolerating one another even when you don't want too. You can love a mate unconditionally, whether the relationship is good or bad. It's nothing your mate can do is wrong. Love brings about companionship with one another for a lifetime. For whatever reason, a person's love it should come from the heart. The heart is where your deepest feelings come from. Forgiveness hurts, but you have to let God take away the hurt from you through prayer and his word the Bible. Forgiveness also comes into play when your mate does something contrary to the relationship where you feel is unforgivable. You should think about how many times we ask Christ to forgive us for the sins that we commit. Communication is important in a relationship. It helps you to know what your mate is thinking and feeling inside. Communication helps you to talk freely about anything without the other person throwing what you both talked about in your face. Sometimes you may not communicate all the time, but communication helps you to get to know one another to see what's on a person's mind and bring you closer together as one. Honesty is the best policy because there are no lies between both of you; only the truth is always revealed. When two people are not honest, this can separate the two. When you're honest, there are no secrets hidden in the dark that can destroy your relationship if reveal beforehand to your mate. Honesty keeps you real with yourself, revealing your inner self in how you feel about things, your prospect on issues before you, and what you don't like. Honesty also helps you to say what you mean and mean what you say, so there are no hard feelings between both of you. Understanding is being sympathetic and having a listening ear even when you don't want to be this way. Understanding is about being supportive standing in that person's corner when you disagree in decision making and choices being made. Understanding helps to deal with one another in their line of thinking. Especially if a wrong decision is made, you don't have to blame anyone just be understanding.

Longevity is where you learn to forgive, forget, and move on to remain together —putting up with differences and problems that surface in a relationship taking the bitter with the sweet and remaining together. A person may cheat but refuses to leave the person they're with no matter what because he believes in staying. Whatever happens in a situation at hand can be worked out together to bring about longevity never leaving, getting separated or acceptance is accepting a person for who they are not trying to change the person how you want the person to be if they wear jeans, not suits, do not know how to coordinate the color of clothes, stutter in their speech, can't read or write and what religion they're in. Sometimes we do accept what a person is telling us even though you know they're lying because you love them and want to make the relationship work. When we're in a relationship or marriage and it's hard to reason with our mates when we are going through the motions, we need to accept the person we love, faults, flaws, friction, and mistakes to be made.

Devotion can be brought about if you constantly pray to keep the relationship together and study together as a couple for Bible principles to reflect in your inner lives. When you look to God above the heavens, he's devoted to fixing up, troubles, or problems created in relationships or marriages. Some mates or love couples should always depend on one another in decision making. This means don't tell your family or friends what's going on in your household but keep it between you, husband, and God above —praying over the matter at hand. You need your other partner as your helper. You should not permit anyone to tear the both of you apart from one another having that clinging spirit of never letting go. Devotion is also caring and loving the person you love when they have a heart attack, stroke, diagnosed with cancer, paralyzed from the waist down, shot, or stabbed multiple times just any life-threatening illness. You're not walking out on them but staying there to care for them.

Purification is when you think of being purified, it's being unblemished, totally clean, and no ingredients have to be added. No man can be pure because they're not God. We as Christians can only strive and work at being pure, keeping in line with God's Word the Bible, but we will never get there unless we die, then God can resurrect us in his own like image, then purification will begin to abide in you. While we're still living on earth as humans, we want to keep in mind what the Psalmist David ask God at Psalm 51:10 to create in you a clean heart and renew a right spirit within you. In other words, relationships you want God to create within you is to be a good husband to your mate with a clean and pure heart. No more cheating, beating, or hitting on her, cursing her out but being true, unadulterated, clean and sincere in every aspect. You just being faithful to the person you love and also trying to change your line of thinking watching what you say forth from your mouth always staying within God's Word the Bible and having a sincerity heart displays purification.

Balancing is something hard to obtain when a family is involved. Your work schedule is hard to spend with your loved one because of the children, but you have to set a time aside for you and him to bond together without the children being around to keep your relationship together. In life today, you want to balance your home, life, children, career, and church. Make sure time is spent with your spouse or loved one. If one travels the week and be home on the weekend before the person goes back to work. Make sure extra time is spent with your spouse or loved one. Balance out that time spent with the person you love and know the stress of work. Kids can take a toll on you. Like putting your fruits on the scale to find how many pounds it goes too. You may have to take some fruits out to keep its balance to one, two, or three pounds. In relationships, you have to balance the time spent with one another. Balancing every hour or minutes for both of you to connect with one another when the kids are asleep and when you not at work. If you are too busy you have to stop what you are doing, find the time, search for time, make it happen to spend time with the person you love.

Sexiness is what you took to get him with your looks, sexy clothes, lingerie, sexy panties and bras, and tight clothes. The same stuff you did to get him. The same stuff you have to do to keep him, so your man won't sway away, and that's the real deal. A little sexiness makes your man love the skin you are in. Sexiness keeps the flame and spark burning. Definitely keep up your appearance, hair and nails done, wearing sexy lace panties and bras, girdles, eyelashes, weave hair, makeup, lip gloss, and low cut blouses keep the pizazz about you going which got his attention in the first place. You need to glue your body to his body. Like pin your body on his donkey tail. You don't have to be thin to keep your man just be you. When you find a rare one here, and Christ lives inside of him. It shows what type of person they are if they're not lying, cheating, and beating the one they love. When you treasure love, you seek it, you keep it, and you adore it never letting go. You got to grab the love and keep it dear to your heart, never losing sight of what makes you happy. Love will prevail and come to you eventually. Some men do love you. Sometimes we love people that do not love us. Happiness should be the key to any ones love life in treasuring love. If you treasure disappointment, it will wipe you right out of here. Never finding the love meant for you but accepting what you have for now, and that's just not good enough. If you are disappointed in love, let it go. It will only destroy what type of person you are on the inside. This is what you need to avoid. A relationship is a relationship you so desire and becomes disappointed when you can't find it. When you try everything to make it work, and it still fails. If you not treated right in a relationship, disappointment creeps in. The old saying is that you have four senses that are always the best senses in relationships. Which is think, pray, ponder, and decide. This is what we should do when trying to make changes in our daily lives. Treasure disappointment can always hurt within and can be very devastating to your soul sometimes, you can't bounce back, but there's always hope. If a man or woman can't hold you up, mentor your soul inside, be your inspiration, communicates with you, love you for who you are and not what they want you to be, accept what the person has provided for you within that man or woman means of provisions and not swerve from the love you have developed for on too another one. Then your love for whoever you're with will not be disappointed. It still can be treasured from the way you have grown, starting with a deep root planted in the ground. By all means, do not forget there's no perfect mate, no perfect relationship, and no perfect marriage. Everything takes work by each other for a relationship to sustain. Relationship is a hard course to keep up with or be in. It takes time, money, love, and patience to maintain a relationship. It's something you have to constantly work on a daily basis if you want it to work. Love is a precious thing like a jewel keeping it clean and polish where it sparkles and shines all day long. See, love makes a relationship without it a relationship doesn't exist. Never give up on your mate you been with for many moons because the sparks were just gone out. It can always be relit. When we marry, we have to learn to stay together with one another not giving up on one another, because you have grown apart or the fire went out. Never ever take another person from someone else because it will never work out that person will eventually leave you for someone else or go back to the person they left you for. Then you right where you started at first but only to have thrown away all those years spent together. We got to get back to where our forefathers used to be like staying together to death do you apart set forth in the Bible.

If a person keeps God in their relationship, you will never go wrong. The relationship or marriage will never get off course or spoil like milk does where you have to throw it away. To maintain a relationship, you have to keep prayer in it, praying morning and evening, communicating with one another, and considering how that person may feel about something not just yourself or how you feel but compromising before you make a decision that can affect the both of you. Sex definitely plays an important role in the relationship or marriage even when you don't want to have sex. You just have it anyway because believe it or not, your relationship won't last. If your mate is not having sex with you, he or she is having sex with somebody. If you're not mowing your grass, somebody else definitely is.

This is why it's so important to adhere to what the Bible says at Proverbs 28:13 give up your sins and stop hiding your sins. He that covers his sin shall not prosper. If you are committing fornication or adultery, stop doing this so God can bless you. When you are having sex, too many feelings get involved instead of you holding out on sex until you married. Exodus 20:17 helps us to appreciate thou shall not lust or wish for our neighbor's house, wife, maidservant, and his manservant anything that is his neighbor. All love and fair game in treasuring love for hooking the right man. I used to think you had to go out and find love because love is not going to show up on your doorstep, but now I know by love being treasured as a disappointment with me I believe love will come to you. You just have to be patient and wait on Lord. Remember to always do everything together, going to parties, church, bible study, grocery store, movies, visiting family members whether you want to or not, concerts, plays, comedy shows, playing video games at home, gambling at casinos, holding hands, plenty of kisses and telling one another constantly how much you love each other. All of the above helps you to maintain a wholesome relationship where you can be treasuring love and not be treasuring disappointment.

A VIRTUOUS WOMAN

A virtuous woman fears God, does what's right, and lines her life up with the Ten Commandments to not sin. A virtuous woman is a good, clean, dependable, happy, and contented woman.

A virtuous woman respects herself, and she will not bring shame upon herself, her values, her beliefs, and her faith. She will do everything in Christ Jesus to stay in his grace.

A virtuous woman, if she saw you without water, she would give you water. If she saw you without food, she would give you food. If she saw you without clothes, she would give you clothes. If she saw you without shoes, she would give you shoes.

A virtuous woman prays daily on a routine basis that she displays Christ-like qualities set in Galatians 5:21-26 fruitage of God's spirit. You will know a virtuous woman by the fruit she bears.

A virtuous woman put on God's complete suit of armor before she leaves the house to do her daily chores or go to work.

A virtuous woman never raises her voice. She's slow to anger. She doesn't hold grudges or thinks evil thoughts.

A virtuous woman cooks for her mate, cleans her house, cherishes her kids, iron clothes, wash clothes, treats him better than herself, and makes sure he's fed when he comes home.

A virtuous woman will never take another woman's man or husband.

A virtuous woman does not curse but says everything in a mild temper and a loving tone of voice. You will know a virtuous woman in the way she carries herself because her spirit will be calm and at peace when you notice her. A virtuous woman will always think of ways to please God, husband, and children through prayer, supplication, and fasting.

A virtuous woman has nothing but good inside of her heart. She respects everything God stands for.

A virtuous woman can handle and deal with a lot of obstacles and dilemmas that come at her at one time without freaking out. She goes to the rock to handle whatever problems she's faced with.

A virtuous woman is awesome, rare, and hard to find. If you come across a virtuous woman, you need to try to get with her and keep her because a woman like her, only comes once in a lifetime.

A virtuous woman can satisfy her mate if he tells her and shows her how to please him, so he wont commit adultery or fornication.

A virtuous woman is like a jewel, a strand of pearls connecting the dots in a man's life to completely fulfill his life with deep satisfaction he longed and desire for.

A virtuous woman never steps out of her boundaries but stays in God's guidelines set out in the Bible at Proverbs 31:10-31 showing her to be priceless, trustworthy, good, strong, work hard with her hands, compliments her husband, wisdom, speak kind words and fears God.

A virtuous woman has a forgiving heart that lets things go to keep her mind at peace with God.

A virtuous woman is appreciative and grateful to God for sending her a mate. When she gets him as a husband, she treats him right, not cheat but trust and respect him as the man of the household, not belittle him for what he may not be able to provide for her.

A virtuous woman listens to words of wisdom given to her by elderly women in making smart choices and the right decisions to make sure she stays on the straight and narrow pathway during her course of life.

A virtuous woman recognizes Christ's position and puts him first, not her mate or husband.

A virtuous woman doesn't get angry where the rage comes out but speaks softly, gentle, and mild-tempered with loving-kindness.

A virtuous woman does not mind going the extra mile to get things done properly.

A virtuous woman never allows herself to be mistreated by a man.

A virtuous woman knows a mate wouldn't be where he is today without her being in his life because the virtuous woman will look out for his best interest, and she knows she's a blessing to him.

A virtuous woman is one that will care for you and not leave you when you get sick, have an illness, have an accident where it could leave you paralyzed.

Ruth was a virtuous woman because she just up and left her homeland, followed Naomi to a strange land, and accept her God. By her doing this, Ruth received her blessing in being Boaz's wife. Naomi knew who Boaz was in the beginning.

The Samaritan woman from the well was a virtuous woman because she showed her respect for Jesus, his position, and who he was. See, the Samaritan and the Jews didn't get along or like one another. When Jesus asked the Samaritan woman for a drink of water, she asked Jesus why you ask me for water. She didn't want to draw water for Jesus in Jacob's well, but she did. Queen of Sheba was a virtuous woman because she was obedient to God by listening to God in saving her people from being annulated. She got in with the king. The king fell in love with her and married her. Then this was when God revealed to her how to save her people.

Mary was a virtuous woman because when the Angel appeared before Mary, letting her know she was going to give birth to a baby being conceived by the Holy Spirit. She listened attentively and was very obedient to what the Angel told her. Mary knew she could be stone to death by not being married. Mary and Joseph communicated with one another what was revealed from the angel. Both of them worked the situation out with togetherness. See, God chose Mary to carry the son of man in her womb. This says a lot for Mary's character for God to choose her. Mary displayed obedience, goodness, and acceptance in carrying the son of man in her womb.

We need to follow these footsteps of these examples of virtuous women set in the Bible which will make us different in our conquest for a good man to come into our lives to love, respect and be faithful to us, for him to see us as a blessing to his life.

TWELVE COMMANDMENTS

Thou shall not sleep with another man's wife
Thou shall be loyal, honest and trustworthy
Thou shall be respectful to one another
Thou shall love your love one with your whole heart and soul
Thou shall not lust behind or think about another woman while you have a wife
Thou shall not be manipulative in your relationship
Thou shall not beat thy love one but beat them with words from the Bible
Thou shall not lie or be deceitful
Thou shall be a forgiver of wrong doing like Christ forgives you every day
Thou shall not be an arguer but a listener
Thou shall be with someone that makes you happy not unhappy
Thou shall not be a nagger but a complementar

THESE ARE TWELVE COMMANDMENTS A PERSON SHOULD WORK at in a relationship to maintain it. These twelve commandments should be easy to follow, like a person driving a car without your hand being on the steering wheel. You constant have to pay attention where you're going to not crash into another car. In relationships, you have to steer it onto the right path for it to work with both hands on the steering wheel.

POETRY OF LOVE

Love is something everybody wants to experience
Love is something you can't put a price tag on
Love is something that blossoms in time
Love is something we long for
Love is something we wish we had sometimes
Love will make you cry sometimes
Love gives you peace and serenity in our lives
Love makes you smile
Love makes you count your blessings
Love makes you get right with the one whom you want to share your life with
Love makes you be patient with whom you share your world with
Love makes you wanna spend time, every minute, second and hour of the day with your love one
Love sometimes makes you miss the person you love that's so far away
Love makes you be thankful for what you do have today and not what you want tomorrow
Love is blind like looking through a looking glass but can't see through it starring you right in your face
Love makes you thank the Lord for whom he sends you in our lives today
Love sometimes wanna make you scream and tell the world "I'm In Love"
Love makes you think about what you let go and how to get it back

IN THE END LOVE BRINGS ABOUT COMFORT AND HAPPINESS WHICH our family members, friends, children can't give us if it was not for love where would we be.

RELATIONSHIPS

Relationship is a Relationship that everybody long for not to be an open door.

Relationship is when you can look a man in the eye and know he sparks your ignition.

Relationship is the one can treasure love and not treasure disappointment because, through Christ, all things are possible.

Relationship is when you can close your eyes and dream of the one you love.

Relationship makes you happy, sad, and glad because you gave it a try and not say bye-bye.

Relationship is one you go through the long-distance and not give in to the short distance.

Relationship you can take walks in the parks with the one you can talk too.

Relationship can mean the world to you if you let your feelings overflow in you.

Relationship is a Relationship you can hooray because the Lord bless you with a winner for all eternity.

Relationship is a relationship when you do not have to look over your shoulders because trust dwells there.

Relationship is a Relationship you can brag to your friends and family because the Lord saved him just for you.

Relationship is a Relationship when you do not have to worry about having one foot in the door, and one foot out the door once you in can close the door can take a seat because the relationship is complete.

Relationship can be whatever you want it to be as long as you can say please when appropriate.

Relationship can last to eternity as long as you can turn your head to the cheating game.

Relationship is a Relationship that can grab you by the hand lead to the path of love and commitment.

THANK YOU'S

I WANT TO THANK MY LORD AND SAVIOR FOR GIVING ME THIS GIFT to write to others by telling the truth about issues that come onto our lives and not sugarcoating any words and keeping it real, simple, and plain. I thank the Lord for giving me the strength and endurance to finish this book while working on a job. I want to thank the Lord for showing me grace and mercy through the road I travel going through many storms, trials, obstacles, the distress which came into my life, which made me humble and grateful for what I have and do not have. I want to thank the Lord for letting me share my life story with you all and not feel ashamed. I want to thank the Lord for instilling in me those qualities of love, contentment, and humbleness. I'm just plain grateful to God for what he allowed me to go through in my life to get to this point. I want to thank Pastor Amos of Liberty Baptist church on Fonden Street in Houston, Tx, for instilling in me Bible principles that changed the person within me to a new creature in Christ. I want to thank Pastor Bryon Stephenson at the Fort Bend Church in Houston, Texas, for his words of encouragement. He would always say, "No matter what you're going through, always smile and rejoice while going through your storm." This kept me strong inside, never letting me give up on my dream because storms won't last forever, it'll be over soon. I want to thank my mom for contributing to my success in life. She made me a strong, willed, and determined individual in my life. I want the world to know my mother was a remarkable and very beautiful woman that's where I get my looks from. She transformed her life for the goodness of her community. She owned her own mattress company in Houston, Texas. She was the first Black woman to be a millionaire. She contributed to many political campaigns. The first black woman to bring into play a foundation for women and children with AIDS and people would not give her credit for this. I truly love my mother, no matter what. She always made sure I had the best when I was grown. She gave me black art, diamonds, and furs. She always told me God bless a child that got its own. She told me if you want something in life, you got to make it happen and go get it and don't give up because she didn't raise quitters. I still love her, and if it wasn't for her, I would have never found my gift in life. I realized in life, I only have one mother, so I have to make the best of a mother and daughter relationship. She will always have my love. I Love you, mommie. I want to thank Pastor Brooks at the Word O Truth Revival Church in Houston, Tx, where she prophesized my life and told me the blessing the Lord has for me. She told me to stretch out my hands up toward the heavens and grab my blessing down from the spiritual realm to the natural realm. I want to thank both of my fathers in heaven. One was my real biological father who, was a well-known chef whom I never got to know. My other father was a reverend who raised me, and this is where I got my spiritual gift from him. I want to thank the late Reverend Michael Pradia, my dad, for passing on his spiritual gift to me to help others to come to know Christ, and to know him, it's never too late to come to know the Master above whom has made you from a babe. It's never too late to develop a relationship with God, whether young or old. I miss my dad, he's the only true friend I had here on earth that truly looked out for me wholeheartedly. I solely now depend on my Master above to look after me like I'm his child and to provide for me. Look how far he has brought me. God is awesome. Never give up on him because he will never give up on you. He'll take you places you never seen or been before. He'll make the little faith you have grew bigger, stronger, inward, and outward. All it takes is believing and trusting in your Heavenly Father Above. I want to thank all my readers who purchase my book receive a powerful message from my writings to help inspire you to reach your dreams, goals, make you a better person within your soul improve your relationship with God or with your husband and get all the blessing God has in store for you. Whatever mistakes you made in the past, you can always move forward on a clean slate, leave the past in the past. Just always remember you can be whatever you want to be in your life, whatever situation you may be in, whatever problem you have in life, no matter if you fail, you can always at any moment pick yourself back up do it again and strive forward on a clean slate. May God bless each and every one of you. Thank You from the Bottom of My Heart! This is my story. Thank you, Lord above for making me whole with a clean and pure heart in your worship. I also want to thank my whole Pradia family, my lovely nieces, and my nephews. I also want to thank everybody who helped me to get here with your prayers. I want to thank my wonderful publishing company for believing in me and taking a chance with me. Please always follow your dreams, no matter what, because dreams do come true. My scripture verses and passages come from the Holy Bible, King James Version, Nelson 544BG.

www.ingramcontent.com/pod-product-compliance
Lightning Source LLC
LaVergne TN
LVHW091545060526
838200LV00036B/714

ABRAHAM LINCOLN THE ATHLETE

A Proud Competitor, but a Humble Sportsman

JASON H. SILVERMAN

Charleston, SC
www.PalmettoPublishing.com

Abraham Lincoln the Athlete
Copyright © 2022 by Jason H. Silverman

All rights reserved

This book or any portion thereof may not be reproduced or used in any manner whatsoever without the express written permission of the publisher except for the use of brief quotations in a book review.

First Edition

Printed in the United States

Paperback ISBN: 978-1-68515-124-9

"*The better part of one's life consists of his friendships.*"
—Abraham Lincoln to Joseph Gillespie (1849)

Dedicated to Dick Davis, my dear friend and my éminence grise

IF LINCOLN WERE AN ATHLETE TODAY
From the Cleveland Plain Dealer, 1971
by Robert Dolgan

Abraham Lincoln, the sixteenth president of the United States was born 162 years ago. He was known as a fine athlete in his youth, but there was no organized sport at the time. In a whimsical moment, I found myself thinking about the kind of athlete he'd be if he were alive today. This is how I envision it:

HE'D NEVER ARGUE with umpires or referees, but he'd know the rule book by heart, and if an official made a mistake, he'd point it out to him, reciting the rule and quoting the section and paragraph.

HIS DIGNITY and demeanor would be such that the referee, instead of being angry, would thank him for correcting him. "You're right, Abe," he'd say.

HE'D START OUT as an end in football for he was six-feet, four-inches tall and pretty skinny. But later in his career, he'd be switched to quarterback, because 'he'd be the smartest player in the league.

HE WOULDN'T START FIGHTS on the field, but if a battle began he'd grab hold of one of the antagonists by the scruff of the neck and the seat of the pants and run him out of the melee.

HE'D NEVER PLAY DIRTY but if he tackled, you would hurt for days.

HE'D TALK WITH THE FANS before the game, and he'd never be too busy to sign an autograph afterward.

THE SPORTSWRITERS WOULD LOVE him because he'd make such good copy and provide them with good quotes. Also, he could spell out the big words for them.

HE WOULDN'T HANG OUT only with the big stars on the team, but he would be just as likely to pal around with the lowliest rookie.

HE'D NEVER BE a clubhouse lawyer, but he'd be able to understand the players who hated the manager and try to explain to them that the "skipper" wasn't such a bad guy.

HE'D NEVER MAKE commercials if he didn't really use the product he was endorsing.

HE WOULDN'T BE one of those athletes who gets his hair styled and would writhe at the thought of sitting under a hair net in the barbershop. He'd have a beard, though, and would insist on his right to wear it.

HE WOULDN'T HIRE A LAWYER to do his salary negotiation for him, because he'd be smarter than the lawyer.

HE WOULDN'T TRY to hold up the owner for a huge salary, but he'd want his fair share.

HE'D BE A PITCHER in baseball, and his pants would 'be too short, his sleeves too long, and his cap too small.

HE'D HAVE A BLAZING fast ball and perfect control, and he'd shamble off the field in a comical, slow way after striking out the side with the bases loaded.

HE'D NEVER REACT to the crowd too much, whether things were going well or badly, but sometimes he'd tip his cap after a particularly exciting feat.

HE'D BREAK THE COLOR LINE and ask to room with a black player on trips, but first he'd check with the black player and make sure it would be okay with him.

HE'D BE THE MOST POPULAR MAN in sports, and when fans would tell him that he could be elected mayor if he ran, he'd just smile at them and wink.

TABLE OF CONTENTS

Preface: *"A Proud Competitor, but a Humble Sportsman": Abraham Lincoln, the Athlete* ··································1

Introduction: *Springfield in the Time of Lincoln* ···············13

Chapter One: *"I Have Seen Mr. Lincoln Go into This Sport with a Great Deal of Zest": Lincoln and Town Ball (Baseball)* ············37

Chapter Two: *"I Am the Big Buck of the Lick": Lincoln and Wrestling* ·66

Chapter Three: *"He Could Beat Any of the Boys…": Lincoln and Fives (Handball)* ································104

Chapter Four: *"He Kept Us Small Boys Running in All Directions…": Lincoln, Marbles, and Bowling* ······················123

Chapter Five: *"The 'Great Canon Game'": Lincoln and Billiards* ····137

Chapter Six: *"He Played a Fair Game, but Not a First-Rate One": Lincoln and Chess and Checkers* ·····················166

Chapter Seven: *"One of the Abes was Frightened": Lincoln and Horseback Riding* ····························180

Chapter Eight: *"Mr. Lincoln Never Missed an Opportunity to Join in a Game of Quoits": Lincoln the Athlete* ·236

Acknowledgments ·256
Note on Sources ·260
About the Author ·275

Preface

"A PROUD COMPETITOR BUT A HUMBLE SPORTSMAN":

Abraham Lincoln, the Athlete

"For such an awkward fellow, I am pretty sure-footed. It used to take a pretty dexterous man to throw me," recalled President Lincoln on the night of his reelection as President in 1864. *"I remember, the evening of the day in 1858, that decided the contest for the Senate between Mr Douglas and myself, was something like this, dark, rainy & gloomy. I had been reading the returns and had ascertained that we had lost the Legislature and started to go home. The path had been worn hog-back & was slippery. My foot slipped from under me, knocking the other oneout of the way, but I recovered myself & lit square, and I said to myself, 'It's a slip and not a fall.'"*

For Mr. Lincoln, athletics was not just a way of explaining his political situation. It was a way into politics. He was naturally competitive. Dennis Hanks, a relative who grew up with Lincoln in Indiana, recalled that Lincoln *"was ambitious*

& determined & when he attempted to Excel by man or boy while whole soul & his Energies were bent on doing it."

Harvey Lee Ross remembered: *New Salem, at the time Mr. Lincoln lived there, was a great place of resort for the young men to gather on Saturdays. The Clary Grove boys, the Island Grove boys, the Sangamon River boys, and the Sand Ridge boys, each designated by the part of the country from which they came, would gather there to indulge in horse racing, foot racing, wrestling, jumping, ball playing and shooting at a mark. Mr. Lincoln would generally take a lay-off for part of the day and join in the sport. He was very stout and active and was a match for any of them. I do not think he bet on any of the games or races, but they had so much confidence in his honesty, and that he would see fair play, that he was often chose as a judge to determine the winner, and his decisions were always regarded as just."*

Most celebrated was his 1831 wrestling match with Jack Armstrong, leader of the Clary Grove boys. One New Salem resident recalled that Jack Armstrong *"was considered the best man in all this country for a scuffle. In a wrestle, shoulder or back hold, there was only now and then a man he couldn't get away with. When Lincoln came into this country there was a crowd called the Clary Grove boys, who pretty much had their way, and Jack Armstrong was the leader among them. Most every new man who came into the neighborhood had to be tried. Lincoln was pretty stout and the boys made it up to see what there was in him. They got him to talking about wrestling one day, and he said he could throw any man around there. Bill Clary kept at Lincoln until he got him into a bet of $5. Then he put Jack Armstrong against him. They were pretty well matched, but Abe was a good deal taller and could bend over Jack."* William

Greene recalled that *"after they had worked for a long time, [Jack] caught him by leg [and] got better of him. L said if they wanted to fight he would try that. Jack quailed and called it drawn."*

The match has been the subject of numerous and very different versions. Daniel Green Burner remembered: *"I suppose you have heard of Lincoln's wrestling match with Jack Armstrong. I saw part of that. Armstrong was one of the Clary Grove gang and it was their habit to initiate newcomers into town. Lincoln was tall, ungainly, awkward, and was bantered by this crowd. These fellows would come into New Salem, get drunk, and would handle a novice roughly. Lincoln finally wagered Armstrong $10 that he could find a man who could throw him. The challenge was accepted and the next Saturday was set for the time. When the Armstrong gang arrived Lincoln told them that his man had not yet come. They waited around and became impatient and finally Armstrong demanded of Lincoln the $10. Lincoln replied: 'Look here, Jack, my man isn't here yet, but rather than lose that $10 I will wrestle with you myself.' "They went at it, and Lincoln just fooled with Armstrong until he had tired him completely out. Then he swung his long leg over Armstrong's neck and made Armstrong run around holding him up in that position. Jack finally begged off, admitting he was beaten and offered Lincoln the $10, which Lincoln refused to take. The two were ever afterward warm friends. I saw all the last part of this match, and it was highly amusing. The story about Lincoln rubbing smartweed in his face is untrue."*

"Uncle Johnny" Porter recalled: *"They wrestled a good while, and I think Abe had thrown Jack two points and was likely to get him down. Clary, I expect, thought he was in danger of losing his money for he called out: 'Throw him anyway, Jack.' At that Jack loosed his back hold and grabbed Abe by the thigh threw him in a second. Abe got up pretty mad. He didn't say much, but he told somebody that if it ever came right, he would give Bill Clary a good licking. You see the hold Jack took was fair in a scuffle, but not in a wrestle, and they were wrestling. After that Abe was considered one of the Clary's Grove boys. I believe they called him president of their club. Abe and Jack got to be great friends and Abe used to stay at Jack's house."*

Thompson G. Onstott recalled that the Clary's Grove *"boys began to size up 'Uncle Abe' and concluded to try his metal, so they consulted and made him an alternative. First, he was to run a foot race [with] a man from Wolf. 'Trot him out,' said Abe. Second, he was to wrestle with a man from Little Grove. 'All right,' said Abe. Third, he must fight a man from Sand Ridge. 'Nothing wrong about that,' said Abe.*

An expert foot race was distanced in the race. *After a few minutes rest a Little Grove man stripped for the wrestle. 'What holds do you prefer?' 'Suit yourself,' said Abe. 'Catch-as-catch-can,' said the man from the Grove. They stood about twenty feet apart and went at each other like two rams. Abe's opponent was a short, heavy-set fellow and came with his head down expecting to butt Abe and upset him, but Abe was not built that way. He stepped aside and caught the fellow by the nap of the neck, threw him heels overhead and gave him a fall hard enough to break every bone in his body. This woke the boys up and they retired again to consult. Abe was now getting mad. 'Bring in your man from Sand Ridge,' said he, 'I can do him up in three shakes of a sheep's tail, and I can whip the whole pack of you if you give me ten minutes between fights.' The committee now* came forward and gave him the right hand of fellowship and said, 'You have sand in your craw, and we will take you into our crowd as you are worthy to associate with us.' From that time on Abe was king among them. His word was law. He was their judge in horse and foot races and all of them would have fought for him if Abe had shown the 'white feather.' "

Mr. Lincoln did not stoop to the level of such contemporaries, however. *"Lincoln was as full of fun as a dog is of fleas, and yet he was not guilty of mean tricks,"* recalled Daniel Green Burner. *"I never knew him to perform one. He had no part in the rowdyism of the Clary Grove gang. They had queer notions of fun. I remember that one evening this crowd came in and got gloriously drunk. What did they do but thrust a helpless, drunken old man into a hogshead, nail on the cover, and then started the hogshead rolling down the steep hill toward the mill. Fortunately, part way down the big barrel struck a stump and was broken to pieces, releasing the captive. But for this accident the victim would probably have been drowned in the river. Lincoln would stoop to no such performance as this."* Lincoln's biographer Alonzo Rothschild wrote: *"The pastimes of these wild young fellows, no less than their quarrels, suffered a change under the pressure of Lincoln's authority. He vetoed one of the gang's favorite diversions, that of rolling persons who had incurred their displeasure down a perilously steep hill in a hogshead."*

Mr. Lincoln had other standards. Lincoln scholar David Herbert Donald wrote that Mr. Lincoln *" enjoyed 'scientific' wrestling, a style in which opponents, followed agreed-on-rules, begin by taking holds and attempting to throw each other."*

As a militia officer in the Black Hawk War, Lincoln took a "prominent part" in wrestling matches. *"I think it is safe to say he was never throw in a wrestle. While in the army he Kept a handkerchief tied round him very near all the time for wrestling purposes and Love the sport as well as any man could,"* recalled one fellow soldier. *"Very few men in the army could successfully complete with Mr. Lincoln, either in wrestling or swimming; he well understood both arts."* Another testified that *"His Specialty was Side holds; he threw down all men."* Still another fellow soldier recalled that Lincoln *"was with them all the while in Jumping or foot Racing and Lincoln done the wrestling for the Company against every Bully Brought up."*

Once, Lincoln decided to use his strength against his own men when they threatened to kill an old Indian who came into their camp. Captain Lincoln bravely blocked them. Longtime friend William G. "Slickly Bill" Greene remembered that *"Lincoln stood between the Indian & the vengeance of the outraged soldiers, brave, good & true. When the challenges continued, Mr. Lincoln said 'if any man thinks I am a coward let him test it.' The mob backed down when Lincoln challenged his antagonists to 'choose your weapon.'"*

Lincoln's strength was legendary. *"Physically, Mr. Lincoln was the strongest man I ever knew,"* recalled Daniel Green Burner, *"That is saying a good deal. Let me tell you what I saw him do. He took a full barrel of whisky, containing forty-four gallons, gripping each end with one hand, raised it deliberately to his face and drank from the bunghole. In doing this he won a $10 hat from Bill Green. In the grocery I have often seen him pick up a barrel of whisky, place it on the counter, and then lower it on the other side."*

Joseph Gillespie wrote that *"Physically, Mr. Lincoln was a Hercules. I first saw him in 1832, while he was engaged in a wrestling-match with one [Lorenzo Dow] Thompson, who was a champion, in that line, of the southern portion of Illinois, while Lincoln occupied that position as to what was then the northern portion. It was a terrible tussle, but Lincoln was too much for him."*

William G. Greene recalled: *"We Sangamon county boys believed Mr. Lincoln could throw any one, and the Union county boys knew no one could throw Thompson; so we staked all slick and well-worn quarters and empty bottles on the wrestle. The first fall was clearly in Thompson's favor, but Lincoln's backers claimed that it was what, in those days, was called a 'dog fall.' Thompson's backers claimed the stakes, while we demurred, and it really looked, for some time, as though there would be at least a hundred fights as a result. Mr. Lincoln, after getting up and brushing the dust and dirt off his jean pants, said: 'Boys, give up your bet; if he has not thrown me fairly, he could.' Every bet was at once surrendered, and peace and order were restored in a minute."*

This was a very rare defeat for Lincoln, recalled a contemporary. In 1864, Greene had a conversation with President Lincoln at the White House during which Lincoln asked Greene: *" 'Bill, what ever became of our old antagonist, Thompson, that big curly-headed fellow who threw me at Rock Island?'* When Greene said he didn't know, the President joked that *'if he knew where he was living he would give him a post-office, by way of showing him that he bore him no ill-will.' "*

Among Lincoln's talents was jumping. Lincoln, it was said, *"hopped well—in 3 hops he would go 40.2 on a dead level."* Another friend recalled that *"he was seldom ever Beat Jumping."* William B. Thompson remembered his merchant father was an accomplished athlete when he first met Lincoln in New Salem: *"As he rode up, he noted the number of horses hitched to the rack and saw that the farmers were engaged in the popular amusement of 'three jumps.' This was an athletic performance in which Mr. Thompson excelled. The young merchant from Beardstown lost no time getting into the game. He was astonished to see the new clerk, whom everybody called 'Abe,' toe the mark, swing forward in three standing jumps, and pass his own scratch by some inches. As Mr. Thompson told the story afterward, this was the first time he had ever been beaten at 'three jumps.'"*

Contemporary Jason Duncan wrote: *"Mr Lincoln would wait till all who were disposed to try their muscles had their best jumps, then come forward with a heavy weight in each hand with his long muscular legs raise himself from the ground and light far beyond the most successful champion, indeed so far generally, that the man who would undertake to over reach it, would become the laughing stock of the crowd."*

In middle age, Mr. Lincoln's sport of choice was a game of "Fives" involving two teams of two men each that tried to hit the ball out of their opponents' reach. Dr. Preston H Bailhache recalled: *"Just off the corner of the Public Square the Illinois State Journal publishing house was located, and its big solid brick wall afforded a splendid place for playing a game called 'Fives.' When Mr. Lincoln went to the printing office for a talk or to get a lot of newspapers, he frequently joined with the boys in playing 'Fives.' This game is a sort of handball, in which players choose sides, and is begun by one of the boys bouncing the ball on the ground, and as it bounds back from the wall one of the opponents strikes it in the same manner, so that the ball is kept going back and forth against the wall until someone misses the rebound, which furnishes a very active and exciting contest. Here is where 'Old Abe' was always champion, for his long arms and long legs served a good purpose in reaching and returning the ball from any angle his adversary could send it to the wall."*

Court clerk Thomas W. S. Kidd testified to Mr. Lincoln's love of handball: *"In 1859, Zimri A. Enos, Esq., Hon. Chas. A. Keyes, E. L. Baker, Esq., then editor of the Journal, William A. Turney, Esq., Clerk of the Supreme Court, and a number of others, in connection with Mr. Lincoln, had the lot, then an open one, lying between what was known as the United States Court Building, on the northeast corner of the public square, and the building owned by our old friend, Mr. John Carmody, on the alley north of it, on Sixth street, enclosed with a high board fence, leaving a dead wall at either end. In this 'alley' could be found Mr. Lincoln, with the gentlemen named and others, as vigorously engaged in the sport as though life depended upon it. He would play until nearly exhausted and then take a seat on the rough board benches arranged along the sides for the accommodation of friends and the tired players."*

Patrick Stanley had built an "alley" in the rear of his grocery in the Second Ward, which is still standing, to accommodate his Irish–American friends, who have a native love for the same character of ball sport. On more than one occasion, 'Old Abe' could have been seen walking down there in company with Mr. Turney and others, who had the same fondness for the game, to test their skill with some of Mr. Stanley's more robust friends. Mr. Lincoln was also very fond of the old game of 'corner ball,' and frequently joined these same gentlemen in excursions out of the city to get a pasture in which they might have a quiet game of ball. He was passionately fond of these ball games, not only for the sport they afforded, but for the better reasons that they gave him recreation from office labor and the mental toil in the studious preparations he made for his professional duties and the indefatigable study in other channels by this self-made man. Mr. Lincoln was just as much in earnest in playing these games as he was when on the stump, making a speech before a jury, in the argument of a cause, or when unraveling knotty law points before the court. I have sat and laughed many happy hours away watching a game of ball between him on one side and Hon. Chas. A. Keyes on the other. Mr. Keyes is quite a short man, but muscular, wiry and active as a cat, while his now more distinguished antagonist, as all now know, was tall and a little awkward, but which with much practice and skill in the movement of the ball, together with his good judgment, gave him the greatest advantage. In a very hotly contested game, when both sides were 'up a stump'—a term used by the players to indicate an even game—and while the contestants were vigorously watching every movement, Mr. Lincoln and Mr. Turney collided with such force that it came very near preventing his nomination to the *Presidency, and giving to Springfield a sensation by his death and burial. Both were badly hurt, but not so badly as to discourage either from being found in the 'alley' the next day.*

Lincoln was said to even be playing hand ball as he awaited the results of the presidential nominating convention in Chicago in May 1860. John Carmody recalled about that time: *"An incident took place, during one of those games, which I have retained clearly in* my memory. I had a nephew named Patrick Johnson who was very expert in the game. He struck the ball in such a manner that it hit Mr. Lincoln in the ear. I ran to sympathize with him and asked if he was hurt. He said he was not, and as he said it he reached both of his hands toward the sky. Straining my neck to look up into his face, for he was several inches taller than I was, I said to him, 'Lincoln, if you are going to heaven, take us both.'"

Introduction

SPRINGFIELD IN THE TIME OF LINCOLN

I now felt firmly rooted and determined to seek no further; as I believed I was then in the center of the most extensive body of the richest land in the United States, or perhaps in the world; and don't yet think I was mistaken.

—Elijah Iles

Nine years before Thomas Lincoln and his family migrated north from Indiana to Macon County, Illinois, Elijah Iles, a twenty-five-year-old pioneer, arrived on horseback in what is now Springfield. In 1821, only nine settlers populated this area of maple, hickory, and elm groves surrounded by thousands of acres of prairie. Among them was John Kelly, the first man to build a cabin in Springfield on what are now Jefferson and Second Streets. An enterprising adventurer, Iles left his Kentucky home for St. Louis. He remained there for three years while learning to trade and to keep shop and buy and sell land. Still restless and in search of his ideal home, he traveled from Missouri through the waving grass of the prairie to the rich land of the

Sangamon Country in central Illinois. Iles, being the visionary that he was, saw its potential and decided to settle down here permanently.

He boarded with the Kelly family while he established the first store in this tiny wilderness settlement. He eventually came to be known as the "Father of Springfield." He recalled later that he *"was the first one to sell goods in Springfield. For some time my sales were about as much to Indians as to the whites. For the first two years I had no competition, and my customers were widely and thinly scattered over the territory.... Many had to come more than eighty miles to trade. They were poor, and their purchases very light. There never was a more uniformly hospitable, honest, and industrious class of first settlers [who] ever settled new country."*

In 1823, the federal land office opened at Springfield, then a small village of twenty or thirty log cabins stretched along Jefferson from First to Fourth Streets. When parcels of land were offered for sale, Elijah Iles and three of his friends, Pascal P. Enos, Thomas Cox, and John Taylor purchased four adjoining parcels for $1.25 an acre and had them surveyed into lots that became the original Town of Springfield. They then proceeded to sell the lots.

They named the town's first streets for American presidents, Monroe, Adams, Washington, Jefferson, and Madison, and the village itself "Calhoun" after the popular South Carolina Senator John C. Calhoun. When the little village was legally incorporated in 1832, the name was changed to that of a nearby creek, a name preferred by the residents: Springfield.

In 1824, Springfield was selected as the permanent county seat of Sangamon County. The census recorded just five hundred residents. By now, many transients had left for "less populous" areas where they could not see the smoke from a neighbor's home; it was in this same year that Iles built his first home from logs.

By 1837, thanks to the efforts of Abraham Lincoln and "the Long Nine," a group of legislators all over six feet tall, the state capital was moved from Vandalia to Springfield, closer to the geographic center of the state. This move, which was completed by 1839, would alter forever the history of this frontier village, now grown to two thousand inhabitants.

Naturally, a state capital demanded an appropriate building, so the county courthouse on the public square was demolished, making way for the new capitol, and a new courthouse was erected on the east side of Sixth Street.

Iles continued promoting the rich agricultural potential of the area, but it was his real-estate ventures in town that made him a millionaire. Shrewdly anticipating the town's growth as the new capital, he began the construction, in 1836, of Springfield's first luxury hotel at the southeast corner of Sixth and Adams Streets, and the American House opened its doors in 1838.

A visiting Ohio editor remarked somewhat sarcastically of Iles's hotel that *"everything inside puts you in mind of the Turkish splendor: the carpeting, the papering and the furniture, weary the eye with magnificence."* Its popularity was instant. In one week alone in 1839, when the legislature was in session, 158 people registered at the grand American House. Many of them were legislators who lived too far away for frequent home visits.

With his typical foresight and energy, while the American House was still under construction, Iles began the first of several housing additions (now called subdivisions) that came to bear his name. One contained 436 lots and covered a twenty-seven-block radius. It was here that the now-famous Lincoln Home was built in 1839 and Iles's owned second home.

In 1837, Mary Todd made her second visit to Springfield as a guest of her eldest sister, Elizabeth, wife of Ninian Wirt Edwards, son of Ninian Edwards Sr., first territorial governor of Illinois. In this same year, Lincoln was admitted to the bar and rode with two saddle bags, his borrowed horse, and seven dollars in his pocket from New Salem to Springfield. Now a bona-fide lawyer, he planned on launching his first law practice with Mary's cousin, John Todd Stuart.

This was also a year of other notable events. Eighteen-year-old Victoria became Queen of England and reigned for the next sixty-three years; Chicago incorporated as a city; the electrical telegraph, which later became a great help to Lincoln, was patented; and a financial panic hit the worst since the country's founding, creating a major recession. Unemployment soared, banks collapsed, and many businesses failed.

Despite the country's financial plunge, Mary and Abraham were young and hopeful about the future. But they were disappointed in Springfield. It was nothing like the sophisticated Lexington, Kentucky, the "Athens of the South," where Mary was born and brought up. Lincoln wrote to Mary Owens, whom he had courted in New Salem, that he found the town "a busy wilderness."

Earlier in the decade, the poet William Cullen Bryant, passing through Springfield, had departed with a negative impression: *"The houses are not so good... a considerable portion of them being log cabins and the whole town having an appearance of dirt and discomfort."*

In the absence of sidewalks and paved streets, the pig population wandered freely through the often-muddy streets. While pro-hog and anti-hog factions argued, the porcine population continued to enjoy its freedom, rooting in the dirt and wallowing in the mud. Chickens and dogs sometimes joined in the fun. And in wet or wintry weather, carriages routinely got stuck in the dark sludge of the roadways.

Meanwhile, Simeon Francis, editor of the *Sangamo Journal* and the man who was to bring together Mary and Abraham after their romantic breakup, was optimistic, enthusiastically promoting the exciting growth of the new capital:

> *"The owner of real estate sees his property rapidly enhancing in value; the merchant anticipates a large accession to our population and a corresponding additional sale for his goods; the mechanic already has more contracts offered him for building and improvement than he can execute; the farmer anticipates, in the growth of a large and important town, a market for the varied products of his farm; indeed every class of our citizens look to the .future with confidence that we trust, will not be disappointed."*

From the small square at Second and Jefferson, where Iles's store and the first courthouse had stood, Springfield's new town center expanded its boundaries. The State House moved toward completion. Assisting was brick mason Jared Irwin, later a neighbor of the Lincolns and one of many workmen lured from the East by job opportunities in Springfield. One to three-story buildings were constructed on Fifth Street south from the corner of Washington, as well as along Hoffman's Row, where Lincoln shared an upstairs office with John Todd Stuart. Craftsmen's signs in growing numbers invited customers to purchase hats, shoes, leather goods, and clothing.

Further, the administration of state government and the growing community required more service providers: clerks, doctors, lawyers, mechanics, hoteliers, builders, and shopkeepers. Even a bookstore appeared, a sure sign that culture was coming to the prairie.

Robert Irwin opened a general store, where Lincoln's close friend Joshua Speed had once done business and where Lincoln had made his first home in the community. Irwin's welcomed frequent customers like Mary Todd—a serious shopper who delighted in choosing from the variety that was now available of lovely fabrics, ribbons, straw hats, coffee, and tea.

At the same time, Springfield was becoming a town of politically aware and involved citizens. On every street corner, in shops on the square and in new drinking establishments, lively political discussions took place. During presidential campaigns, tempers ran high. In 1839, during the election campaign of

William Henry Harrison and Martin Van Buren, both the Whigs and the Democrats arrived by the thousands to hold their state conventions in the new capital. Speaking tournaments went on for hours followed by torchlight parades, singing and barbecues until midnight.

Mary Todd and Abraham Lincoln flourished in this milieu. *"This fall,"* she wrote, *"I became quite a politician, rather an unladylike profession, yet at such a crisis, whose heart could remain untouched while the energies of all were called in question?"*

And people partied. When in session, the legislature included many eligible bachelors. This meant a lively social life attracting marriageable young women like Mary Todd and her sisters. The home of her sister Elizabeth and brother-in-law Ninian Wirt Edwards was a popular venue for many entertaining gatherings of what Mary called the "the coterie," including awkward Abraham Lincoln, his friend Joshua Speed, and the brilliant young politician Stephen A. Douglas. Isaac Arnold, a legislator remembering Springfield of those early capital days, said, *"We read much of 'Merrie England,' but I doubt if there was ever anything more 'merrie' than Springfield in those days."*

As the city grew, so did the churches and their need for bigger and better buildings and new ministers. The local Episcopal Church, seeking a new pastor contacted Reverend Charles Dresser of Virginia. He accepted the position and moved with his wife, Louisa, and two sons to Springfield in 1838. The following year, he decided to build a home and purchased Lot 8 in Block 10 of the Elijah Iles's Addition. The lot Dresser purchased had been owned originally by Iles himself. It was bought by Dr. Gershom

Jayne, Springfield's first physician, who then sold it to the Dressers. In order to accommodate the building plans, Dresser paid ninety dollars to Francis and Emeline M. Wester Jr. for an additional ten-foot-wide strip off the south side of the lot.

The home Dresser built faced Eighth Street and was a modest cottage of one and a half stories that extended 150 feet north down Jackson Street. It stood on a rise above the unpaved street. Shutters flanked the set of two windows on each side of the walnut front door.

On the ground floor, the home contained a parlor, a sitting room with fireplaces for heating, and a kitchen. Above, in the half loft, there were two low-ceilinged bedrooms under the slanting roof. Reverend Dresser added an outhouse and possibly a barn in the back, along with a well and cistern for collecting rainwater.

By November 4, 1842, Mary Todd and Abraham Lincoln had passed through their stormy courtship and engaged Reverend Dresser to perform their marriage ceremony in her sister's parlor. At this time, Reverend Dresser had his own problems. He was struggling with debts and eager to sell his Eighth and Jackson property. Lincoln would most certainly have visited the home and probably found it to his liking, but the time was not right for him to make this kind of financial commitment.

Rather than become homeowners, the newlyweds took up residence at the Globe Tavern, an inn and stagecoach office, where Mary's sister Frances and her husband, Dr. William Wallace, had lived for a time as well. However, after a year and the birth of Robert Todd Lincoln, the family rented somewhat larger quarters, a three-room cottage nearby on the east side of South Fourth Street between Adams and Monroe. Here Mary was able to afford help, and she enjoyed some space of her own.

THE GLOBE TAVERN WHERE NEWLYWEDS ABRAHAM AND MARY TODD LINCOLN RESIDED.

In 1844, Reverend Dresser was still in financial difficulties and unsuccessful in selling his home. Mary's father helped solve the problem for Dresser and Lincoln. On his only visit to Springfield to see his daughters, Robert Todd of Lexington, Kentucky, made possible the purchase of the Dresser home by a generous monetary gift honoring the birth of Robert Todd Lincoln. He wished his grandson well with the words, "May God bless and protect my little namesake."

On Tuesday, January 16, 1844, Abraham Lincoln, age thirty-five, and the Reverend Charles Dresser entered into a contract for the sale of Dresser's house at Eighth and Jackson

Streets. Lincoln agreed to pay Dresser $1,200 in cash and to convey a lot worth $300 on Adams Street in the business section that he and Stephen T. Logan had acquired two years earlier.

On May 2, 1844, Reverend Charles Dresser deeded the property to the Lincolns. And so, the Lincolns purchased the only house they would ever own. It was hardly *"an upper-class existence in an upper-class environment,"* as a biographer once described the locale, but it was a delighted Mary who, in the lovely spring of that year, babe in arms, passed over the threshold of her modest new home. She had all the basics for a happy domestic life: "a nice home, a loving husband and precious child."

The only home Abraham Lincoln ever owned, Eight and Jackson Streets, Springfield, Illinois.

Lincoln was now practicing law with his new partner, William Herndon, in the Tinsley Building on the square. He must have been pleased that his new home was an easy six-block walk to work.

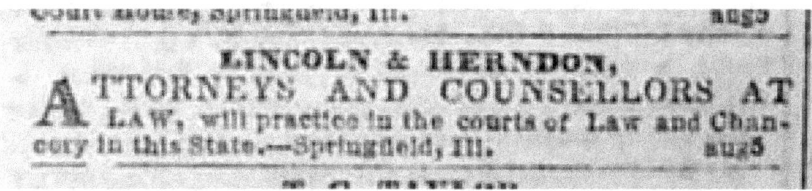

ADVERTISEMENT IN THE LOCAL SPRINGFIELD NEWSPAPER.

LINCOLN-HERNDON LAW OFFICES IN THE
TINSLEY BUILDING, SPRINGFIELD.

At this time, the neighborhood was on the outskirts of town, mostly empty lots, owned but not improved. This would come in the next decade. The streets were still unpaved and muddy, and no sidewalks or gutters appeared until Lincoln and neighbor Charles Arnold, then sheriff of the county, agitated for improvement. Until 1851, when an ordinance forced livestock to be penned, Springfield allowed pigs and other farm animals to roam freely in the unpaved streets. Mary remarked to a domestic, *"At least my guests won't have to wade through cow and hog tracks to get to my parties, thus ruining my carpets. The law has taken a hand and made those folks who have hogs and cows keep them home."*

Although not the elegant mansion of her native Lexington, Mary was delighted to have a place of her own at last. For Lincoln, who cared little for physical comfort, who had grown up in woods and log cabins, slept on plank floors and shared beds in boardinghouses with other itinerant lawyers, it must have felt a bit strange mounting the plaque "A. Lincoln" on his door. He may have felt some pride of ownership for he wrote to his father-in-law, Robert Smith Todd, "that he was going to housekeeping." At the time the Lincolns moved in, a family of three—Reverend Francis Springer, his wife, Mary, and one child—lived across Jackson on the southeast corner of Eighth. By 1844, Reverend Springer had officially closed the English and Classical School that he ran from this home. It is thought, but not proven, that a young Robert may have studied briefly with Reverend Springer there. Lincoln and Springer established an enduring friendship that continued during the Civil War, when Springer was an army chaplain.

The public entertainments within a community are a good barometer of how its residents use their free time and what type of entertainments draw them together. In early Springfield on long winter nights, the folks not only enjoyed the entertainment but also welcomed an opportunity to get out of a cooped-up winter house and pass some time with other Springfieldians in a night out of "entertainment."

The population of Springfield in 1830 was less than 1,000. During that decade much of the "entertainment" was in the form of lectures by local residents. In step with a national phenomenon, the creation of local lyceums, two lyceums were formed and provided a platform for Springfield men to learn and debate topics of current interest. Some lectures were free and open to the public. Others were open only to "members," and sometimes, in the early days, women were excluded. There were occasions when women were invited to attend, but they were never invited to lecture. That honor was reserved for men. During the 1830s, the locals lectured, debated, sang songs, participated in choirs, and performed popular theatrical pieces.

By 1840, Springfield's population had grown to 2,579. During that decade as well as the preceding decade, there was no "place" dedicated to indoor performances. Entertainments were held in churches and other public places. The hall of the House of Representatives and the chamber of the Senate in the State Capitol were favorite venues after about 1844.

The Springfield population in 1850 had grown to 4,533. That decade saw the coming of the railroad and after about 1853 specific places were dedicated to the commercial performing arts. These were not public places, but rather private entrepreneurial businesses. They were usually on the upper floor of a three-story building around the Public Square. There were a number of these: the Concert Hall on the north side of the Public Square, Cook's Hall on the East Side of the Square, and the Masonic Hall at Fifth and Monroe. When the Metropolitan Hall opened in early 1856, it was the largest amusement hall in Illinois with 1,200 seats.

Springfield was fortunate to be on the tour route of many traveling entertainments as they moved between Chicago and St. Louis, often stopping in Springfield for a "gig." These "entertainments" were more of a commercial venture requiring the purchase of tickets to be entertained by traveling artists in an astounding variety of performing arts: singers, family bell ringers, opera singers, minstrel singers, magicians, pantomimes, lecturers, violin and flute concerts, holiday celebrations and balls, readers of plays and performers of plays from Shakespeare to Irish farce, band concerts, and balloon ascensions, Fourth of July celebrations, and celebrations of the birthdays of Washington, Franklin, and Robert Burns.

There were other forms of entertainment: circuses, the annual state fair when it was held in Springfield, and a slew of dancing classes.

Many of the names of those "entertaining" in Springfield are familiar to us even today. Horace Mann would be surprised to know that 150 years after his 1859 lecture in Springfield, one of its principal businesses is Horace Mann Insurance. Titans in mid-nineteenth-century America's political and intellectual life lectured, and among them were Albert T. Bledsoe in 1842, Ralph Waldo Emerson in 1853, Bayard Taylor in 1854, Henry Ward Beecher in 1855, Theodore Parker in 1856, Park Benjamin in 1857, and Joshua A. Giddings in 1860.

The names of most entertainers, however, are not recognized by today's reader. One minstrel is said to have been Mark Twain's model for his descriptions of minstrel shows. Another, a French Entertainer in Lincoln's Springfield, is said to have been the aeronaut for Emperor Napoleon III in the Franco-Austrian War, a year after his appearance in Springfield.

Some of the itinerant entertainers were scoundrels, leaving unpaid advertising bills from their local stay. One soprano had been the former wife of the King of Bavaria and the mistress of many European notables. When she lectured on "fashion," William Herndon did not like that at all. He lectured the night following her appearance, scolding those who had attended about their wayward standards and the decline in community standards.

But, the most interesting salacious tidbit from all of the entertainments involved a pianist, Sigismund Thalberg, who had been decorated by every European potentate. While touring Illinois, the mother of a young member of Thalberg's troupe shot at him for "fiddling" with her daughter. The report is that Thalberg quietly left Illinois and headed back to Europe on the sly and in disgrace.

The saddest story involves a young boy named Nicholas Goodall, a flute player genius. Nicholas appeared at the Masonic Hall in Springfield on February 21, 1855. He was wildly popular, had extended his Springfield stay, and was invited to parties in private homes. There is no evidence to put Abraham Lincoln at any of his concerts, but he was in Springfield during this time and may have attended.

On the evening of April 14, 1865, Nicholas was said to have been present at Ford's Theatre where his father was first violinist in the orchestra that evening. It is said that young Nicholas witnessed the assassination of Lincoln and thereafter fell into a hopeless depression. His father placed Nicholas in an institution for the insane and there, and in the local alms house, Nicholas lived until his death at age 32 in 1881.

The Lyceum Movement

The Lyceum Movement was named for the place where Aristotle lectured to the youth of ancient Greece. From 1826 until after the Civil War, hundreds of informal associations were established in the Northeastern and Midwestern United States for the purpose of improving the social, intellectual, and moral fabric of society.

The first American lyceum, "Millbury Branch Number 1 of the American Lyceum," was founded in 1826 in Millbury, Massachusetts, by Josiah Holbrook, a teacher and lecturer. Holbrook was a traveling lecturer and teacher who believed that education was a lifelong experience, and he intended to create a National American Lyceum organization that would oversee this method of teaching. As conceived by Holbrook, each lyceum was to contribute to the spread of learning, especially of the natural sciences. A major topic in early years was the establishment of public schools.

The lyceum movement was led by voluntary local associations, including lyceums, mechanics' institutes, and agriculture organizations. At first, the lyceums were local ventures with local citizens lecturing and debating. Prominent local men, and those who hoped to be prominent, were invited as speakers. Topics included science, culture, health, history, and politics. Participants discussed such questions as whether to abolish the death penalty, whether newspapers could be trusted, and whether married people were happier than single people.

Promoters hoped their Lyceums would disseminate knowledge and encourage civic responsibility. Townspeople hoped attendance would help them climb the ladder of middle-class respectability. Aspiring local leaders used them as forums for honing their oratorical and analytic skills. Springfield had two Lyceums—the Sangamon County Lyceum, founded in 1833, followed a few years later by the Young Men's Lyceum. A few weeks before his twenty-ninth birthday, Abraham Lincoln addressed the Young Men's Lyceum. He responded to the question, "Do the signs of the present times indicate the downfall of this Government." His remarks, known as the "Lyceum Speech," are an important Lincoln text, containing clues about the developing mind of the future president.

At the Lyceum, young men like Abraham Lincoln could simultaneously pursue their professional and social advancement. They gave people an opportunity to hear debates and lectures on topics of current interest. They multiplied rapidly and numbered 3,000 by 1834.

By 1840 they had become professionalized institutions with outside lecturers to whom fees were paid. Noted lecturers, entertainers, and readers would travel the "lyceum circuit," going from town to town or state to state to entertain, speak, or debate in a variety of locations. Among the well-known speakers who traveled from state to state were Ralph Waldo Emerson, Frederick Douglass, Henry David Thoreau, Daniel Webster, Nathaniel Hawthorne, and Susan B. Anthony. Many of Emerson's essays were originally written as lyceum lectures. This contributed significantly to the education of the adult American in the nineteenth century.

The Lyceum Movement reached the peak of its popularity before the Civil War. After the Civil War, it blended indistinguishably into the Chautauqua Movement, which had begun in the 1870s.

Entertainment

Social life in Springfield had zest and liveliness beyond that of any other city in the state. Socially, as well as in law and politics, it was the capital of Illinois.

What sort of a place was this in which so much of the state's life centered? Fortunately, there were visitors who recorded what they saw. Among them was an Ohio editor who wrote with such glowing enthusiasm that one is inclined to suspect him of an investment in Springfield real estate. At any rate, this is what he recorded after a visit in the early autumn of 1839.

Springfield lies on the edge of a large prairie. On the left, as you enter the village from the South, is a delightful grove, where the rills are more lively, and the ground more undulating than usual.... Approaching the southern part of the town, you leave a great sweep of verdant landscape behind you, and behold almost as great a natural meadow to your right. No one can conceive the grandeur and beauty of the scenery, unless he has wandered through a prairie country, at a season when an immense carpet, spangled with very bright yellow and vermilion flowers, and fringed along the line of the horizon with a darker timber, is spread over a very gracefully rolling surface, beneath a vast sky half covered with lowering clouds painted by the sun, and the other half as serene and clear as if no vapor had ever stained its azure.

But in the suburbs of Springfield there is a paradise in miniature, which compensates for the loss of the boundless prospect left behind. Small clusters of infant trees, which nature has planted with all the regularity, and more than the taste of art, rise like bowers of romance to hedge in the village with beauty. They extend, like arms from the main grove, not continuously, but like a chain of islands, gradually diminishing in size, and sheltering from a powerful noonday sun, the softly chiming rivulets. Here the man of leisure comes to steal pleasant thoughts from the cool shade, and the man of business for a while gives his care to the refreshing breezes that always carry on a rapid commerce over the heated plains. On Sunday the shady retirements are thronged with visitors in fine broadcloth, who find a place most inviting to contemplation.

Passing them reluctantly, you glance forward at the throng of stores, taverns, and shops, some wearing their titles on their fronts, some on long arms projecting from their sides, and some in the usual style of tavern signs, beneath the picture of a bird or beast, on a black board swinging from a miniature gallows. Before reaching the centre of business, you behold to your right an agreeable assemblage of dwelling houses very neatly painted, most of them white, and situated somewhat retiringly behind tasteful front yards. To the left, at a distance, are seen more showy edifices, the principal expense of which seems to have been their decoration, standing rather proudly apart from the throng of neat but humble mansions. Passing a modest-looking meeting house, which speaks more for the simple piety of the inhabitants, than the ostentatious taste of the citizens, you now approach an area fenced from the street by a long stone-cutter's shop, eloquent with the music of scores of pick axes, shaping the rudiments of the new State House.

Turning to the east you see the comfortable buildings, apparently young and certainly tasteful, gradually dwindling in size and becoming more scattered until the town melts away into the level monotonous plain. Several miles across the prairie is seen another grove, and along its margin clever farmhouses are strung in quite a picturesque manner. Toward these centers of rural felicity, narrow black paths wind through the desolate green. Along this edge of the town runs the Central Railroad, now under contract. Follow this, in a northerly direction a short distance and then turn to the left, and new clusters of neat little dwellings attract your attention, many of them labelled as the residences of dealers in pills and legal advice. Towards the grove, the town assumes a more consolidated and antiquated appearance. Here is seen the rarest of all landscapes; crowded squares alive with shrubbery and tasteful ornaments, decorating alike the little remnant of twenty years ago, and costly edifices of last year. Every house is separated from the street by a neat front yard, and from its neighbor by a clean little garden; roses greet the visitor with a blush as he enters the gate, and pushing the door, he finds himself under a bower of honeysuckles. Old shackly buildings are concentrated as the temples of Flora. The sun of contentment and happiness seems to shine on all, and gives the abodes of simple elegance a charm to which mere magnificence must be a stranger.

The new State House, even though unfinished, dominated the town. Although two years had elapsed since the cornerstone was laid, the second story was not yet completed; while tool sheds and stone piles littered the square. Still, thirty or forty men were at work, and the clinking of their hammers was merry music to the young capital.

Of scarcely less interest, especially to the visitors, were the hotels and taverns. Typical of most of these was the Globe Tavern, a plain, two-story wooden structure which also served as an office for several of the stage lines operating through Springfield. Whenever a stage arrived, or a private conveyance for that matter, the clerk would ring a large bell mounted on top of the house, and the stable men would run out from the rear to take charge of the horses.

Completely overshadowing such a modest structure as this was the American House, which Elijah Iles built on the southeast corner of Sixth and Adams streets. Its size alone created a sensation. When it was opened, *in November, 1838, two hundred citizens dined with the manager, J. Clifton, 'late of Boston.'* " The Ohio editor, who wrote so kindly of Springfield, commented on it with mixed awe and irritation. *"Near the State House,"* he wrote, *"is a gigantic building, called the American House, intended perhaps as the tavern for Legislators—Politics and politeness hover round this splendid affair. Everything inside puts you in mind of the Turkish splendor, the carpeting, the papering, and the furniture, weary the eye with magnificence. The building itself is distinguished more for the harmony and simplicity of its proportions, than the richness of its exterior. A fine place for those who are troubled with a superabundance of silver."*

Chapter One

"I HAVE SEEN MR. LINCOLN GO INTO THIS SPORT WITH A GREAT DEAL OF ZEST."

Lincoln and Town Ball (Baseball)

"...Exultations and mortifications... are but temporary; the victor shall soon be vanquished, if he relaxes his exertion; and... the vanquished this year may be the victor next, in spite of all competition."

Abraham Lincoln, 1859

My interest in Abraham Lincoln and a Washington baseball club has occupied most of my life. In the 1950s, an elementary school project on Lincoln and a Cub Scout trip to Griffith Stadium in Washington, D.C., home of the hapless Washington Senators until 1961, coincided nearly perfectly. From that point on, I was hooked on both.

To no one's surprise, Lincoln proved more loyal and reliable to me. The Senators moved once in 1961, but they were replaced by an expansion team that was not great, but acceptable. They moved again in 1971, this time leaving me without a baseball team for thirty-four years before the appearance of the Washington Nationals, who, incidentally, won the World Series in 2019 after a drought of ninety-five years. Anyone who has ever attended a Nationals game knows that one of the promotions is the racing presidents in the middle of the fourth inning of every game. Lincoln, Jefferson, Washington, and Teddy Roosevelt all race around the park to the entertainment of all who watch. At limited times Taft, Coolidge, and Hoover joined the mix, but were eventually phased out in favor of the Mt. Rushmore four. Lincoln, again to no one's surprise, and to my delight, had won more races than any of his fellow presidents. To me, it is only fitting.

Lincoln leads the way in the President's Race during a Washington Nationals game.

What few people know, however, and what has been largely neglected in the great pantheon of Lincoln literature, is that the real Abraham Lincoln was a baseball fan and, according to eyewitnesses, played the game, or a derivation thereof, quite competently.

Some historians have claimed that Lincoln played baseball and watched baseball near the White House while President as the game grew in popularity during the Civil War. The White House history website reports that *"The president and son Tad watched a baseball game between the Quartermaster's Department and the Commissary Department"* in the summer of 1862 *"from a spot along the first base line, cheering with their fellow fans and also receiving an ovation from the crowd."*

As detractors denounced baseball in the nineteenth century for drunkenness, gambling, and bad behavior, there were numerous attempts to link the game to Abraham Lincoln. These stories, many of which were apocryphal, linking the martyred president to baseball helped contribute to its acceptance and popularity.

George Kirsch, in *Baseball in Blue & Gray*, tells the following tale: *"Certainly as president, Lincoln had ample opportunity to see a baseball game. Before, during, and after the war baseball clubs competed on the President's Grounds near the White House in Washington, D.C."*

The *Baseball Almanac* mentioned this story: *"At about six o'clock, the President, who was prevented from appearing earlier on account of the semi-weekly Cabinet meeting, came on the ground and remained until the close of the game (Washington 28 vs Brooklyn Excelsiors 33), an apparently interested spectator of the exciting contest.*" The story even includes an interesting detail of Lincoln and his son eating peanuts at the game and the ground around their feet being covered in peanut shells. While Lincoln might have indeed attended a game with his son, Tad, and consumed enough peanuts to cover the ground, this particular game, however, took place in 1866, and the president in attendance was Andrew Johnson.

One story widely circulated even had Lincoln skipping out of cabinet meetings to play baseball on the White House lawn, impressing everyone with his athletic abilities. Yet, no evidence has ever been found that even remotely hints of this being accurate.

Thus, many of Lincoln's connections to baseball were more invention than fact. In A.G. Spalding's 1911 book *America's National Game*, he tells this story:

> *It is recorded that in the year 1860, when the Committee of the Chicago Convention which nominated Abraham Lincoln for the Presidency, visited his home at Springfield, Illinois, to notify him formally of the event, the messenger sent to apprise him of the coming of the visitors found the great leader out on the commons, engaged in a game of Base Ball. Information of the arrival of the party was imparted to Mr. Lincoln on the ball field.*

'Tell the gentlemen,' he said, 'that I am glad to know of their coming; but they'll have to wait a few minutes 'till I make another base hit.'

LINCOLN'S NOTIFICATION

ABOVE LINCOLN LEARNS OF HIS NOMINATION, 1860, BY HOMER DAVENPORT. THE BACK PANEL OF A WHEATIES CEREAL BOX FROM 1939, WHICH TELLS THE STORY OF HOW LINCOLN RECEIVED THE REPUBLICAN NOMINATION IN 1860.

Newspapers across the country carried a slightly different version of the Spalding story. The *San Francisco Daily Evening Bulletin* was indicative of this. Under the headline *"How Lincoln Received the Nomination,"* the newspaper reported: *"When the news of Lincoln's nomination reached Springfield, his friends were greatly excited, and hastened to inform 'Old Abe' of it. He could not be found at his office or at home, but after some minutes the messenger discovered him out in a field with a parcel of boys, having a pleasant game of town-ball. All his comrades immediately threw up their hats and commenced to hurrah. Abe grinned considerably, scratched his head and said 'Go on boys; don't let such nonsense spoil a good game.' The boys did go on with their bawling, [sic] but not with the game of ball."*

However, the contemporary story is almost certainly untrue. Soon after his assassination, Lincoln's law partner William Herndon commenced writing Lincoln's biography. His research included interviews and correspondence with persons who knew Lincoln. Several of those included accounts of what Lincoln was doing on the day of his nomination as he anxiously awaited word from the party convention. The most likely interpretation of the story is that it was pure political propaganda. It was a manufactured story showing Lincoln to be a man of the people, unconcerned with personal ambition. From the perspective of baseball history, this is interesting as it shows town ball's status in American culture. "Town ball" required no further explanation and claiming that a man such as Lincoln was playing it was taken to be plausible and a political asset.

Stories that Lincoln mentioned baseball on his death bed as well as the 1914 claim by Rachel Billington, an alleged former neighbor of Lincoln, that he played baseball regularly and *"could hit the ball every time it was pitched to him"* have been thoroughly discredited.

Mrs. Billington claimed to live only a few doors away from the Lincoln family at Springfield and also knew Lincoln later as a lawyer in Decatur. *"In those days,"* said Mrs. Billington, *"the batter stood with his back to a wall and Lincoln could hit the ball every time it was pitched to him."* The most interesting thing here is that the game that Mrs. Billington saw played had the batter standing against the wall.

Lincoln has been joined with baseball since an 1860 Currier and Ives political cartoon showed the newly elected president with ball in hand, standing on home plate as his three defeated rivals, John C. Breckinridge, Stephen A. Douglas, and John Bell looked on. Lincoln has hit a home run using a bat representing his party's platform, while the others have all been called out using much weaker bats.

In the cartoon, each has a bat in his hands. Lincoln also has the ball and is saying, *"Gentleman, if ever you should take a hand in another match at this game, remember that you must have a good bat to strike a fair ball and make a clean score and a home run."* On Lincoln's "bat" were the words *"Equal rights and free territory."*

CURRIER AND IVES CARTOON, 1860.

While the 1860 convention met, Lincoln had been trying, in one way and another, to keep down the excitement that was pent up within him—playing billiards a little, town ball a little, and story-telling a little. It is obvious then those sports provided Lincoln with an outlet for stress and anxiety. The eminent Lincoln historian, David Donald describes wonderfully the image of Lincoln waiting as the Republican convention was meeting.

> *"While the Republican National Convention was in session, Lincoln went quietly about his business in Springfield, but he eagerly sought to learn what was going on in Chicago. Up early on Friday, May*

18, the day when nominations were to be made, he passed some time playing "fives"—a variety of handball—with some other men in a vacant lot next to the Illinois State Journal office. Learning that James C. Conkling had unexpectedly returned from Chicago, he went over to his law office to hear the latest news from the convention. Stretched out on an old settee, so short that his feet stuck out over the end, he listened to Conkling's prediction that Seward could not be nominated, and that the convention would choose Lincoln. Lincoln demurred, unwilling to tempt fate by being overoptimistic, and said that either Bates or Chase would probably be the choice. Getting up, he announced: 'Well, Conkling, I believe I will go back to my office and practice law.'

At the Lincoln & Herndon office [Edward L.] Baker, of the Illinois State Journal, came in with telegrams announcing that the names of the candidates had been placed in nomination and that Lincoln's was received with great enthusiasm. Shortly afterward, a new telegram announced the result of the first ballot.... Giving no indication of his feelings, Lincoln went over to the telegraph office, where a report on the second ballot was just coming in.... Lincoln then awaited the results of the third ballot in the Journal office. As he had anticipated this was the last ballot.

> Seward retained most of his strength, but nearly all the other delegates flocked to Lincoln..."
>
> 'I knew this would come when I saw the second ballot,' Lincoln remarked as he accepted the congratulations of his fellow townsmen. Emerging from the Journal office, he said jokingly to the ball players who broke off their game to congratulate him: 'Gentlemen, you had better come up and shake my hand while you can—honors elevate some men.' "

Baker was the editor of the *Journal* and was with Lincoln for a great deal of the day: *"Met Lincoln and we went to ball alley to play at fives-alley was full-said it was pre-engaged; then went to excellent beer saloon near by to play game of billiards; table was full and we each drank a glass of beer; then went to Journal office expecting to hear result of ballot...."* Nearly ninety years later, Branch Rickey made sure that a portrait of Lincoln loomed overhead when he signed Jackie Robinson to a professional contract with the Brooklyn Dodgers.

Lincoln's actual connection to the sport ranges from credible accounts of him watching games and even playing baseball to the preposterous tale of the dying president giving the fast-growing sport his blessing.

Radio sportscaster Bill Stern used to regale listeners with the story of Lincoln rallying from his deathbed to tell Abner Doubleday: *"Keep baseball going; the country needs it."* Lincoln, of course, never regained consciousness after being shot at

Ford's Theatre on April 14, 1865. Doubleday, meanwhile, was nowhere near the theater.

Interestingly, Doubleday was stationed in Washington at the time of the assassination and, while Lincoln and Doubleday never met, Doubleday travelled with Lincoln to Gettysburg in November of 1863 and was at social events with Lincoln during the war years.

Historian Jules Tygiel, who has written frequently about baseball, says he had heard stories of Lincoln arriving in his carriage with his son Tad to see a game in 1862. Another time, Tygiel said, Lincoln supposedly joined a group of boys for a game in Silver Spring, Maryland.

Much as we would like to picture Lincoln setting aside the monumental burdens of the Civil War to play a little baseball or catch up on some baseball news, Lincoln never mentioned baseball in his letters or his speeches. Yet, there are enough accounts from his contemporaries to indicate that Lincoln greatly enjoyed playing and watching baseball.

One can almost see Lincoln looking south from the windows of the White House to distract himself from the dismal news he regularly received from the battlefields by watching the original Washington Nationals run the bases. The newly formed baseball team played on what is now the South Ellipse, then called the White Lot, which, appropriately enough, was enclosed with a whitewashed fence.

Because he knew the team's founder Edmund F. French, quite well, Lincoln was almost certainly a Nationals fan. When Lincoln served his only Congressional term in the House of

Representatives from 1847 to 1849, he lived in a boardinghouse facing the Capitol on the current site of the Library of Congress. It was known as "Abolition House" for being a center of antislavery activists in Washington. Among Lincoln's daily dinner companions were Rep. Joshua Giddings of Ohio, the leading abolitionist in the House, who helped Lincoln write a bill for emancipation in the District of Columbia, along with a variety of Whig members and federal employees.

French, a clerk at the Treasury Department, lived in the house with Lincoln and regularly joined Lincoln for meals. In 1859, while still working at Treasury, French wrote the Constitution and bylaws of the National Baseball Club of Washington, D.C. It was the founding document of the Washington Nationals and therein laid down the rules for sportsmanlike conduct as well as the charge for monthly dues. Dated November 27, 1859, it specified that only gentlemen could join, and they had to be sponsored by another member. The initiation fee was 50 cents and the monthly dues were 25 cents.

Most of the rules concerned fines of 10 cents to 25 cents for such ungentlemanly acts as cursing, disputing the umpire, and missing practice.

French was also a player on the team composed of other government clerks, who suited up in the late afternoons in uniforms consisting of pantaloons and high-collared shirts. The leather-covered ball with a center of India rubber wound with yarn could not weigh more than six ounces or measure more than 10 inches in circumference. The wooden bat could be of any length but no thicker than two and one half inches.

In 1862, French became the Nationals' first president and President Lincoln invited French to various White House social occasions. French's brother, Benjamin Brown French, appointed the superintendent of public buildings by Lincoln, planned Lincoln's inaugurations and later his trip to dedicate the cemetery at Gettysburg.

Lincoln loved baseball. He had played a primitive and popular version of the game called "town ball" as a young man and lawyer in Springfield, Illinois. His friend James Gourley, a Springfield boot maker, who had known him since 1834, in later years recalled: *"We played the old-fashioned game of town ball—jumped—ran—fought and danced. Lincoln played town ball—he hopped well—in 3 hops he would go 40.2 [feet?] on a dead level.... He was a good player—could catch a ball ... and be a hitter too."*

Abraham Lincoln the Athlete

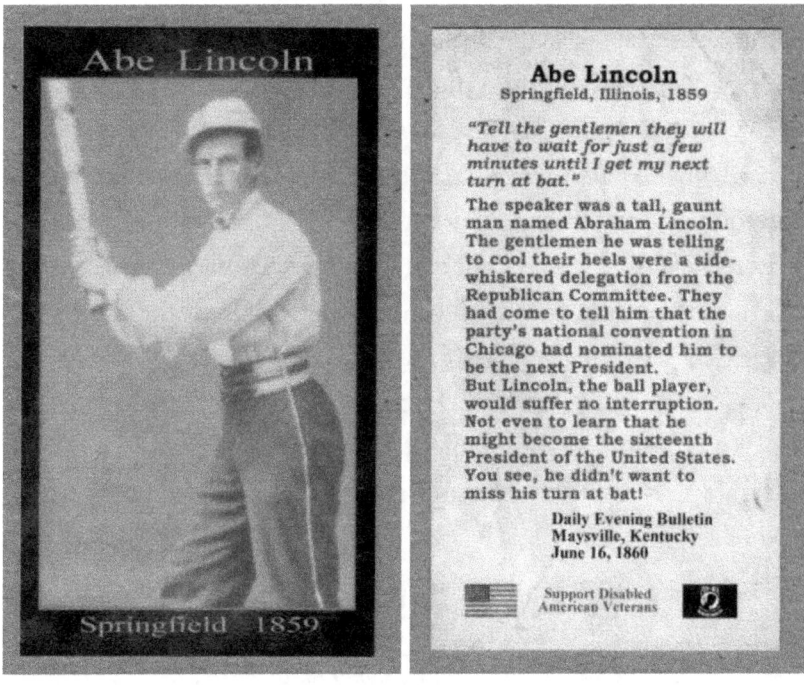

FRONT AND BACK OF A FACSIMILE BASEBALL CARD FROM 1987.

When he moved to Illinois, Lincoln arrived in a community that had a vibrant ball-playing culture. A baseball variant that the locals specifically remembered as being called town ball was played in central Illinois in the 1820s and 1830s. Other ball games that were played during the antebellum era included bullpen, cross out, and long town. Lincoln had a reputation of being a good fives player. Ball playing was a large part of the culture of central Illinois, and it would have been atypical of Lincoln not to take part in these games.

There are numerous accounts of pioneer life in the Illinois County in the decades before the Civil War, and many of them contain references to ball playing. In the histories of Menard County, Mason County, Fulton County, McLean County, and Henry County, there are several references to town ball and bullpen as favorite pastimes. All these counties were in the Sangamon River valley, just north and west of Springfield, Illinois. But together, they describe a lively ball-playing culture existing among the Yankee settlers of central Illinois that began in the 1820s and continued into the Civil War era.

County histories provide rich detail about the sports being played as Lincoln matured into adulthood. For example, a history of Sangamon County describes this in detail.

> "The principal game among the boys was 'bullpen,' a kind of ball. The party was equally divided. A field was laid out with as many corners, or bases, as there were men on a side. They tossed for choice, the winners' side taking the corners, or bases, the others going into the 'pen.' The game was this: The men on the bases, tossing the ball from one to another as rapidly as they could, threw and struck one in the 'pen' whenever they could. If one threw and struck no one, he was out; but if he struck one, the men on the bases all ran away, and if the one struck first did not throw and hit one in return, he was out; though if he did, both kept their places. So the game went on till all on the 'corners' were out; the others then took the bases. This was a rough, but lively and amusing game. Those in the 'pen' often had their ribs sorely battered with the ball; but many

became such adepts in the art of 'dodging' the ball when thrown at them, that it was almost impossible to strike them. The game was, in time, abandoned for a game called 'town ball'; the present baseball being town ball reduced to a science."

Almost all sources agree that bullpen was a popular game in central Illinois during the pioneer era. A close reading of the county history mentioned has town ball growing in popularity in the 1820s.

"Canton was incorporated as a town Feb. 10, 1837. Upon that day an election was held to vote for or against incorporation, resulting in the adoption of the measure by a majority of 34, there being 46 ballots cast. Immediately thereafter the following five Trustees were chosen: David Markley, Joel Wright, Thomas J. Little, William B. Cogswell and Franklin P. Offield. They held this first meeting March 27, 1837, 'at Frederic Mennerts' inn…' Under by-laws adopted by this Board, revenue was to be raised by a tax on all real estate within the boundaries of the town, which, it was provided, should be assessed at its true value, and upon the assessment 'an ad-valorem tax of not exceeding fifty cents on every one hundred dollars should be levied by the President and Trustees annually.' Section 36 of the ordinances provided that 'any person who shall on the Sabbath day play at

> *bandy, cricket, cat, town-ball, corner ball, over-ball, fives or any other game of ball, within the limits of the corporation, or shall engage in pitching dollars or quarters, or any other game, in any public place, shall, on conviction thereof, be fined the sum of one dollar'".*

Another county history states that *"The boys didn't play base ball in 1835. It hadn't been invented. Where I lived… we played 'town ball.' There was a pitcher and catcher. We ran in a circle, and being hit by the ball was out, or the man running the bases could be 'crossed out,' by throwing the ball across his path ahead of him as he ran. They also played 'one-old-cat' and 'two-old-cat' with ball and bat."*

There's a great deal of evidence, then, of ball playing in Illinois before Lincoln arrived and while he was living there. There is also much less evidence of ball playing in Indiana and Kentucky during Lincoln's youth. However, in 1866, William Herndon interviewed Burnbry B. Lloyd, who appears to have known the Lincolns while they lived in Kentucky. Lloyd mentioned that people in Kentucky, during that time, played ball and specifically mentioned *"corner ball, called bullpen, cat & town ball."*

This is significant for two reasons. First, this is evidence that Lincoln was exposed to ball games from a very young age and may have participated in these games while he was a child in Kentucky. More importantly, if Lloyd is speaking about Kentucky during the time when Lincoln lived there, as he appears to be doing, then this is evidence of ball playing in western Kentucky prior to 1816.

John H. Littlefield, an aspiring artist, who was once a clerk in the Lincoln-Herndon law office and ultimately painted a famous portrait of Lincoln remarked, *"As a relaxation from professional cares he would go out and play ball. The game was what was called barn ball, and it consisted of knocking the ball against the side of a building and then hitting it again on the rebound. I have seen Mr. Lincoln go into this sport with a great deal of zest."*

Sometimes on sunny afternoons, such as those in early June 1856, Ben McQueston, a clerk at J.W. Matheny's store, would call up the stairway to the law office, *"Mr. Lincoln, we are going to play ball."* Unless something very pressing was on the table, Lincoln gladly trotted down to a field with the others and played whatever game was on, often a version of "town ball" or rudimentary baseball. *"Everybody played ball,"* McQuestion said. *"There was nothing incongruous about a leading lawyer like Lincoln joining in with tradesmen, clerks, and professional men for an afternoon's amusement. Everyone had time for recreation and business did not suffer."*

There are several accounts of him playing in towns throughout the Eighth Judicial Circuit of Illinois, where he traveled as a lawyer during the 1850s. *"Here Abraham Lincoln and his friends played town ball,"* reads a marker placed before the Postville Park, Illinois, courthouse by the Illinois Historical Society in 1965.

A fire in 1857 destroyed Logan County's records, so little is known about the cases Lincoln handled at Postville. Once, when Lincoln was absent from a court session, Judge Treat sent the sheriff, Dr. Deskins, to find him. Deskins finally found Lincoln in Postville Park, *"playing town ball with the boys."*

Postville, Illinois, was the county seat of Logan County and was part of the Eighth Judicial Circuit that Lincoln travelled while practicing law. Riding the circuit, Lincoln would have been in Postville twice a year from 1839 to 1847.

Historian and Judge, Lawrence Stringer, described Lincoln's social activities at Postville Park: *"Lincoln was always a leader in athletics and played ball and various games with the boys. Scores of old residents can remember seeing him out in the Postville Park, after court had adjourned, indulging in a game of 'town ball'—baseball had not then been invented. He was also quite fond of throwing the maul and frequently entered into a contest of this kind with John Allison. Allison always claimed that he could throw the maul two feet farther than could Lincoln, but John Mann, of Lake Fork, came into the game one day and threw the maul farther than either Lincoln or Allison"*

ILLINOIS STATE HISTORICAL MARKER, POSTVILLE PARK.

Lincoln liked playing town ball even as president, especially with the boys. He took long rides out to the Maryland home of Francis Preston Blair, called Silver Spring, to consult with the venerable political guru, who had been a member of Andrew Jackson's Kitchen Cabinet and helped found the Republican Party and to cavort in games of town ball. Lincoln had appointed Blair's son, Montgomery, to his cabinet as Postmaster General.

One of the Blair grandchildren, Frank B. Blair, recalled how a group of the children eagerly awaited his visit: *"We boys, for hours at a time, played 'town ball' on the vast lawn, and Mr. Lincoln would join ardently in the sport. I remember vividly how he ran with the children; how long were his strides, and how far his coat-tails stuck out behind, and how we tried to hit him with the ball, as he ran the bases. He entered into the spirit of the play as completely as any of us, and we invariably hailed his coming with delight."*

In 1857, the President's "Indian Peace Medal" received a new design that has become a monument of baseball history. A new reverse to the medal was commissioned from engraver Joseph Wilson, who created an emblematic design featuring an Indian chief in full headdress manning a plow, a farm and a church in the distance, a simple home with a woman standing in the doorway and a baseball game being played in the background. Although Wilson died in the year that this medal was issued, Lincoln chose this design for the reverse of his Indian Peace Medal. This domesticated vignette was ringed by a bow, arrows in a quiver, an Indian woman, a peace pipe, and a grisly depiction of one Indian brave scalping another. The vignette indicated the possible taming of the wild through American ways in religion, farming, and adoption of its favorite game.

ABOVE IS THE FRONT AND BELOW IS THE REVERSE OF
PRESIDENT LINCOLN'S INDIAN PEACE MEDAL. NOTE
THE BASEBALL GAME IN THE BACKGROUND.

During the Civil War, Union soldiers in their camps played the newly regularized game of baseball. In Washington, organized teams like the Nationals played in the White Lot. But less formal teams of federal employees also played. Winfield Scott Lamer, a journalist for the *Indianapolis Journal* and later a clerk in the United States Customs Office in St. Louis, observed Lincoln at a baseball game and wrote one of the few detailed accounts of Lincoln, the loyal and enthusiastic fan:

> *"It was at Sixth and K streets. The quartermaster's department was playing the commissary department.... This lot was an old circus grounds. The game was progressing merrily. There were no stands. Ropes kept the cord back.*
>
> *The well-known black carriage drawn by two black horses came along. I saw the president get out of the conveyance and, taking his little son, Tad by the hand, walked over to see the game. This was before the days when cavalry escorts accompanied Mr. Lincoln wherever he went.*
>
> *There was no enclosed stand, not even a seat. Unobtrusively and unseen by the crowd, Mr. Lincoln sat down in the sawdust left by the circus back of first base, crossed his feet, and sat his little son up on them, between his knees.*

He arrived when the game was young and stayed to the finish. It was the custom then for teams to give three cheers for each other after the game was finished. The custom was observed on this occasion.

Lincoln took off his hat and joined in the cheering. Then someone saw him and called for 'Three cheers for Old Abe.' Needless to say, they were very heartily given.

The President thanked the crowd, saying 'Boys it was a very good game and I enjoyed it very much.' He took little Tad by the hand and walked back to the carriage.

I have heard that Mr. Lincoln played a good first base.... President Lincoln did like baseball."

Cornelius Savage probably had one of the few unique experiences of playing baseball in President Lincoln's backyard along with the President himself. "*I used to meet the President two or three times a week and walk with him,*" Savage recalled. "*I was in the Ordnance Department and on the way to the Adjutant General ... [Lincoln] frequently made the trip from the White House to the War Department building, and in this way I passed him many times. The president came to recognize me and ... I commenced to fall in next to him and walk with him.*"

Savage formed a baseball team with a number of his friends from Brooklyn, New York, and played their games right behind the White House less than a hundred yards away. "*While we were out there playing ball,*" Savage went on, "*we would often see the figure of the resident standing in back of the White House, dressed in his black coat and with his stove-pipe hat on. Many times he seemed to be watching the game with great interest, and on one day he actually walked down to the field from the White House, and, standing in the back of the catcher's cage, he threw the ball onto the field. We counted that quite an event.* President Lincoln apparently did this several more times in the coming days as he enjoyed participating in the game "with the Brooklyn boys quite a lot," Savage believed.

Soon thereafter, according to Savage, a new Commissioner of Public Buildings told the ball players that they would have to move their games and play elsewhere because they were too close to the President and his home. "*A few days later I met the President on his walk,*" Savage said, "*and I told him that the Commissioner had ordered our ball games away from his house. Then Mr. Lincoln said; 'Don't go away until I tell you so.' And he never did tell us to go.*"

Lincoln was surrounded by men who followed baseball. The journalist to whom he was closest, Noah Brooks, whom he planned to appoint as his private secretary in his second term, went on to write the first novel about baseball, *Our Base Ball Club and How It Won the Championship* that was the first novel devoted entirely to baseball. Throughout the story, intense town rivalry forces the Catalpa, Illinois, community, and its ball club to confront game-throwing players and to enter the debate about amateur versus professional teams. In his introduction to the book, A. G. Spalding champions Brooks' vivid portrayal of the ups and downs, the trials and the triumphs of a baseball club, concluding *"that while nothing is really needed to popularize the game, I am sure the story will commend itself to every lover of pure and wholesome literature."*

"That's beautiful: the hurrah game!," wrote Walt Whitman, "well—it's our game: that's the chief fact in connection with it: America's game: has the snap, go, fling, of the American atmosphere—belongs as much to our institutions, fits into them as significantly, as our constitutions, laws: is just as important in the sum total of our historic life." Whitman spent many mornings waiting outside the White House to see Lincoln coming and going. No writer since has exceeded these extravagant and fervent claims for the game. Whitman's baseball credo could only have been spoken by a man who grew up with the sport and saw it develop from its slower, more sedate forms into a demanding game of hardball with "snap and go."

And yet, it was perhaps a scandal involving a minor league player that became Lincoln's most direct and familial link to the national pastime. There is no doubt that Warren Wallace Beckwith led an interesting life. Born in Mount Pleasant, Iowa, in 1874, his father was a wealthy railroad executive, and Beckwith was said to have inherited a fortune upon his father's death in 1905. He played college football at Iowa Wesleyan, played baseball and football professionally, and served in the Spanish-American War and World War I.

WARREN WALLACE BECKWITH.

But his life literally became a captivating national news story in 1897 when he eloped with Jesse Lincoln, granddaughter of the late President. Her father Robert Todd Lincoln, former Secretary of War, was quoted calling Beckwith a "Baseball Buffoon."

The Beckwith–Lincoln marriage played out like a soap opera in the newspapers for the next decade. Beckwith spent most of 1897 playing in the Texas League with Dallas, Paris, and Denison/Sherman/Waco teams. *The New York Times* reported that Beckwith's nicknames in Texas were "The Dude" and "Lady Killer," and that "He would never go into a game to pitch without first combing or brushing his hair faultlessly."

Beckwith made headlines again when he enlisted in the military service when war was declared with Spain. When he returned from Cuba, and after the birth of the couple's first child, a daughter, he joined Sacramento in the California League, which resulted in another round of stories about Robert Todd Lincoln's disapproval of his son-in-law's profession. According to contemporary news reports, neither Robert Todd Lincoln nor his wife, Mary Eunice Harlan Lincoln, daughter of former United States Senator from Iowa, James Harlan, ever accepted the marriage.

News stories announcing the couple's divorce in 1900 turned out to be premature and they had a second child, Robert Todd Lincoln Beckwith, who, upon his death in 1985, was the final direct descendent of President Lincoln.

Beckwith and Lincoln did divorce in 1907. Beckwith never played professionally after 1899 but played extensively on semi-professional teams in Illinois and Iowa. Beckwith's final appearance in organized ball was as the manager of Oshkosh in the Wisconsin State League for part of the 1905 season.

After serving in France in World War I, Beckwith settled in La Jolla, California. He died in La Jolla in 1955 and was buried at the Forest Home Cemetery in Mount Pleasant.

On the anniversary of his birth in 1920, the *Ottawa (IL) Herald* marked the occasion with a front-page story recalling different aspects of his life.

"*Play baseball, yes Lincoln played baseball,*" the newspaper said. "*He would leave his [Springfield law] office any time of the day and it used [to be said about] him that he left the courtroom during court to engage in a game of ball. He could play too.*"

Lincoln's love of sports and baseball called attention to his character traits, wrote John Sayle Watterson in *The Games the*

Presidents Play. In whatever sport he watched or participated, Lincoln demonstrated *"sociability, ambition, competitiveness, and a sense of fair play. In much the same way as he [once] reacted when his son kicked over a chess game [in which the president was playing], letting fly all the pieces, Lincoln was able as president to pick up the pieces after military defeats and begin again."*

Strong evidence, then, suggests that Abraham Lincoln deserves to be called the first "baseball president."* Indeed, it is altogether appropriate that on December 13, 1865, eight months after Ford's Theatre, when a record ninety-one baseball clubs gathered in New York for the National Association of Baseball Players convention, that the players raised a glass to the late president who enjoyed their sport and who many considered might have been a pretty fair player himself.

> *Nevertheless, credit must be given where it is due and it was Andrew Johnson, Lincoln's successor, who would become the first president to invite a baseball team inside the White House and also the first president on record to call baseball "our national game."*

Chapter Two
"I'M THE BIG BUCK OF THIS LICK"

Lincoln and Wrestling

A DEPICTION OF LINCOLN WRESTLING IN NEW SALEM, ILLINOIS.

South central Illinois is gorgeous in the summer and fall. The gently rolling hills are heavily populated by beautiful trees of all sizes and shapes. It is a peaceful area. It is also a land that harbors some very important historical secrets.

Located about twenty miles northwest of Springfield is the restored village of New Salem. Situated on a bluff that overlooks the small and winding Sangamon River, it is now little more than a collection of memories. Yet, what memories they are.

The original village was a tiny pioneer settlement that flourished and then faded away, all in a short period of time in the 1830s. It was founded in the fall of 1828 when James M. Camron and his uncle, James Rutledge, sailed down the river in search of a good location to build a gristmill. They liked the western bank of the river and, in particular, the ridge that overlooked the bank. They walked up the hill, scouting the land, and decided that this would be their new home.

Within two months, they had each built a small cabin up on the ridge and also filed claim with the Illinois State legislature in Springfield to build a dam across the river.

They received permission to do so and soon constructed a small gristmill and sawmill. The gristmill's purpose was to grind up corn from the nearby fields and the sawmill was designed to slice trees into planks to be used for building.

At about the same time, William Clary arrived on the scene. He too was in search of a spot to start a small business. He decided to open a general store on the location and sell liquor, as well. Meanwhile, his brother, John, became the founder of a small farming community about five miles to the west. It became known as Clary's Grove.

William's store quickly became a gathering place for the area's toughest men. Cock fighting, dice throwing, storytelling, and wrestling were all popular activities for the men who worked hard all day in a variety of occupations and sought distractions at night. The Clary's Grove boys were among his best customers.

Life in New Salem was demanding, both physically and emotionally, and only the most determined could survive. There were few amenities to speak of, and there was always the threat of an Indian uprising. Many tribes lived in the area, and a constant vigilance was demanded.

The little village died out after a brief existence. If it had not been home at one time to a young fellow named Abraham Lincoln, it would be of no interest at all today; it would be just another tiny settlement that faded into oblivion.

Lincoln was born on February 12, 1809, in a small cabin that was a few miles south of Hodgen's Mill Kentucky. His father, Thomas, and mother, Nancy, owned some three hundred acres of land called Sinking Spring Farm.

He was the second of two children, having an older sister named Sarah. When Lincoln was six, the family moved to Little Pigeon Creek, a wilderness settlement in southern Indiana. Lincoln's mother died there on October 5, 1818.

Fourteen months later, Thomas married Sarah Bush Johnson, a widow, and she brought her three children to live in the Lincoln cabin with Thomas and his two children. In March of 1830, the family moved to a spot near Decatur, Illinois. A year later, Lincoln, just twenty-two years of age, set out looking for both adventure and opportunity. He and two other men, his stepmother's son, John D. Johnston, and John Hanks, agreed to take a flatboat of goods down river to New Orleans for a man named Denton Offutt. About four miles from Springfield, they met up with Offutt. Since he had not yet bought a flatboat, they wound up building one for him.

It was on April 19, 1831 that Lincoln had his first look at New Salem. The flatboat he was on got hung up on the small dam on the Sangamon River, just a couple of hundred yards from the ridge where the village sat. The New Salem residents straggled down to the river's edge to watch the tall young man and his companions struggling to force the flatboat off the dam. Abe figured out a way to move the boat and soon they resumed their voyage to New Orleans.

While the boat was hung up on the dam, Offutt took a brief look at the little village on the ridge and he liked what he saw. On the way to New Orleans, he told Lincoln that he was going to come back to New Salem and start a general store. He asked Lincoln if he would like to be a clerk in the store; having no other plans, the future president readily accepted the offer.

Lincoln was known to use his unnatural strength to his advantage for profit in other ways besides a job, on one occasion betting a later close friend Bill Greene a fur hat that he could drink a shot from a barrel of whisky by lifting the entire thing above his head and drinking straight from the hole. Greene felt this would be an impossible feat of strength, but one which Lincoln pulled off easily.

Displays of brute strength like this didn't go unnoticed by Lincoln's employer, Denton Offutt, who bragged to neighbors and anyone who would listen that Lincoln was not just the most intelligent man in the region but also strong enough to beat up anyone in town, a claim that eventually piqued the interest of a local bully said to be able to "lick anybody" called Jack Armstrong.

It was this decision by the strapping young frontiersman that laid the foundation for his legendary wrestling match with Jack Armstrong.

Wrestling had come to the New World with the first colonists, back in the early 1600s. Colonists were by nature (and necessity) a tough and hardy breed of people; imagine the courage it took to get into a small ship and set sail out over the rugged Atlantic Ocean. The voyage could take over thirty days, with the constant challenge of fierce storms and fear of strange beasts uppermost in everyone's thoughts.

Wrestling was a sport for the strong of heart. It flourished along the eastern seaboard and moved west with the men who carved out the wilderness. By 1831, wrestling was very popular as both a test of manhood and as a form of entertainment in small villages like New Salem, Illinois. Among the more adventurous types, it was also an excellent excuse for betting.

On the American frontier, the sportsmanlike collar and elbow gave way to a catch-as-catch-can style that required less skill and more brute strength. The matches were decided when an opponent was thrown off his feet. In the name of civic pride, and, of course, some friendly wagering champions from each county were pitted against each other. Lincoln progressed swiftly in this rougher style of wrestling, though he often helped conquered opponents to their feet or gave them water after the matches. "He was a proud competitor but a humble sportsman," recalled one contemporary. And when his wrestling skills diminished, Lincoln's leadership qualities emerged.

Abraham Lincoln had the perfect physique for wrestling. Tall and lean, he was wiry and very strong from his years of swinging an axe. He had tremendous foreman strength and little body fat. He also had developed considerable endurance and a fierce pride, two more key ingredients in a wrestler's makeup. He probably had many impromptu tussles while growing up in Kentucky and Indiana, but they were not recorded and are lost in the mists of time.

However, a book entitled *Life of Lincoln and Stories of the Lincoln Trail* claims that he was already an accomplished wrestler by the time he arrived in New Salem. Talking about the Lincoln family settling in Little Pigeon Creek, Indiana, the book says: *"Here Lincoln lived until he was twenty-one, going to school 'by littles,' reading his dozens of books by the light of an open fireplace, and earning came as a rail-splitter, storyteller, and rassler."*

LINCOLN PORTRAYED AS A ROUGH AND TUMBLE FIGHTER.

Though he had no dreams of sporting grandeur, the future president, like many of his contemporaries who worked manual labor jobs, enjoyed physical activities like wrestling as a leisure activity. But just like in his political career, Lincoln was a calculated and ambitious wrestler. Still, conversely to his political persona, the young Lincoln was a confident sportsman who could be simply described as cocky. Lincoln's confidence in his ability stemmed from his mastery of the "catch-as-catch-can" manner of wrestling, a brawling and combative style known for its bull-like aggressive rushes and hand-to-hand combat tactics to the opponent. Nevertheless, this bar-fight style of wrestling still needed more than a hint of skill to pin a rival. Lincoln's rare mix of thin and wiry but broad, strong, and smart athlete made him nearly impossible to beat.

And so it was in the summer of 1831, William Clary was selling liquor from his store and doing well. He charged twelve cents for a drink of brandy, gin, or whiskey and twice that for his best wine. He developed a good and steady business of local customers and visitors from off the river. When river travelers came up the bluff for a break in their journeys, they were looking for a place to drink a bit and swap tales. Offutt chose to build his store very close to Clary's and the two men competed for business. Clary's store was at the top of the bluff, about forty feet in front of Offutt's store. Travelers had to make a choice between them as to which was the best place to spend their small amount of money.

Then one day in July, Lincoln walked into the village with very few belongings and little hope of anything substantial on the horizon, other than having a job in hand. Within a short period of time, he would become involved in what must be considered one of the most intriguing sporting events in all of American history.

Lincoln impressed Offutt with his wiry strength. Offutt had seen Abe pick up large barrels of whiskey and other bulky items and carry them with ease. At six feet and four inches of height and carrying close to one hundred and eighty pounds, he was a very large man for the time. *"He sure was the big buck of this lick,"* said a New Salem resident. *"He can outrun, outlift, outwrestle and throw down any man in Sangamon County,"* said Bill Green, a store clerk in New Salem, as he watched the twenty-two-year-old Lincoln whip all comers one day in 1831.

Good natured and conversational, Abe made friends quickly. But he also made a few enemies, probably without even being aware of it. Offutt was a man who liked to talk a lot. He was very proud of his new helper and boasted to William Clary that Abe was the strongest man he knew. Moreover, Lincoln matched his reputation as an in-ring force with his uncharacteristic, to today's view of him, loud public trash talking. After decisively defeating another opponent with a single toss in the ring, Honest Abe being as honest as he could be looked into an entire crowd and challenged any and all who dared to face him. Lincoln shouted, *"I'm the big buck of this lick. If any of you want to try it, come on and whet your horns."*

This quote comes from the biography *Abraham Lincoln: The Prairie Years*, which was written by poet and author Carl Sandburg in 1926. Lincoln reportedly said this phrase after a raucous battle with his stepbrother, John Johnston, which was initiated by a man named William Grigsby. This fight of Lincoln occurred earlier in his life when his family were the only people not invited to a double wedding involving two brothers, Rueben and Charles Grigsby, who were marrying a pair of sisters, Matilda and Elizabeth Hawkins. Hurt by this perceived slight at his family, Lincoln penned a sarcastic poem in which he accused the third Grigsby brother, William, of being gay. His reputation as a heterosexual man besmirched, William challenged Lincoln to a wrestling match.

Perhaps feeling bad about the whole thing or maybe just wanting to insult him more, Lincoln, who was a clear head taller than his challenger, suggested that this wouldn't be fair to William and instead suggested William fight his stepbrother, John D. Johnston who wasn't near the fighter that Abe was. William accepted.

When the day arrived for the hotly anticipated showdown, as soon as the fight began, Grigsby quickly gained the upper hand and placed Johnston in a painful hold. It was at this point that, Lincoln barreled through the crowd, grabbed Grigsby from behind and duplexed him into the ground.

As Carl Sandburg tells it, Lincoln defeated Johnston, went searching for Grigsby in the crowd, threw the man into the middle of the ring, and then sparked an all-out brawl when he issued this challenge to the crowd: *"The two fighters, stripped to the waist, mauled at each other with bare knuckles. A crowd formed a ring and stood cheering, yelling, hissing, and after a while saw Johnston getting the worst of it. The ring of the crowd was broken when Abe shouldered his way through, stepped out took hold of Grigsby and threw him out of the center of the fight ring. Then, so they said, Abe Lincoln called out, 'I'm the big buck of this lick,' and his eyes sweeping the circle of the whet crowd he challenged. 'If any of you want to try it, come on and your horns.' "*

Jason H. Silverman

S.T. DADD'S ILLUSTRATION OF LINCOLN
WRESTLING FROM THE
STORY OF ABRAHAM LINCOLN (1900)

A DEPICTION OF LINCOLN ABOUT TO THROW ONE OF HIS OPPONENTS. FROM AN EARLY BIOGRAPHY OF LINCOLN

No one stepped forward.

But Clary knew a few strong men, as well. They were men of a different temperament than Abe: loud and belligerent when the liquor took effect. They enjoyed rough-and-tumble pastimes. There is little doubt that Lincoln soon heard about the wild goings-on next door to his store, and he was most likely a spectator at some of the events.

Wrestling was the best way to determine what a man was made of. The bouts in the thick grass between Clary's store and Offutt's store were a regular occurrence, in a true frontier style. The ringleader of the bunch was a rugged farmer from Clary's Grove named Jack Armstrong.

The Clary's Grove Boys *"thought that had found only another subject by which this band could display its strength and prowess,"* observed John T. Stuart, who was Mr. Lincoln's mentor and first law partner. *"The champion of the clan, Jack Armstrong was selected to wrestle with Lincoln and to show him that although six feet three he was no man at all compared with the 'Boys.' It did not take Jack long to discover that he had got hold of the wrong customer; and when it was evident that Lincoln was getting the better of their champion the whole Band pitched in and gave Lincoln several blows which had no very salutary effect on the strength of his legs. Lincoln however took all this in perfect good humor and by laughing and joking displayed such an excellent disposition that he at once won their hearts and was invited to become one of the company. This was the turning point in Lincoln's life."*

Shorter than Lincoln, Armstrong was much thicker and heavier. A biography of Jack at the Illinois State Historical

Society reports that he was *"a man of medium weight, below medium height....(and) endowed by nature with that peculiar and perfect coordination of nerves and muscles which gave him an excess of physical strength for his weight."*

At age twenty-seven, he was also five years older than Lincoln. Little is known about his wrestling expertise other than the fact that he was considered the roughest of the gang of young men who resided at Clary's Grove.

Within a short amount of time from Lincoln's arrival, a match was brewing, and the talk soon reached the point that if either man shied away, then he would be branded a coward. Lincoln accepted the challenge, getting up from behind his counter, and prepared to wrestle the feared Armstrong. Offutt offered to bet anyone ten dollars that Lincoln would win. Money, drinks, and various items were soon being wagered around the village.

Finally, the two men, Lincoln and Armstrong, met on the grassy area between the two stores to settle the talk. The spot is approximately forty yards long and twenty yards wide and is thick with trees and bushes on both sides of the clearing. As many as one hundred men may have gathered to see the contest, as it was undoubtedly a major source of discussion in the little village and the surrounding area.

Despite their physical differences, Abe and Jack were equally matched. While Abe had the advantage in height and leverage, Jack had the edge in experience and attitude. He was undoubtedly a more seasoned grappler and fighter, according to all reports.

There were several types of wrestling that were engaged in on the frontier. One style was where the two men agreed to take a hold on each other and see who could throw who first. If either man was tossed or lost his grip, then he was the loser. Some historians think this is how the match was contested and that it was more of a sport than a battle.

But there was another style more popular with rowdies. The rough-and-tumble sort of men, like the Clary's Grove boys, preferred a no-holds-barred style of match, which means anything was acceptable except kicking, eye gouging, and biting. It was perhaps a bit of the elbow-and-collar style of wrestling that was very popular in Vermont, and which spread west with the settlers.

If it was the latter style of match, then the two men probably circled one another warily, sizing each other up. After a few feints and attempts to get the other man down, they would have grabbed hold and begun real wrestling. Pushing, pulling, and yanking, the spectators shouting all the time, each man tried to trip the other to the ground.

In 1939, a popular movie called "Abe Lincoln of Illinois" was made from the Pulitzer Prize–winning play of the same name, written by Robert Sherwood. In this version of the story, Lincoln, who was played superbly by Raymond Massey, tangled with Armstrong who was played by Howard da Silva. Armstrong throws Lincoln with a move like an under-arm spin, tossing him hard to the ground. Lincoln stands up, wipes his hands on his trousers, and then tosses Armstrong with a similar move. Then the two men began brawling, rolling to the ground, and gripping one another's head and arms in an effort to gain control. At last, Lincoln throws Armstrong heavily to the ground. Exhausted, Armstrong surrenders. It was a dramatic version that looked good on film.

Annoyed by the lack of sportsmanship, Lincoln lost his temper and, according to legend, won the match by grabbing Armstrong by the neck, raising him above his head, shaking him around, and slamming him on the ground. The crowd was shocked by Lincoln's clear victory, and the rest of the Clary's Grove Boys were angered by the result. Enraged, the Clary's Grove Boys began to threaten Lincoln. Many stories have Lincoln on his feet, looking down at the defeated Armstrong. The Clary's Grove boys advanced on Lincoln, shouting at him and raising their fists. An all-out fight appeared imminent.

Lincoln supposedly stood with his back against one of the two stores, fists clenched, and declared he would take them on one at a time, if need be. However, Armstrong came to Lincoln's side and told his pals that Abe had beaten him fairly, and that he had proven that he was worthy of their respect. *"Boys, Abe Lincoln is the best fellow that ever broke into this settlement. He shall be one of us,"* Armstrong reportedly said. The Clary's Grove boys backed off and Lincoln gained a new status in the little village. He was known from then on as a man not to be trifled with, despite his infectious grin and considerate good humor. The fact was, it seemed, that Lincoln could defend himself and gained immense stature due to his wrestling abilities!

Abraham Lincoln the Athlete

LINCOLN LIFTS AND THROWS JACK ARMSTRONG IN THIS PICTURE.

Another version of this story can be found in the biography *Abraham Lincoln: Redeemer President*:

> "When Offutt (Lincoln's boss at the time) began boasting that his new clear could whip any rough-houser in New Salem, several of them put up their champion, Jack Armstrong, to wrestle Lincoln. Just how the match was fought, or even who exactly won, is

probably unsure, Armstrong later admitted 'that he threw L. but did not do it fairly'; what does seem sure is that Lincoln came away with the admiration and probably the store business, of even New Salem's roughest lot and the lifelong loyalty of the Armstrongs. 'He won us by his bearing and boldness,' Royal Clary recalled, "Jack and [Lincoln] were the warmest friends during life."

Here's how David Herbert Donald described the fight in his biography of Lincoln:

"None were wilder than the boys from Clary's Grove, a few miles to the west, whose leader was the stalwart Jack Armstrong.... When Offutt, enchanted with his new assistant, began boasting that Lincoln was not merely the smartest man in New Salem but also one of the strongest, the Clary's Gove boys called his bluff. They cared not at all about Lincoln's mental superiority, but they dared him to test his strength in a wrestling match with their champion, Jack Armstrong. Lincoln was reluctant, because he said he did not like all the 'wooling and pulling' of a wrestling match, but the urging of his employer and the taunts of his rivals obliged him to fight. In the collective memory of New Salem residents the contest was an epic one and various versions survived: How Armstrong defeated Lincoln through a trick; How Lincoln threw Armstrong; how

Armstrong's followers threatened collectively to lick the man who had defeated their champion until Lincoln volunteered to take them all on, but one at a time. The details were irrelevant. What mattered was that Lincoln proved that he had immense strength and courage, and that was enough to win the admiration of the Clary's Grove gang. Thereafter they became Lincoln's most loyal and enthusiastic admirers."

Biographer and one of Lincoln's personal secretaries, William O. Stoddard, wrote this of the match:

"The episode was full of important consequences to Abraham Lincoln. His courage and prowess had been thoroughly tested and had made a deep impression upon the minds of his rough neighbors. He was in no danger of further challengers from any of them, and Jack Armstrong avowed himself the fast friend of the man who had given him so good a shaking."

The impact of that 1831 wrestling match at New Salem is exciting to ponder. One of the men died twenty-three years later without ever having claimed any degree of fame, other than his role in the contest. The other fellow went on to become the sixteenth President of the United States. Abraham Lincoln is generally regarded as the greatest of all Americans. A Gallup poll in 1958 declared him as such, and his reputation has grown since then.

"Lincoln, by far, is America's favorite president," said James Horgan, a Florida history professor and an expert on presidents, in a newspaper article in the 1990s. Lincoln has become such a powerful figure in American and world history that he is the subject of more books than any other person. It is estimated that over sixteen thousand books and pamphlets have been written about him. And many of those books contain at least some mention of the wrestling match in 1831.

But how much truth lies behind the stories that Lincoln wrestled Jack Armstrong in New Salem in the summer of 1831? *"There is just too much documentation that it took place to doubt it,"* said Candy Knox, at the Lincoln New Salem Historic Site who leads tours through the site. *"What we have deduced from all our research is that the match took place in the little grassy area between the Clary and Offutt stores."*

In fact, there is an informational sign posted above the Clary store entrance that refers to the popular events going on in New Salem at the time. It reads, in part: *"Gambling, cock fights, gander pulls and wrestling matches were all very common activities at the store."*

Other noted Lincoln historians also accept the fact that the wrestling match was a real event. According to Ira Berkow, a national columnist who authored a story that appeared in the *New York Times* several years ago, *"Lincoln established his reputation as a wrestler in 1831 in a dramatic confrontation with one Jack Armstrong, the leader of a rowdy bunch known as the Clary's Grove Boys."*

Carl Sandburg, a native of Illinois who was one of the nation's most respected writers, wrote a highly-praised six-volume biography of books on Lincoln. He even claimed Lincoln scored a pin. Sandburg wrote that

> *"Lincoln lifted him up by the throat ... shook him like a rag, and then slammed him to a hard fall. Armstrong, short and powerful, aimed from the first to get in close and use his thick muscular strength. Lincoln held him off with long arms, wore down his strength, got him out of breath, surprised and 'rattled.' They pawed and clutched in many holds and twists till Lincoln threw Armstrong and had both shoulders on the grass."*

Sandburg did add that "some claimed it was a draw." Armstrong acknowledged: " *'He's the best feller that ever broke into this settlement,' and the fight was over."*

From then on Lincoln often appeared in the role of sports arbiter during the six years he worked in New Salem. His reputation for fairness—and for having the strength to back up his decisions—made him a popular referee, and there was not a local foot or horse race, cockfight or gander pull that he didn't preside over was rare.

"Lincoln didn't do sports per se," said Charles Strozier, a noted Lincoln scholar, *"but he was very strong and wiry—about six feet four inches, very tall for those times, and weighed about 184 pounds. He could hold a heavy ax at arm's length for such a long*

period of time that people were struck by the feat. "And Lincoln was a noted wrestler. There's enough testimony to trust it."

Thomas Schwartz expressed the same sentiment. *"I don't think there's any doubt Lincoln was a wrestler of some renown,"* said Schwartz. *"There is enough evidence to support that."*

The main thrust of the bout could be described like this: Lincoln didn't really want to wrestle Armstrong because he felt it was being built up too much as a "fight" and not strictly a good-natured contest. But when he saw how everyone was talking about the match and making it such a big deal, he knew it was bound to take place eventually.

"In those days, there was a lot of pressure to prove yourself in manly contests," said local historian Raymond Montgomery. *"I think Offutt promoted the match as a way of drawing attention to his store. I think Lincoln didn't have much choice."*

The match took place on a hot sunny afternoon. It may have started out with an agreement for each of the men to take holds, but that seems unlikely given the reputation of the Clary's Grove boys. By all accounts, they liked their "rassling" rough and tumble and Armstrong most likely would have wanted a contest with few rules.

However, once the match started, it's a fairly safe bet that it quickly turned into a wide-open affair. Lincoln, by most accounts, got the best of Armstrong. One popular storyline says that Armstrong, frustrated by his inability to penetrate beyond Lincoln's long arms, stomped on Abe's foot and that the match became rowdy from that point on.

As previously stated, some historians suggest they battled to a draw, but most of them say Lincoln finally got Armstrong down and made him give up.

"I think the fight may have been a draw," said Strozier. *"But the fight gave him (Lincoln) legitimacy in the neighbor hood, and nobody bothered him anymore when he sat reading under a tree."* Whatever the outcome, Lincoln was totally accepted by the rowdies. Some scholars even suggest the wrestling match was a key element in the fortunes of the future president. Way back in 1860, a former law partner, John T. Stuart, said the event was "the turning point" in Lincoln's life.

Shortly after the match, New Salem sent a company of men up to northern Illinois, around the Dixon area, to fight in the Black Hawk War. Jack Armstrong and several other Clary's Grove boys were in the group. The men elected Lincoln their captain, a great honor for a relative newcomer to the area.

Whatever happened on that distant day in 1831, the match was a defining moment in the life of Abraham Lincoln and a great moment for wrestling enthusiasts everywhere. The fact is that the man many consider the finest of all Americans wasn't a soccer player, basketball player, football player or golfer, but he certainly was a wrestler. And, there exists considerable evidence to support that conclusion.

A SPECULATIVE DRAWING OF LINCOLN WRESTLING AT A COUNTY FAIR THOUGH NO EVIDENCE EXISTS TO SUGGEST THAT HE DID SO.

The sport of wrestling often helps the men who battle one another to build strong bonds of friendship, just like Gilgamesh and Enkidu in The Epic of Gilgamesh. And such appears to be the case with Jack Armstrong and Abe Lincoln.

By wrestling their best man, Lincoln earned the respect of the Clary's Grove boys. After the contest, Lincoln often visited the Armstrong cabin about four miles from New Salem and sometimes helped Jack with farm work. He liked to bring candy to the children and would even rock the baby's cradle from time to time. Jack's wife, Hannah, would sew Abe's clothes when they needed mending and insisted that he join the family for supper.

> *"There's no doubt that Lincoln and Armstrong became good friends,"* said Montgomery. *"In fact, I think the best friends Lincoln ever had in life came from his New Salem days ... and Jack was among the best of them."*

The biography of Armstrong in the Illinois Historical Society Library also notes that he was *"extremely sociable in his disposition"* and that he loved to have Lincoln stop by. At times, if he heard Lincoln was not busy, Armstrong would even send word to him to come visit and stay awhile.

Even though Lincoln moved away from New Salem in 1837 and took up residence twenty miles southeast in Springfield, his connection to the Armstrong family was not severed. Twenty-one years later, William "Duff" Armstrong, one of Jack and Hannah's twin sons, was charged with murder. It was an incident that resulted from a late-night brawl. Lincoln wrote to Hannah Armstrong and offered to take the case.

> *"I have just heard of your deep affliction, and the arrest of your son for murder. I can hardly believe that he can be capable of the crime alleged against him. It does not seem possible. I am anxious that he should be given*

a fair trial at any rate; and gratitude for your long-continued kindness to me in adverse circumstances prompts me to offer my humble services gratuitously in his behalf. It will afford me an opportunity to requite, in a small degree, the favors I have received at your hand, and that of your lamented husband, when your roof afforded me a grateful shelter without money and without price."

The trial was held in the town of Beardstown, about twenty-five miles west of New Salem. Even though the killing occurred late at night, a key witness had declared in court that he could identify Duff as the murderer by the light of the moon. Lincoln consulted an almanac and found out that there was very little moonlight on the night of the murder. On May 7, 1858, the jury found Duff innocent of all charges.

When Mrs. Armstrong asked Lincoln how much she owed him for his work, he reportedly responded, *"Why, Hannah, I shan't charge you a cent—never. Anything I can do for you I will do willingly and without charge."*

The last known link between Lincoln and the Armstrong family came in 1863. Duff Armstrong was a member of the 85th Illinois volunteers during the Civil War. He was ill in a hospital in Louisville when Hannah appealed to the president to help him get discharged. Lincoln's loyalty to his friends was evident when he stopped what he was doing to come through for the Armstrong family once again.

It is obvious that there was a very strong relationship between Abe Lincoln and the family of Jack Armstrong that developed from the wrestling match and endured through the years.

Jack never lived to see Abe Lincoln declared as president of the United States. He died of a lingering illness on September 9, 1854, at the age of fifty. He is buried in the Old Concord Cemetery in Petersburg, just two miles from New Salem. But Armstrong's place in history is secure, thanks to an informal wrestling match held almost two centuries ago on a hot summer's day in a little village in the American heartland.

Feeling more confident after his wrestling match with Armstrong and gaining acceptance by the community as a whole, Lincoln began to mature rapidly. He labored over his reading and studies and polished his conversational skills. He began to contemplate a future that extended far beyond the boundaries of the little village on the ridge.

He spent six years in New Salem and got his first taste of political life there. On August 6, 1832, he decided to run for the Illinois State legislature on the Whig ticket. Though he carried his own district by a margin of 277 votes to 7, he lost the overall election.

When the Offutt store quickly failed, Offutt moved away to begin a horse-selling business. That fall, Lincoln went into partnership in another general store with William Berry, another New Salem resident. Abe called on his wrestling skills again when a loudmouth came into the store and used profane language in front of the women. Lincoln asked him to hold his tongue, but the man continued and even boasted that no one could make him stop.

Finally, his patience worn thin, Lincoln invited the man outside. Abe flung him to the ground and stuffed weeds into his mouth to shut him up. It did the trick.

On May 7, 1833, Lincoln was named postmaster of New Salem. He used to walk through the village with the letters stuffed inside his hat, handing them out to residents when he came across them. On August 4, 1834, he ran for office again, and this time he was elected to the state legislature.

During that term, Lincoln found the opportunity to use his wrestling prowess when he needed to protect a New Salem friend who was on hand to hear him give a speech at a little town called Pappsville, located just a little west of New Salem. Just as Lincoln was getting ready to speak, a fight broke out in the crowd and his friend was roughed up. Lincoln jumped off the platform, grabbed his friend's assailant, tossed him a few feet, then strode back to the platform and gave what amounted to the first political speech in his career.

Many people have speculated that the great love of Lincoln's life was a New Salem resident by the name of Ann Rutledge. Her father had come to New Salem in 1828 and established a tavern in his house. It became a popular meeting place and Abe boarded there for a year. Though he was a nondrinker, Abe spent many a night with Ann in the tavern, talking about a variety of topics. A great affection grew between them. He was shocked and saddened almost beyond words when she became ill and died at the tender age of twenty-one, on August 25, 1835.

Shortly after her death, he wrote: *"I can hardly be reconciled to have the snow, rains and storms beat upon her grave! My heart is buried there."*

In 1836, Lincoln won re-election to the statehouse and began to set his sights on a career in law and politics. On April 15, 1837, Abraham Lincoln rode out of New Salem to begin a new life in Springfield. He was now on a course with destiny.

Local historian Raymond Montgomery, a lifelong resident of the area and a student of Lincoln's days in New Salem, sees those seven years as a part of a magnificent plan for both Abraham Lincoln and the young nation he was to serve during its most critical test of existence.

> *"It is my feeling that there had to have been some power stronger to have created New Salem,"* said Montgomery. *"I've always thought it was placed there to educate the man who was to become the sixteenth President of the United States and to prepare him for the trials and tribulations that lay ahead. There is no way this man could have survived the rigors and demands of life in New Salem without the support of all the people there. He had no money and very few material possessions. He survived by his ability to make people like him and want to help him. They all rallied around him. I believe there is no way the Union could have survived without Abraham Lincoln leading the way. Abe Lincoln's political prowess really flowered in New Salem.*

And the wrestling match with Jack Armstrong may well have been the thing that proved he was the type of man to be followed."

Montgomery sees another fascinating element to Lincoln's years in New Salem. *"It's very interesting that the village came into existence and endured only as long as Lincoln lived there,"* he said. *"It was a beautiful spot for a town but once Lincoln left the village withered and died, almost immediately. It's like it was placed here for a reason."*

COVER OF THE 1958 *CLASSICS ILLUSTRATED* COMIC BOOK.

Near Bethany, Missouri, however, lies the grave of a man named Lorenzo D. Thompson, whose distinction was that he defeated Lincoln at wrestling. But, like many "almost undefeated" champions, Lincoln had supporters who claimed that the one famous defeat wasn't really a defeat at all.

Carl Sandburg describes it in his epic biography, *Abraham Lincoln, The Prairie Years:*

> "Lincoln's friends bet money, hats, whiskey, knives, blankets and tomahawks. On the day of the match, as the two wrestlers tussled in their first feel-outs of each other, Lincoln turned to his friends and said, 'Boys, this is the most powerful man I ever had hold of.' For a while Lincoln held him off; then Thompson got the 'crotch hoist' on him, and he went under, fairly thrown. The match was for the best two out of three falls. In the second grapple, Lincoln went to the ground, pulling Thompson down with him. It looked like a 'dog fall' [a draw]; Lincoln raised his head and said: 'Boys, give up your bets. If this man hasn't throwed me fairly, he could.' And his men paid their bets to the last dollar or jackknife ... but still went on claiming it was a dog-fall wrestle...."

Pvt. Lorenzo Dow Thompson was the St. Clair County, Illinois, wrestling champion whom Lincoln met when he was a Captain during the Black Hawk War. Upon hearing of Thompson's prowess at wrestling, Lincoln was certain in his own ability and *"told my boys I could throw [Thompson]."* As confident as ever, Lincoln set up a match between himself and the private when both of their regiments had down time from fighting. Unfortunately, much like how Armstrong underestimated Lincoln, Lincoln underestimated Thompson. Though still in his physical prime, Lincoln realized rather quickly after the match began that he was wrestling *"a powerful man"* in Thompson, and that *"the struggle [of winning] was a severe [one.]"* Shockingly, Lincoln, for the first time in his career, was thrown out of the ring and lost the match. When his men came to the defense of their captain claiming Thompson had cheated, Lincoln laughed and said Thompson won fairly.

With their hero defeated, Sangamon's troops cried foul and prepared for the brawl that often followed wrestling matches. Lincoln, showing the poise and character that would sustain him later as president, held up his hands and halted the hostilities.

In fact, when Lincoln was reminiscing about his wrestling days while on the campaign trail in 1860, he told Risdon Moore, a college professor whose father served with Lincoln during the Black Hawk War, that he was undefeated until he was thrown by a man named Lorenzo Dow Thompson:

> *"Gentleman, I felt of Mr. Thompson, the St. Clair champion, and told my boys I could throw him, and they could bet what they pleased. You see, I had never been thrown, or dusted, as the phrase then was, and, I believe, Thompson said the same to the St. Clair boys, that they might bet their bottom dollar that he could down me. You may think a wrestle, or 'wrastle,'*

as we called such contests of skill and strength, was a small matter, but I tell you the whole army was out to see it. We took our holds, his choice first, a side hold. I think realized from his grip for the first time that he was a powerful man and that I have no easy job. The struggle was a severe one, but after many passes and efforts he threw me. My boys yelled out 'a dog fall,' which meant then a drawn battle, but I told my boys it was fair, and then said to Thompson, 'now it's your turn to go down,' as it was my hold then, Indian hug. We took our holds again and after the fiercest struggle of the kind that I ever had, he threw me again, almost as easily at my hold as at his own. My men raised another protest, but I again told them it was a fair down. Why, gentlemen, that man could throw a grizzly bear."

Incidentally, another account—one by a close friend of Lincoln, the aforementioned "Slicky Bill" Greene,"who witnessed the fight—asserted that Thompson overcame Lincoln the second time by getting "the crotch lock on Mr. Lincoln." After getting "the crotch lock" on him, Lincoln, "slid off." In the process of sliding off, Thompson managed *"to grab Lincoln and throw him down as easy as church on Sunday."*

"We can only find one recorded defeat of Lincoln in 12 years," says Bob Dellinger, director emeritus of the National Wrestling Hall of Fame in Stillwater, Okla., where Lincoln is enshrined in the

Hall of Outstanding Americans. *"He was undoubtedly the roughest and toughest of all the wrestling presidents."**

While Lincoln's temper cooled as he matured, he never lost his fighting spirit, and even when he was the president, Lincoln liked to challenge people to impromptu tests of strength. One of Lincoln's favorite tricks, which dated all the way back to his childhood, was to pick up a woodcutting axe and hold it "at arm's length at the extremity of the [handle] with his thumb and forefinger." He would apparently challenge whomever he was with to do the same and see who could hold it longer. As for Lincoln, he could apparently hold this pose for several minutes, a feat few could match.

Lincoln, of course, eventually moved to Springfield and lived there for twenty-three years, from 1837 through 1860. On November 6, 1860, he was elected president of a very nonunited nation. When Lincoln departed Springfield on February 11, 1861, for Washington, D.C., the country was torn in a bitter struggle over several matters, including state rights and slavery. Addressing the crowd that came to the Springfield train station to bid him farewell, Lincoln made an emotional speech:

> *"My friends, no one not in my situation can appreciate my feeling of sadness at this parting. To this place, and the kindness of these people, I owe everything. Here I have lived a quarter of a century and have passed from a young man to an old man. Here my children have been born, and one is buried. I now leave, not knowing when or whether ever I may return, with a task before*

> *me greater than that which rested upon Washington. Without the assistance of that Divine Being who ever attended him, I cannot succeed. With that assistance, I cannot fail. Trusting in Him who can go with me, and remain with you, and be everywhere for good, let us confidently hope that all will yet be well. To His care commending you, as I hope in your prayers you will commend me, I bid you an affectionate farewell."*

Abraham Lincoln never returned to Illinois alive. He was shot and killed by actor John Wilkes Booth while attending a play at Ford's Theatre in Washington, D.C. He died on April 15, 1865. Remarkably, even in death there was evidence he could have been a fine wrestler. *"Even after his assassination, the physicians marveled at the fifty-six-year-old's tough, lean muscular build,"* said Dave Petrie, a college professor at Gettysburg College in Pennsylvania. Petrie added that Lincoln's body fat percentage was a remarkable seven percent, similar to elite athletes of today.

Shortly after his death, a pastor in Brooklyn, New York, Henry Ward Beecher, spoke of the impact this man had on the nation and the world:

> *"Four years ago, O Illinois, we took from your midst an untried man and from among the people. We return him to you a mighty conqueror. Not thine any more, but the nation's; not ours, but the world's. Give him place, O ye prairies. In the midst of this great continent*

his dust shall rest, a sacred treasure to myriads who shall pilgrim to that shrine to kindle anew their zeal and patriotism."

Lincoln's formative years in New Salem are a huge part of what made Abraham Lincoln such a man.

The village has been restored to the way it appeared in the 1830s, due to the work of hundreds of volunteers. The historic site includes the sixty acres of the original village and a total of three hundred and twenty acres overall. It is managed by the New Salem Lincoln League under the auspices of the Illinois State Historic Preservation Agency.

Strolling through the narrow village up on the ridge above the Sangamon River, it's not difficult to imagine what Lincoln saw when he first arrived there. On each side of the dirt road that meandered through the village sat a smattering of small, wooden buildings. Most were one or two-room cabins where the citizens lived. But there were also a few small buildings where work was done. There were shops for a blacksmith, carpenter, leather maker, barrel maker, and a hat shop (where a man made hats from beaver pelts), as well as a school, two general stores, two taverns, two mills and an estimated twenty-three family dwellings. Vegetable patches and small pens for horses and pigs were a common site. Several of the small cabin homes hosted church meetings on Sundays.

The village ran in a line that was relatively straight. The primary path through the village was merely a trail of hard-packed dirt and could turn into a muddy quagmire after a heavy rain. At first, Lincoln found a little spot in the back of Offutt's store to sleep and barely had room to maneuver his lanky six-feet, four-inch frame. He probably owned very little in the way of personal effects, just a few good books and a change of shirts.

Today, some 650,000 people a year visit the restored site at New Salem. Visitors can walk the very path that Lincoln trod in the years 1831 to 1837. They can imagine the long, lanky figure of the young man loping along the dusty path that served as the village's main street, tipping his hat to passing women and sitting on porches to swap tales with friends.

Perhaps they can visualize walking into a store and seeing Lincoln behind the counter, reaching out a large hand to greet them. Then they can stroll on down the tree-lined path to Offutt's store and glance over to where the Clary store sits.

If they try really hard, they may be able to envision Lincoln and Jack Armstrong walking to the center of the small grassy area, with men surrounding them and shouting out encouragement. The image may form of Lincoln and Jack circling each other, sizing each other up, and then coming to grips in the most meaningful wrestling match in American history.

Wrestling was and is today The Sport of Lincoln. No other sport can boast of such a powerful identification with the man many consider the most important person to ever live in the history of the United States.

One of the finest places in the world for studying the history of wrestling is the International Wrestling Institute and Museum in Newton, Iowa. The museum opened its doors on September 18, 1998, with the following mission statement:

> *The International Wrestling Institute and Museum will preserve, maintain, and promote the long and illustrious heritage of Mankind's Oldest Sport in a manner which will benefit the sport, educate and entertain the public and financially support the Institute and its activities.*

In the first five years of its existence, an estimated 25,000 fans visited the museum. In the lobby, visitors are greeted by a larger-than-life-sized mural of Abe Lincoln wrestling Jack Armstrong in New Salem.

One of the most popular areas of the museum is the wall called "The Sport of Lincoln." It was painted by noted artist Jack Bender and his wife, Carole, of Tulsa, Oklahoma. The wall also offers eight different artists' renditions of Lincoln and Armstrong wrestling in New Salem as well as a few other Lincoln artifacts.

"*It is our opinion that people should know of the association between Abraham Lincoln and wrestling,*" said Kyle Klingman. "*Abraham Lincoln had an immense impact on the history of our great nation, and all wrestlers should be aware of his association with wrestling and proud of it. One of our primary goals is to let people know that wrestling is indeed the sport of Lincoln.*"

Moreover, the importance of Lincoln as a wrestler transcends something more than an interesting tidbit of information about America's greatest president. Lincoln learned about his own strength and confidence as well as humility through the sport. Writer and historian David Fleming said it best, noting that "*when his wrestling skill diminished, Lincoln's leadership qualities emerged."* Without what he learned from wrestling, Abraham Lincoln would not have been the same man who became America's sixteenth president.

Chapter Three
"HE COULD BEAT ANY OF THE BOYS..."*

Lincoln and Fives (Handball)

Serious Lincoln fans have likely heard a reference to the "alley by the journal office" a few times over the years but may not know much about it. Abraham Lincoln was known to be a sportsman for most of his life in an age when organized sports were hard to find. Undoubtedly, it is common knowledge that Lincoln was a skilled wrestler and possessed extraordinary strength as a young man. He was also known to "roll ten pins" (bowling) and play billiards and chess (to be discussed in following chapters) but admitted that he never excelled at any of them. Lincoln engaged in these games for exercise and amusement, both physically and mentally. During play, he routinely regaled those present with jokes, western anecdotes, and stories, which made him popular with opponents and teammates alike.

Lincoln was also an enthusiastic handball player, but details have always been hard to find. The game of handball was much better suited to Lincoln. At six-feet-four-inches tall, his long legs and gangly arms served the rail splitter well. Muscles honed while wielding an axe as a youth were kept tight and toned as an adult.

Lincoln milked his own cows and chopped his own wood even though he was a successful, affluent lawyer with little time to spare.

In the years before Lincoln was elected president, he was a successful Springfield lawyer and often played handball in an alley by the *Illinois State Journal* newspaper office to ease his stress load. The paper occupied a three-story building at 116 N, Sixth Street. The building next door immediately south was a three-story building that housed a store operated by John Carmody. The next building south was known as the Logan building, owned by Judge Stephen T. Logan. (See the following map.)

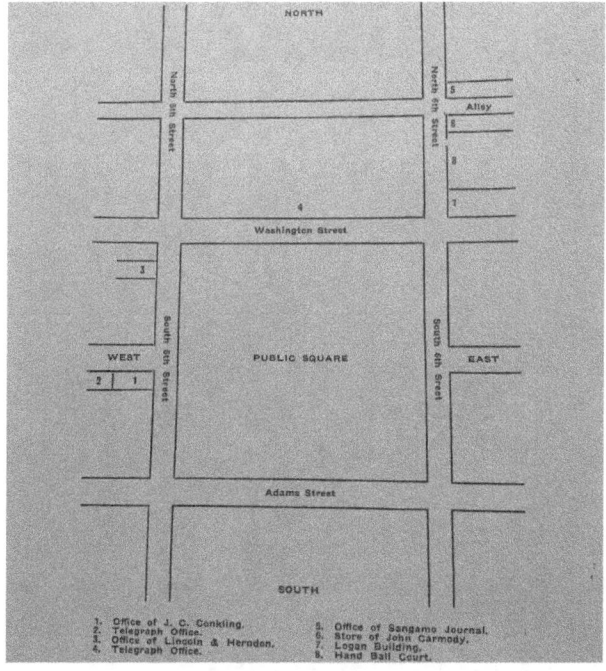

A MAP OF THE BUILDINGS SURROUNDING THE ALLEY WHERE LINCOLN PLAYED FIVES TAKEN FROM A 1924 PAMPHLET "DID MR. LINCOLN PLAY HAND BALL DURING THE NATIONAL CONVENTION OF 1860"

The large vacant lot between these two buildings was the site of the storied impromptu handball court used by lawyer Lincoln and his friends. The brick walls of the Carmody store and Logan building formed at the front and back walls of the handball court and the other two sides were enclosed by wood fences standing six to eight feet high. The fences also had wooden bench seats for visitors watching the matches or for players waiting their turn to take on the winner.

LINCOLN ON THE COVER OF THE 1971 OFFICIAL MAGAZINE OF THE US HANDBALL ASSOCIATION.

The term handball really didn't exist in Lincoln's day. It was called a "game of fives" by Abe and his contemporaries. When Lincoln went to town, he frequently joined with the boys in playing handball. In the Springfield version, players choose sides to square off against one another. The game is begun by one of the boys bouncing the ball against the wall of the Logan building. As it bounced back, and opponent strikes it in the same manner, so that the ball is kept going back and forth against the wall until someone misses the rebound. "Old Abe" was often the winner, for his long arms and long legs served a good purpose in reaching and returning the ball from any angle his adversary could send it to the wall. The game required two, four, or six players, spread equally on each side. The three players who lost paid 10¢ each, making it 30¢ a game. So, the games got pretty serious.

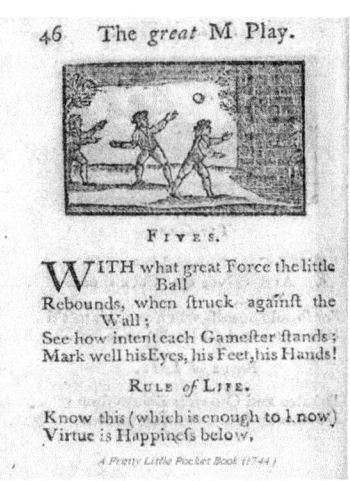

THIS ILLUSTRATION FROM *A PRETTY LITTLE POCKET BOOK*, A 1744 PUBLICATION THAT DEMONSTRATES THAT THE GAME OF FIVES EXISTED LONG BEFORE LINCOLN WAS BORN.

Clerk of Court, Thomas W. S. Kidd, spoke of Lincoln's love of the game: *"In 1859, Zimri A. Enos, Esq., Hon. Chas. A. Keyes, E. L. Baker, Esq., then editor of the Journal, William A. Turney, Esq., Clerk of the Supreme Court, and a number of others, in connection with Mr. Lincoln, had the lot, then an open one, lying between what was known as the United States Court Building, on the northeast corner of the public square, and the building owned by our old friend, Mr. John Carmody, on the alley north of it, on Sixth street, enclosed with a high board fence, leaving a dead wall at either end. In this 'alley' could be found Mr. Lincoln, with the gentlemen named and others, as vigorously engaged in the sport as though life depended upon it. He would play until nearly exhausted and then take a seat on the rough board benches arranged along the sides for the accommodation of friends and the tired players."*

In May of 1860 the most noteworthy game of handball in our country's history took place on this court. The Republican National Convention, held in a wood frame building specifically designed for use known as the "wigwam," had kicked off in nearby Chicago on May 16. The Whig party had imploded, the free soilers were migrating, and the anti-Catholic populists from the Know Nothing party were flocking to the Republican Party with its antislavery message. Even though this promised to be a raucous convention, the eventual Republican nominee, "Abram Lincoln," decided to stay home and play handball instead. According to Lincoln, he *"was too much of a candidate to go to Chicago and not enough of a candidate to stay away."*

Most Lincoln scholars agree that Abe played handball all three days of the convention (May 16–18) to relieve stress while waiting for news to arrive by telegraph at the *Illinois State Journal* newspaper offices. The last day of the Republican convention, Friday, May 18, 1865, Lincoln arose bright and early and headed downtown. Although nervous and anxious, Lincoln greeted neighbors and friends on the streets and on the square around the Illinois Capital Building.

At 8:30 a.m., Lincoln nervously visited the second-floor office of lawyer James C Conkling located at 119 S, Fifth Street. Mr. Conkling had just returned from Chicago, and Lincoln was anxious to hear any news from the convention. Conkling told Lincoln to relax, assuring him that he was sure to be nominated that day. Lincoln, however, was not so confident and told Conkling, "*Well, Conkling, I guess I'll go back to my office and practice law.*" But here is where the narrative takes a mysterious turn.

Lincoln did not arrive back to his law office until just before 10 a.m. We know this from accounts of the many well-wishers, friends and supporters who were waiting the arrival of their candidate on the corner of Sixth and Adams on the square. Shortly after ten, Edward L Baker, one of the editors of the *Illinois State Journal*, appeared at the office of Lincoln and Herndon with two bulletins in his hand. The first one announcing that the delegates were filing back into the wigwam; the second that the names of the candidates for president had been presented to the chairman of the convention.

The initial news was not good. When voting for the nomination began, William H. Seward led on the first ballot with 173 votes. Lincoln was a distant second tallying 102 votes. There were 465 delegates at the convention, making 233 votes necessary for the nomination. Simon Cameron received 50; Salmon P. Chase got 49, and Edwin Bates had 48. Witnesses claimed that, upon hearing the news, Lincoln threw himself upon a horsehair couch in the office without expressing any opinion on the news. By all accounts, Lincoln was very guarded in all of his statements that morning.

After a few minutes, Lincoln arose from the chair and said: "*The dispatches appear to be coming to the Journal office.... Let us go over there.*" When the Lincoln entourage arrived at the foot of the stairway leading to the telegraph office on the north side of the public square, Lincoln said: "*Let's go up; it must be about time for the second ballot.*" The results of the second ballot were coming across the tickertape as Lincoln entered the room. The telegraph operator handed the news to Mr. Lincoln. On the second ballot, most of the Pennsylvania delegation jumped over to Lincoln, putting him in a near-tie with Seward (184 for Seward and 181 for Lincoln). Although silent, witnesses remember a look of satisfaction appearing on Lincoln's face.

News soon arrived that on the third ballot many additional delegates switched to Lincoln, and he won the party's nomination. Lincoln was nominated and would be elected the nation's 16th president.

But where was Lincoln from 8:30 a.m. to 10 a.m.? His longtime friend and bodyguard Ward Hill Lamon was the first to say that Lincoln was playing handball during that period. Henry Wirt Butler confirmed that he was engaged in a game with the candidate at Lincoln's request while awaiting news from the convention. When young Butler was born, Lincoln was a practicing attorney in Springfield living at the home of Butler's parents. He had just finished reading the *Life of William Wirt* and suggested that the baby be named after the former U.S. Attorney General. When the boy whom Lincoln had named grew to be a young man, he became a favorite of the Great Emancipator's and read law for some time in his office. It should be noted that Wirt was barely twenty years old, and Lincoln was fifty-one at the time of the game.

EARLY PHOTOGRAPH OF YOUNG MEN PLAYING A GAME OF FIVES.

Lincoln's friend, Dr. Preston H Bailhache, recalled a handball game played on a court built by Patrick Stanley in an 'alley' in the rear of his grocery in the Second Ward, which is still standing. *"Just off the corner of the Public Square the Illinois State Journal publishing house was located, and its big solid brick wall afforded a splendid place for playing a game called 'Fives.' When Mr. Lincoln went to the printing office for a talk or to get a lot of newspapers, he frequently joined with the boys in playing 'Fives.' This game is a sort of handball, in which players choose sides, and is begun by one of the boys bouncing the ball on the ground, and as it bounds back from the wall one of the opponents strikes it in the same manner, so that the ball is kept going back and forth against the wall until some one misses the rebound, which furnishes a very active and exciting contest. Here is where "Old Abe" was always champion, for his long arms and long legs served a good purpose in reaching and returning the ball from any angle his adversary could send it to the wall.*

I have sat and laughed many happy hours away watching a game of ball between Lincoln on one side and Hon. Chas. A. Keyes on the other. Mr. Keyes is quite a short man, but muscular, wiry and active as a cat, while his now more distinguished antagonist, as all now know, was tall and a little awkward, but which with much practice and skill in the movement of the ball, together with his good judgment, gave him the greatest advantage. In a very hotly contested game, when both sides were 'up a stump'—a term used by the players to indicate an even game—and while the contestants were vigorously watching every movement, Mr. Lincoln and Mr. Turney collided with such force that it came very near preventing his nomination to the Presidency and giving to Springfield a sensation by his death and burial. Both were badly hurt, but not so badly as to discourage either from being found in the 'alley' the next day."

PHOTOGRAPH OF WHAT IS BELIEVED TO BE A
HANDBALL USED BY ABRAHAM LINCOLN.

Another eyewitness was the unofficial gatekeeper of the Handball Court, William Donnelly, a nephew of John Carmody. Years later, Donnelly offered this account to a reporter,

> "I worked in the Carmody store and usually had charge of the ball court. I smoothed the wall and leveled the ground. I made the balls. Old stockings were rolled out and wound into balls and covered with buckskin. Mr. Lincoln was not a good player. He learned the game

when he was too old. But he liked to play and did tolerably well. I remember when he was nominated as though it were yesterday. It was the last day of the convention and he was plainly nervous and restless."

Donnelly continues: "He played handball a good deal during every day of the convention, evidently to relieve the over-strained mind. I was standing down in front of the Carmody store when Edward L. Baker, Charlie Zane (Judge) and one or two others brought word from the telegraph office that he was nominated. It was the bulletin showing the result of the third and last ballot. I naturally followed the crowd upstairs to the editorial room on the second floor. The stairway was in the alley outside the building. The telegram was read and then handed to Mr. Lincoln who read it out aloud again. After a lot of hand shaking, we returned to the street below. Mr. Lincoln appeared anxious to get away. When he came to the entrance of the ball court, the players gathered round, congratulated him and pledged him their support."

The account continues: "He thanked them, looked at the telegram he had in his hand and said: there's a little woman over on eighth Street that will be glad to hear the news; if you'll excuse me, I'll go and tell her. He then left for home. I can see him now as he went away. He leaned forward and walked mighty fast. The boy that went with him had to run almost to keep up with him. Mr. Lincoln never came back to the court or played handball after the day he was nominated. I did not vote for Mr. Lincoln in 1860. There were only three Irishmen who did. They were called Irish Republicans and were regarded as curiosities."

John Carmody recalled another handball game: "An incident took place, during one of those games, which I have retained clearly in my memory. I had a nephew named Patrick Johnson who was very expert in the game. He struck the ball in such a manner that it hit Mr. Lincoln in the ear. I ran to sympathize with him and asked if he was hurt. He said he was not, and as he said it, he reached both of his hands toward the sky. Straining my neck to look up into his face, for he was several inches taller than I was, I said to him, 'Lincoln, if you are going to heaven, take us both.'"

For years a myth circulated that Abraham Lincoln was playing handball when he was notified that he was nominated for president. Obviously that legend must be filed alongside the myth that Lincoln wrote the Gettysburg address on the back of an envelope on the train ride to Gettysburg. Neither story is wholly true but there is a grain of truth in each. Lincoln was playing handball at the time the delegates in Chicago were voting and he edited the Gettysburg address on the train.

On the last day of the convention, Lincoln was "down town" bright and early. He talked on the streets with neighbors and friends as had been his wont for many years. He was anxious and depressed. The anxiety and depression disappeared, however, upon his reading the bulletin showing the result of the second ballot.

The first event worth recording of which we have any account, was the visit he made to the law office of James C. Conkling at about 8:30 a.m. This office was located on the second floor at 119 South Fifth Street. There was a telegraph office on the same floor to the rear. There was, also, a telegraph office operated by another company, on the north side of the public square where telegrams and bulletins were received from the wigwam.

Conkling had been in Chicago for several days and had returned home unexpectedly. When Lincoln heard this, he was quite anxious to see Conkling and learn the news. It is now known that Conkling assured Lincoln that he would be nominated that day; but, Lincoln was not so sanguine.

Lincoln returned to the office of Lincoln & Herndon about 10:00 a.m. where several friends and supporters had gathered. Where had he been during the interim? Had he come directly from the law office of Conkling? Or, from the hand ball court? When did he play handball? Ward Hill Lamon says that he played handball early in the day. It is clear that he never returned to the handball court after his nomination. It follows, then, he must have played before going to the office of J. C. Conkling.

The proof is positive that Lincoln walked rapidly southward on the east side of sixth street; he met and shook hands with the cashier of the old Marine bank; a little farther along, a messenger boy "sawed off" a telegram which Lincoln received and went on his way. This telegram was probably the first official announcement of his nomination.

Mrs. Lincoln had already heard the news and was holding a reception for neighbors and friends who hurried over to extend their congratulations. What were Lincoln's emotions as he returned to the modest home at the corner of eighth and Jackson streets? We have heard a great deal regarding the domestic life of the Lincolns; and, if the family life was not all that it might have been, this incident is clear to the effect that the girl upon whom he had bestowed the ring inscribed with the words 'Love is Eternal' was always first and uppermost in his thoughts.

After the nomination of Lincoln, artists came to Springfield to paint his portrait and sculptors came to model his bust. Lincoln had not the time for a separate sitting for each artist, so he agreed to open his mail every morning in representative hall where the artists could place their easels and perform a certain amount of work every day. This plan was accepted.

Among the artists who came to Springfield was George F. Wright, who painted the portrait afterward purchased by Lincoln and presented to the Butler family with whom he had boarded in earlier days. It was a special gift to William Butler, the state treasurer of Illinois and a close Springfield friend.

PORTRAIT OF LINCOLN BY GEORGE FREDERICK WRIGHT AND PRESENTED TO THE BUTLER FAMILY. IT IS SAID THAT THIS WAS THE ONLY PORTRAIT OF HIMSELF THAT LINCOLN EVER PURCHASED.

In an affidavit signed by Henry Wirt Butler regarding the history of the Lincoln portrait, he includes the statement that he played hand ball with Lincoln on the last day of the convention and that he played at the personal request of Lincoln, himself.

Mr. Clinton L. Conkling was a man of many admirable qualities. No one who knew him could believe that he would knowingly or intentionally distort a fact or claim a preferment to which he was not entitled. Yet, it must be said, he put forward a most surprising pretention that involved him in a hopeless inconsistency.

Conkling's misfortune arose from the belief that he, himself, was the first person to notify Lincoln of his nomination. He related this interesting story in private conversations and public speeches, without eliminating the points of contradiction. On February 12, 1920, he delivered a memorial address before the constitutional convention, which was in part as follows:

> "On Friday morning, May 18, 1860 the third day of the convention.... James C. Conkling who had been in Chicago, several days arrived home.... About half past eight o'clock, Mr Lincoln came into the office and inquired for him ... being told that Mr Conkling was not in but probably would be in an hour, Mr Lincoln said he would go out on the street and come again as he was anxious to see Mr. Conkling. Presently, the latter came in and Mr Lincoln again called....
>
> "After discussing the situation at some length, Mr Lincoln arose .... and said: "Well, Conkling, I believe

I will go back to my office and practice law." He then left the office*. "A moment after Mr Lincoln left, the wires in the adjoining telegraph office brought the news of his nomination and I rushed down the stairs after him. I met him ... just a few steps away ... all unconscious of the news. I cried to him: 'Mr Lincoln, you are nominated.' Taking my outstretched hand in his ... he looked down upon me and said: 'Well, Clinton, then we have got it.'*

Then the excited crowds surged around him and I dropped out of sight."

No one questions the motives of Conkling. But it must be evident that his oft repeated statement amounts to a contradiction in itself. Lincoln was not nominated for more than three hours after he left the office of James C. Conkling. The convention did not assemble until ten o'clock. There were the usual nominating speeches, after which three ballots were taken. The nomination was made in the early afternoon. Addison G. Procter, the last known living delegate who sat in the convention, states that it occurred about 1:00 p.m. although, he cannot give the exact time.

Lincoln was in the office of Lincoln & Herndon, when the bulletin showing the result of the first ballot was received. He read the bulletin of the second ballot in the telegraph office on the north side of the public square. He was in the editorial room of the *Sangamo Journal* when Edward L. Baker brought in the bulletin of the third ballot; it was read aloud, then handed to

Lincoln whereupon he exclaimed: *"I knew it would come when I saw the second ballot."*

The literature relating to this last hour is extensive and will repay a most careful study. Historians confirm that Abraham Lincoln never returned to that handball court after that day. Years later, President Lincoln spoke about his athletic prowess on the night of his reelection as President in 1864: *"For such an awkward fellow, I am pretty sure-footed. It used to take a pretty dexterous man to throw me."*

PHOTO OF THE HANDBALL USED BY LINCOLN LOCATED IN THE BEHRING CENTER, NATIONAL MUSEUM OF AMERICAN HISTORY, WASHINGTON, D.C.

In October of 2004, the Smithsonian Institution displayed Abraham Lincoln's handball as part of their exhibit "Sports: Breaking Records, Breaking Barriers." It's small (about the size of a tennis ball), dirty and well-worn and really old. The ball has "No. 2" stamped on the side but it is unclear if the stamp was on the ball when Lincoln handled it or if it was stamped on the side for reference years later. It came from the Lincoln Home in Springfield, where Lincoln lived with his family from 1844 until 1861.

The ball was found in the 1950s in a dresser drawer when Lincoln's Springfield home was being restored. Smithsonian officials say the descendants of one of the men who played handball with Lincoln donated it to the Lincoln Home. A contemporary newspaper article verified that the ball was indeed one of those used by Lincoln to play handball in the alley.

Eerily enough, on May 18, 1860, while Lincoln was having a friendly neighborhood game of "fives" to calm his nerves, just a few blocks from the Wigwam, on the second night of the Republican Convention, the McVicker's Theater just a few short blocks away was opening "Our American Cousin," the play Lincoln would be watching at Ford's Theater his last night on Earth.

Although Assassin John Wilkes Booth was not in the production, he would appear at the McVicker's four times in different productions between 1862 and 1863 while Lincoln was in the White House. Ironically, the McVicker's Theatre was the very first place where actor Harry Hawk began theater work as a call boy or stagehand. Hawk was the actor on stage alone at the moment of Lincoln's assassination and likely uttered the last words Mr. Lincoln ever heard. Who knew a well-worn piece of leather sports equipment could have so many connections?

*"*He could beat any of the boys wrestling, or running a foot-race, in pitching quoits, or tossing a copper; could ruin more liquor than all the boys of the town together, and the dignity and impartiality with which he presided at a horse-race or fist-fight excited the admiration and won the praise of everybody that was present and participated. I sympathized with him because he was struggling with difficulties, and so was I. Mr. Lincoln served with me in the Legislature in 1836 when we both retired, and he subsided, or became submerged, and was lost sight of as a public man for some year."* Stephen A. Douglas in the First Lincoln–Douglas Debate, Ottawa, Illinois, August 21, 1858.

Chapter Four

"HE KEPT US SMALL BOYS RUNNING IN ALL DIRECTIONS...."

Lincoln, Bowling, and Marbles

Watercolor painting of Lincoln playing marbles with a young boy. This watercolor illustration by Rick Tuma appears in the video short "Lincoln: Recollections and Reminiscences," featured in the McLean County Museum of History exhibit, "Abraham Lincoln in McLean County."

Jason H. Silverman

BOWLING

DURING 1847–1848, WHILE SERVING IN THE U.S. HOUSE OF REPRESENTATIVES, LINCOLN OFTEN BOWLED WITH OTHER CONGRESSMEN AT A WASHINGTON HOTEL CALLED THE CONGRESS HALL REFECTORY.

"If the young man of the house spends some, of his evenings at the bowling alleys, don't discourage him. He is merely following in one or two of the footsteps of Abraham Lincoln. Those were the days when Lincoln was only a congressman. He served In the House from 1847 to 1849 and apparently wanted to continue, but there was no overwhelming demand for him in his Illinois district.

While In Washington for those two years, however, he took keen delight in hurling the old cannon ball down the alley. And he was fairly good at it. Judging from the few accounts of his prowess now available. He bowled match games with other members of congress at the alley in James Caspari's hotel, known as the Congress Hall

Refectory, on Capitol Square, opposite the House of Representatives. The hotel has long ago disappeared, and its site is now a part of the Capitol grounds.

Lincoln was always watched by the crowds. 'He played the game with great gusto,' according to the only account of Congressman Lincoln's sporting activities here that this writer can locate. 'Whether he won or lost, it was all the same to him. His gaunt figure added to the bystanders' entertainment. When he played, a crowd gathered, especially to hear his jokes, some of which were reduced to the appreciation of a mere man.'

The records don't seem to disclose whether Lincoln learned to bowl here or at the Illinois state capital while a legislator. Lincoln had prodigious strength, and in his early Illinois days was fond of physical recreation of the simpler sort, such as wrestling.

'In sports requiring either muscle or skill he took no little interest.' wrote Herndon, his law partner and

biographer. He indulged in all the games of the clay, even to a horse race or a cock fight."

Text of newspaper clipping below.

By RODNEY DUTCHER
NEA Service Writer

WASHINGTON — If the young man of the house spends some of his evenings at the bowling alleys, don't discourage him. He is merely following in one or two of the footsteps of Abraham Lincoln.

Those were the days when Lincoln was only a congressman. He served in the House from 1847 to 1849 and apparently wanted to continue, but there was no overwhelming demand for him in his Illinois district.

While in Washington for those two years, however, he took keen delight in hurling the old cannon ball down the alley, and he was fairly good at it, judging from the meager accounts of his prowess now available.

He bowled match games with other members of congress at the alley in James Caspari's hotel, known as the Congress Hall Refectory, on Capitol Square, opposite the House of Representatives. The hotel has long ago disappeared and its site is now a part of the Capitol grounds.

Always Watched by Crowds

"He played the game with great gusto," according to the only account of Congressman Lincoln's sporting activities here that this writer can locate. "Whether he won or lost, it was all the same to him. His gaunt figure added to the bystanders' entertainment. When he played, a crowd gathered, especially to hear his jokes, some of which were reduced to the appreciation of a mere man."

The records don't seem to disclose whether Lincoln learned to bowl here or at the Illinois state capital while a legislator. Lincoln had prodigious strength, and in his early Illinois days was fond of physical recreation of the simpler sort, such as wrestling.

"In sports requiring either muscle or skill he took no little interest," wrote Herndon, his law partner and biographer. "He indulged in all the games of the day, even to a horse race or a cock fight."

Dr. Samuel Clagett Busey told the story in his memoirs, *Personal Reminiscences and Recollections of Forty-Six Years' Membership In The Medical Society of the District of Columbia, Residence in this City, DC.*

When Lincoln was a Congressman in the Thirtieth Congress (1847–1849), he lived in a boarding house on First Street, E., run by a Mrs. Spragg. At that time, her place was both a popular residence and an eatery for young Whig lawmakers and other professionals.

Dr. Busey, a new surgeon in Washington City at that time, was setting up his first practice. He took his meals at Mrs. Spragg's, *"occupying a seat at the table nearly opposite Abraham Lincoln, whom I soon learned to know and admire for his simple and unostentatious manners, kind-heartedness, and amusing jokes, anecdotes, and witticisms."*

Busey described Lincoln, the bowler.

> "*Congressman Abraham Lincoln was very fond of bowling, and would frequently join others of the mess, or meet other members in a match game, at the alley of James Casparis, which was near the boardinghouse. He was a very awkward bowler, but played the game with great zest and spirit, solely for exercise and amusement, and greatly to the enjoyment and entertainment of the other players and bystanders by his criticisms and funny illustrations. He accepted success and defeat with like good nature and humor, and left the alley at the conclusion of the game without a sorrow or disappointment.*"

Much has been written about Lincoln, the fierce competitor who hated to lose. However, from Busey's description, it appears that in bowling, the one sport at which Lincoln did not excel, he was fairly laid back regarding his failures and successes competitively.

This description actually bears out if one examines how Lincoln accepted his defeats as a state legislator, a lawyer, a Congressman, a debater, and as president. He didn't LIKE losing, and we know that he learned from each failure. Outwardly, however, he accepted those results with great equanimity.

Although Lincoln didn't shine on the lanes in that bowling alley, he certainly did so on the sidelines.

When it was known that he was in the alley, there would assemble numbers of people to witness the fun which was anticipated by those who knew his fund of anecdotes and jokes.

When in the alley, surrounded by a crowd of eager listeners, he indulged with great freedom the in the sport of narrative, some of which were very broad. His witticisms seemed for the most past impromptu, but he always told the anecdotes and jokes as if he wished to convey the impression that he had heard them from someone; but they appeared very many times as if they had been made for the immediate occasion.

Twelve years later, it was Lincoln's sport of narrative that mattered, not bowling.

MARBLES

Marbles have been with us in some form since ancient times. Small, hard balls of clay have been discovered in European caves. Egyptian tablets have depicted people playing with marbles, and some have been found in pharaohs' tombs. The Romans, including Augustus Caesar, played with them. Marble games are mentioned in two of Shakespeare's plays, and it has been a tradition to play marbles on Good Friday in England, where it is still sometimes called Marbles Day.

American Indians used smooth, round pebbles for marbles; early settlers made them out of clay. George Washington, Thomas Jefferson, and Abraham Lincoln were all avid marble players. During the Civil War, some soldiers carried marbles in a bag suspended from their belts and played with them between battles.

Around the turn of the century, most marbles were handmade in Germany by expert glassmakers. They were very beautiful and are now valuable collectors' items. If you should come across a marble that has a little circular nub of glass, or pontil, on each end, the marble was handmade. The pontil shows where a special tool called a marble scissors snipped hot molten glass from a long rod to form the marble.

After World War I, machines were invented to make marbles, and since that time most marbles have been mass-produced in factories.

Lincoln often appeared in the role of sports arbiter during the six years he worked in New Salem. His reputation for fairness—and for having the strength to back up his decisions—made him a popular referee, and a local foot or horse race, cockfight or gander pull that he didn't preside over was rare.

When he wasn't refereeing or defending his wrestling and crowbar-throwing championships, Lincoln played a game that seems incongruous for a man of his size and strength—marbles. But like everything he attempted, he did it better than anyone else.

While Lincoln played marbles with the youngsters in the New Salem area, he also shone against men. In those days marbles were popular with all ages. The game was played on a square marked off on the ground with a stick. Lines were drawn diagonally across the square, connecting its corners, a small marble placed at each corner and a larger one (Old Boler) put at the spot in the center where the lines intersected. From the taw line, at a previously agreed-upon distance from the square, Lincoln could hit Old Bowler with his taw (shooter) four times out of five.

The marbles used were irregular, homemade ones fashioned from rounds of clay and baked in the embers of a fireplace. Sometimes a bullet mold was used to shape the marbles; otherwise, the clay was rolled between the hands.

Once, after he had become president and was burdened with worries about the Civil War, Lincoln found relaxation in a makeshift game of marbles. He was walking toward Army headquarters in Washington with a telegraph clerk and one of his sons. Picking up a smooth, round stone from the street, he challenged them to a contest of shooting stones ahead, marble fashion, to see who could get his stone to the headquarters steps in the least number of shots. When they reached the steps, Lincoln had won and had found in a simple game a respite from presidential pressures.

Dr. Edwin M. Colburn, an early Bloomington physician, recalled the popularity of marbles and other games in the early 1840s. Not among children, mind you. No, he was talking about elected officials.

"*I saw, day after day,*" Colburn related in a reminiscence from 1883, "*the sheriff, county clerk and other officers in the streets playing marbles and pitching quoits*" (the latter was similar to horseshoes, only played with metal rings). Marbles, or at least small spherical objects made to be knocked around with the flick of a thumb or finger, have been around since time immemorial. To cite several representative examples, marbles have turned up in excavations at ancient Mesopotamian and Egyptian sites, and references to them appear in Roman literature.

This amusing diversion was all the rage among Bloomington's adults in the 1850s, recalled one old-timer in 1879.

"*Boston ring and long taw were the favorite games, and the public streets were often filled with the young businessmen of the city, with coats off, engaged in playing marbles with as much enjoyment and interest as if selling calico and molasses at a good profit.*"

The 100 block of East Front Street (where Rosie's Pub is today) was said to be the "great resort for the marble players of early Bloomington."

"*Many of the best players are now among the oldest and most esteemed citizens of the city,*" added Colburn in 1879, looking back over a quarter century. Indeed, if his recollection is to be believed, Bloomington's accomplished marble players of the pre-Civil War era included David Davis, Asahel Gridley, Dr. G.W. Stipp, Leonard Swett, Allen Withers, and others.

There are several accounts of Abraham Lincoln playing marbles, both as a young man and then as an attorney on the Eighth Judicial Circuit. In New Salem, Lincoln boarded with cooper Henry Onstot. T.G. Onstot, Henry's son, knew Lincoln well. *"My first knowledge of him was as a great marble player,"* he recalled in a 1902 reminiscence. *"He kept us small boys running in all directions gathering up the marbles he would scatter."*

Ivory Pike recalled an older Lincoln playing marbles in Bloomington. Pike's uncle, Meshach, owned the Pike House at Center and Monroe streets, a hotel the future sixteenth president frequented. *"It was just like Lincoln to stop on his way to the courtroom and play marbles with a group of boys,"* Pike remembered back in 1931, at the age of 86. *"He was a good mixer and seldom forgot a face. It was easy for him to become acquainted with anyone."*

Abe Williams, born in Bloomington in 1870, penned a richly detailed reminiscence when he was 80 titled "Up through Boyville in the Old Home Town." His family home at 1409 North Main Street was "Boyville headquarters," he recalled. Their yard included a *"fine place in the shade for pitching horseshoes and playing marbles, either 'little ring,' 'bull ring,' or 'pat,' the three common marble games."*

It's been said that a good definition of the game of marbles is "any game played with marbles." In the nineteenth century, there were hundreds of different games and hundreds of variations of each game, as "house rules" altered from region to region, city to city, and even neighborhood to neighborhood.

Marbles were tolerated by local officials, as evidenced by the fact that one of the more popular venues for the amusement was the county courthouse basement. One such game held on February 13, 1879, drew the attention of the local press.

> *"John Wesley VanShoick, age 40, wagered and lost a bushel of peanuts to local tailor William Nightwine, 59.*
>
> *As one would expect, tempers sometimes flared. On March 17, 1879, while playing marbles in the courthouse basement, Charlie Smith hit fellow player Tommy Halligan in the head with a nice-sized chunk of coal cinder. Young Halligan's wounds were dressed by janitor Newell and at last accounts he was doing well.*

For boys, railroad tracks were a popular spot to play marbles, as the hard, compact surface between the rails and ties proved an ideal "pitch" to stage everything from a fleeting game to an all-day tournament. Marbles were a big sport in the warehouse district south of downtown Bloomington. *"Complaint is made that the boys congregate on the Big Four and Lake Erie tracks near Lee Street to play marbles,"* reported the March 28, 1895, *Pantagraph*. *"No objection is made to the marbles, but (the boys) become so interested in their games that they become oblivious to oncoming trains, and they are in continual danger of being run over."* Asphalt streets were also a popular surface for marbles, though this too posed dangers. In February 1912, area motorists complained that boys were playing marbles smack in the middle of busy streets, unmindful of approaching traffic.

Boys played marbles mostly outdoors, so the first games were often as good a sign of approaching spring as the robin. When cement sidewalks began appearing in the early 1900s, they became a popular place to shoot marbles.

Even so, boys still gravitated to railroad tracks, if for no other reason than to be far from the watchful eye of parents and other meddlesome adults. In mid-March 1917, a group of small boys was spotted playing marbles on the Illinois Central tracks in Normal (now Constitution Trail). *"It is true that some games have been played upon the concrete walks about town, but these are not the real signs of spring,"* observed the *Pantagraph*. *"They are merely sporadic cases, but when the boys congregate upon the right of way and play 'keeps' with pewees, glassies and agates (three types of marbles), it's a sure sign that spring is here."*

For many older men, marbles were a part of childhood they could never quite let go. *"There is many a man who even today, should you visit him, will lead you to his den,"* reflected the March 26, 1918, *Pantagraph*, *"and there, in his archives which have become his holy of* holies because they contain the mementos of a happy, youthful existence, he will proudly exhibit a chest filled with marbles of all descriptions."

As previously mentioned, Lincoln's favorite marble game, and one he played to alleviate stress while he was the president was Old Bowler (or Boler). Lincoln enjoyed the game immensely, and the rules, according to the *A Guide to the History of Marbles*, were as follows:

> *Mark off a 3-5 Foot circle with a 1-foot square in the middle. Set a marble on each corner of the square and a favorite marble, 'Old Bowler,' in the middle.*
>
> *Shooting from outside the ring, players try to first knock the corner marbles out of the square. If you knock a corner marble out of the square, add it to your pile and shoot again from outside the ring. But don't hit "Old Bowler." If you do, add one of your marbles to the corner. Return Old Bowler to the middle and your turn is over.*
>
> *Once the corner marbles are gone, the player to knock Old Bowler out of the box wins the favorite marble.*

Horatio G. Cooke, a soldier from Iowa and a skilled escape artist was brought from the battlefield to the White House to be appointed by President Lincoln a scout for the Union Army. Before embarking on his assignments, Cooke observed Lincoln shooting marbles on a table in his office. Lincoln asked Cooke if he played, and the soldier demurred. *"I saw the burdens of war in the cragged, weary face of the president,"* Cooke recalled later in his life, *"and it seemed to be that for a brief moment President Lincoln retreated to the days of his youth playing marbles. As quickly as that look came it faded away and we talked about my going behind the enemy's lines."*

Lincoln had Cooke perform some of his escape tricks and was so delighted that the president said, the Confederates *"would have to 'go some' to hold you if you should fall into their hands.' That remark seemed prophetic and was fulfilled afterwards."* Then Lincoln promptly handed the young magician a $2 greenback as a souvenir telling Cooke *"to keep it always and to remember 'Uncle Abe'… and that he was going to keep an eye on [him] for something better as he grew older."*

Late in his life, Cooke would always fondly remember Lincoln and he would always associate the game of marbles with the war-weary president.

Chapter Five
"THE 'GREAT CANON GAME'"

Lincoln and Billiards

In his introduction to Henry C. Whitney's *Life on the Circuit with Lincoln,* historian Paul M. Angle explains that few men *"knew Lincoln well, and of those who did only six, Herndon, Lamon, Whitney, Arnold, Nicolay, and Hay wrote extensively of his life."* Of these six, Angle contends that *"Only Herndon and Whitney are intimate, realistic and convincing."* Although many have challenged the accuracy and appropriateness of this type of distinction, Angle's endorsement of Whitney's work still carries weight. In addition to Whitney's personal association with Lincoln, Angle continues, *"The fact that Whitney's work deals mainly with the most colorful part of Lincoln's pre-presidential career, his life as a circuit lawyer, and with the most crucial years of his political life ... [makes] its claim to recognition ... obvious."*

Whitney and Lincoln met in the fall of 1854 and *"for the next few years the conditions under which lawyers then earned a livelihood brought the two men together frequently."* Whitney traveled the circuit *"with Lincoln and other lawyers, particularly when court traveled to Champaign, Danville, and Paris, among other county seats."* Angle notes that despite being twenty-two years younger than Lincoln, Whitney *"seems to have been accepted by the ruling coterie—David Davis, Lamon, Swett, and Lincoln. Days of association in court, and nights of companionship in small taverns, easily led to familiarity. Moreover, though conditions were changing rapidly, enough of the old conviviality, or the self-made amusement of men away from home, remained to bring the little group of travelers into close personal relation.*

Their seven years together on the circuit, then, gave Whitney first-hand knowledge of the circumstances in which they passed their spare time, undoubtedly with Lincoln spinning his web of stories.

Late in his memoir, Whitney observed that Lincoln *"was very eccentric and uneven in his friendships."* As one example, he alleged that in Lincoln's distribution of patronage, some friends like Ward Hill Lamon were handsomely rewarded with desired appointments, while others such as Leonard Swett were not. He then gave another example of this trait: *"For instance, he did not like the best lawyer in one of our county seats at all, and the latter did not like him: but a drunken fellow who turned lawyer late in life, and settled there, Lincoln used to seek out and play billiards with, by the hour...."*

Jesse W Weik, who coauthored Herndon's classic biography of Lincoln, cites the same story as being *"further illuminative of Lincoln's peculiarities."* Weik's phrasing is essentially identical to Whitney's, and he presents it as Whitney's story. Likewise, Cart Sandburg draws from Whitney stating:

> *[Lincoln] picked his companions by what they could do for him at the time he wanted something done,* Whitney also noted. *'As a constant habit he chose as his opponent at billiards a bibulous lawyer of no merit save the negative one of playing billiards as awkwardly and badly as Lincoln himself; it was a strange but not unfamiliar sight to see these two men, who had nothing else in common, playing billiards in an obscure place, sometimes for hours together.' And Whitney also wished to note that billiards was the only 'non-utilitarian thing' that he ever knew Lincoln to indulge in."*

The Whitney-Weik account appears related to a letter from Henry C. Whitney to William H. Herndon, dated August 27, 1887, in the Herndon-Weik Collection, which names Lincoln's billiards partner. Several years after Lincoln's death, and in anticipation of a book on his famous law partner, Herndon contacted a broad range of Lincoln's colleagues, friends, and associates, including Whitney, and asked them to forward their reminiscences of Lincoln. Amid a wide-ranging series or reflections, Whitney commented that *"Lincoln & George Lawrence a worthless, drunken lawyer- used to play billiards together: one played about as well as the other."*

Lawrence was from Danville, the seat of Vermillion County and a regular circuit stop. There are other discussions of Lincoln's circuit-riding in the region list Lawrence (often with no first name or initial) as a member of the legislative delegation. Two pages after his handwritten reference to Lawrence as Lincoln's billiard opponent, Whitney turned his attention to Lincoln's intimacies. After noting that his "*memory is good*" and that he "*took to Lincoln on the circuit from the start,*" and claiming to have personally "happened to have rather more intimacy with him than ordinary," Whitney continued, *"[David] Davis and [Leonard) Swett were more intimate [with Lincoln]— Lamon, Weldon, Parks, Moore, Hogg, Vorhees, McWilliams less so. Oliver L. Davis of Danville he despised, and Oliver hated him."*

Altogether, the Whitney-Weik passage has seven elements, of which six are either directly verifiable or entirely consistent with the idea that Lincoln did indeed play billiards and often did so with George Lawrence. In fact, Lincoln's seven-year circuit colleague Whitney says that "*Lincoln used to seek out*" his partner in billiards, rather than the other way around, a distinction that billiard aficionados will notice and find poignant. The only element that cannot be verified here is whether Lawrence was a "drunken fellow." It is known, however, that drinking alcoholic beverages was quite popular during the period, with many members of the traveling bar adhering more to the rule than the exception, Lincoln, of course, excluded.

On Friday, May 18, 1860, the Republican National Convention in Chicago turned to the issue of nominating a candidate for the presidency or the United States. By all accounts, Lincoln was unusually anxious that day. He arose early from his Springfield bed and roamed the town while waiting for word of the Chicago results, visiting his law office, James C. Conkling's law office (to see what Conkling knew upon his surprise return from Chicago), the telegraph office, and the office of Edward L. Baker, editor of the *Illinois State Journal*.

Much has been written about what Lincoln did during his anxious wait on that Friday. How did he seek comfort or serenity while passing the time on that fateful day? When cue-sport devotees undergo such stress, they typically head to the billiard hall to find peace in a threatening world, where they often drink a beer in the process. This is apparently what Abraham Lincoln did as well.

As word spread of Lincoln's nomination, his fellow townsmen began to congregate at the *Journal* office and his house. To some of the billiard players who interrupted their game to congratulate Lincoln, he quipped, *"Gentlemen, you had better come up and shake my hand while you can—honors elevate some men."*

Accounts of Lincoln's activities that day differ only slightly. Edward L Baker gave the following description to William Herndon:

> *I left Chicago on night train; arrived here [Springfield] in morning before balloting began. Met Lincoln and we went to ball alley to play at fives—alley was full—said it was pre-engaged; then went to excellent beer saloon near by to play game of billiards; table was full and we each drank a glass of beer; then went to Journal office expecting to hear result of ballot; waited awhile; but nothing came and finally we parted; I went to dinner.*

Herndon himself later wrote:

> *The news of his nomination found Lincoln at Springfield in the office of the Journal. Naturally enough he was nervous, restless, and laboring under more or less suppressed excitement. He had been tossing ball – a past time frequently indulged in by the lawyers of that day, and had played a few games of billiards to keep down, as another has expressed it 'the unnatural excitement that threatened to possess him.'*

Two key points are evident. First, it is clear that Lincoln, at a minimum, made an attempt to play billiards during this anxious day. Many historians have acknowledged that he played "fives" (a version of handball) to pass the time on that Friday, but most have ignored the other sport he set out to play—billiards. Second, whereas Baker said that he and Lincoln set out to play handball and billiards but found the handball alley and billiard table full, Herndon maintained that Lincoln and Baker did in fact play "*a few games of billiards*" in order to "*keep down 'the unnatural excitement that threatened to possess him.'*"

It is likely that both passages come from the same interview of Edward L. Baker by Herndon. Herndon's notes on the interview billiards passage state:

> *"he got here on the night train the day before the nomination: that Lincoln and himself went to what is called the ball alley to play at 5's—that the alley*

> *was full—that they went to an excellent and neat Beer Saloon to play a game of Billiards. That the table was full and took a glass of Beer. That they then went to the Journal office and there read the first dispatch stating the result of the first ballot and finally they parted, each his own way. Baker to dinner—Lincoln to his paper [or "people"].*

Accordingly, Herndon cites Baker to the effect that he and Lincoln passed the time that day by drinking a beer in "an excellent and neat Beer Saloon," when unable to play billiards and after being unable to play "fives" earlier. The act of drinking beer would have been somewhat unusual for Lincoln but could be taken as another sign of Lincoln's nerves at that anxious time.

It is quite possible that both passages are accurate. After all, Lincoln's intent to play billiards being blocked at one point in the day does not preclude his having played at some other time during that day. Either way, in all probability Abraham Lincoln set out to play billiards, and may have accomplished his goal, as he waited to hear whether he was nominated for the presidency of the United States.

In late November 1859, Lincoln left Springfield for a visit to Kansas Territory. He wanted to try out the speech he would give at the Cooper Institute in New York in February 1860, without having it come to the attention of the Eastern press, as well as to see "Bleeding Kansas" and perhaps win over its six delegates to the upcoming Republican national convention.

At Atchison, his fourth tour stop, he spoke for two hours and twenty minutes at the Methodist Church on the evening of December 2, 1859. According to two eyewitnesses, Lincoln's speech on the imperative of preserving the Union was "profound." When he attempted to finish ninety minutes into his remarks, the audience would not let him stop, and afterward many of them followed him to the Massasoit House hotel, where a prolonged reception took place.

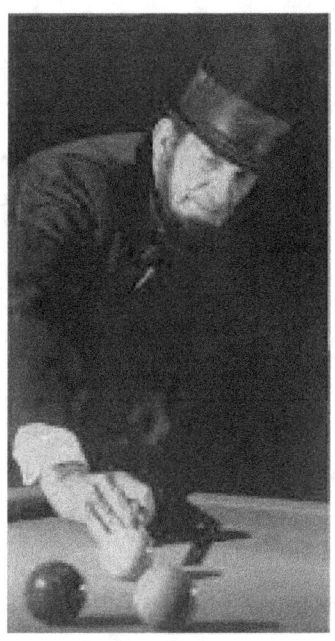

Lincoln playing billiards as portrayed by Harry Hahn of Mt. Pulaski, Illinois. (Photo by Sam B. Davis)

Years later, a brief article appeared under the bold print heading "Beat Lincoln at Billiards." This undated clipping, probably appeared in the "Kansas Topics" section of the Kansas City, *Missouri Journal*. No more is known about the piece but it states that when Lincoln visited Atchison in 1859, he stopped at the Massasoit House kept by the Thomas Murphy after he delivered his speech at the old Methodist Church where he played billiards with the landlord. Several years later, when Lincoln was president, Thomas Murphy was appointed superintendent of Indian affairs for Kansas and Indian Territory. The appointment was presented to Lincoln by Kansas Senator Samuel C. Pomeroy. "*Who is Murphy?*" Lincoln asked. Pomeroy told him he was the proprietor of the Massasoit Hotel at Atchison, Kansas, whereby Lincoln replied, *"Oh, is that the little Irishman who beat me playing billiards when I was at Atchison?"* The source of the story is John B. Murphy, son of Thomas Murphy.

Obviously, newspaper articles based on the memories of family members may include any number of historical inaccuracies. Many elements of the story can be verified, however. Lincoln was in Atchison, Kansas, in 1859, and delivered an address at the Methodist Church. He stayed at the Massasoit House, which was built in 1858 and burned in 1873. The Massasoit House was the finest hotel in Atchison at the time and has been described variously as a "pretentious hotel" and a "magnificent establishment." Likewise, Thomas Murphy was the proprietor of the Massasoit House and was appointed Superintendent of Indian Affairs for Kansas and Indian Territory during Lincoln's administration. Samuel C. Pomeroy "was destined to be one of the first United States senators from Kansas" and he served in the Senate during Lincoln's tenure in the While House."

A consistent, though admittedly inconclusive, pattern between the article and the known facts is evident here. As to the critical point, that Lincoln "went back to the hotel and played billiards with the landlord," it is indeed possible that the alleged match could have occurred there. Atchison, with an estimated population of 4,000, had at least four billiard establishments, including the "Massasoit Billiard Room" located "under" the Massasoit House. Although this does not prove that the Lincoln–Murphy match occurred, it shows that the opportunity existed.

And was Lincoln's Kansas trip a success? He achieved his primary objective, in that he tested, practiced, and polished what would become his great Cooper Institute speech, and he also got a first-hand look at "Bleeding Kansas." He did not, however, win over any of the six Kansas convention delegates, who remained firmly in the Seward column. And if the billiard match with Murphy did in fact occur, with Lincoln the loser, the future president was only two-of-four among his important Kansas endeavors.

Lincoln's impending election to the presidency in 1860 meant that the nation's gain would be Illinois's loss. On September 20, 1860, the *Central Transcript* of Clinton, Illinois, noted that when the Circuit Court next commenced:

> *"We cannot hope to have the presence of the noble form, the genial face, or listen to the ready wit, the convincing eloquence, the close deflecting argument—as is our wont—of that greatest living statesman Honest Old Abe Lincoln. Mr. Lincoln has probably amused the people or Clinton for the last time with his awkward attempts at billiard playing, or his incomparable manner of telling a good story. The last time we saw him in Clinton, he was walking past our office door when he was accosted by an old acquaintance who apologized for naming a very ugly looking hound dog, 'Abe Lincoln.' 'Well,' said Lincoln, 'I don't care anything about it if the dog don't.'"*

What is significant here is the editor's selection of the personal features most characteristic of Abraham Lincoln. In a list of otherwise undeniably accurate and well-known traits, he included billiard playing right along with the others. The implications are unmistakable; how likely is it that a passage written to honor such an admired and unique individual, which would be read by people personally acquainted with him, would have mentioned Lincoln's billiard playing if it were an activity only casually, passingly, or peripherally associated with him?

On January 20, 1909, the *Illinois State Journal* reported the story of "Lincoln's first Billiard Game." The article, which depicts life on the circuit, is based on the recollections of Henry Russel, who, as a young man, worked at an Urbana hotel and stage house. The proprietor of the Champaign House was Russel's uncle, James S. Gere. Lincoln and company resided at the Champaign House in Urbana, Illinois, in May 1848, during their circuit travels, and Lincoln's billiards opponent was a young local attorney named J. C. Sheldon. The event took place at "a new billiard hall and the first that had ever been in Urbana...." Apparently, neither one had played billiards before and they *"jollied and bantered ... that they were behind the times."*

Word of the match soon spread and *"the hall was soon comfortably filled with spectators."* No one else played on other tables during the Lincoln–Sheldon match, in order to watch. The match was to 100 points, with Russel unable to remember who won. Later, Russel reminisced,

I seen Mr. Lincoln play his first game of billiards. I heard him say it was the first game he had ever played. A new billiard hall and the first that had ever been in Urbana had opened, and some how a bantering conversation opened between some of a group of attorneys and citizens of the town, when Mr. Lincoln stated he had never played billiards and J. C. Sheldon, a young attorney made the statement that he had never played a game of billiards. They were jollied and bantered to begin now, that they were behind the times. They took the jollying pleasantly and agreed to play a game. All the crowd followed and soon other citizen s hearing that Lincoln and Sheldon were playing a matched game of billiards, the hall was soon comfortably filled by spectators. I have always felt sure they told the truth, for the game was I think, one of the most awkward and laughable billiard games I ever witnessed even among amateurs. Mr. Lincoln, being tall and angular and Sheldon short and stocky, made the contrast amusing at start, and soon the game furnished plenty of amusement and laughter; no matter where a ball lay Mr. Lincoln could lean his whole body over the rail and reach with his long arms a ball anywhere on the table, while Sheldon's large prominence came in contact with the rail so that he could not lean over, and would try to lay on the table. That position was prohibited, and Sheldon was compelled to use a bridge so frequently that it was very amusing. The game of one hundred points lasted until too late for any other playing and no one wanted to play while the Lincoln–Sheldon game lasted. I do not recall which won the game.

Judging from the Urbana man's description of the game, Lincoln would never have become a champion billiard player.

The problem is that Lincoln was not traveling the circuit in May 1848 and was not in Urbana during the entire month of May 1848. It's a fine article, but Lincoln simply was not there at the specified time. This does not mean, of course, that these events did not occur at some other point in time. Lincoln was in Urbana in May of 1850–52 and 1854–57, as well as other times, and he and his circuit colleagues did regularly frequent the Champaign House hotel during their stays there. Although the Champaign-Urbana city directories from 1850 make no specific references to billiard halls; there are several references to inns, saloons, and taverns, which often included billiard tables, as did hotels like the Champaign House. Likewise, James S. Gere *"came to Urbana, Champaign County, in 1845 or 1846, and for several years kept the Champaign Hotel."* Gere even had an interest in the law, and *"practiced to a considerable extent in the lower courts."* Also, Henry M. Russel lived in Urbana during the period in question, having moved there *"in 1847, shortly before attaining his majority ... The next year he was in the employ of his uncle, James Gere, assisting him in conducting the old time 'Champaign Hotel' and in farm work."* Lincoln's alleged opponent, J. C. (Jairus Corydon) Sheldon, presents another problem. In 1848, he lived in Ohio, where he apprenticed as a ship builder. However, by May 11, 1853, he was living in Urbana, where he began legal apprenticeship in 1855. It is clear that his path crossed that of Lincoln, because Lincoln composed *"the committee appointed to examine him"* when Sheldon was admitted to the bar during the fall term of 1855. Further, in an 1880 thesis on Lincoln in Champaign County, Henry M. Beardsley wrote:

> *"Once in a while he [Lincoln] would play a game of billiards. I remember an old citizen tell me. 'the first game I ever played [was] with him. When it came my turn to play, he said to me in a legal-like manner. 'Now if this were my case, I would hit this ball, make it roll against that one, have it hit the cushion and then roll back against the third ball there.' "*

Presumably, the unnamed "old citizen" cited here was Sheldon, who would have been 52 or 53 in 1880. So what is to be made of this? Although the hotel, its proprietor, and Russell's presence can all be verified, and the probability that a billiard table or hall existed in Urbana during the period is high, it is nevertheless clear that Lincoln and Sheldon did not play billiards in Urbana in May 1848. The match quite likely took place, but on some different date.

Map of Lincoln's Eighth Judicial Circuit Prior to 1847

THIS MAP TRACES LINCOLN'S TRAVELS ALONG THE EIGHT JUDICIAL CIRCUIT. THE LIFE OF A CIRCUIT-RIDING LAWYER PROVIDED AMPLE OPPORTUNITY TO INDULGE IN BILLIARDS.

On February 11, 1949, the La Salle, Illinois, *News Tribune* ran an article with the opening line, *"Here is the story of Lincoln playing billiards in La Salle, which Charles Ulysses Gordon has so kindly sent us."* It contends that "one day in October 1858," Lincoln "by chance" met Frederick L. Fake at the Hardy House in La Salle while *"detained a few hours for the lack of transportation."* Three games were played *"to the keen amusement of the large crowd which soon gathered."* Lincoln proposed the game and refused Fake's offer of a spot (i.e., handicap) of "forty points in the hundred" in order to play. Lincoln *"divested himself of coat, waist-coat, collar, and necktie, rolling his shirt sleeves to his shoulders."* When shooting, he *"very carefully squared himself."* The game was played on a *"table being of the ancient six pocket pattern"* and Lincoln talked and told stories, perhaps several of them, much to the delight of the large crowd in the "little room," as he played. Fake apparently won the first game, because Lincoln refused the offer of a 50-point spot (in a game to 100) for the second game, *"saying he had not played his best game, etc."* They *"divided the expense at the finish."* Much storytelling went on by Lincoln, particularly *"of what he did not know of billiards, making everybody happy with a performance long to be remembered."* The participants later "went to Ottawa" where Lincoln and Douglas spoke *"in the public park that evening to a large audience."*

As with the Urbana story, the La Salle article lacks credibility because in October 1858, Lincoln was not there. He may have been in the area twice during the month. On October 27th he gave an address in Vermont, Illinois, and on October 28th made a "hurried visit" to the Tremont House in Chicago *"for a few moments ... on his way to Petersburg."* That trip could possibly have taken him through La Salle and Ottawa, but there is no such indication (nor or a speech or any kind). Otherwise, he was only within 50–60 miles of La Salle one time that month, at Toulon, Illinois, on October 8th; but his movements to and from that location originated toward the southwest (i.e., Galesburg to Toulon, Toulon to Oquawka, Illinois, and Burlington, Iowa). Likewise, the article's reference to Lincoln's giving a speech with Douglas in Ottawa during October 1858 is suspect. He did debate with Douglas all across Illinois in 1858 at Ottawa, Freeport, Jonesboro,

Charleston, Galesburg, Quincy, and Alton. Ottawa seems to jump out here, but that debate took place on August 21, and Lincoln entered town for the debate from Morris to the east of Ottawa (La Salle is west of Ottawa). The La Salle article has Lincoln entering Ottawa the wrong month and from the wrong direction.

On August 12, 1948, the Neosho *Missouri Times* said the following: *"Abraham Lincoln, who played billiards regularly, pronounced it as 'a healthy-inspiring, scientific game, lending recreation to the otherwise fatigued mind.'"* Lincoln had every reason to offer an opinion on this subject. Nevertheless, the search for the origin of this passage has been unsuccessful.

A more reliable, first-hand account of Lincoln conversing about billiards was recorded by J. Hubley Ashton, United States Assistant Attorney General from 1864 to 1869. According to Ashton, *"on a bright morning in May 1864 ... I accompanied my Chief to the White House for the purpose or being presented to the President."* Lincoln, who *"was in the hands of the barber"* at the time, *"drew his feet from the chair on which they had been resting, and wrapping one leg around the other, turned to us as for conversation."* The president outlined a problem regarding his authority to intervene in a contractual matter between a federal agency and a private vendor, and asked his Attorney General, Edward Bates, and Ashton their opinions. Ashton suggested a strategy by which the president could achieve his objective through indirect means.

Lincoln then changed the subject and with a wry look on his face asked Ashton *"Do you ever play billiards?"*

"I replied that I did not. 'Well,' he said, 'I thought you did, for your answer reminds me of the performance in billiards I saw the other day,

where the fellow caromed on the white and hit the red on the opposite side of any object placed in the middle of the table,' and slowly drawing himself out or his chair, with the barber's towel still under his chin, he proceeded to show us, with the aid of a pen, a hat, and two inkstands, how the player he spoke of could strike a ball, on one side, and hit another ball on the opposite side of the hat, without touching the hat."

This account, written shortly after the pertinent event by a high-ranking member of Lincoln's administration, shows both that Lincoln watched billiards while in the White House and used billiards as a metaphor through which to explain more substantive matters of law and presidential authority. Both points confirm Lincoln's interest in billiards.

The game of billiards was enormously popular during the era of Lincoln. Billiards historian Mike Shamos has written:

> "During the 1850s, interest in billiards increased to the point that public competitions were held for paying spectators. In 1858 the New York Times began reporting the results of matches. The following year, thousands of people filled Fireman's Hall in Detroit to see (Michael) Phelan himself beat John Seereiter for the astronomical prize of fifteen thousand dollars (by contrast, the first prize in the U.S. Open Pocket Billiard Tournament held 130 years later was only ten thousand dollars).... Based on newspaper and magazine articles of the day, as well as the number of billiard licenses issued and tables sold, it appears that

billiards was the chief sport for men in the United States from the 1850s until the 1930s."

Quite obviously, Lincoln's involvement with billiards would have been diminished had there been no place for him to play, but the game was apparently quite popular in Springfield as well. The first *Springfield City Directory*, published in 1857, lists two "Billiard Saloons," the "St. Nicholas, under St. Nicholas Hotel" and "Hickox's, over Fosselmans." Two years later, the second *City Directory* (for 1859) listed two "Billiard Saloons," but with different owner-operators, "L[e]nvenson, J." and "Smith, J.P." Keeping in mind that many billiards tables of the era were located in inns, taverns, hotels, and in the homes of exceptionally prosperous individuals, who would have had no reason to be listed in the *City Directory* as billiards establishments, it is highly likely that other tables were in use during the period.

In contrast, the White House did not have a table during Lincoln's presidency. The first billiards table in the White House was placed there amid much controversy in 1825, by John Quincy Adams. With his defeat in 1828 at the hands of Andrew Jackson, who made the table a campaign issue by arguing that it showed Adams' aristocratic nature, gambling tendencies, and extravagant use or public funds—which was untrue, as the table was actually a privately purchased used model—the table was removed. The While House remained without a billiard table until Ulysses S. Grant's personal table was installed in 1869. Nevertheless, billiard tables would have been available in any number or public and private venues in Lincoln's Washington.

Abraham Lincoln was a billiards player. The evidence leaves no doubt of this. To argue that he was not personally involved in the sport would necessitate ignoring the personal recollections of Lincoln's seven-year circuit companion Henry C. Whitney, the experiences of his long-time law partner William H. Herndon, the testimony of editor Edward. L. Baker (with whom Lincoln spent time on the day he was nominated for president), and the recollections of Assistant Attorney General Ashton. Further, one would need to discredit not only the suspicious La Salle account but also the highly plausible reports or matches in Clinton and Atchison. It is true that the recollections of seemingly all of Lincoln's companions have been criticized, including those of Whitney and Herndon. Whitney, for example, has been accused of exaggerating his personal intimacy with the man to whom he looked up, and Herndon's reputation has likewise been scathed. But in the case of Lincoln's billiards playing, they are not alleging anything remarkable about the man. They are neither purporting to have some secret inside track to his friendship or confidence nor claiming any particular insight into his motivation or the rationale underlying some great event of state. They are simply saying that Lincoln liked to play this game as corroborated by Baker, Ashton, and others. In fact, if there were any reason for these associates to distort the record of Lincoln's billiards playing, it would be to contend that he did not play, thereby shielding him from the two contradictory stereotypes or the era: that billiards was either an unsavory game of the masses or the elitist pastime of the idle aristocracy.

Lincoln did not appear to be a particularly skilled player. The references to Lincoln's game are nearly unanimous in describing it as "awkward." Henry Russel, for example, described the Urbana match as *"one of the most awkward and laughable games I ever witnessed."* Perhaps the kindest, if backhanded, comment about his game is Whitney's contrast between Lincoln and Lawrence, explaining that *"one played about as well as the other."* It is obvious from these accounts that the great man almost certainly lacked great billiards technique.

This is not at all surprising given other accounts or his coordination and movements. Whitney called Lincoln *"an awkward specimen of manhood"* and said that *"his legs and arms were disproportionately long, his feet and hands were abnormally large, he was awkward in his gait and actions."* He walked "crookedly" and was "infernally awkward" on horseback. So, the contention that Lincoln was awkward, which is certainly not a characteristic associated with billiards success, is nothing new.

But to say that he did not appear to be skilled is not to say that he was necessarily a poor player. As an athlete, Lincoln was no slouch: *"in any sports that called for skill or muscle he took a lively interest,"* one historian has written. The accounts of his athleticism as a young man are widely known; he is said to have excelled at throwing things like crowbars and cannon balls, and to have been *"obviously proudest or his wrestling talent, which was demonstrated time and again."* While billiards and wrestling are quite different sports, strength is an asset in both. As an adult in Springfield, Lincoln played catch, ball, and fives, apparently with regularity and interest. Catch and handball are difficult for people without minimal levels of coordination, so Lincoln's fondness for them suggests that his awkward demeanor may not have been as relevant to his billiards skills as might first appear.

Likewise, as all cue-sport enthusiasts know, pool and billiards are games calling for mental toughness, even over physical coordination. In that regard Lincoln stood out. As historian William Barton relates, *"Lincoln's ... frequent feeling of awkwardness, must have made him realize very early that to succeed in life he must cultivate intrinsic mental ... traits."* By another account, Lincoln had an unparalleled ability to focus his mind. *"No man had greater power of application than he,"* wrote the eminent scholar Merrill Peterson. *"Once fixing his mind on any subject, nothing could interfere with or disturb him."* Or, as Whitney put it, *"his mental vision was perfect.... Inside [his mind] all was symmetry and method."* Combined with his *"great fondness for geometry,"* it is possible that Lincoln's mental strength may have at least partially offset the awkwardness with which he moved and may have produced better billiards skills than would otherwise be expected.

In the preface to his Lincoln biography, Whitney explained that after Lincoln's death, Lincoln biographer, J. G. Holland, spoke with Lincoln's neighbors and others who knew him well, for the purpose of determining *"what manner of man he was."* What Holland found, Whitney reported, was

> *"the queer result that the more he extended his inquiries and the deeper his research, the more entangled and obscure became his knowledge, and the more hopeless the difficulty of gaining any intelligent and satisfactory*

data upon which to base an analysis of his subject ... he found out that Mr. Lincoln was an able man, and also that his ability was meager; that he was a profound, and likewise a superficial, lawyer: that he was a Christian and also an atheist; that he possessed a refined, and likewise a coarse, nature; that he was a profound dialectician, and that he was very shallow, and so on. On no one trait, did even those who saw him daily, for twenty years, agree."

Herndon likewise sought the input of many who knew Lincoln, but found that no two *"agree in their estimate of him. The fact was that he rarely showed more than one aspect of himself to one man. He opened himself to men in different directions."* Well over a century later, with all the scholarly work that had transpired, Merrill Peterson can still write of the impossibility of producing a definitive picture of Lincoln:

"Paradoxically, the more [scholars] wrote about Lincoln, the more blurred, confused, and problematic the image became. It almost seemed as if the modus operandi was to disagree....All the work devoted to illuminating and elucidating particular subjects tended to obscure the forest for the trees."

An engraving by John Tenniel of Abraham Lincoln dressed as Uncle Sam playing pool with Jefferson Davis who is getting the better of him. But this cartoon was published in the London *Punch* Magazine on May 9, 1863, on the eve of the great Union victories at Gettysburg and Vicksburg in early July, 1863.

BEAUTIES OF BILLIARDS BY CURRIER AND IVES
HAND-COLORED LITHOGRAPH, C. 1869.

ANTIQUE POOL TABLE. A RESTORED NINETEENTH-CENTURY POOL TABLE
IN A MODERN GAME ROOM. THIS IS A BRUNSWICK & BALKE FROM 1878.

President Lincoln was the exact contemporary of Charles Darwin, who also had a billiard table installed in his home, Down House. After a day of thinking, correspondence, and experiments, he would play billiards with his butler as relaxation before dinner. So apparently did George Washington, who according to various sources, wrote about his winnings and losses in his diary. Jefferson also seems to have had a billiards table at Monticello.

Mark Twain's *The Innocents Abroad* writes about playing in Europe on atrocious tables. This, by the way, was in 1867, shortly after the Civil War. Here's an excerpt describing billiards in Paris.

> *"At eleven o'clock we alighted upon a sign which manifestly referred to billiards. Joy! We had played billiards in the Azores with balls that were not round and on an ancient table that was very little smoother than a brick pavement—one of those wretched old things with dead cushions, and with patches in the faded cloth and invisible obstructions that made the balls describe the most astonishing and unsuspected angles and perform feats in the way of unlooked-for and almost impossible "scratches" that were perfectly bewildering. We had played at Gibraltar with balls the size of a walnut, on a table like a public square—and in both instances we achieved far more aggravation than amusement. We expected to fare better here, but we were mistaken. The cushions were a good deal higher than the balls, and as the balls had a fashion of always stopping under the cushions, we accomplished very little in the way*

> *of caroms. The cushions were hard and unelastic, and the cues were so crooked that in making a shot you had to allow for the curve or you would infallibly put the "English" on the wrong side of the hall. Dan was to mark while the doctor and I played. At the end of an hour neither of us had made a count, and so Dan was tired of keeping tally with nothing to tally, and we were heated and angry and disgusted. We paid the heavy bill—about six cents—and said we would call around sometime when we had a week to spend, and finish the game."*

So what game exactly was Lincoln playing? A billiard, strictly speaking, is when you hit an object ball after first caroming the cue ball off another ball, or sink a ball by caroming it off another one Lincoln may well have played some kind of pool (in his younger days), but "billiards" (which covered a lot of ground in those days) is what respectable folks, like Abraham Lincoln, played.

> *Briefly these are the most significant historical references to Lincoln's Billiard Playing:*

William H. Herndon and Jesse W. Weik, *Herndon's Lincoln: The True Story of a Great Life*, 3 vols. 1889; William H. Herndon and Jesse W. Weik, *Herndon's Life of Lincoln,* Paul M. Angle ed. 1930 and 1963; Carl Sandburg, *Abraham Lincoln: The Prairie Years,* 3 vols. 1925–26; Jesse W. Weik, *The Real Lincoln: A Portrait,* 1922; Henry Clay Whitney, *Life on the Circuit with Lincoln,* Paul M.

Angle, ed., 1940; "Lincoln's First Billiard Game," *The Illinois State Journal* (Springfield, Ill), 20 January 1909; Walter B. Stevens, "Recollections of Lincoln: Lincoln's Game of Billiards," *St Louis Globe-Democrat*, 31 January, 1909, Magazine Section; "Lincoln Was a Billiards Fan," *The Illinois State Journal*, 1 August 1947; Bazy Miller, "The Starter," *La Salle (Ill.) Tribune*, 11 February 1949; "Beat Lincoln at Billiards," *Kansas City Journal*; copy in Lincoln-sports-billiards file, Illinois State Historical society; *Central Transcript* (Clinton, Ill.) 20 September 1860 as cited in Maurice Graham Porter, "Portrait of a Prairie Lawyer: Clifton H. Moore 1851-1861 and 1870-1880, A Comparative Study" (LL.B. thesis, University of Illinois, 1938; Neosho *Missouri Times*, 12 August 1948; Henry M. Beardsley, "Abraham Lincoln in Our Own County," (M.L. thesis, Illinois Industrial University, 1880); J Hubley Ashton, "A Glimpse of Lincoln in 1864,' *Journal of the Illinois State Historical Society* 69 (February 1976).

Chapter Six

"HE PLAYED A FAIR GAME, BUT NOT A FIRST-RATE ONE":

Lincoln and Chess and Checkers

Although the documentation on this aspect of Lincoln's activities is rather sparse and anecdotal, Abraham Lincoln was known to have been a chess and checkers player. Excerpts from key sources will be shown below. They demonstrate the instances where Chess crossed paths with Lincoln.

As a reticent individual, Lincoln did not provide the researcher with many examples of his recreational activities. Hence it was left up to other observers to provide a glimpse into Lincoln, the chess and checkers player.

The Every-day Life of Abraham Lincoln, by Francis Fisher Browne 1913:

> "Mr. G.W. Harris, whose first meeting with Lincoln in a log schoolhouse has been previously described in these pages, subsequently became a clerk in Lincoln's law office at Springfield and furnishes some excellent reminiscences of that interesting period.... Mr.

Lincoln was fond of playing chess and checkers, and usually acted cautiously upon the defensive until the game had reached a stage where aggressive movements were clearly justified."

Lincoln and His World, by Richard Lawrence Miller, 2013:

"A contemporary report said he 'plays a very fair game, but not a first rate one ... While playing chess, Mr. Lincoln seems to be continually thinking of something else. Those who have played him say he plays as if it were but a mechanical pastime to occupy his hands while his mind is busy with some other subject.... He plays what chess players call a "safe game." Rarely attacking, he is content to let his opponent attack while he concentrates all his energies in the defense—awaiting the opportunity of dashing in at a weak point, or the expenditure of his adversary's strength.... He is the model of a chess general."'

Abraham Lincoln: A Life, by Michael Burlingame, 2013

"When Hatch recommended Nicolay (as a personal secretary), Lincoln found it easy to accept the advice, for he regarded the young man as 'entirely trustworthy' and had often conversed and played chess with him in Hatch's office, which served as an informal Republican headquarters."

Abraham Lincoln, the War Years, by Carl Sandburg, 1939

"One of them was a gleaming, vital creature, Katherine Jane Chase, known as Kate and born under strange stars. She had grown to be his chum and helper, playing chess with him, walking with him to the office, telling him what she got from a newly read book..."

Katherine Jane Chase was the daughter of Lincoln's Secretary of the Treasury, Salmon P. Chase. Often called the "American Queen," she worked surreptitiously behind Lincoln's back to win the 1864 Republican nomination for her father. However, in the interval the 21-year-old toast of Washington, D.C., and Honest Abe were chess partners.

The Story-life of Lincoln, by Wayne Whipple, 1908

"An old friend of Mr. Lincoln once related to me another of his stories which shows not a little of his character. This gentleman was conversing with the President at a time during the War when things looked very dark. On taking leave, he asked the President what he should say to their friends in Kentucky—what cheering news he could give them of him. Mr. Lincoln replied:

'That reminds me of a man who prided himself greatly on his game of chess, having seldom been beaten. He heard of a machine called the "Automaton Chess Player," which was beating everyone who played against it. So,

he went to try his skill with the machine. He lost the first game, so with the second, and the third. Then, rising in astonishment from his seat, he walked around the machine and looked at it a few minutes. Then, stopping and pointing at it, he exclaimed, 'There is a man in there.' "Tell my friends,' said Mr. Lincoln, 'there is a man in here!'"

The chess automaton, the Turk, had been destroyed by fire in 1854.

Honest Abe   Judge Samuel Treat

Abraham Lincoln with Robert Todd

LINCOLN AS A CHESS PLAYER FROM "THE AMERICAN CHESS MAGAZINE," 1897:

"Mr. Lincoln was very partial to and quite skillful in the game of chess, and a few years before he was made President, Judge Samuel H. Treat, a grave and learned gentleman, then Chief Justice of the Illinois Supreme Court, was his frequent antagonist, and probably a little his superior as a player, writes G. M. McConnel in the Chicago Times-Herald. In the hot months of summer, Springfield was a sleepy place, and one sweltering summer noontide these two friends were having an engrossing game in the still, deserted Supreme Court room, with the board on their knees between them. In the critical stage of the closely contested game, while Treat was deeply pondering a move, Lincoln's son 'Tod,' [sic] then probably 8 or so years old, came suddenly into the room and, laying his hand on his father's shoulder, said, insistently:

'Pa! Ma says for you to come down some right away. She wants you.' 'All right, Tad,' said his father, abstractedly, 'you run home and tell her I'll be there in a minute.' The boy had probably some experience of what 'in a minute' meant when chess was in question, and he muttered something with an ominous shake of the head but walked quietly to the door and waited there several minutes. Treat did not stir, but studied the board with the closest attention, and Lincoln sat motionless. Presently the boy came back, gave his father a little shake, and repeated: 'I say, ma wants you to *come down some right away! She wants you now!' 'Sh-sh! Tad! Yes-yes—in a minute—in a minute,' said his father, with a deprecatory wave of his hand, but without taking his eyes from the board. The boy stood for a minute or two in petulant impatience, and then, suddenly lifting his foot, with a vigorous kick he sent the board and the chessmen flying about the room. Treat sprang to his feet, his usually quiet visage flaming with wrath, but clinched his teeth and said nothing. Mr. Lincoln dropped back in his chair with a curious laugh of amused dismay, looked up with unruffled good humor and said: 'Well, Judge, I guess that's Tad's game! You set 'em up again and we'll have it out some other day. Come along, Tod. Let's go see what ma wants,' and without other words he took the boy by the hand and strode calmly away toward home. Lincoln was thought to be a very good chess player."*

An excerpt from an article in *The New York Times* from November 15, 1860, discusses traits of the next President who had been elected on November 6, 1860: "THE NEXT PRESIDENT.; LETTERS FROM MR. LINCOLN'S HOME. What his Neighbors Think of his Election—A Personal Interview—A Characteristic Visitor—Col. Ellsworth in a New Character, &c.":

"Speaking of custom, reminds me of a curious custom of Mr. LINCOLN while playing chess—for be it known to the disciples of CAISSA, the devotees of MORPHY,

PAULSEN, ANDERSON, STAUNTON, LICHTENHEIN, *and the army of chess players, that Mr. LINCOLN takes delight in the movements on the ordinary, as well as of the political chess board, and plays a very fair game, but not a first-rate one. He has a habit of whistling and sing musical ability being confined to one tune, and that tune, I sagely suspect, is "Dixie's Land." While playing chess, Mr. LINCOLN seems to be continually thinking of something else. Those who have played with him say he plays as if it were but a mechanical pastime to occupy his hands while his mind is busy with some other subject, just as one often twirls a cane, or plays with a string, or as a pretty coquette toys with her fan. The way any man plays, either at a game of skill or of chance, is generally a pretty fair index to his character. Success or defeat—the chances—the variations in the probability of triumph—the turning point in the struggle—the exhibition of temper under all circumstances—the stubborn defence in hopeless resistance—the spirited attack with the weaker force, and all the incidents of mimic warfare contribute to develop the strong points of a man's disposition. Nor does Mr. LINCOLN suffer by judgment under this rule. He plays what chess players call a "safe game." Rarely attacking, he is content to let his opponent attack while he concentrates all his energies in the defence—awaiting the opportunity of dashing in at a weak point, or the expenditure of his adversary's strength, self-reliant in adversity, magnanimous in success, and undaunted by defeat, he is the model of a chess general. His abstractedness, however, must not be regarded as applicable to ordinary pursuits. He seizes a point in conversation with remarkable quickness—often anticipating the meaning before the sentence is concluded.*

A few years before Lincoln became President, he played chess with Judge Samuel H. Treat (1811–1887), Chief Justice of the Illinois Supreme Court. According to Treat, whom Lincoln biographer Jesse W. Weik interviewed in 1883:

From *The Real Lincoln*, by Jesse W. Weik.

One morning Lincoln came to his office and joined him in a game of chess. The two were enthusiastic chess players and when the opportunity offered indulged in the game. On the occasion named they were soon deeply absorbed, nor did they realize how near it was to the noon hour until one of Lincoln's boys came running in with a message from his mother announcing dinner at the Lincoln home, a few steps away. Lincoln promised to come at once and the boy left; but the game was not entirely out; yet so near the end the players, confident that they would finish in a few moments, lingered a while. Meanwhile almost half an hour had passed. Presently the boy returned with a second and more urgent call for dinner; but so deeply engrossed in the game were the two players they apparently failed to notice his arrival. This was more than the little fellow could stand; so that, angered at their inattention, he moved nearer, lifted his foot, and deliberately kicked board, chessmen, and all into the air. "It was one of the most abrupt, if not brazen, things I ever saw," said Treat, "but the surprising thing was its effect on Lincoln. Instead of the animated scene between an irate father and an impudent youth which I expected, Mr. Lincoln without a word of reproof calmly arose, took the boy by the hand, and started for dinner. Reaching the door he turned, smiled good-naturedly, and exclaimed, 'Well, Judge, I reckon we'll have to finish this game some other time,' and passed out. Of course, I refrained from any comment," continued Treat, who, by the way, was old and had never been blessed with a child," but I can assure you of one thing: if that little rascal had been a boy of mine he never would have applied his boots to another chessboard."

According to The Lincoln Institute, Mr. Lincoln enjoyed and excelled at both physical and mental games. Mr. Lincoln was a participant in the debating club organized in New Salem in 1832, and he was one of the founders of the Young Men's Lyceum in Springfield.

From *The Every-day Life of Abraham Lincoln*, by Francis Fischer Browne.

George Washington Harris, a clerk in Lincoln's law office in Springfield recalled: *"Mr. Lincoln was fond of playing chess and checkers, and usually acted cautiously upon the defensive until the game had reached a stage where aggressive movements were clearly justified. He was also somewhat fond of ten-pins, and occasionally indulged in a game."*

From *Lincoln: The Biography of a Writer*, by Fred Kaplan.

George Harrison, a friend of Lincoln, wrote of their time in the militia during the Black Hawk War, *"We passed our evenings by jumping, playing checkers, chess, swimming our horses."*

One of Lincoln's chess sets is displayed in the Smithsonian. He did play an occasional game at the White House. One time he was playing chess with Judge Samuel. H. Treat, Chief Justice of the Illinois Supreme Court. Lincoln's son, Tad, was sent by his mother to say dinner was ready. When his father continued with his chess game, Tad went over to the game and kicked the chess board off the table or laps of the two players. The judge was speechless, but Lincoln said mildly, "Come, Tad," and they walked away together to have dinner. Lincoln bought a chess set for his son Tad, which is on display at the National Museum of American History.

There was an item "Abraham Lincoln as a Chess Player" in *Our Folder*, November 1, 1920 (the publication of the Good Companion Chess Problem Club). Before relating an anecdote, the article stated:

Abraham Lincoln was very partial to and quite skillful in the game of chess, and a few years before he was made President Judge Samuel H. Treat, a grave and learned gentleman, then Chief Justice of the Illinois Supreme Court, was his frequent antagonist, and probably a little superior as a player.

The same issue had the following illustration:

A Chess Board decorated with the portraits of the Generals and Admirals of the Union forces in the Rebellion. Pres. A. Lincoln, Commander in Chief of the Army and Navy.

Frederick Douglass had this to say about another nineteenth century, three-dimensional chess master, Lincoln. The occasion was the dedication of the still-controversial Emancipation Memorial in 1876 in Washington, D.C.

Douglas said, *"Abraham Lincoln was not, in the fullest sense of the word, either our man or our model. In his interests, in his associations, in his habits of thought and in his prejudices, he was a white man.*

His great mission was to accomplish two things: first, to save his country from dismemberment and ruin; and second, to free his country from the great crime of slavery. To do one or the other, or both, he must have the earnest sympathy and the powerful cooperation of his loyal fellow-countrymen.

Viewed from the genuine abolition ground, Mr. Lincoln seemed tardy, cold, dull, and indifferent; but measuring him by the sentiment of his country, a sentiment he was bound to as a statesman to consult, he was swift, zealous, radical, and determined."

Douglass knew who Lincoln was and who he wasn't. Lincoln was a chess player and that was reflected in his politics. More importantly, he and Lincoln understood who and what White America was. What Douglass and Lincoln were playing for, in their own ways, was everything. And when you're playing for everything, you say what you have to say, you do what you must do to carry the day. *"The only question you ever really must answer is: Do you want to be right or do you want to win?"*

The Lincolns did not play cards as they were considered a form of gambling, but based on archeological finds in the backyard, they did play chess and possibly checkers. The pieces were stored in their games table such as the one below. The top spins

90 degrees and flips open to make a square top. Underneath is a storage area for game pieces.

MID-NINETEENTH-CENTURY GAMES TABLE THAT COULD
BE SEEN IN THE HOMES OF PROFESSIONALS.

After the heartbreaking death of his son, Willie, Abraham Lincoln, and his family fled the gloom that hung over the White House, moving into a small cottage outside Washington, on the grounds of the Soldiers' Home, a resident for disabled military veterans. Lincoln lived at the Soldiers' Home for a quarter of his presidency, and for nearly a quarter of the critical year of 1862.

At his secluded cottage, Lincoln complained to his closest aides, recited poetry to his friends, reconnected with his wife and family, conducted secret meetings with his political enemies, and avoided assassination attempts. Perhaps most importantly, he forged key friendships with the soldiers that helped to renew his flagging spirits. The cottage became a refuge from the pressures of the White House, a place of tranquility where Lincoln could refresh his mind.

One way of doing this, Lincoln found, was in games of chess and checkers with the recuperating soldiers. Private Albert See, one of the infantry guards at the Soldiers' Home remembered seeing Lincoln and his son, Tad, playing checkers on the porch of the president's cottage one evening while he was on sentinel duty. Lincoln asked if he wanted to lay down his gun for a moment and "take a game," an offer the young soldier proudly accepted.

Other soldiers as well recalled similar stories. Lincoln not only told stories while he played but also attentively listened to the soldiers' stories about themselves, their families, and the war in which they had been fighting. By virtually all accounts, Lincoln enjoyed the camaraderie created through the games of chess and checkers with the soldiers.

Chapter Seven
"ONE OF THE ABES WAS FRIGHTENED:" LINCOLN AND HORSEBACK RIDING

TWO ILLUSTRATIONS OF THE ICONIC LINCOLN WITH HIS HORSE, OLD BOB.

Abraham Lincoln was certainly no stranger to horses. The President was quite fond of the animals. History tells us that there was a fire at the White House stables. In fact, the stables were engulfed by fire. President Lincoln tried to run into the burning stable to save his son's ponies. President Lincoln had to be physically restrained.

A young Abraham Lincoln riding his horse in New Salem, Illinois.

Thomas Tad Lincoln on one of his ponies.

Lincoln's children Willie and Tad had several ponies. Willie had a pony at the White House and insisted on riding it every day. Tad also rode the pony; he was so small when he learned to ride it that his feet stuck straight out from the saddle. On Tad's tenth birthday, April 4, 1863 (after Willie had died), a new pony arrived at the White House. The Lincolns still had Willie's pony, but this new pony became Tad's.

Lincoln owned several horses throughout his life, including Tom, Belle, Old Buck, and a reddish-brown horse named Robin (who was called "Old Bob"). Lincoln rode Old Bob when on the circuit as a lawyer. He left Old Bob in Springfield. He owned Old Bob prior to his presidency, when he was still practicing law in Springfield, Illinois. He was a carriage horse that Lincoln used in his travels to places that the railroad was not yet connected to.

Old Bob was a replacement for Old Buck, who Lincoln retired when he became too old for regular use. Old Buck was kept by Lincoln in his home stable with another one of his horses named Old Tom. Prior to his move to D.C. after being elected president, Lincoln sold Old Bob to John Flynn, so he stayed behind in Illinois when Lincoln left.

Old Bob was put out to pasture by Flynn in 1865. He was brought out of retirement to participate in a parade on April 4, 1865, celebrating that capitalization of Richmond as the capital of the Confederate States. Old Bob was decked out in red, white, and blue for the occasion.

Following Lincoln's assassination, Old Bob was brought out of retirement one more time to follow behind the hearse at Lincoln's funeral. Old Bob wore a drape of black and silver and was led by a family friend, Henry Brown. Behind Old Bob in Lincolns funeral procession was a carriage carrying Lincoln's son Robert. It has been said that Old Bob and Young Bob, the president's son, were his only family that attended the funeral.

There is no confirmed information of Old Bob's final years, though stories have been told that many showmen offered to purchase Old Bob to use in their performances. Flynn refused all offers.

When Lincoln went to Washington, D.C., he got a new horse, whom someone named "Old Abe." When Abraham Lincoln went to the Soldier's Home just outside of Washington, it was on Old Abe that he rode. Lincoln told this story to Marshal Lamon about an assassination attempt while on his way to the Soldier's Home:

> *"I was jogging along at a slow gait, immersed in deep thought, when suddenly I was aroused—I may say the arousement lifted me out of my saddle as well as out of my wits—by the report of a rifle. [He heard a bullet whistle past his ear.] Old Abe, with one reckless bound, unceremoniously separated me from my eight-dollar plug-hat, with which I parted company without any assent, expressed or implied, upon my part. At a break-neck speed we soon arrived in a haven of safety.*
>
> *I can truthfully say that one of the Abes was frightened on this occasion, but modesty forbids my mentioning which of us is entitled to that honor.*

Lincoln's horse Old Bob, on the day of Lincoln's funeral in 1865, held by Rev. H. Brown

Lincoln's horse "Old Bob," on the day of his funeral in 1865, held by Rev. H. Brown.

In 1865, Abraham Lincoln was honored by the inclusion of a caparisoned horse at his funeral. When Lincoln's funeral train reached Springfield, Illinois, his horse, Old Bob, who was draped in a black mourning blanket, followed the procession, and led mourners to Lincoln's burial spot. A riderless horse or caparisoned horse (in reference to its ornamental coverings, which have a detailed protocol of their own) is a single horse, without a rider, and with boots reversed in the stirrups, which sometimes accompanies a funeral procession. The horse follows the caisson carrying the casket. A riderless horse can also be featured in military parades to symbolize fallen soldiers. The custom is believed to date back to the time of Genghis Khan, when a horse was sacrificed to serve the fallen warrior in the next world. The caparisoned horse later came to symbolize a warrior who would ride no more.

In the United States, the caparisoned horse is part of the military honors given to an Army or Marine Corps officer who was a colonel or above; this includes the president, by virtue of having been the country's commander in chief and the Secretary of Defense, having overseen the armed forces. Alexander Hamilton, former Secretary of the Treasury (1789–1795) was the first American to be given the honor. Historian Ron Chernow noted that Hamilton's gray horse followed the casket "with the boots and spurs of its former rider reversed in the stirrups." Abraham Lincoln was the first president of the United States to be officially honored by the inclusion of the caparisoned horse in his funeral cortege, although a letter from George Washington's personal secretary recorded the president's horse was part of the president's funeral, carrying his saddle, pistols, and holsters. Traditionally, simple, black riding boots are reversed in the stirrups to represent a fallen leader looking back on his troops for the last time.

This statue of Abraham Lincoln and his horse, Old Bob, was created by Ivan Schwartz. The statue is made of bronze. It is life size and done as true to the times as possible. It should also be noted that old photos, clothing, and skulls were studied. The skills of a forensic scientist were also used by New York-based StudioEIS. For the statue of Lincoln, Mr. Schwartz and his team examined all the photos taken of the president and the life casts of his face and hands from 1860. Lincoln's surviving coat and top hat, now in the collection of the Smithsonian's National Museum of American History, were measured to accurately reflect the president's daily garb. *"For the statue of Lincoln, Mr. Schwartz and his team examined all the photos taken of the president and the life casts of his face and hands from 1860. Lincoln's surviving coat and top hat, now in the collection of the Smithsonian's National Museum of American History, were measured to accurately reflect the president's daily garb. 'He was 6 feet 4 inches, and wore a size 14 shoe,"* noted the artist. The saddled horse next to the sculpted Lincoln also took intensive research. The artists studied nineteenth-century equestrian statues in New York City and a photo of Old Bob, Lincoln's favorite horse. In consultation with equine experts, they chose an American Standardbred as the model for the sculpture."

The following photos of the statue of Lincoln and Old Bob are located outside President Lincoln's Cottage at the Soldiers' Home National Monument in Washington, D.C.

Young Abraham Lincoln Reads on a Horse.

The above statue was sculpted by Anna Hyatt Huntington and given to Lincoln City on the condition that the town never change its name. According to a plaque at its base, Lincoln was offered the governorship of the Oregon Territory in 1849 but turned it down and returned to his law practice. He would tour the circuit from town to town, and along the way he would read books while riding his horse. The statue of Abe Lincoln reading on a horse is 15 feet tall and was given to the city on the condition that it always face west.

Lincoln and horses were not always a total success story. Abraham Lincoln owned several horses throughout his life and was known to take good care of them, give them nicknames and even made sure that the one he could not take to Washington was boarded properly during his absence.

Not always, however, did the horses pay back that kindness received from their owner. There are four known incidents in which Lincoln's steeds—more or less successfully—tried to abandon him, thus leaving Lincoln without his favorite mode of transportation.

The first time Abraham Lincoln lost a horse was right after the Black Hawk War when Lincoln tried to make his way back home to New Salem. The horse disappeared during the night and from then on, it was walking home on foot or using a canoe.

The second flight episode occurred in 1836—and a rather insolvent Lincoln even placed an ad in the local newspaper asking for help in the case of the runaway horse that had disappeared from a livery.

Times three and four both took place in Washington and during Lincoln's commute to and from his summer residence, The Soldier's Home. Even more embarrassing—the second time, on his way into the city, someone saw the runaway horse with its rider clinging to the reigns and dutifully reported the incident to the newspaper *Evening Star*, which printed it on September 13, 1862.

To save the President's honor, the paper described the horse as a "spirited and powerful beast."

Abraham Lincoln the Athlete

> services in that capacity.
>
> ALMOST A SERIOUS ACCIDENT TO THE PRESIDENT.—When coming into the city this morning from the Soldier's Home on horseback, the President had a narrow escape. His steed, a spirited and powerful beast, ran off with him, and came very near throwing him in the race, in which Mr. Lincoln lost his hat, but succeeded in checking the animal's career at the cost of a sprained wrist in so doing.
>
> PERSONAL.—Capt. J. R. Goldsborough, U. S.

LINCOLN WAS A SKILLED HORSEMAN. HERE HE RIDES AS A CIRCUIT LAWYER.

The horse's importance to Abraham Lincoln is revealed in many of Lincoln's jokes and stories. In March 1863, the famed Confederate battalion known as Mosby's Rangers raided Fairfax, Virginia, and captured a Union brigadier general, two captains, and number of soldiers and horses. Upon learning the news, the president supposedly commented: *"Well, I am sorry for the horses."* He then explained: *"I can make a brigadier general in five minutes, but it is not easy to replace a hundred and ten horses."*

Here are a few other stories and jokes in which Lincoln reflected on the importance horses.

Horse Trade: While a young lawyer in Illinois, Lincoln got to joking with a judge about making a trade of horses. They finally agreed to do so at a predetermined time and place, stipulating that the horses would not be seen beforehand and that if either man backed out of the trade at that point, he would have to pay $25. At the appointed time and place, the judge appeared with the sorriest-looking horse ever seen in those parts. The crowd soon broke out in laughter as Lincoln arrived carrying a wooden sawhorse upon his shoulders. The laughter only grew when Lincoln, after surveying the judge's horse, put down the sawhorse and exclaimed: *"Well, Judge, this is the first time I ever got the worst of it in a horse trade."*

Horse Chestnut: During the first Lincoln-Douglas debate, at Ottawa, Lincoln accused Stephen Douglas of misrepresenting his position through *"a specious and fantastic arrangement of words, by which a man can prove a horse chestnut to be a chestnut horse."*

McClellan's Fatigued Horses: Although General George B. McClellan proved himself a remarkably fine organizer of the troops, he exasperated Lincoln and many others by his reluctance to engage the Confederates in combat. When McClellan gave the excuse that he couldn't act because half of his horses were fatigued, lame, ill, and undernourished, and this more than a month after the last fighting, Lincoln sent him a somewhat sarcastic telegram asking: *"Will you pardon me for asking what the horses of your army have done since the battle of Antietam that fatigue anything?*

The Horse as Rider: A few months earlier, McClellan had written Lincoln a letter offering him advice on how to carry out the affairs of the nation. Lincoln didn't reply directly to McClellan, but *supposedly remarked that it made him think of the man whose horse kicked up and stuck his foot through the stirrup; the man said to the horse, "If you are going to get on, then I will get off."* Lincoln had no intention of 'getting off' but wished that McClellan would understand that he was only a general, not a dictator.

Swapping Horses Mid-Stream: Two years later, Lincoln and McClellan were facing off in the 1864 presidential election and Lincoln made use of another horse and rider allusion. He made the case for his re-election while the country was still at war by noting: *"I have not permitted myself ... to conclude that I am the best man in the country; but I am reminded, in this connection, of a story of an old Dutch farmer who remarked to a companion once that 'it was not best to swap horses while crossing streams'."*

The term "horse whisperer" has long been a part of equestrian vernacular, traditionally applied to persons who have an almost mystical affinity with horses, able to tame even the most cantankerous animals through sympathetic handling. Since many such persons were seen to confront their subjects face-to-face and apparently communicate with them silently or in low voices, they were designated "horse whisperers."

Denton Offutt of Kentucky, is perhaps best known to history as the man who, in 1831, befriended and gave young Abraham Lincoln his first real job as a clerk in his store at New Salem, Illinois. There can be little doubt that Offutt—garrulous and good-natured, often impulsive or even reckless, and an inveterate schemer—had a significant influence upon the future president. It was more likely as an example to avoid rather than one to emulate. During his own lifetime, Offutt was better known as an expert horse trainer, and he is the first American who can be identified as an authentic "horse whisperer." Many of Offutt's skills he no doubt passed on to the future president.

Offutt's brief sojourn as a merchant and entrepreneur at New Salem and his relationship to the future president has not been overlooked by historians. His subsequent career as a well-known horse tamer has generally been dismissed as inconsequential by historians unfamiliar with the equestran world of the nineteenth century. The distinguished Lincoln historian Michael Burlingame considered Offutt, in post–New Salem life, as no more than *"a confidence man, peddling a magical expression that would allegedly tame horses when whispered in their ears."* William G. Greene, who was Lincoln's assistant in Offutt's store, described Offutt as *"a wild, recless [sic], careless man, a kind of wandering horse tamer."*

Yet such prominent statesmen as Lincoln and Henry Clay of Kentucky and some of the most prominent horsemen of the country who knew Offutt personally praised his amazing ability with horses; such men would be difficult to deceive. Though fame and fortune always eluded the hapless Offutt during his lifetime, his methods spawned countless imitators, some genuine horse whisperers, others no more than charlatans.

During much of history, the use of fear and pain as horse-training methods have generally defined the human–equine relationship. The process of training a horse to accept human control, whether as a mount to be ridden or to labor in harness, has traditionally been known as "breaking" the horse. Although still in common usage today, the term is suggestive of both the philosophy and methods from which it derived, methods that would now be considered unnecessarily harsh, or even cruel. Horse training was intended to "break" the independent spirit of the animal through the use of coercion and render it submissive and obedient. Treatment was liable to be especially severe if the subject was a grown horse, either a feral animal captured from the wild or a domestic animal considered to be unruly or vicious. The trainer, in such cases, might resort to beatings, confinement, starvation, sleep deprivation, or even bleeding in an effort to render the horse manageable.

During the nineteenth century, more benign methods of training horses began to replace the brute-force approach, part of a larger social movement toward more humane treatment of animals that began in Britain early in the century and spread to the United States much later. Influential British equine authorities, such as John Lawrence and William Youatt, urged patience and kindness in the training of young horses, deploring the barbarity of cruel treatment. *"The restive and vicious horse,"* Youatt wrote, *"is made so by ill-usage, and not by nature."* Contributing to this shift toward a gentler approach were certain trainers, often known as "horse-tamers" or "horse whisperers," whose successes in domesticating notoriously ill-tempered animals brought them widespread fame and focused attention on their methods. These "whisperers" often cloaked their methods with secrecy, so that many observers attributed the taming of a vicious horse to the use of mysterious charms or potions or to an occult "animal magnetism" unique to the trainer. Only gradually came the realization that such men relied upon a keen understanding of equine psychology and an approach based upon sympathy and kind treatment. Such methods, known today as "natural horsemanship," are intended to cultivate trust and harmonize with the natural instincts of the horse.

The designation "horse whisperer" was first applied to the Irishman James Sullivan, a horse-tamer who practiced his art in the Duhallow district of County Cork, Ireland, during the late eighteenth and early nineteenth centuries. As he was often seen to speak softly into the ear of those animals he wished to subdue, Sullivan came to be widely known as "The Whisperer" and was frequently employed by the Lord Doneraile (Hayes St. Leger) of Doneraile, County Cork, to tame obstreperous horses at his stables. According to one observer, Sullivan was able to achieve dramatic and lasting effects within a very short time spent in communion with the animal. Although sometimes he performed openly before spectators, Sullivan preferred privacy in his work. Horatio Townsend recalled,

> "When sent for to tame a vicious beast, for which he was paid more or less, according to distance, generally

> *two or three guineas, he directed the stable, in which he and the object of the experiment were placed, to be shut, with orders not to open the door until a signal was given. After about half an hour, during which little or no bustle was heard, the signal was made, and, upon opening the door, the horse appeared lying down, and the man by his side, playing familiarly with him, like a child with a puppy dog. From that time he was found perfectly willing to submit to any discipline, however repugnant to his nature before."*

Sullivan's ability appeared to be so magical in nature that his parish priest feared for his soul and threatened to denounce him as a sorcerer dabbling in the black arts if he did not reveal his secret. Sullivan died some time prior to 1810, confiding his secret only to a different priest with instructions that it be passed on to his eldest son.

Although Sullivan's method remains obscure and the results were doubtless exaggerated in the telling, accounts describing his activities are striking in their similarity to those of later practitioners. In the United States, Denton Offutt developed, taught, and promoted a distinctive style of natural horsemanship in the antebellum era, a style that he preferred to call "gentling" rather than the customary "breaking" of a horse. One of his early pupils was Abraham Lincoln whose gentle and compassionate character coincided nicely with Offutt's suggestions.

Teenaged Alexander Keene Richards, a resident of Georgetown, Kentucky, who became one of the most significant thoroughbred breeders of the nineteenth century, described Offutt as *"a queer genius ... an uneducated man but full of originality."* The time Richards spent with Offutt, receiving practical instruction in the care and training of horses at the hands of a master, was an important formative period in the young man's life. More than fifteen years after taking lessons, Richards still carried Offutt's book of instructions and training philosophy with him when he traveled abroad on horse-buying expeditions.

Offutt had visions of great wealth to be made from the resources of the region. The fertile prairie lands of Illinois were ideally suited for production of abundant crops of grain, but there was at this time no practical way to transport produce to outside markets except by the rivers. Offutt proposed to purchase grain and pork in Illinois and take it by flatboat to market in New Orleans. To accomplish this, he needed to hire an experienced boatman and a capable crew. Through his inquiries, Offutt learned that there was just such a man in the vicinity, John Hanks of Kentucky, who lived in Macon County five miles northwest of Decatur.

Hanks had come to Illinois in 1828, and it was his glowing reports of the region that persuaded Thomas Lincoln and many members of the closely associated Hanks family, who were then living along Little Pigeon Creek in southern Indiana, to migrate to Illinois in March 1830. Before their arrival, John Hanks selected a tract for the Lincoln family, located about five miles further west on a bluff overlooking the Sangamon River, and he cut some timber to be used in construction of their cabin. At the time of their move, Thomas Lincoln's son Abraham had just passed his twenty-first birthday.

Offutt paid a call upon Hanks at his cabin in February 1831 and outlined his proposal. *"He wanted me to go badly,"* Hanks later recalled, *"but I waited a while before answering. I hunted up Abe, and I introduced him and John Johnston, his stepbrother, to Offutt. After some talk we at last made an engagement with Offutt fifty cents a day and sixty dollars to make the trip to New Orleans."* John Hanks and his cousin, Abraham Lincoln, set out on the first of March, floating down the Sangamon River in a canoe to Judy's Ferry, five miles east of Springfield, where they met up with Johnston. From the ferry, the three men walked to Springfield, where they found Denton Offutt comfortably settled in "The Buckhorn," the best inn in town.

According to their agreement, Offutt was to have arranged for the building of a flatboat at Springfield, but, dallying in the congenial company at the inn, he had neglected to have this done. Offutt was contrite over his failure to provide the boat and engaged the three men to build the boat themselves at wages of twelve dollars a month each. They spent two weeks cutting timber on public land and floated the logs down the river to old Sangamo Town, about seven miles northwest from Springfield, where they were sawed into planks at a local mill.

Within four weeks, the newly constructed flatboat, eighty feet long and eighteen feet wide, was ready to launch. With a cargo of pork packed in barrels, bacon, corn, and live hogs, Offutt and his three employees set off down the Sangamon River, but they ran into trouble on April 19 when they reached New Salem and the boat hung upon a milldam. They had to unload most of the cargo into another boat and then transfer it back again once their flatboat had been freed from the dam.

A few miles farther downriver, they put in to shore at a place known as the Blue Banks, about a mile above the confluence with Salt Creek and eight miles north of Petersburg. Here Offutt purchased a herd of about thirty hogs from Russell Godbey, but the experienced stock-handler was confounded in trying to drive the balky swine back to the flatboat. The young men managed to herd them back into their pen and were rather at a loss as to what to do next, until reportedly Offutt conceived the bizarre idea to sew their eyelids shut. *"Abe held the head of them, I the tail,"* John Hanks recalled, *"and Offutt sewed up their eyes."* Even after this drastic experiment, the hogs refused to be driven, so they at last loaded them, a few at a time, onto a cart. Johnston and Hanks hauled the hogs to the flatboat, where Lincoln received them and cut the stitches from their eyes. Although Lincoln himself recalled the incident in his brief autobiographical notes, many historians consider this to be no more than a frontier "tall tale." Even if wholly fabricated by Lincoln tongue-in-cheek, the story certainly provides insight on Lincoln's perception of his employer as wildly impulsive on occasion.

With the hogs safely aboard, the flatboat continued its voyage, passing from the Sangamon to the Illinois River and then into the current of the Mississippi. At St. Louis, Lincoln recalled, John Hanks decided go ashore and head back home, *"having a family and being likely to be detained from home longer than at first expected."* The three remaining men floated down the great river, stopping briefly at Memphis, Vicksburg, and Natchez, and they arrived at New Orleans early in May. They remained in the city for a month, disposing of their cargo and enjoying the sights and attractions of the city. In June, the Offutt party boarded a steamboat bound upriver to St. Louis. Offutt remained behind at St. Louis while Lincoln and his stepbrother John Johnston set out on foot across Illinois to Coles County, where Thomas Lincoln had recently moved. Lincoln did not remain long at his father's home but came to New Salem in late July to await the arrival of Denton Offutt.

During the leisurely flatboat voyage down the Mississippi, Lincoln recalled (writing in the third person) that Offutt *"conceived a liking for A[braham], [and] contracted with him to act as clerk for him, on his return from New Orleans, in charge of a store and mill at New Salem."*

The community of New Salem at this time had been in existence for less than two years. The plan of the town was laid out in October 1829 by John M. Camron and his uncle James Rutledge. The town site was on the high ground overlooking the Sangamon River, near the grist and sawmill erected by Camron and Rutledge during the previous year. The first store building opened in the autumn of 1829, and the post office was established on Christmas day of that year. In July 1831, after parting company with Lincoln and Johnson, Denton Offutt purchased a stock of merchandise at St. Louis for his proposed store, arranging for it to be shipped to Beardstown, located on the Illinois River near its junction with the Sangamon. Offutt then came up the Illinois River on a boat to Beardstown and continued on to Springfield by stagecoach. On July 8, he obtained a merchant's license from the County Commissioners' Court of Sangamon County to keep store at New Salem.

Offutt returned to New Salem soon after Lincoln's arrival there, having been delayed by the need to return briefly to Kentucky, to assist in the settlement of his mother's estate; she had passed away in February 1831. On September 2, he was back in Illinois and paid ten dollars for a town lot in New Salem on which to erect his store building, located on the east bluff overlooking the Sangamon River. Lincoln began his new service in Offutt's employ by assisting in the construction of a log store building. This accomplished and having received no word regarding the arrival of Offutt's merchandise at Beardstown, Lincoln took temporary employment assisting a local doctor in rafting his family and possessions down the Sangamon to Beardstown. At the Beardstown freight office, Lincoln discovered Offutt's trade stock had arrived, and so immediately set out overland back to New Salem to arrange wagon transport. Halfway there, he encountered wagons on the road sent by Offutt, who had been informed of the arrival of his goods during Lincoln's absence. Lincoln gave the head carter a note authorizing delivery and hurried back to New Salem to prepare for receiving the merchandise. The store was soon open for business, and Offutt added other enterprises to his new empire, such as leasing the Camron and Rutledge mill operation.

Young Abraham Lincoln initially slept in the store building, later arranging to board with various families in New Salem. To assist Lincoln at the store, Offutt hired two local youths as assistants, nineteen-year-old William G. Greene, and Charles Maltby. Offutt apparently left the day-to-day operation of the store to his employees and devoted his time to traveling back and forth between Springfield and New Salem, intent on hatching new schemes. Lincoln spent much of his time tending to business at the gristmill, while Greene and Maltby ran the store in his absence.

At Offutt's direction, Lincoln cut timber and split rails to build a stock pen near the mill large enough to contain a thousand hogs. Offutt purchased a great deal of corn that he stored at the mill; he intended to fatten hogs for markets downriver.

Unfortunately for Offutt's dreams of entrepreneurial glory, none of these endeavors prospered. The Sangamon River was too shallow for steamboat navigation, so that the anticipated trade never materialized, and the store location, on the outskirts of town, was poorly chosen. Offutt's store did little business, even at first, and trade fell off considerably during ensuing months.

In the spring of 1832, a penniless and disillusioned Denton Offutt made a hasty departure from New Salem, leaving Lincoln behind to deal with angry creditors. Lincoln, by agreement among the creditors, was left in charge of the store to sell out the stock and other assets to pay Offutt's debts. In less than a decade, the entire community of New Salem was abandoned, many of the inhabitants relocating to nearby Petersburg.

Many Lincoln biographers consider his early friendship with Offutt to have been an important formative influence in the life of the future president. Lincoln's law partner, William Herndon, described Offutt as an *"odd character,"* but *"good at heart and a generous friend of Lincoln."* Offutt would remain in periodic contact with Lincoln for the rest of his life. Although Offutt did not again return to New Salem, he evidently remained in the upper midwest region for some time afterward, as the next report of his whereabouts places him at Vincennes, Indiana, in December 1834.

Knox County sheriff John Purcell placed a notice in the *Western Sun* offering a twenty-five-dollar reward for the capture of Denton Offutt, who had escaped from jail on the thirteenth of the month. The reward would be paid out to any person who was able to deliver the fugitive to the sheriff or to secure him in any Indiana jail.

$25 REWARD!

ESCAPED from the Jail in Knox county, state of Indiana, on the 13th inst. a man by the name of Denton Offutt: supposed to be between thirty and thirty-five years of age, about six feet high, dark complected, black hair; is very talkative and wishes to pass for a gentleman; one of his upper fore teeth is out. He will probably make his way to the state of South Carolina or Georgia. The above reward will be given if he is secured in any jail without this state, or delivered to me in Vincennes.

JOHN PURCELL, Sh'ff. K.c.
Dec. 15th, 1834—49–tf

DENTON OFFUTT, THE WANTED MAN. *WESTERN SUN* [VINCENNES, INDIANA], DECEMBER 27, 1834.

This advertisement provides the only known physical description of Offutt, who was reported to be about six feet tall, with black hair and a dark complexion, *"very talkative and wishes to pass for a gentleman."* The exact nature of Offutt's offense cannot be determined, but it most likely involved debts he was unable to pay. Despite later detractors who described him as a "con man," there is no evidence to suggest that Offutt ever deliberately set out to swindle anyone. Instead, it appears that Offutt was simply a well-intentioned dreamer who often naively made great plans beyond his ability to achieve and who could sometimes persuade others to invest.

Offutt apparently never again traveled to the upper Midwest, where he had left scores of angry creditors behind. Soon after his jailbreak, he returned home to his family in Kentucky. He spent the next five years training horses and driving them to out-of-state markets for his brothers, Otha and Sam, each of whom owned a farm in the Bluegrass Region. In 1840, by his own recollection, Denton embarked upon a career as a professional horse trainer and soon became well known through the region. Unlike many prominent trainers of the era, Offutt was not concerned primarily with conditioning racehorses for the track, but he worked with horses of any sort: draft horses, carriage horses, saddle horses, stock horses, and hunters, as well. His distinct specialty was to tame "unbroken" horses so that they could be safely handled and ridden. These included young horses which had yet to be saddled, formerly free-roaming feral horses which had had no previous human contact, and older horses which, from ill-treatment or bad disposition, were vicious or otherwise unmanageable.

In the autumn of 1841, Offutt submitted a short exposition of his philosophy and methods as a letter to the *Spirit of the Times*, the leading sporting magazine of the day. In this essay, he revealed some of the basic methods that in later years he endeavored to guard as trade secrets. *"My secret for Taming Vicious Horses is gentleness and patience,"* he began, *"which removes fear and gives the animal confidence in man."*

Offutt's methods recognized that horses were not mere dumb brutes but sensitive and intelligent creatures, possessed of needs, desires, dislikes, and fears. Horses are genetically programmed to flee from danger when possible, and to fight when they cannot run. For a horse, the human world is filled with strange sights, sounds, and smells, and that which is unfamiliar is best treated as potentially dangerous. Through an approach that combines a soothing voice and gentle handling, Offutt believed, the horse can be conditioned to trust the trainer. *"Rubbing a horse in the face will cause him to present his head to you, and talking kindly to him will attract his attention,"* he wrote. *"I suppose in some horses it is important to whisper to them . . . you may use any word you please, but be constant in your tone of voice."* Through gradual introduction and repetition, accompanied by gentle handling and reassurance, a horse can be brought to calmly accept that which once was strange or even frightening, such as blankets, saddles, or even gunfire.

The methods described in his 1841 letter to the *Spirit of the Times* were set out more fully in a pamphlet, published during the following year, titled *Denton Offutt's Method of Gentling Horses, and Curing Their Diseases*. This pamphlet was not copyrighted until 1846 but was advertised throughout the United States by a handbill printed in Washington, D.C., in 1843, which contained endorsements from numerous horsemen in Kentucky and elsewhere in the country. In 1848, his pamphlet was enlarged to a full-scale volume, *A New and Complete System of Teaching the Horse on Phrenological Principles.* In a handbill printed in Lexington in April 1853, Offutt solicited subscriptions for a greatly expanded treatment of his methods, noting that *"The work will be published as soon as a sufficient number of subscribers have been obtained to justify it, and on a large clear print, and well bound in cloth ...offered to subscribers at the moderate price of $5."* Copies of this notice were published in a number of agricultural journals. The volume was published in March of the following year.

Offutt was himself barely literate as can be seen by his later letters to Abraham Lincoln and a letter published verbatim in the *Spirit of the Times* in 1859, which lacked punctuation and were so filled with bizarre spelling and grammatical errors as to be nearly incoherent. He obviously must have had considerable assistance in the preparation of these manuscripts, although the identity of the ghostwriter is unknown. A memorable chapter from *The Educated Horse,* titled "Dialogue between man and Horse," presents the perspective of the horse and is intended to lead readers into considering how their actions may be perceived by a different species.

> *Man, I wish to put my hands on your face, and come near you.*

> *Horse, If so, you must let me see that you will not hurt me, nor will have anything about you that will, nor anything that smells badly. I am a stranger to you; all that will offend any of the five senses, I will be compelled to guard against, and those senses must have the proof that you will not hurt me, before I will allow them to be on me.*

Man, I wish to put my hands all over you.

Horse, This you may do, by commencing at the face. Commence rubbing on the face, and repeat it; then pass down the neck, first as slight as possible, and as I become used to it, rub the harder. Remember always to rub the way the hair lies smooth. My tail is, when I play, to be held up high; as my pride and beauty, you must be careful in handling it. But after you raise it, be sure to repeat it, and raise it and put it down several times, until it goes up quietly. It becomes habituated by use.

Man, Then the more I rub you, and repeat it, the quieter you get?

Horse, It is so with all beasts. The dialogue continues for some length and is quite remarkable in its understanding of equine psychology.

Advertisements such as the 1843 and 1853 handbills were not intended to place Offutt's book in the hands of the general public but to promote the man himself and to gain publicity, pupils, and patrons. Offutt had come to realize that his methods were a marketable product and that it might be of greater financial benefit to impart his secrets for a fee to a select group of students than to give them away freely by unrestricted publication. Accordingly, his books were made available only to his pupils and others he trusted. A notation on the flyleaf of the 1846 pamphlet reads, *"Persons having received instructions of me, and one of these books, are expected not to divulge the secrets or lend the book out of their families."*

In a preface to the 1848 edition, Offutt instructed his students to *"Place this book among your private papers, or in some place where others will not get it ... If you lose or destroy one, I hope you will not call on me for another, for those who are not careful of a few things are not deserving of many."* Recipients of *The Educated Horse* were required to sign a lengthy pledge of confidentiality, bound by law and their personal honor to keep his secrets and to pay a financial penalty should they violate the agreement. Offutt retained a copy of the pledge with the signatures of all his students recorded thereon:

> *"We, the undersigned, have each of us purchased of Mr. Denton Offutt a copy of his book in relation to educated horses, laws of mind and physiology and diseases of animals, which he has disposed of to us on the express condition that all its contents are to be kept secret from all other persons, with certain exceptions hereinafter mentioned, and under a specified penalty."*

The exceptions were limited to "a son or daughter of the paternal family" and to servants caring for horses, who might be provided with simple instructions, but not the book itself.

By 1857, Offutt had taken up residence in Tennessee. Testimonials from his handbills and other sources indicate that he made tours through many of the southern states, including the Carolinas, Virginia, Mississippi, and Texas, where he demonstrated his ability to tame even the most bad-tempered and cantankerous horses. Writing in 1873 to Lincoln biographer William H. Herndon, Maryland physician James Hall recalled seeing Offutt in Baltimore during the 1850s, *"advertising himself in the city papers, as a veterinary Surgeon, & horse tamer, proposing to have a secret to whisper in the horse's ear, or a secret manner of whispering in his ear, which he could communicate to others, & by which the most refractory & vicious horses could be gentled & controlled. For this secret, he charged five dollars, binding the recipient by oath not to divulge it. I knew several persons, young fancy horsemen, who paid for the trick. Offutt advertised himself not only through the press, but he appeared in the streets on horse back & on foot in plain citizens dress of black, but with a broad sash across his right shoulder of various colored ribbon, crossed on his left hip under a large rosetta of like material, rendering his appearance most ludicrously conspicuous."*

His old friend Abraham Lincoln gained national attention during the 1856 presidential election when Lincoln was nearly chosen as the vice-presidential nominee to run with John C. Frémont, the first candidate of the newly organized Republican Party. Failing to secure the nomination, Lincoln spent some time campaigning for the party and then returned to his law practice in Springfield with his partner, William Herndon. A young man from the New Salem area, Tom McNeely, came into his office one morning in August or September 1857. McNeely, who had heard of Denton Offutt from his father, had met and introduced himself to Offutt in Mississippi where the horse-tamer was giving an exhibition in the spring of 1857. According to McNeely's recollection:

"When I told Offutt that I resided at Petersburg, Illinois, on the very edge of New Salem, and had frequently seen Mr. Lincoln, he lost his interest in his crowd and the horses. We had a long talk about Lincoln and the old settlers, but Mr. Lincoln was the center of Offutt's thought and conversation. Offutt had not seen anyone who knew Mr. Lincoln for about twenty-four years. He had heard something of Mr. Lincoln in politics during the Fremont campaign of the preceding year. He said that after leaving Lincoln at New Salem he had gone South and taken up the business of treating wild and fractious horses and had followed it."

As the crowd of spectators grew restless over this prolonged conversation and called for the horse-tamer to resume his demonstration, Offutt, learning that McNeely planned to return to Illinois soon, gave him a message to pass along to Lincoln for him, should the opportunity present itself.

McNeely told Lincoln of meeting Offutt and gave him his regards but was rather hesitant to repeat Offutt's message verbatim. Lincoln seemed quite pleased to hear of Offutt, being instantly transported in his memories to the old days in New Salem. At last, encouraged by William Turney, clerk of the Illinois Supreme Court who was also present in the room, McNeely finally delivered Offutt's message. *"He told me to say to you,"* McNeely said, with some embarrassment, *"tell Lincoln to quit his damned politics and go into some honest business, like taming horses [for I have taught him well]."* Lincoln laughed out loud upon hearing this. *"That sounds like Offutt,"* he said, and from that day on, whenever Lincoln met McNeely, he referred to Offutt's message and laughed again.

Grateful clients provided Offutt with numerous testimonials and accolades, which he had made up into advertisements such as the handbills of 1843 and 1853, and another printed in February 1859. The latter included a recommendation given to Offutt a decade before from the noted Kentucky statesman Henry Clay, who wrote:

Ashland, Ky., Oct. 17, 1849

The bearer hereof, Mr. Denton Offutt, of Kentucky, being about to travel in other parts of the United States, and perhaps in Europe, I take great pleasure in recommending him as a person of uncommon skill in the treatment of horses and domestic animals, especially in training, breaking, and curing them of diseases.

Such is the extraordinary effect of his system in the management of the horse, that he will, in a very short time, render the wildest animal gentle and docile, insomuch that he will subject it to his easy control and direction. Mr. Offutt has been many years engaged in the study and practice of his remarkable method of dealing with the horse, and has given many satisfactory evidence of his great success.

H. Clay

It would, however, be more than a decade before Offutt traveled to Europe, and then not under the best of circumstances.

In addition to his clients for his services as a trainer, Offutt began taking on pupils as early as 1840. *"The perfect art of training horses,"* he wrote in his execrable prose to the *Spirit of the Times* in 1859, *"sens [since]1840 which I commens [commence]teaching it ther[e] has now som[e] Ten or more Teachers of Art At that time 42 to 1848 in Cincinnati Ohio."* His handbill of 1843 stated. *"Other persons can be taught the same management, as many of his pupils are equally as successful as himself."*

When Hamilton Busbey, editor of the New York–based sporting journal *Turf, Field and Farm,* visited Keene Richards at his Georgetown estate in October 1877, Richards showed him a copy of *The Educated Horse,* which bore a publication date of 1854. This was probably not the first, nor the only, copy of Offutt's book that Richards possessed. In conversation with Busbey, Richards recalled his tutelage under Offutt as among his "earliest memories." This suggests that he learned the "gentle" methods of horse training and management as a teenager. Richards would have been thirteen years old in the summer of 1841, and very likely he began his training with Offutt at about this time and was thus among his first pupils.

A list of Offutt's pupils would include not just young boys and horse breeders but successful men in a variety of professions.

Besides his informal student, Abraham Lincoln, among the men who completed a course of instruction and received copies of his book, who signed the pledge of confidentiality never to reveal Offutt's secrets, were Sam Houston, U.S. senator from Texas

(1846–59) and later governor of the state (1859–61); Thomas J. Rusk, also a senator from Texas (1846–57); John Minor Botts, three-term U.S. representative from Virginia (1839–43, 1847–49); and John S. Rarey, who at the time of his first acquaintance with Offutt was a little-known horse trainer from Ohio.

Born on December 6, 1827, to a prosperous farm family in Franklin County, Ohio, John Rarey demonstrated a remarkable affinity for horses as he grew up and, while yet in his teens, developed a local reputation as a horse trainer. As Keene Richards later recalled, Rarey came to Georgetown in 1850 with a traveling circus, with which he was probably employed as a horse handler. When the circus moved on, Rarey remained in Georgetown to study with Offutt, and in due time "graduated" and received his copy of Offutt's book. He then returned to Ohio, where his reputation continued to grow as he took on many more clients and began to instruct others in his methods. In 1855, Rarey traveled to Texas and spent several months there helping to capture and tame the wild mustangs of the prairie.

In 1851, he published a book, *The Modern Art of Taming Wild Horses*. The book, which was written with greater literary skill than Offutt's work, was by no means plagiarized from Offutt, but it described essentially the same principles and methods, working in harmony with the horse's natural instincts and using gradual familiarization to promote acceptance of objects and situations. Like Offutt, Rarey referred to these methods as the "gentling" of horses. In his book, Rarey gave no credit to Offutt for these methods and, in fact, made no mention at all of his former mentor. Like Offutt, Rarey bound his pupils to a pledge of confidentiality in regard to his methods. Rarey was a more aggressive promoter than Offutt; his book was first published in Columbus, Ohio, and during the next three years was reprinted in several editions across the country. Later, after he had achieved considerable fame in England during his visit there from 1857 to 1860, Rarey's book was published in London, and, in translation, in Paris and Copenhagen. Rarey released his students from their secrecy pledge after his book was published in England.

Despite the publication of his book, prior to 1858 Rarey was still not well known outside Ohio, nor was he financially successful. According to Dennis Magner, who interviewed many persons who had known Rarey, *"he traveled alone on foot from town to town, carrying a satchel and meeting with but indifferent success. His wages were $3.00 and he was ready to teach one or more at a time, as he had opportunity, at this rate."* Rarey decided to pursue fame and fortune by taking his methods to Europe. He secured a letter of introduction from Ohio governor Salmon P. Chase, and traveled to Toronto, where he gave an exhibition before Sir Edmund Head, the governor-general of Canada, and a group of army officers. They were impressed by his demonstration and provided him with endorsements and letters of introduction to prominent men in England. Before leaving Canada, Rarey formed a partnership with Rollin A. Goodenough, a Toronto merchant and amateur horse-breeder, described as a "sharp, hard-fisted New Englander," who accompanied him abroad and acted as his manager and promoter in return for a share of the profits.

Rarey and Goodenough arrived at Liverpool on November 29, 1857, bearing letters of introduction to Sir Charles York of the

Horse Guards of London and to Sir Richard Airy, quartermaster general. In short order, Rarey received an invitation from Queen Victoria to exhibit his skills, and in two performances at Buckingham Palace in January 1858 quite enthralled the royal family and court. Shortly after entertaining the queen, Rarey capitalized upon the attendant publicity and acclaim by opening an office at Tattersall's (near Hyde Park Corner in what was then the outskirts of London), promising to begin teaching his methods as soon as five hundred subscriptions had been received. More than two thousand persons quickly signed up, each depositing ten guineas (about fifty dollars) to learn his system.

On March 2, the *London Morning Post* challenged Rarey to attempt to tame the most vicious horse then known in the kingdom, an animal known as Cruiser. So savage was Cruiser's reputation that for the past three years he had worn a heavy iron muzzle and was kept in a brick stall. It was alleged that he had bitten an iron bar in half and torn bricks out of the walls of his stable with his teeth; he had also been known to *"often lean against the side of his stall and scream and kick as if insane."* Cruiser's owner, wishing to breed him, had been contemplating blinding the horse to make him more approachable. Over a period of about two weeks, Rarey transformed the homicidal beast into a horse allegedly as gentle as a kitten, and after subsequently taming a zebra at the London Zoo, there no longer remained any doubt as to his abilities.

CRUISER TAMED.

JOHN S. RAREY TAMES CRUISER *HARPER'S NEW MONTHLY MAGAZINE*, APRIL 1861.

Rarey gave his first class for subscribers on March 21 at the Riding School of the Duke of Wellington in the Knightsbridge area of London; the list of participants read like a Who's Who of British aristocracy, including not only lords and ladies but earls, viscounts, marquises and the odd admiral or member of parliament. Classes were held several times a week, at first hosted by the duke and later moved to the Roundhouse, an establishment on Kennerton Street leased by Rarey. Later in the spring, the Ohio horse-tamer began the first of his public "lectures" or demonstrations. Successful beyond their wildest dreams, in August Rarey and his manager quarreled over the division of profits, and the irate Goodenough took his share and returned to Canada. After Goodenough's departure, Rarey took his show across the English channel, where he was feasted and feted by the courts of Europe.

Fame and fortune, however, had so far eluded Offutt, despite his own efforts at promotion. In February 1854, he had attended a meeting of the United States Agricultural Society in Washington, D.C., where he introduced a resolution for the appointment of a committee on animal physiology, and for *"the general improvement in all respects of domestic animals."* Colonel Charles B. Calvert of Maryland seconded this motion and provided testimony as to Offutt's ability in regard to horses, which he had recently witnessed at the Maryland State Fair in Baltimore. Whether through "mesmerism, or magnetism," the colonel recalled, Offutt had transformed an animal well known for its vicious nature *"almost instantaneously"* to *"gentleness and tractability."* The motion was referred to the committee of the society, which later reported that Offutt *"possessed wonderful powers over untamed animals,"* but they *"had not been able to understand enough of the plan to report favorably in recommendation."*

Offutt made several determined efforts to promote his unique methods and obtain sponsorship from government at both state and Federal levels. While in New Orleans on December 31, 1850, Offutt wrote to the governor of Texas, offering, for an unspecified financial consideration, to improve the various breeds of livestock in the state, horses, mules, cows, hogs, and sheep, using a superior breeding system he claimed to have discovered. He requested the governor to place his request before the Texas legislature and enclosed a printed copy of a similar petition he had recently submitted to the General Assembly of the Commonwealth of Kentucky.

In the Kentucky petition, Offutt asserted that he had devoted many years of his life to the study of domesticated animals. *"By patient investigation and numberless experiments,"* read the document, *"he has become perfectly master of the secret laws that control their action; and that those animals so essential to the various wants of human life, can be greatly improved in all their physical adaptations, their social affections and mental habitudes, whereby they can be rendered perfectly submissive to the will of man."*

Bad temperament and vicious habits, he observed, were caused by want of proper knowledge and kind feeling in their owners and keepers. Offutt, being *"anxious to do all the good within his limited power for the advancement of science, the welfare of his fellow-man, and the prosperity of this great and noble commonwealth,"* offered to teach this "perfect science" if "a reasonable and just compensation" were to be granted to him out of the public treasury. Offutt may well have submitted petitions to the legislatures of other states in addition to Texas and Kentucky, but, given the fantastic and unsubstantiated nature of his claims, apparently no action was taken in any case.

Offutt had no more success in gaining the support of the United States government, which he petitioned on three separate occasions, offering to disclose the particulars of his system of improving "the breed of all domestic animals" for an appropriate financial compensation. These petitions were all virtually identical in wording to that sent to the General Assembly of Kentucky in 1850. His first petition to Congress was introduced in the Senate on

December 9, 1850, by Senator Joseph R. Underwood of Kentucky; his second, by Senator Sam Houston of Texas on March 13, 1854, and his final attempt, which included an offer to provide copies of his book for five dollars each, was introduced in the House on December 10, 1858, by Representative Humphrey Marshall of Kentucky. This latter petition would have been in reference to the new edition of his book, *The Educated Horse*, which had just been published. In each case, the petitions were referred to the committee on Agriculture, and eventually tabled without further action. Although Offutt without question possessed a genuine gift for handling horses, he simply could not resist grandiose exaggeration and so those who had not witnessed his skills at firsthand could not take him seriously. In all his efforts to profit from his abilities, Offutt truly was his own worst enemy.

By the time of his latest petition to Congress, Denton Offutt had been hearing of Rarey's English celebrity with increasing anger, no doubt fueled by reports of the enormous sums garnered by his former pupil. Telling Lincoln, who had become a successful Springfield lawyer and was inching toward his political career, that he had never released Rarey from his pledge of secrecy, and so he considered Rarey's public performances to be a serious breach of contract.

After seeking Lincoln's legal advice, Offutt finally had enough, and in mid-April 1859 boarded a ship for England, armed with a bundle of endorsements, intending to denounce Rarey as a fraud and villain. The *Spirit of the Times* took note of his departure, referring to him as *"the original horse-tamer of the United States,"* whose purpose in traveling abroad was to *"teach his art of taming vicious animals to the nobility and gentry of Albion, and he claims that he can do all that was ever accomplished by Rarey, and something more."*

Unfortunately for Offutt's ambitions, the British public gave little attention to his presence, viewing him as just one more of the many imitators who had sprouted there in the wake of Rarey's fame. Perhaps the only man in England who recognized his true worth was Keene Richards, then in the country to purchase thoroughbred horses for his stable in Georgetown. Having arrived when the Rarey mania was at its height, Richards may have attended one of Rarey's performances out of curiosity. He acknowledged that Rarey's system was of value, but certainly took every opportunity to set the record straight where his former teacher was concerned.

At the height of the excitement about Rarey, Richard Ten Broeck came to visit Keene Richards in his rooms in London. Ten Broeck was a personal friend of Richards, the former manager of the Metairie race course in New Orleans, and had generated quite a bit of excitement among American horsemen when, in 1856, he became the first American to bring native-bred thoroughbreds across the Atlantic to pit against English horses. Ten Broeck asked Keene Richards what he thought about the idea of taking lessons from the celebrated horse-trainer Rarey. As Richards later recalled,

> *"I frankly told him that I thought the system which Rarey taught would prove of great assistance to him in the management of his stable but added that it was not necessary for him to go to Rarey for instruction. I then explained to him what I knew of Rarey and Offutt and wound up by placing Offutt's book in his hands. He*

took it home with him, and he afterwards informed me that he sat up all night reading it. He also pronounced it a wonderful book." If Offutt and Richards were able to renew their acquaintance while in England, the reunion was brief, since Richards departed not long after Offutt's arrival.

Denton Offutt became increasingly embittered by the indifferent reaction to his reception, even as John Rarey continued to be lionized in the British press and was invited to visit the estates of the nobility. So invisible was Offutt during his stay in England that, only three years later, one British commentator, reacting to the news of the Offutt–Rarey lawsuit across the Atlantic, wrote, *"Does Denton Offutt exist? or is he the vain offspring of some penny-a-liner's brain? Has he vanished into thin air? We can make nothing of him, we admit. We can get no information upon the subject."*

While in England, Offutt dashed off several angry letters to the *Spirit of the Times* which were not published, but in mid-June a missive was received whose contents were just too juicy to resist. Well aware of his literary deficiencies, Offutt included a request for the correction of his text, but the editors of the *Spirit* reproduced the letter verbatim with all its grotesque spelling and structure. Offutt's letter, titled *"To people a Warning: Against Swindlers in the Teaching of Art of Training Horses Selling a Book,"* was a lengthy and nearly undecipherable diatribe against Rarey. He declared that he had begun teaching and published a book on his methods long before Rarey, and that *"sens that time he has taken all that is worth anything in his Book is min and he not smart enough has changed and in every leson maid it wors."* Rarey was guilty of *"robing my coppy right,"* Offutt wrote, and reported that he had confronted Rarey at the state fair in Richmond, Virginia, with an offer to compare their respective books. *"He wold not show it I compard it to many all say he is copped from mind I publickly declared him a Rober to his fase and Advertst him with the bove, rober, swindler and Ignorant."*

Why the editors of the *Spirit* chose to embarrass Offutt in this manner is rather puzzling. Despite the publication of Rarey's book in several American editions, he was still relatively unknown in this country prior to visiting England since, like Offutt, his book was made available only to his students who were bound by a pledge of secrecy. Possibly, the editors were reacting to the frenzy of adulation stirred up among their English cousins, expecting to ride a similar wave of Rarey-worship in this country. A glib commentary upon Offutt's letter was published in the same issue of the *Spirit,* in which the editors acknowledged him to be the "original" horse tamer, but at the same time rather smugly insisted, *"We do not care to involve ourselves in the controversy."* After making a number of sarcastic jokes concerning Offutt's tortured prose, they concluded that, beneath all this "brilliancy," was the "hardest kind of horse sense." Certainly, Denton Offutt never again contributed any item to the *Spirit of the Times.*

Offutt returned to the United States shortly after his letter was published, reaching New York on August 13, 1859, aboard the steamer Liverpool. From a hotel in Paris, Kentucky, on September 7, he wrote to Lincoln asking for his assistance in collecting a debt of fifty dollars owed to him for demonstrations made at the

1858 Agricultural fair in Richmond, Virginia, offering to split it equally if Lincoln could collect.

Rarey, in the meantime, left England again in autumn 1859 and gave a series of lectures in Paris, France. Having a great desire to see Arabian horses in their native land, Rarey continued on to Rome, and thence to Alexandria, Egypt, visiting Cairo briefly, and he finally ended up in Jerusalem. From Jerusalem, Rarey made an excursion to the Dead Sea, and northward up the Jordan Valley to Damascus. He concluded his eastern tour with a visit to Constantinople and returned to England in spring 1860. Rarey gave a farewell lecture on October 27 at the Crystal Palace in London to a crowd estimated at eight thousand and took passage to New York, accompanied by the now-famous horse Cruiser. Arriving at New York on December 8, he received a hero's welcome, and then hurried off to Ohio to spend the Christmas season at home.

At the beginning of the new year, Rarey was back in New York, beginning a series of lectures before overflow crowds for an admission of fifty cents to a dollar a person. His first performance was on January 5 at Niblos Garden, a theater on Broadway, to a crowd of approximately 3,200 persons. He gave four more lectures at the Niblos and then changed venue on January 23 to the Brooklyn Academy of Music.

A "typical" Rarey lecture consisted of, first, the introduction of cruiser, who stood quietly while a long discourse was delivered upon the habits and tendencies of horses in general and of the specific history of "this once-so-wicked creature." Next, a relatively mild-mannered horse was led in and put through various paces to display Rarey's complete control. After this, two Shetland ponies were brought onto the stage, the smaller carried in the arms of an enormous African American assistant and the other, larger, pony led in on a halter.

While the audience admired these miniature horses, Rarey would explain "how and why" they became so small. The eagerly awaited climax came after the Shetlands were taken away. There then followed the introduction of a true hellion, *"some terrible and outrageous horse, whose vile tendencies, evil disposition and fiendish propensities are vouched for in a letter by some consummate wag."*

For the performance at the Academy on January 23, the *New York Times* reporter noted that the *"last fight was a good one. The contest with this animal was terrific. His heels were in all directions three minutes out of every four; his mouth was savage, his tail was very whiskey; his mane was stiff, and his eye was like that of a maniac. For ten minutes he and his opponent struggled, twisted, fought, kicked, squealed, snorted, stamped, ran, wheeled, and wrestled. His physique was very powerful—his limbs were unbendable except for their own purposes, and his intelligence was keen and quick. His time had come—he was conquered, he yielded, and with one wild outcry, he laid himself down, while RAREY, with tumbled hair, saw-dusted clothes, and an agitated voice, announced a second performance for Friday evening at 7-1/2 o'clock."*

Denton Offutt was still livid over the whole Rarey situation, and now that his nemesis was back in America, after seeking Lincoln's advice, he took legal action against his former pupil for breach of contract. In a suit filed with the New York Supreme Court in late January 1861, Offutt asserted that he was the originator of the system of horse-training publicized by John S. Rarey.

The plaintiff's petition stated that *"previous to the year 1850, [Offutt] had discovered and perfected a new and before that time unknown method of taming unruly or wild horses, mules and other animals."* His secret method was made known to others only upon payment of a stipulated fee and a pledge of secrecy secured by a bond providing a penalty of fifty dollars for each violation of the agreement.

"On or about the 16th day of September 1850 John S. Rarey... *applied to plaintiff to be instructed in his misterious and wonderful art of Taming horses mules &c"* and executed and delivered his bond to Offutt. Offutt charged that *"said Rarey has from the date of said bond up to the present time constantly and daily violated said agreement by imparting the said secret to Twenty thousand persons in Europe and America."*

As a further cause of action, Rarey, who had been provided with a copy of Offutt's book under the same bond and pledge of secrecy, *"soon thereafter published what he claimed to be a book containing his Rarey's System of Horse Training, of which the said Rarey was the discoverer, but that in truth and fact said book ... contained in detail, substance and effect the said System of plaintiff for taming horses."*

Offutt asked for a judgment against Rarey in the amount of one hundred thousand dollars in damages, with Rarey to be enjoined from selling any more copies of his book or from making any public demonstrations of horse-taming.

In a carefully worded card placed in the *New York Herald* in response to these allegations from *"a person from the South,"* Rarey asserted that a lifetime of *"assiduous labor and study"* had gone into the development of his own skills. *"I have been constantly beset by [those] claiming to be the originators of the system I teach and to have taught me all I know about horse-taming,"* Rarey stated, but he did not specifically deny having been Offutt's pupil.

On Saturday, February 2, Rarey gave his "farewell performance" at the Academy. Five thousand persons paid a dollar apiece, and as advertised, half of the proceeds were donated to the New York Asylum for Widows and Orphans. During the performance, something new was added, the exhibition of two Arabian horses, a stallion and a colt, belonging to U.S. senator William H. Seward. While on vacation in the Holy Land in 1859, Seward had expressed an interest in acquiring Arabians to Ayoub Bey Trabulsky, a high-ranking Syrian official, as a personal favor that would also be to the agricultural benefit of the United States.

When Rarey attempted to apply his methods to the stallion, the result was both *"interesting and amusing. The horse seemed to understand his intentions, and more in fun than in anger, resisted all attempts to entrap him."* Once Rarey had succeeded taking the horse off its feet, it *"betrayed singular intelligence—placed his forelegs about RAREY'S neck—drew him up close to him, while with his nose he fondled and caressed him."* At the conclusion of the show, Rarey announced his immediate departure for Philadelphia and other cities of the seaboard.

Aware of Rarey's intention to leave the state, Offutt's attorney, Edward W. Packard, filed a motion on February 1 to require Rarey to give testimony before the court prior to his departure. In a letter to the *Times*, Packard disclosed that he had in his possession copies of both Offutt's and Rarey's books, as well as the original bond signed by Rarey and would welcome a public examination of the evidence to determine which of the two men was the originator of the horse-taming system practiced by Rarey. On the fifth, the Court denied Offutt's motion to examine Rarey before his departure from New York on the grounds that, as Rarey had not yet made answer, there was as yet no issue in the court between the parties.

On February 11, writing from Baton Rouge, Louisiana, Offutt contacted Lincoln again, apparently hoping that his friend, now the president of the United States, might be able to give him some assistance. *"My prosperity I have lost,"* he wrote, and he noted that *"I have sued John S Rain [sic], of Ohio at N York for $100,000 Dollars he has large mounts."* If the courts ruled against him, he hoped to obtain an appointment as *"physiologist of this State,"* which would allow him to remain in a warm climate.

Should this not be possible, perhaps Lincoln could find him a position in his administration? *"I hope you think me worthy of the Trust of office. I hope you will give me one Pattent office or the office of Agriculteral Department or the Commisary for Purchais of Horses Mules Beef for Army or mail agent I can do more for the Advansment of Selecting good Animals all others And more to Improve the breads of Animals."* Lincoln's reply is lost to us, but, as much as he might wish to help his old friend, he had enough experiences with Offutt many years before and had more sense than to place Offutt in any position of responsibility. Offutt's suit worked slowly through the court system; two years after the action was filed, the complaint was dismissed on April 18, 1863.

Other than indirectly through the existence of the New York legal action, Denton Offutt disappeared from the historical record after the spring of 1861. The simplest explanation is that Offutt may have died during 1862, and this may, in fact, be the primary reason for the termination of the suit. Lincoln biographer William Townsend notes that Offutt was *"old, broken financially, and in the late stages of consumption [pulmonary tuberculosis]"* in February 1861 when he penned his last letter to Abraham Lincoln. Townsend did not provide a citation for this information, and confirmation could only be found in Offutt's previous letter to Lincoln in September 1859, when he mentioned that *"I am in good helth but lean recovering from cough."*

Offutt appears to have spent most of his last years as a resident of Louisiana, apparently seeking a warmer climate for his health. Hamilton Busbey, editor of *Turf, Field and Farm*, wrote in 1878 that *"Denton Offutt has been in his grave a good many years,"* suggesting a date of death at least a decade prior to his observation.

Rarey, as always with the legendary Cruiser as his opening act, continued to give performances to sellout crowds in the northern states throughout 1861 and 1862. Using a significant part of his newly acquired wealth, Rarey built a fine mansion on the site of the house in which he had been born, on the farm near Groveport, Ohio, not far from Columbus. On December 12, 1862, at the request of Major General Henry W. Halleck, Rarey traveled to Virginia to evaluate the condition of the horses and mules of the Army of the Potomac, there finding himself in the middle of the battle of Fredericksburg. Under the circumstances, he later reported to the general, he was unable to assess the general management of army horses, but *"I had the opportunity to see them on duty."*

For the last three years of the war, Rarey remained closer to home and performed only occasionally, but in the summer of 1865, he gave what proved to be his final farewell at Zanesville, Ohio. The local paper announced his imminent arrival with *"Rarey is Coming! The Great Innovator and World renowned Tamer of Wild and Vicious Horses!"* Soon afterward, in December, Rarey suffered a severe stroke that left him partially paralyzed, and from which he never fully recovered. On October 5, 1866, while visiting friends in Cleveland in the company of his niece, he went outside for a walk and returned shortly, complaining of a pain in his head. His niece assisted him in taking a seat, and after a few moments he said, *"I am dying."*

Less than two hours later, John Solomon Rarey was dead at the age of thirty-eight; his remains were conveyed to his home at Groveport. Cruiser survived him by nine years, dying at last in his twenty-third year on July 6, 1875, at the Rarey farm.

When Hamilton Busbey visited Keene Richards at Blue Grass Park in Georgetown, Kentucky, in October 1877, dinner-table conversation turned to the subject of horse-taming, and he became "deeply interested" in what he was told about Denton Offutt. Richards, one of the most influential horsemen in Kentucky, claimed Offutt was *"the founder of the horse-taming school."* Richards agreed to loan his copy of *The Educated Horse* to Busbey if it would be used *"in doing justice to a former citizen of Georgetown."* Busbey took it with him back to New York, and was so impressed by its contents that he mentioned the book to Robert Bonner, editor of the *New York Ledger* and one of the richest men in America.

Bonner was an expert horseman with a sizable stable of trotting-horses who had taken lessons from John S. Rarey. Bonner took the book with him when he left the offices of the *Spirit of the Times,* and on the next day, Busbey received a note that stated, *"There are some very interesting things in Offutt's book—some things that are entirely new to me and well worth copying. The 'Dialogue between man and Horse' contains the substance of all that Rarey ever taught. He evidently based his system on that."* According to Busbey, Bonner kept the book for ten days, and read and reread it numerous times.

Hamilton Busbey took Robert Bonner at his word, also believing that Offutt's book was "worth copying." On January 4, 1878, he announced the forthcoming serialization of *The Educated Horse* in the pages of *Turf, Field, and Farm,* noting that whereas Offutt's students had been bound by a pledge of confidentiality, *"The time has come for the veil of secrecy to be torn aside. The claims of Denton Offutt to the foundership of the horse-taming school can be established in no other way."* The first installment appeared in the January 11, 1878, issue of *Turf, Field, and Farm.* The byline was attributed to Denton Offutt of Georgetown, Kentucky, *"the preceptor of Rarey."* Offutt, who had been unable to establish his claim during his lifetime, was at last vindicated.

A brief postscript is in order. The successor to Offutt and Rarey as America's most famous tamer of "wild and vicious horses" was Dennis Magner, who came to national attention shortly after the Civil War. Magner's book, *The Art of Taming and Educating the*

Horse (1886) is considered to be one of the best of the numerous horse-training books published in the nineteenth century. Unlike Rarey, Magner openly acknowledged the debt that he and all other trainers of the "gentling" approach owed to Denton Offutt. Magner had a similar flair for the dramatic and was every bit as accomplished a performer as Rarey, giving demonstrations across the country and taking on pupils.

While giving homage to Offutt, Magner considered Rarey to be a fraud and did not hesitate to say so in print. *"[Rarey's] great pretended secret was the same as that known and practiced long before him by Fancher, Offutt, and others,"* Magner wrote, *"and was obtained by him of Offutt. He was simply a bold pretender."* He had observed that horses "tamed" by Rarey had a disturbing tendency to revert to a bad disposition after some time, and so undertook some rather extensive research to determine the truth of the matter.

Magner took the opportunity to witness one of Rarey's last performances at Pittsburgh in the early summer of 1865, having given a series of demonstrations of his own methods during the previous week. Rarey's technique was much as he had expected a method already well-known: the use of a strap attached to a foreleg which is used to bring the horse to its knees and then forced to lie down, after which *"handled and caressed ... until submissive to control."*

Three years later, when in Columbus, Ohio, Magner made a side trip to the Rarey farm and spent several hours studying the aging Cruiser, who had again become unmanageable after the death of Rarey. In 1872, while giving demonstrations in New York, Magner unexpectedly made the acquaintance of Rollin A. Goodenough, who was then living in the city and had come to the exhibition.

Upon his return to North America in late 1859, Rarey's former promoter came to New York and used his share of the profits to establish the Goodenough Horse-Shoe company, manufacturing a patented new style of shoe which was applied cold and better designed to fit a horse's foot. The Goodenough horseshoe was widely adopted and enjoyed several decades of popularity in the United States and abroad.

Magner asked Goodenough whether Rarey had, indeed, subdued Cruiser using the methods described, and was told there was little truth in the published reports. He had been with Rarey at the time, and it had taken the two men two days to subdue the horse by putting him on the ground and leaving him to struggle bound and helpless until he was exhausted: *"his fore-legs tied up . . . a collar put on, and his hind legs tied forward to it."*

Magner again interviewed Goodenough in 1881 and was given more details on Rarey's career, obtaining a signed statement attesting to the truth of the account. Magner observed that any method aimed at lowering the strength of the horse, *"bleeding, starving, depriving of sleep, etc."* may temporarily subdue the animal for a time, but *"after the strength is regained, the character is liable to become as bad as before."* With such evidence, and given that Rarey's public performances were often described in the press as violent struggles or "fights," Rarey's actual methods, despite his claims, were apparently anything but "gentle" and bore little resemblance to the natural horsemanship practiced by Offutt.

In 1869, one British writer commented that Rarey was *"a lion tamer, not a horse educator, as his dupes discovered."* Offutt's results, in contrast, were attested to by men such as Henry Clay, who had observed his efforts over a period of years.

Neither Goodenough nor Magner, of course, can be considered strictly impartial in their accounts. Goodenough parted company with Rarey, not on the best of terms, and returned to North America while his former partner remained in England to glory in public acclaim. Goodenough's claims that he was himself as much responsible for Rarey's greatest triumphs may contain little truth. Magner, on the other hand, was a tireless self-promoter, and anything that might diminish the lingering shadow of Rarey could only work to his own benefit and position as America's newest celebrity horse-tamer. Fraud or not, Rarey's most significant legacy—and through him, his teacher Denton Offutt—was a heightened sensitivity by the public on both sides of the Atlantic for animal welfare in general and horses in particular.

Support for societies for the prevention of cruelty to animals was strengthened as a consequence of the great publicity attendant upon Rarey, and cavalry horses in the military received better treatment.

There can be little doubt that Denton Offutt had a significant influence on Abraham Lincoln and the American horsemen of his era. Although modern practitioners of natural horsemanship express a similar philosophy and use many of the methods he developed, the man himself is seldom acknowledged and is largely forgotten. Offutt's historical legacy is that he was the first person, on either side of the Atlantic, to formulate and publish a system of training based upon principles of natural horsemanship. For this accomplishment, he has truly earned the title of America's first "horse whisperer."

Chapter Eight

"MR. LINCOLN NEVER MISSED AN OPPORTUNITY TO JOIN IN A GAME OF QUOITS"

Lincoln the Athlete

Young Abe Lincoln played this ring-toss game when he was living in Illinois. The official game is played with metal stakes called hobs and rubber or metal rings called quoits.

"There were two elements in the place," wrote historian Benjamin Thomas about New Salem. *"One was a rough and boisterous, happy-go-lucky crowd known as the Clary's Grove boys. They lived in and around the community of that name, but came to New Salem to drink, gossip, trade and play. Physical strength and courage were their ideals. In individual and free-for-all fights they had demonstrated their superiority over the boys from other settlements, and they ruled the town when they chose to."* Senator Stephen Douglas made a similar observation in the 1858 debate at Ottawa, saying Mr. Lincoln could *"beat any of the boys wrestling, or running a foot-race, in pitching quoits or tossing a copper; could ruin more liquor than all the boys of the town together; and the dignity and impartiality with which he presided at a horse-race or fist-fight ... won the praise of everybody that was present and participated."*

In the autobiography that Lincoln prepared in June 1860 for John Scripps, he wrote: *"A's father, with his own family and others mentioned, had, in pursuance of their intention, removed from Macon to Coles county. John D. Johnston, the step-mother's son, went to them; and A. stopped indefinitely, and, for the first, as it were, by himself at New-Salem, before mentioned. This was in July 1831. Here he rapidly made acquaintances and friends. In less than a year Offut's business was failing—had almost failed—when the Black Hawk War of 1832—broke out. A. joined a volunteer company, and to his own surprise, was elected captain of it. He says he has not since had any success in life which gave him so much satisfaction."*

New Salem gave Mr. Lincoln his first set of adult friends. The respect of that group of young men meant a great deal to him—even nearly three decades later. Some of these men were men of education and accomplishment—Dr. John Allen, Preacher John M. Berry, Justice of the Peace Bowling Greene and farmer James Short. A key group in Mr. Lincoln's social and political development was the young men he came to know in New Salem and Springfield in the 1830s.

Mr. Lincoln's popularity with "the boys" was not tied to his indulgence in their vices. Indeed, he eschewed gambling, smoking, and drinking. Mr. Lincoln managed to be one of the boys without being exactly like the boys. *"Salem in those days was a hard place for a temperate young Man like Mr Lincoln was and I have often wondered how he could be so [extremely] popular" without drinking and carousing,"* one friend wrote, *"Mr. Lincoln "did not in those days even smoke or chew Tobacco."* Contemporary biographer William H. Herndon concluded that it was *"difficult for a young man of ordinary moral courage to resist the temptations that beset him on every hand. It remains a matter of surprise that Lincoln was able to retain his popularity with the hosts of young men of his own age, and still not join them in their drinking bouts and carousals."*

There was a code of conduct by which Mr. Lincoln lived. Biographer Alonzo McDonald wrote of an incident during his Lincoln's first legislative election: *"A crowd of voters that had collected at Papsville, getting full of whiskey and enthusiasm, began a general fight. Among those who were roughly handled was a follower of the New Salem candidate. Jumping from the platform, Lincoln rushed through the melee, seized his friend's assailant as if to make him 'walk Spanish,' tossed him off ten feet or so, resumed his place on the stand, and calmly began his little speech. This prelude, it is safe to say, did not lessen the warmth of his welcome from an audience akin to 'the bare-footed boys,' the huge-pawed boys,' or 'the butcher-knife boys,' who, in the elections of those days, so often held the balance of power."*

Some of those whom Lincoln met in New Salem took a somewhat paternal interest in him. Democratic Justice of the Peace Bowling Greene was called an almost a second father to Lincoln by businessman Abner Y. Ellis and as a lending library by James Short. Ellis said that Lincoln said that *"he owned more to Mr Green for his advancement than any other Man."* New Salem chronicler Thomas P. Reep wrote how Justice Greene gave Mr. Lincoln an unusual lesson in the law. The case involved ownership of a hog that was claimed by both Jack Kelso and the Trent brothers. *"Lincoln, appearing for the Trent brothers, proved by three witnesses that the hog belonged to them. Kelso testified that the hog belonged to him, but he was unsupported by witnesses."* To Mr. Lincoln's surprise, Greene ruled for Kelso. *"Mr. Lincoln "then called the attention of the court to the rule of evidence, which required a case of fact to be determined in accordance with the greater weight of preponderance of the testimony. Green replied, 'Abe, the first duty of a court is to decide cases justly and in accordance with the truth. I know that shoat myself, and I know it belongs [to] Kelso and that the plaintiffs and their witnesses lied."*

Jason H. Silverman

HOW ATHLETIC WAS ABRAHAM LINCOLN?

How Athletic was Abraham Lincoln? Civil War YouTube Talk by Reading Through History, October 30, 2018.

Historian Michael Burlingame noted that *"In Greene's court, Lincoln argued minor cases even before he had obtained a license. The rotund judge loved jokes, and Lincoln's sense of humor amused him vastly; he also respected the young man's intellectual ability and allowed him to peruse the law books in his small personal library. Although he was the leading Democrat in New Salem, Greene urged Lincoln, a Whig, to make his second run for the state legislature [in 1834]. A temperance advocate, Greene was a cultivated man of refined manners, and his authority as an arbiter of disputes was widely respected."*

At Bowling Greene's Masonic funeral in 1842, Mr. Lincoln was called to give a eulogy: *"He looked down a few moments at the face of his friend,"* wrote fellow attorney Henry Rankin. *"His whole frame began trembling with suppressed emotion. He then turned and faced the friends who filled the room and crowded the doorways and stood outside around the open windows. He spoke a few words, broken sentences only, tremulous vibrations of the thoughts he found it impossible to coherently articulate. Tears filled his eyes. He vainly struggled to regain that self-control under which he had always held his feelings before these friends on so many occasions. He had no words that could express adequately the thoughts that thronged him as he stood beside the body of his friend whose life had been so near his and had meant so much to him.*" At the funeral's conclusion Lincoln took Mrs. Greene on his arm and escorted her to the cemetery.

The man who brought Lincoln to New Salem was entrepreneur Dennis Offutt who was described by one resident as a *"gassy—windy—brain rattling man"* and by another as a *"wild, harum-scarum kind of man."* As previously mentioned, Lincoln first brought a raft of goods down the Mississippi River to New Orleans in 1830 and later served as a clerk in Offutt's store. Judge Thompson Ware McNeeley Lincoln's first New Salem employer in Mississippi in the late 1850s:

> *"When I told Offutt ... that I resided at Petersburg, Ill. on the very edge of New Salem, and had frequently seen Mr. Lincoln, he lost his interest in his crowd and the horses. We had a long talk about Mr. Lincoln and the old settlers, but Mr. Lincoln was the center of Offutt's thought and conversation. Offutt had not seen any one who knew Mr. Lincoln for about twenty-four years. He had heard something of Mr. Lincoln in politics during the Fremont campaign of the preceding year. He said that after leaving Lincoln at New Salem*

> he had gone South and taken up the business of treating wild and fractious horses and had followed it. The crowd with horses to be tamed became impatient and broke in on the conversation with calls for Offutt. As we separated I told him I was going back to Illinois in May. Offutt's parting request was: "Go and see Mr. Lincoln and tell him about me and give him my best wishes. Tell him for me to quit his damned politics and go into some honest business like taming horses."

The truth was that Lincoln enjoyed and excelled at both mental *and* physical games. Lincoln was a participant in the debating club organized in New Salem in 1832. And he was one of the founders of the Young Men's Lyceum in Springfield. G.W. Harris recalled: "Mr. Lincoln was fond of playing chess and checkers, and usually acted cautiously upon the defensive until the game had reached a stage where aggressive movements were clearly justified. He was also somewhat fond of ten-pins, and occasionally indulged in a game."

Lincoln was a regular participant in chess games—especially with federal judge Samuel Treat. In New Salem, he found many mentors for his mental development. Jack Kelso, for example, was the fishing bard of New Salem. Kelso appeared to work no harder than necessary; he preferred hunting, fishing and doing odd jobs. "Lincoln had no musical ability, but had an ear for rhythm. He fished now and then with Kelso, and oftener sat with Jack and visited in the evening. Lincoln's taste in poetry up to this time had been principally for jingles, and rhymed nonsense." He began *"to appreciate some of the real beauties to be found in the writings of great poets,"* wrote Lincoln biographer William E. Barton.

But the youthful Lincoln was better known for physical challenges. *"Attaining manhood entailed more than reaching a certain age; in practice it meant proving oneself physically in contests with other boys and eventually with other men."* wrote Lincoln scholar Douglas Wilson in *Honor's Voice*. Lincoln was indeed a very good athlete, and he was well remembered for his skill in jumping, running, wrestling and playing ball. *"His playful hours for these years,"* recalled New Salem resident Mentor Graham, were *spent "pitching quoits—jumping—hopping—Swimming—Shooting—telling Stories…"* Another resident, Hardin Bale, said Mr. Lincoln would play at various *"games—jumping—running—hopping."* Abner Ellis knew Mr. Lincoln in New Salem where he used *"to run footraces & jump with the boys and also play ball."* And, Rowan Herndon said Lincoln was fond of exercise and all kinds of fun.

"On more than one occasion," recalled Springfield contemporary Thomas W.S. Kidd, Lincoln's head came *"in contact with heads as yet unknown to fame in his eagerness to catch the flying ball. He argued in earnest; played his game of ball in earnest; tried his case, made his political speech, or told his humorous story, each characterized by the same peculiar earnestness."* Mr. Lincoln's neighbor James Gourley recalled playing ball with Lincoln and Edward D. Baker in 1844, *"the game was Called fives—Striking a ball with our hands against a wall that Served as alley. In 1860 Lincoln & myself played ball—this game."* Fred T. Dubois, son of State Auditor Jesse Dubois, later wrote:

The game would start with one player throwing the ball against the rick wall below the chalk line, and the next player would take it on the bound with his open hand and drive it against the wall, always under the chalk line. It was a very strenuous game, quite similar in some respects to the present game of tennis. These men would play it in the evening just before the evening meal, and there was always a large crowd on the sidewalk and in the street outside of the vacant lot to watch.

Illinois State Journal employee Joseph D. Ropers remembered Lincoln's *"love of handball. Immediately south of the Journal office there was a vacant piece of ground some 85 x 100 feet, the south end of which was the solid wall of a three-story building. The door or entrance to the ball alley as it was called was at the north end."* According to Roper: *"My memory is clear that Mr. Lincoln got as much or more real enjoyment in these games than any of the others. His suppleness, leaps and strides to strike the ball were comical in the extreme."* Another Springfield observer, John Langdon Kaine, was more complimentary of Lincoln's athletic style*: "His agility was surprising in view of his usual deliberate, almost indolent manner; and his long legs and long arms gave him a remarkable range of play. He was entirely democratic here, taking the inevitable chaffing of the Irish players and spectators amiably, and sometimes returning it."*

Helen Nicolay, daughter of one of Lincoln's personal secretaries John Nicolay, wrote of the scene in Springfield on the climatic day of the 1860 Republican National Convention: *"There is a legend, entirely in keeping with his character, that on the 18th of May, the day the nominations came before the convention, he was playing a desultory game of ball with some boys, when a young messenger, carrying a telegram, came charging down the flight of steps that led from the telegraph office, shouting at the top of his lungs: 'Mr. Lincoln! Mr. Lincoln, you're nominated!'"*

A famous part of the Lincoln legend, of course, Lincoln's wrestling match with Jack Armstrong of the Clary's Grove boys. *"This was the turning point in Lincoln's life,"* attorney John T. Stuart told a Columbus, Ohio newspaper reporter in 1860—thus determining its place in the Lincoln mythology. Biographer Benjamin Thomas wrote that the fight gave Mr. Lincoln *"the reputation for courage and strength that was so essential to success on the frontier, and convinced his associates that he 'belonged.'"* Historian Douglas L. Wilson wrote an extensive analysis of fight in *Honor's Voice*:

> "The Clary's Grove boys, Stuart explained, were the regulators of the neighborhood and 'took it upon themselves to try the mettle of every new comer and ascertain what sort of stuff he was made of.' But Lincoln had proved an exceptional case, and it didn't take Armstrong long, according to Stuart, 'to discover that he had got hold of the wrong customer, and when it was evident that Lincoln was getting the better of their champion, the whole band pitched in and gave Lincoln several blows which had no very salutary effect on the strength of his legs. Lincoln however took all this in perfect good humor, and by laughing and joining displayed such an excellent disposition that he at once won their hearts and was invited to become one of the company."

Harper's Weekly shows Lincoln swatting he Copperhead nemesis Clement Vallandigham out of the North and into the South. No evidence has been found that Lincoln played Shuttlecock.

In 1860, James Q. Howard interviewed other New Salem residents whose somewhat different accounts were incorporated into a campaign biographer written by William Dean Howells. According to Wilson, *"While [Howells] modified Stuart's version of the story (in which the match ends with Lincoln's pummeling) and merged it Green's, Howells did not hesitate to draw the conclusion suggested by Stuart: that in giving Lincoln 'a reputation for courage necessary in a new country' and gaining him a core of loyal and politically useful friends, his wrestling match with Armstrong 'seems to have been one of the most significant incidents of his early life.'"*

According to fellow store clerk William Greene, Mr. Lincoln's election as captain of his company during the Black Hawk War was partly a reflection the animosity that the Clary's Grove Boys felt toward his opponent, William Kirkpatrick: *"At one time, Abe had been employed by Kirkpatrick for a few days to move some saw logs. It was customary then, in moving logs, to have what was called cant hooks, and Kirkpatrick was to furnish one of these. When Lincoln was ready to start the work, this hook had not been furnished. Kirkpatrick agreed that if Lincoln would move the logs without it, he would pay him $2 additional at the end of the job, which is what the cant hook would have cost. But when the job was completed, Kirkpatrick refused to do this."* The result was that the company choice between Kirkpatrick and Lincoln, the Clary's Grove sentiments were not only overwhelming for Lincoln; they were against Kirkpatrick.

Henry Clark, who served with Mr. Lincoln in the Black Hawk War told William Herndon that he was Lincoln's friend and "he was my frind [sic]" Lincoln once served as Clark's second in a fight with Ben Wilcox after Clark and Wilcox had engaged in a lawsuit. *"After the conflict the seconds conducted their respective principals to the river washed off the blood, and assisted them to dress,"* Robert B. Rutledge later told William Herndon. *"During this performance, the second of the party opposed to Mr Lincoln [John Brewer] remarked – 'Well Abe, my man has whipped yours, and I can whip you.' Now this challenge came from a man who was very small in size. Mr. Lincoln agreed to fight provided he would 'chalk out his size on Mr. Lincoln's person, and every blow struck outside of that mark should be counted foul'. After this sally there was the best possible humor and all parties were as orderly as if they had been engaged in the most harmless amusement."* The match was to have important consequences for Lincoln's social acceptance and political success.

When New Salem friend William G. Greene went to Washington during the Civil War, he told President Lincoln that Clark was opposing him in the upcoming election. *"Bill, when you get back home, go see Henry Clark and tell him I sent you,"* said the president. *"Say to him that at one time when he had a hard fight on his hands, I stood by him and now that I have a hard fight on, I want him to stand by me!"* When Clark got the message, he told Greene: *"Tell Abe Lincoln that Henry Clark remembers, and that he and his house will stand by him!"*

About 16 years after he first came to New Salem, Lincoln tried to convey the lessons he had learned coming up the political ladder. *"Now, as to the young men. You must not wait to be brought forward by the older men. For instance, do you suppose that I should have ever got into notice if I had waited to be hunted up and pushed forward by older men? You young men get together and form a "Rough and Ready Club' and have regular meetings and speeches,"* Congressman Lincoln wrote Billy Herndon in June 1848. *"Let every one play the part he can play best—some speak, some sing, and all hollow."*

A LITTLE GAME OF BAGATELLE, BETWEEN OLD ABE THE RAIL SPLITTER & LITTLE MAC THE GUNBOAT GENERAL.

LINCOLN PLAYING A GAME OF BAGATELLE, A FORM OF BILLIARDS, AGAINST UNION GENERAL GEORGE B. MCCLELLAN.

The advice fell on disgruntled ears back in Springfield. In response to a complaint from Herndon about the old men of the party, Mr. Lincoln replied on July 10: *"I suppose I am now one of the old men; and I declare on my veracity, which I think is good with you, that nothing could afford me more satisfaction than to learn that you and others of my young friends at home were doing battle in the contest and endearing themselves to the people and taking a stand far above any I have been able to reach in their admiration."* He added that *"I was young once, and I am sure I was never ungenerously thrust back ... The Way for a young man to rise, is to improve himself every way he can, never suspecting that any body wishes to hinder him."*

As he got older, Lincoln's concern for the development of young men was also dramatically evident in his work as an attorney. George Minier recalled this incident:

"In the spring term of the Tazewell County Court in 1847, which at that time was held in the village of Tremont, I was detained as a witness an entire week. Lincoln was employed in several suits, and among them was one of Case vs. Snow Bros. The Snow Bros., as appeared in evidence (who were both minors), had purchased from an old Mr. Case what was then called a 'prairie team,' consisting of two or three yoke of oxen and prairie plow, giving therefor their joint note of some two hundred dollars; but when pay-day came refused to pay, pleading the minor act. The note was placed in Lincoln's hands for collection. The suit was called and a jury impanelled. The Snow bros. did not deny the note, but pleaded through their counsel that they were minors, and that Mr. Case knew they were at the time of the contract and conveyance. All this was admitted by Mr. Lincoln, with his peculiar phrase, 'Yes, gentlemen, I reckon that's so.' The minor act was read and its validity admitted in the same manner. The counsel of the defendants were permitted without question to state all these things to the jury, and to show by the statute that these minors could not be held responsible for their contract. By this time you may well suppose that I began to be uneasy. 'What!' thought I, 'this good old man, who confided in these boys, to be wronged in this way, and even his counsel, Mr. Lincoln, to submit in silence!' I looked at the Court, Judge [Samuel] Treat, but could read nothing in his *calm and dignified demeanor. Just then, Mr. Lincoln slowly got up, and in his strange, half-erect attitude and clear, quiet accent began: 'Gentlemen of the Jury, are you willing to allow these boys to begin life with this shame and disgrace attached to their character. If you are, I am not. The best judge of human character that ever wrote has left these immortal words for all of us to ponder:*

'Good name in man or woman, dear my lord,

Is the immediate jewel of their souls:

Who steals my purse steals trash; 'tis something, nothing;

'Twas mine, 'tis his, and has been slave to thousands;

But he that filches from me my good name

Robs me of that which not enriches him

And makes me poor indeed.

Then rising to his full height, and looking upon the defendants with the compassion of a brother, his long right arm extended toward the opposing counsel, he continued: 'Gentlemen of the jury, these poor innocent boys would never have attempted this low villainy had it not been for the advice of these lawyers.' Then for a few minutes he showed how even the noble science of law may be prostituted. With a scathing rebuke to those who thus belittle their profession, he concluded: 'And now, gentlemen, you have it in your power to set these boys right before the world.' He plead for the young men only; I think he did not mention his client's name. The jury, without leaving their seats, decided that the defendants must pay the debt; and the latter, after hearing Lincoln, were as willing to pay it as the jury were determined they should. I think the entire argument last not above five minutes."

William Green said of Mr. Lincoln in 1860: *"Whenever he could find a young man he put him on right course, encouraged morality integrity and honesty—all that have looked up to him as an oracle have succeeded well...."* At the end of his 1860 trip to New York City for the famous Cooper Union speech, Lincoln visited the "House of Industry" in the infamous Five Points section of Manhattan. After the 1860 election John V. Farwell recalled that Mr. Lincoln visited a Mission Sunday School which Farwell ran for delinquent children in Chicago. Although Lincoln had asked that he not be called upon to speak, he did, according to Farwell: *"My little friends, I am glad to see you in such a place as this, surrounded by men & women who seem to be intent upon nothing but doing you good. While I have never made a profession of religion, I do not hesitate a moment in recommending you to follow the advice of these teachers, and* to say to you that the poorest boy among you may aspire to the highest positions in the gift of the people if capacity & energy are linked with honesty in the development of character."

In many of his speeches to young men and women, Lincoln stressed the need for physical strength to promote mental strength. Lincoln would use these occasions to reminisce a bit about all the games that played in growing up and as a young man in Springfield. Excelling on the field of play, Lincoln would emphasize, would engender respect among one's peers and pay many dividends down the road. He needed only to talk about his own life to emphasize the point. As young people listened attentively Lincoln, the master storyteller, captivated them and regaled them with his experiences in playing fives, town ball, wrestling, and how by developing the strength to excel at those games he was able to master the discipline that such mental games as check and checkers required. Billiards and bowling provided him the coordination and dexterity to play such as marbles and quoits.

So, was Abraham Lincoln a great athlete? According to one contemporary, Lincoln was *"hard as nails, a good horseman, ball player, runner, swimmer, crowbar heaver, wrestler, and master jumper."* But it's always best to let Lincoln speak for himself whenever possible.

In 1859, after his failed senate run against Stephen Douglas, a disappointed Abraham Lincoln became a minor political celebrity due to his impressive, and eventually legendary, debate performances against Douglas. The Wisconsin Agricultural Society was hosting its ninth annual State Fair and invited him to give a speech. Lincoln came up from Illinois on September 29 and

Lincoln was brought out to the fairgrounds where he mounted a wagon-turned-stage underneath a tree to deliver his speech to the crowd. He spoke about farming and about winning and losing the agricultural contest that was about to be awarded. In his usual Lincoln style, even when speaking about something as simple as fair contest winners, he delivered lines of remarkable eloquence that have lingered in history.

> *"Some of you will be successful, and such will need but little philosophy to take them home in cheerful spirits; others will be disappointed and will be in a less happy mood. To such, let it be said, 'Lay it not too much to heart.' Let them adopt the maxim, 'Better luck next time;' and then, by renewed exertion, make that better luck for themselves.*
>
> *And by the successful, and the unsuccessful, let it be remembered, that while occasions like the present, bring their sober and durable benefits, the exultations and mortifications of them, are but temporary; that the victor shall soon be the vanquished, if he relax in his exertion; and that the vanquished this year, may be victor the next, in spite of all competition.*
>
> *It is said an Eastern monarch once charged his wise men to invent him a sentence, to be ever in view, and which should be true and appropriate in all times and situations. They presented him the words: 'And*

this, too, shall pass away.' How much it expresses! How chastening in the hour of pride! – how consoling in the depths of affliction! 'And this, too, shall pass away.' And yet let us hope it is not quite true. Let us hope, rather, that by the best cultivation of the physical world, beneath and around us; and the intellectual and moral world within us, we shall secure an individual, social and political prosperity and happiness, whose course shall be onward and upward, and which, while the earth endures, shall not pass away."

Yes. Abraham Lincoln was a gifted athlete who, most importantly, knew how to graciously and humbly win *AND* dignifiedly and respectfully lose. That's assuredly the definition of greatness.

ACKNOWLEDGMENTS

The genesis of this book began in the long COVID-inspired sequestration of 2019–2020. With libraries and archives shuttered and travel all but nonexistent, there were a number of logistical problems that few researchers and scholars had faced before; surely, I hadn't.

Yet, I have prided myself on finding topics about Abraham Lincoln that have not been studied before in book-length works. My previous two books on aspects of Lincoln and immigration were such and the current book, a true labor of love, is another.

I found myself very much missing college and professional sports during 2020. As a lifelong sports fan and former athlete, I experienced a true sense of loss with March Madness, college and professional football games, Major League baseball, and the like being cancelled on a regular basis. To fill the loss and satisfy my need for sports, I found myself wondering about Abraham Lincoln, the man I have devoted my career to studying, as an athlete. One thing led to another and before I knew it, I was deep into research, albeit electronically, on this understudied, if not historically neglected, aspect of Lincoln's life. Bits and pieces about Lincoln's athletic prowess exist, but heretofore, no one had attempted to put it all together in a book.

Although writing is a solitary endeavor, researching relies on the assistance and cooperation of librarians and archivists across the country certainly more than ever during these *still* surreal times. And I am very happy to say that when it was safe to return to their work, I was the beneficiary of a number of helpful individuals and institutions.

Phillip Hays, Data Analysis and Reference Librarian/Access Services Coordinator at Dacus Library, Winthrop University, my academic home for over thirty-three years before I retired, did yeoman work for me. He graciously helped me get articles from Interlibrary Loan as well from the university's online catalogue which, as an emeritus professor, I could not access without a current Winthrop email address.

Lawrence Mott and Michael Lynch of the Lincoln Memorial University Abraham Lincoln Library and Museum scanned numerous manuscript documents for me and mailed them to me on a flash drive. I am deeply indebted to them for their generous work on my behalf.

Emily Rapoza, Senior Archivist at the Lincoln Financial Foundation Collection, in Fort Wane, Indiana, and numerous Archivists and Librarians at the Library of Congress, the National Archives, and the Abraham Lincoln Presidential Library and Museum in Springfield, Illinois, all helped by answering my email queries and by emailing copies of items whenever they could, and I am grateful for their taking the time to do so. Elizabeth Ratigan of the Kiplinger Research Library of the DC History Center provided me with valuable information about their Edmund French Collection as soon as she could, and it arrived at a crucial time in my writing.

Along the way, I made some new cyber friends. Al Hunter, columnist for the *Weekly View* became a regular email correspondent as he works on his very important book on Osborn Oldroyd. Al generously shared with me a number of his files and notes, especially about wrestling and handball, and, although we haven't yet met in person, he has become a trusted and respected friend. Jess MacDonald, whom I have also not yet met in person, made me an honorary member of the storied Springfield, Illinois Abe Lincoln Hand Ball Club and sent me several very attractive logo shirts to prove my membership!

Speaking of friends, Lincoln was very correct when he said the best part of one's life consisted of their friendships. I would be very remiss if I didn't mention my very closest friends. Matt Fike, professor of English at Winthrop University and an exemplary scholar kept me informed about the happenings at my former academic home. My email correspondence with Matt was always something to which I looked forward, and I am so grateful for his friendship and sage advice. Bob Gorman, baseball historian extraordinaire, has been my best friend and racquetball partner for well over thirty years. Since moving after my retirement, to say that I miss our twice weekly "r-ball games" is a vast understatement. Perhaps, more importantly, I miss seeing my best friend! Thanks must also go to "the Mayor," Eddie Lee, my friend and former colleague whom I have known for over thirty years. While working away on this book I could always count on Eddie for news from Winthrop and Rock Hill and to make my job as book review editor for the *Lincoln Herald* much easier because of his reliability and his willingness to review the many times I asked.

Dick Davis, my former student, and one of the most generous human beings it has ever been my pleasure to know, became a very dear and trusted friend. His enthusiastic support for my writing and teaching has lifted me up during some dark times and I will forever be grateful. His emails always inform and amuse, and it is to him that I gratefully dedicate this book.

I consider Bill Pederson, editor of *Abraham Lincoln Abroad* and Tom Turner, editor of the *Lincoln Herald*, close and respected friends. They always get first dibs on what I write, and I want to thank them for their willingness to publish my essays and for their friendship and support over the years. Both men are truly gentlemen and scholars.

This is the second book in a row that I have published with Palmetto Publishing Group, and every book I write will go to them because of the thoroughly professional and impressive jobs they do and the respect they show to their authors. I would especially like to thank Jack Joseph and Erin Miller for all their hard work and enthusiasm for all my publishing projects. An author could not ask more from a publisher.

I thank my wife of thirty-five years, Susan, and our son, Alex, for welcoming Mr. Lincoln into our home for yet another extended stay and for once again indulging my interest in "living" in the nineteenth century. Their regular assistance, when I experienced my all too often techno-issues, repeatedly saved me from giving up on computers, Microsoft Word, and technology in general. May the circle always be unbroken.

And to Mr. Lincoln, another hearty thanks for being such a fascinating, albeit challenging, person to study. As I have said since my son was a little boy, "Abraham Lincoln is the founder of the feast!"

NOTE ON SOURCES

Anyone who has ever studied Abraham Lincoln encounters the same problem; he didn't leave any diaries, journals, or extensive reflections. *"He was the most secretive, reticent, shut-mouthed man that ever lived,"* said his law partner, William H. Herndon.

Recently, Richard C. White in his very important new book, *Lincoln in Private: What His Most Personal Reflections Tell Us About Our Greatest President,* uncovered Lincoln's "best thoughts," in the short notes he wrote to himself. Lincoln would work out his personal stances on the biggest issues of the day, never expecting anyone to see these frank, unpolished pieces of writing, which he'd keep close at hand, in desk drawers, and even in his top hat.

The profound importance of these notes has been overlooked, because the originals are scattered across several different archives and have never been brought together and examined as a coherent whole.

These notes do not only showcase Lincoln's brilliance and empathy indeed but also his very human anxieties and ambitions. Yet, and understandably so, they deal with the biggest issues Lincoln faced: slavery, his debates with Stephen A Douglas, reflections on his lost bid for a U.S. Senate seat, the new Republican Party, the secession crisis, and his theological ruminations.

However, for a book such as this, these private reflections, the closest one can come to Lincoln's mind and soul, unfortunately do not add measurably to the topic of this book.

Thus, as with my previous books on Lincoln, I have had to do some extensive historical detective work. Digging into hitherto neglected county histories, personal recollections, and reminisces of Lincoln by his lesser famous contemporaries revealed a treasure trove of information about Lincoln the athlete and games player. On more than one occasion, Lincoln was observed in an informal setting in which he was relaxing and playing, something he was not often able to do with the nation severed into two and war all around him. Some observations were amusing while others were poignant. Some, as explained herein, were apocryphal as the authors of those memories faded, and yet they wished to touch somehow the memory of the martyred president.

Some memories were repetitive and contradictory to others. Yet, all demonstrated a side to Abraham Lincoln not seen normally in studies about the man. Indeed, a more human side in which Lincoln demonstrated an interest in observing and participating in a variety of sports and games with an often-childlike enthusiasm and vigor. All told, the memories of those lesser figures who observed him make a compelling case for an even more likeable and awe-inspiring human being: a man who was able to relax, albeit briefly, and have a bit of fun during his difficult younger years and during the nation's darkest hour.

Although this is somewhat of an unconventional listing of many lesser-known sources, readers who wish to pursue specific topics somewhat further will be able to follow throughout the book consulting the listings below. They are in the order in which I used them.

Michael Burlingame and John R. Turner Ettlinger, editors, *Inside Lincoln's White House: The Complete CivilWar Diary of John Hay.*

Douglas L. Wilson and Rodney O. Davis, eds., *Herndon's Informants: Letters, Interviews, and Statements about Abraham Lincoln.*

Roy P. Basler, ed., "James Quay Howard's Notes on Lincoln," *The Abraham Lincoln Quarterly,* Volume IV, December 1947.

Daniel Green Burner, "Lincoln and The Burners at New Salem," in Charles Hubbard, ed., *The Many Faces of Lincoln.*

Michael Burlingame, ed., Walter B. Stevens, *A Reporter's Lincoln.* David Herbert Donald, *"We Are Lincoln Men" Abraham Lincoln and His Friends.*

Osborn H. Oldroyd, *The Lincoln Memorial: Album Immortelles*

Harvey Lee Ross, *The Early Pioneers and Pioneer Events of the State of Illinois.*

Thomas W. S. Kidd, "How Abraham Lincoln Received the News of His Nomination for President," *Journal of the Illinois State Historical Society,* April–July 1922.

G. Onstott, *Pioneers of Menard and Mason Counties,* p. 72–73.

Alonzo Rothschild, *Lincoln, Master of Men*, p. 23.

"Lincolniana Notes: Recollections of a Springfield Doctor," *Journal of the Illinois State Historical Society*, June 1954, p. 60.

Michael Aubrecht, "Civil War Baseball: Baseball and the Blue and Gray," *Baseball Almanac*, August 2016.

David Donald, *Lincoln*.

Herbert W. Forster, "He Knew Lincoln: New Yorker Who Played Baseball with Civil War President as Spectator," *The New York Times*, November 20, 1921.

Edmund F. French Baseball Scrapbook and Memorabilia, 1859–1871. Special Collections Finding Aid, The Historical Society of Washington, D.C. MS 595.

Frederic J. Frommer, *The Washington Nationals: 1859 to Today*.

Frederic J. Frommer, Frederick J., "When Baseball Was Bigger Than Politics," *Politico*, October 22, 2019.

Weekly Kansas City Star, February 18, 1920, "Fought Fires with Lincoln Sixty-Five Years Ago."

History of Fulton County, Illinois.

History of Henry County, Illinois.

History of Menard and Mason Counties, Illinois.

George Kirsch, *Baseball in Blue & Gray: The National Pastime During the Civil War.*

"[Lincoln] Was a Baseball Fan," *Kingston (NY) Daily Freeman*, June 3, 1914.

Steve Light, "150 Years Ago, the Civil War Began...And Baseball Became Part of Soldiers' Lives," National Baseball Hall of Fame website. http://baseballhall.org/news/history/battling-diamond.

Edward George Lowden, *History of the 71st Regiment, New York*

"The Lines of Arlington," *The New York Times*, September 15, 1861.

William B. Mead and Paul Dickson, *Baseball: The Presidents' Game*

George C. Rable, "Patriotism, Platitudes and Politics: Baseball and the American Presidency," *Presidential Studies Quarterly*, 19 (Spring 1989): 363–372.

James C. Roberts, *The Nationals Past Times.*

San Francisco Daily Evening Bulletin, June 16, 1860.

Smith, Curt. *The Presidents and the Pastime: The History of Baseball & the White House.*

A. G. Spalding, *America's National Game.*

Washington National Republican, August 28, 1865.

Washington Post, "Baseball in the Sixties: Reminiscences of the Game in Washington 25 Years Ago," January 22, 1888.

Washington Post, "Baseball of Long Ago: How Washington Amateur Teams Came Together Back in 1866," March 10, 1890.

Washington Post, "A Historic Grand Slam," May 23, 2000.

John Sayle Watterson, *The Games Presidents Play: Sports and the Presidency.*

Christopher Klein, "10 Things You May Not Know About Abraham Lincoln," History.com (A&E Television Networks, November 16, 2012), https://www.history.com/news/10-things-you-may-not-know-about-abraham-lincoln).

Susan Bell, "Lincoln's Looks Never Hindered His Approach to Life or Politics," *USC News* (USC, February 19, 2015), https://news.usc.edu/75846/lincolns-looks-never-hindered-his-approach-to-life-or-politics).

"The Railsplitter: Abraham Lincoln: An Extraordinary Life," National Museum of American History (National Museum of American History, n.d.), https://americanhistory.si.edu/lincoln/railsplitter).

Bob Dellinger, "Wrestling in the USA," National Wrestling Hall of Fame (National Wrestling Hall of Fame, n.d.), https://nwhof.org/stillwater/resources-library/history/wrestling-in-the-usa/).

David Fleming, "The Civil Warrior," *Sports Illustrated* https://vault.si.com/vault/1995/02/06/the-civil-warrior-on-the-us-frontier-young-abe-lincoln-was-a-great-wrestler-and-sportsman).

Michael Burlingame, Abraham Lincoln: A Life, 2 vols. Lincoln: A Life.

William Greene interview with William H. Herndon, May 30, 1865, *Herndon's Informants: Letters, Interviews and Statements About Abraham Lincoln*, ed. Douglas O. Wilson and Rodney O. Davis (Urbana, 1998), 18. William H. Townsend was one of the few historians to give much notice to the life of Denton Offutt before and after his time at New Salem; see his *Lincoln and the Bluegrass: Slavery and Civil War in Kentucky*

Diane L. Beers, *For Prevention of Cruelty: The History and Legacy of Animal Rights Activism in the United States*.

John Lawrence, *The Horse, His Varieties and Uses*.

William Youatt, *The Horse, With a Treatise on Draught.*

"Taming Wild Horses," John S. Skinner, *American Turf Register*, 1838.

Horatio Townsend, *Statistical Survey of the County of Cork*

"Rranger" [pseud.], "The Whisperer," *New Sporting Magazine* [London, England] July 1838.

Hamilton Busbey, "Denton Offutt and His Book," *Turf, Field and Farm*, January 4, 1878.

Denton Offutt, *A New and Complete System of Teaching the Horse on Phrenological Principles.*

James S. Offutt, "Denton Offutt: Employer and Friend of Lincoln at New Salem," (typescript, n.d., n.p.). Multiple copies of this typescript exist, one in the Abraham Lincoln Presidential Library in Springfield, IL.

Nellie Offutt Chesley, "The Offutt Family [typescript, 8 vols.], 3:74; 4:53, 56-57, 77, 95, 128, 130, 132–33, 162, 182 (photocopy of original at the Jane C. Sween Research Library, Montgomery County Historical Society, Rockville, Maryland).

Kentucky Reporter, February 10, 1827.

Jessamine County Will Book D, 30 (October 30, 1830).

William E. Barton, *The Life of Abraham Lincoln*.

William H. Herndon and Jesse W. Weik, *Herndon's Lincoln: The True Story of a Great Life*.

Abraham Lincoln, "Autobiographical Notes," May–June 1860, series 1, general correspondence, 1833–1916, Abraham Lincoln Papers, Library of Congress, Washington, D.C.

Lincoln "Autobiographical Notes"; John Hanks interview by Herndon, June 13, 1865, in *Herndon's Informants*.

Thomas P. Reep, *Lincoln at New Salem*.

Kentucky Reporter, March 2, 1831.

Robert Mazrim, Dennis Naglich, and Curtis Mann, "Looking for Lincoln's Property at New Salem: Archaeological Investigations at the "East Ridge" Locale," *Lincoln's New Salem State Historic Site, Fieldwork and Technical Reports Bulletin* Number 14 (Salisbury, IL, 2007), 102–6.

Charles Maltby, *The Life and Public Services of Abraham Lincoln*.

Henry C. Whitney, *Lincoln, the Citizen*.

Vincennes (Ind.) *Western Sun and General Advertiser*, December 27, 1834.

Denton Offutt, "To People a Warning Against Swindlers in the Teaching of the Art of Taming Horses Selling a Book," *Spirit of the Times*, June 25, 1859, 230.

Denton Offutt, "Best and Cheapest Book on the Management of Horses, Mules, Etc.," handbill, Library of Congress, Printed Ephemera Collection, portfolio 197, folder 34.

Denton Offutt, *Denton Offutt's Method of Gentling Horses, and Curing Their Diseases.*

Denton Offutt, *The Educated Horse: Teaching Horses and Other Animals to Obey at Word, Sign, or Signal, To Work or Ride; Also, the Breeding of Animals, and Discovery in Animal Physiology, and the Improvement of Domestic Animals.* Denton Offutt, "Discoveries in Animal physiology," *The Valley Farmer* [St. Louis, Mo.], April 1853, 144.

"The Original Horse Tamer," *Spirit of the Times*, June 25, 1859.

Denton Offutt to Abraham Lincoln, September 7, 1859, and February 11, 1861, available at Abraham Lincoln Papers at the Library of Congress, manuscript Division (Washington, D.C., American memory project [2000–2002] http://memory.loc.gov/ammen/index.html

Denton Offutt, "Phrenology & Physiology of Animals," handbill included in September 7, 1859, letter to Lincoln, Abraham Papers at the Library of Congress.

Thomas B. Thorpe, "Rarey, the Horse Tamer," *Harper's New Monthly Magazine,* April 1861.

Sara L. Brown, "Rarey, the Horse's Master and Friend," *Ohio Archaeological and Historical Quarterly* 25 (1916).

John S. Rarey, *The Modern Art of Taming Wild Horses.*

Dennis Magner, *Facts for Horse Owners: A Pictorial Encyclopedia of Practical Instruction* and *The Art of Taming and Educating the Horse.*

"The American Horse-Tamer," *London Times,* January 25 and 29, 1858.

"Mr. Rarey, the Horse-Tamer," *London Times,* April 9, 1858.

London Times, March 22, April 22, November 15, 1858.

"United States Agricultural Society," *New England Farmer,* April 1854.

"United States Agricultural Society," *Horticultural Review and Botanical Magazine,* 1854.

"Petition of Denton Offutt, Relative to Improving the Breed of Domestic Livestock." Records, Governor Peter H. Bell, box 301-20, folder 16, Archives and Information Services Division, Texas State Library and Archives Commission, Austin, Texas.

Senate Journal, 31st Cong., 2nd sess., December 9, 1850, 27; 33rd Cong., lst sess., March 13, 1854; May 2, 1854, 357.

House Journal, 35th Cong., 2nd sess., December 10, 1858; January 4, 1858.

Senate Committee on Agriculture, 33rd Cong. 1st sess., S. Rept. 253, May 2, 1854.

"Look Out, England!" *Spirit of the Times*, April 23, 1859, 26.

Richard Ten Broeck, "Some Personal reminiscences, Incidents and Anecdotes," *Spirit of the Times* December 27, 1890.

John Dizikes, *Sportsmen and Gamesmen*.

"The Biter Bitten," *Baily's Magazine*, January 1862.

Siva Vaidhyanathan, *Copyrights and Copywrongs: The Rise of Intellectual Property and How It Threatens Creativity*.

Passenger Lists of Vessels Arriving at New York, New York, 1820-1897, NARA microfilm publication 27, roll 194, Records of the

U.S. Customs Service, Record Group 36, National Archives, Washington, D.C.

Denton Offutt to Abraham Lincoln, September 7, 1859, Abraham Lincoln Papers at the Library of Congress; Brown.

"Mr. Rarey's first lecture," *New York Times*, January 5, 1861.

"The Horse-Tamer in Brooklyn," *New York Times*, January 24, 1861.

Denton Offutt vs. John S. Rarey, New York Supreme Court, index no. LJ1863O24, Division of Old Records, New York County Clerk, New York, NY.

Brooklyn Daily Eagle, January 31, 1861.

"The Secret of Horse-taming—Rarey's Case Before the Court," *New York Times*, February 2, 1861.

"The Great Rarey Suit," *Wilkes' Spirit of the Times*, February 9, 1861.

"Rarey's Farewell," *New York Times*, February 4, 1861.

"These Arabian Horses," *New York Times*, August 6, 1860.

Transactions of the New York State Agricultural Society for the Year 1860.

"The Horse-Tamers in Court—Mr. Offutt's Suit Against Mr. Rarey," *New York Times*, February 5, 1861.

Denton Offutt to Abraham Lincoln, February 11, 1861, Abraham Lincoln Papers at the Library of Congress.

"Decisions: Supreme Court," *New York Times*, May 13, 1862.

Denton Offutt vs. John S. Rarey, New York Supreme Court.

Zanesville (Ohio) Daily Courier, June 28, 1865.

"General News," *New York Times*, December 20, 1865.

"Sudden Death of Prof. J. S. Rarey," *New York Times*, October 8, 1866.

E. J. Edwards, "Robert Bonner," *American Monthly Review of Reviews*, August 1899.

Robert M. Miller and Rick Lamb, *The Revolution in Horsemanship, and What it Means to Mankind.*

"The Goodenough Method of Shoeing Horses," *London Times*, December 10, 1868.

Buck Brannigan, *Believe: A Horseman's Journey.*

Bill Dorrance and Leslie Desmond, *True Horsemanship Through Feel.*

Klaus F. Hempfling, *Dancing With Horses.*

John Lyons, *Lyons On Horses.*

Mark Rashid, *Considering The Horse.*

Robert M Miller and Richard A. Lamb, *Revolution in Horsemanship.*

Monty Roberts, *The Man Who Listens To Horses.*

ABOUT THE AUTHOR

Jason H. Silverman is the Ellison Capers Palmer Jr. Professor of History Emeritus at Winthrop University, where he taught for over thirty-three years. Prior to that he taught at Yale University for four years. Author or editor of eleven books, several of which were nominated for national book awards, his recent works are *When America Welcomed Immigrants: The Short and Tortured History of Abraham Lincoln's Act to Encourage Immigration* (2020) and *Lincoln and the Immigrant* (2015, 2020), a volume in the Concise Lincoln Library series published by Southern Illinois University Press. The latter was awarded *The Immigrants' Civil War Award* by Hofstra University's *Long Island Wins*, a nonprofit communications organization that focuses on immigration issues on Long Island and beyond. Of the 16,500, and counting, volumes published on Abraham Lincoln, Silverman's is still the first, and only, full-length study of its kind. This volume inspired *American by Belief*, a museum exhibit at President Lincoln's Cottage at the Soldier's Home National Monument in Washington, D.C.

His current book-length project is *Lincoln's Magician* that studies the friendship between Lincoln and Captain Horatio Green (Harry) Cooke, America's first escape artist, a Union spy with the Lincoln Federal (Jessie) Scouts, and a mentor to Harry Houdini.

Dr. Silverman received his undergraduate degree at the University of Virginia and his graduate degrees at Colorado State

University and the University of Kentucky. Among his teaching awards, he has received *Winthrop's Outstanding Junior Professor Award*, been named the *University's Distinguished Professor*, received the *Pi Kappa Phi Excellence in Teaching Award* three times, and, in 1990, became the first person in Winthrop's history to be named *South Carolina Professor of the Year*. In 2011, Dr. Silverman was named the inaugural *Ellison Capers Palmer Jr. Professor of History* at Winthrop.

In 2018, he was awarded *The Order of the Silver Crescent*, the state of South Carolina's highest civilian award for "significant contributions, leadership, volunteerism, and lifelong influence within a region or community. The Order of the Silver Crescent is a once in a lifetime achievement."

Dr. Silverman is Chairman of the Scholarly Advisory Group for President Lincoln's Cottage at the National Soldier's Home Monument in Washington, D.C., coeditor of *Abraham Lincoln Abroad* and on the editorial boards of *The Lincolnator, North & South*, and the *Lincoln Herald*, where, in January 2018, he became the Book Review Editor and quarterly columnist.

For eight years, Dr. Silverman also served two elected terms on the Rock Hill School Board 2002–2010).

www.ingramcontent.com/pod-product-compliance
Lightning Source LLC
LaVergne TN
LVHW011806060526
838200LV00053B/3682